CW01212512

FIR LODGE

SEAN MCMAHON

This is a work of fiction. Names, characters, businesses, organisations, places, events and incidents are either the product of the author's imagination, or are used in a fictitious manner. The one exception is Fir Lodge itself, which the author has been given express permission to reference within these pages by written agreement from the owner of the lodge.

Any resemblance to actual events or persons, living or dead, is purely coincidental, or referenced satirically.

Author's note: utilising the abilities of a Restarter to alter the timeline to amend author-ownership is strictly prohibited.

For more information, visit:

www.restarterlodge.com

ISBN-13: 978-1985333208

ISBN-10: 1985333201

Dedicated to The Gang, the real-life heroes, who forever inspire me.

CHAPTER ONE

Restarting the Past

165th Restart – Saturday Evening, 8:39pm

With less than twenty-three minutes of guaranteed existence left, there was no margin for error.

"Glass breaks, watch for the balloon, move the yellow ball, *then* the red," thought Kara, "but not *too* much."

She had spent no less than seven Saturdays finding the perfect angle so that Jon would finally pot the yellow pool-ball that would spark the chain of follow-up shots which, in turn, would ultimately have him facing the right way, at just the right time. It had taken another two Saturdays before that, learning to move them at just the right speed, so he wouldn't notice her meddling. Then, what felt like countless weekends memorising the order he would work through the remaining yellow balls left on the table, gently moving the bright-red, spherical obstacles out of his way.

In the early days, it had taken far more effort and concentration to remember the correct sequence. A minor problem greatly exacerbated by the fact that pool wasn't her game to begin with.

But this was far from the early days, and with a wry smirk, she was once again reminded of a thought she couldn't help but entertain; that given enough time, she could have truly perfected the double into the centre pocket.

Hal shot her a playful scowl, as he jumped the final four steps of the staircase.

'The irony *still* isn't lost on me either,' remarked Hal, 'but if you could nudge the cue-ball like, yesterday, that would be–'

'Already done,' said Kara, 'less talking, more hot-tub-tripping maybe?' but he was already gone. 'Such a backseat Restarter,' she mumbled, to no one in particular.

'I heard that!' shouted Hal, as he made his way into position, waiting patiently to carry out his next task.

It was a dance now. They moved with an elegant precision that could only come from countless hours of practise and repetition. Moving in time with the music, that Hal had selected before he had descended the stairs, which was now echoing throughout the lodge, Glenn Miller's "In the mood" was today's soundtrack of bad-assery. They'd admitted to each other a long time ago that, despite its twee undertones, they were glad that Jon had added music from his annual RAF ball to the group playlist. Music was everything to them these days, not least because of the way it inexplicably blasted through the muffling-fog unlike anything else they'd encountered. Hal theorised that this was due to the ebb and flow of the reverberations and varying changes in decibel levels. Kara, on the other hand, didn't care why.

Things were already changing, and Hal and Kara

had to adapt their plan in subtle ways. The champagne flute that always broke, now *never* did, meaning Hal now had to knock over a wine bottle every time, just to keep their plan in motion. As if to highlight the point, a cork flew past Kara's field of view, but was plucked from the air before it could reach its target.

'Right on time Pete,' said Kara, as Peter walked past her, and then out of sight.

Their friends were in disarray, as they reacted to the smashed bottle of wine that Hal had dutifully knocked over. Daisy, meanwhile, was busy having to duck under and around the helium-filled roadblocks that had sprung up in front of her face, eventually losing her balance and spilling the contents of the glass she was clutching all over Stacey. All of these things culminated to serve one, singular purpose; to cause a temporary pile-up of people, to prevent anyone from accessing the communal stairway that led to the lower-level.

It had taken them both a long time to perfect these seemingly simple alterations to the timeline. If their friends had descended the stairs sooner, it would have sent events a few degrees off course, and they'd be right back where they started. Literally. Just one of the many pieces of the ever-shifting puzzle that she and Hal were attempting to manipulate, in order to acquire the precious seconds that they needed so that they–

"Stop thinking and keep working Kara!" she said to herself sternly.

Of all the hindrances the fog presented, the thing she hated the most was how it caused her mind to wander. Even in its distilled state, the fog was not to be taken lightly; her charge would only keep its effects at bay for so long. Hal reasoned that this was due to–

Kara was thrust back into the present, her tangential thoughts cut short, as the hot tub in the rear communal-area of the lodge became silent, the rhythmic hum instantly replaced by the all-too-familiar whinging of Robert. His groans were notably more muffled than last time; another by-product of the ever-present fog, which Hal regularly joked was potentially an ethereal manifestation of Robert's sardonic wit.

'Kara! You still with me?' said Hal, running back

into the hallway from the rear garden.

'Yeah, sorry. It's–'

'I know. The music, remember? Anchor yourself!' said Hal. 'Last chance,' he added with a wink, 'it's still not too late, we could just *kill* Robert instead?'

Kara rolled her eyes, but couldn't hide her smile.

Taking advantage of the fact that Will and Jon were facing away from him, due to Kara's repositioning of the pool balls changing the way the game would play out, Hal walked through the open double front doors. He turned around, gently closing them behind him, the latch catching softly with a barely audible "click".

Will was displaying his frustration over not being able to sink a shot that was, as Jon was taking great pleasure in reminding him, a shot that "even Kara could make." With a sullen look on his face, Will remained completely oblivious to the fact that the cause of his failure was a direct result of Kara's unseen intervention.

As Jon aligned his follow-up shot, Will leant against the doorframe of the side entrance, resigned to the fact that he wouldn't be getting to have another go anytime soon. It was at this moment that Alex appeared, but with Will now blocking the doorway, he was unable to enter the lodge. Not wishing to disturb the flow of the game, Alex reached into his pocket, lighting a cigarette instead.

By Hal and Kara's design, this resulted in Alex being *just* within Robert's line of sight, and earshot.

'Can you hit the trip switch Alex?' shouted Robert. 'Tub's gone off again!'

'Don't worry,' shouted a voice that sounded both immediately familiar to Kara, and completely alien to Hal. 'I'll sort it.'

It was one thing hearing a recording of his own voice, which made Hal cringe at the best of times. It was another thing entirely, hearing your own voice emanating from a duplicated version of your own voice-box.

"This is it," thought Hal, now an outsider looking in, both literally and figuratively, as he stood on the driveway, beyond the front doors of Fir Lodge. Hal mouthed the words "For Rohan" through the glass to Kara, and she replied as she always did, every time Hal fired off a reference she didn't understand, from a film or television show she hadn't seen; with a look that heavily implied *I still don't know what that means*, which she rounded off with a half-hearted salute.

And then, in a moment between moments, *he* arrived.

As the physical embodiment of the cause, and potential solution, to *all* of this presented himself, they both felt a chill that made the hairs on their arms and the back of their necks stand up, a sensation only made possible by their current, retained charge. Their stomachs lurched, as they experienced the feeling of time slowing for just a fraction of a second, coupled with a sudden, understandable sense of dread.

Jerry was standing there as he always did; in the dark, just beyond the now-closed front doors, directly in front of Hal, whom Jerry barely acknowledged. Standing on the gravel with welcoming eyes, Jerry yawned idly, and then coughed to get someone's attention. Without Kara's past-self there to notice him, and the doors blocking his access, it was Jon that caught sight of him first.

Jon walked slowly towards the front entrance, and opened one of the glass-panelled doors, curious to see what their unexpected visitor wanted.

No longer impeded, Jerry strutted his way past Jon, and into the lodge, completely ignoring the common courtesy of formal greetings, and made his way to the pool table.

Kara tapped the pleat of her skirt impatiently, counting down the twenty-two seconds until, finally, right on cue, an identical copy of herself casually walked down the stairs, and stood directly in front of her.

Kara's doppelganger called out for Hal, who arrived as intended, a minute later than he should have done, joining her in the hallway, his reflection in the glass of the front door not actually a reflection at all.

To the casual, untrained Restarter, it would have been reasonable to speculate that the true cause of their unease was in direct correlation with the paradigm shift caused by Kara and Hal themselves, who had just walked into a room they were *already* occupying. But the truth behind their fear was that the arrival of Jerry meant one of two things; that in just over twenty-two minutes, they would either both be erased from the current timeline, unceremoniously sent back to where this all began, forced to start their plan over from scratch…or, alternatively, the terrifying possibility that there would be no more second chances at all, and they would simply be erased entirely, forever.

CHAPTER TWO

Arrival

Friday Afternoon, 12:04pm

After a two-hour drive, Robert was relieved to finally see the sign for Pentney Lakes. Situated amidst 275 acres of beautiful woodland and unbelievably picturesque lakes in Norfolk, he was looking forward to seeing where they'd be staying for the long weekend.

His wife, Daisy, was meticulously directing him through the quiet wilderness, reciting Rachel's detailed directions from the email on her phone.

Following her final instruction, Robert turned left onto the driveway of the property, the shingle dispersing beneath his tyres with a satisfying crunch.

He pulled up, parking to the left-hand side of Jasmine's car, just as Kara, Hal, and Jasmine herself were yanking their cases and bags of shopping from the boot, and taking them into the lodge.

Robert had been bringing up the rear of the convoy, observing Jasmine's scrappy implementation of vehicular manoeuvring, whilst Peter and Fearne had knocked back the beers and vodka jelly shots respectively, in the back seats. Will and Stacey were parked directly in front of him and, as convoy leaders, they were indulging in the privileges their head-start had afforded them, cracking open their first bottle of wine on the front balcony.

As Robert killed the engine, he noticed his passenger-side wing mirror had been knocked inwards. He knew for sure that this was a tell-tale sign that Daisy had clearly had another near miss with a parked vehicle, and made a mental note to readjust the mirror on Sunday.

"Not long now…" he thought, with the

reinvigorated thrill that inevitably follows a two-hour drive, knowing you have a bottle of twelve-year-old whisky in the boot of your car.

His good mood was accentuated by the knowledge that Daisy had agreed to drive home at the end of the long weekend. They'd left their daughter with Robert's parents for the duration of their trip and, with a second child on the way, he knew this would be his last chance to fully let loose for a while. It was something that he by no means resented, but fully intended to embrace wholeheartedly.

Robert bounced out from behind the wheel, his stocky, muscular frame causing the car to groan as he did so, and took the opportunity to stretch out his back, being sure to add extra emphasis to the sigh he made, to ensure that he really hit home the fact to his wife that he had done his husbandly duties and deserved, without recompense, to get utterly shit-faced.

'Don't forget the cases,' said Daisy, as she made her way into the cabin.

'No problem babe,' he said, running his hand through his number-three-all-over brown hair, and continuing his seemingly never-ending inventory of chores for the afternoon.

Rachel and Jon, who were the masterminds behind the gang's weekend away, had arrived long before their guests, and were busy showing everyone to their rooms, ensuring drinks were readily available, if not already free-flowing.

Jon worked as a high-ranking officer for the Royal Air Force, doing "important" work that the rest of the group didn't ask him too much about. Not because they weren't interested, but because he wasn't really at liberty to divulge as much about the finer details as he would have liked. Thanks to the nature of his work, Jon was in great physical shape, his athletic and toned frame perfectly in proportion with his six-foot height, his black hair kept to an easily maintained short length, yet effortlessly smart at all times.

Rachel, meanwhile, worked as a Technological Support Officer for a small firm, a gig she took up so that she could move in with Jon, which finally allowed for her to cut out the two-hour round-trip to Newark that she was making every weekend to see him. A warm-hearted, slim woman with a bubbly personality, the mood of the natural-brunette could often be gauged by her fluctuating choice of hair-colour, which was sometimes red, sometimes dark-purple, and sometimes black altogether.

The excuse, not that they ever needed one, for the weekend of serious drinking and tomfoolery, was to celebrate Rachel's thirtieth birthday. The gang had known each other for over a decade (some longer than that), and their relationships had transcended beyond the moniker of mere "mates". They were the family they had chosen, and their bond was unbreakable, even if Robert regularly played it down, by always referring to everyone as "at best, acquaintances." A long-running, unfunny joke which had stemmed from the fact that the majority of them had predominately met through work many years prior. Most of them had moved onwards and upwards to other careers, despite the joke itself refusing to die.

Hal, Kara, and Jasmine were the oldest, reaching the giddying heights of their mid-thirties, with only Jasmine seemingly being at peace with that fact. They were also the only three whose partners could not attend.

Jasmine's partner, David, was currently at a remote location in a humble village on the outskirts of Essex, trying to find the final fish on his checklist of what he described as being "a 17-piece puzzle" at the fishing lakes near to their home town.

Hal's other half, Jess, was looking after their three-year-old fur baby, a Staffordshire Bull Terrier named Shelby. Despite their efforts, they were unable to secure a dog-sitter, and they were not keen on placing their precious rescue dog into a kennels for the weekend. After weeks of searching for alternatives, they were forced to admit defeat, with Jess agreeing to take one for the team by sitting this one out.

Kara, meanwhile, had only recently got the ball rolling with her boyfriend Greg, and as the lodge was already filled to capacity, they'd mutually decided to do their own thing.

Will and Stacey had scored a home-run by dropping their three-year-old (and considerably more human) little girl with their parents. A fraction taller than Hal, with sweeping brown hair and a physique that Will referred to as his "textbook dad-bod", Will was legendary for the drunken persona he often adopted when he embraced intoxication, much to the chagrin of his incredibly-tolerant wife, Stacey. Only Hal had ever come close to reaching the same level of infamy within the group dynamic whilst drunk, but Will would always be king.

However, Hal and Will were determined not to be the ones to ruin Rachel's thirtieth, and were secretly planning on reining it in this time around. Though this was exactly what they always said, usually about fourteen seconds before one of them ruined an evening by drinking just a shot too much, and tipping themselves over the edge.

Hal entered through the large double doors to the lodge, as Rachel appeared and greeted him, and he noticed her hair was a vibrant red, indicating she was fired up and in party-mode.

Every single one of Hal's friends brought something special and different to the group. But for Hal, Rachel was unique in that she always seemed to know what he was thinking. They often joked that they were two sides of the same coin, and that she was his female-counterpart. Not only did she possess the same sense of humour that he did, she could tell just by the look on his face what he was thinking in any given situation. They had met through work and, by an extreme instance of good-fortune, she and Michaela, who would be arriving the next day, were there for him when his last long-term relationship ended in a blaze of predictably-average failure. That disaster, however, was the best thing that had ever happened to him, as it led to him forming friendships he would never have found. He couldn't bring himself to imagine an alternate-timeline version of his life, one without these people in it...

'Hal, you made it! How was the drive?!' said Rachel, who was positively beaming.

It was a well-established fact in Britain that there were only two potential responses when using descriptive terminology to quantify traffic; either it was "an absolute nightmare", or "it wasn't too bad actually." There was no in-between.

'Hey Rach'!' said Hal. 'Well, Jasmine was driving scrappy…but other than that, it wasn't too bad actually!'

Rachel pulled Hal in for a hug, and kissed him on the cheek.

'If you want to dump your bag, your room's just there,' she said, pointing to the room to the right of the pool table. 'You're sharing with your brother. Jon's out back setting up the hot tub if you want to say "hey."'

Hal hugged her again, then moved to the side to allow his other friends the opportunity to discuss their own interpretation of the traffic with Rachel, and made his way to his designated room for the weekend.

He entered the bedroom, pushing the door behind him with his foot, so that it was partially closed, as he heard Robert's booming voice all the way from the hallway.

'Traffic was an absolute nightmare,' he heard Robert saying to Rachel.

Hal chuckled, and tossed his case onto the bed that he had decided would be his.

"First dibs," he thought.

Hal freshened up a little in the bathroom, and

headed further down the hall into the rear garden. The hot tub didn't disappoint, an eight-seater beast that sat opposite what he would later discover to be a sauna and steam room.

'Jon mate, this place is awesome!' said Hal.

'Ah man,' said Jon, laughing in agreement. 'I can't wait to get on it tonight! How you doing? Drive okay?'

'It wasn't too bad actually!' said Hal, as they bear-hugged each other.

Hal was glad to see him. Due to Jon's line of work, he was often deployed during the gang's gatherings. This was the first time in a long while that the stars had aligned, and Jon was able to attend one of their spectacular blowout parties.

'Hot tub looks great!' noted Hal, casually leaning his weight against it.

The seemingly innocuous action immediately caused the tub to shake, generating a menacing clunking noise that clearly meant nothing good. The jets slowed, causing the bubbles to dwindle away feebly until, eventually, the water was perfectly still.

'What'd I do?!' said Hal in horror.

Fearful that he had already managed to ruin Rachel's thirtieth birthday, he recoiled away from the tub, and inspected his hands, as if he had inherited a dastardly form of destructive telekinesis.

'Ha, oh nothing mate,' said Jon, 'I think the power just tripped,' he added reassuringly, tapping on the control panel of the tub to see if the digital display would come back to life.

After a short while, the display obliged, flashing happily, as the jets started back up again.

'I'll keep an eye on it,' he added. 'If it keeps doing it, I'll call the owner out to take a look.'

'Fair play,' said Hal. 'Where's the breaker box anyway? In case we need to restart it?'

'Through that door, in with the sauna and steam rooms,' said Jon, pointing to the door directly behind Hal, who nodded, and absconded to the garden, which seemed to extend into infinity.

Hal plonked himself down on one of the picnic benches, feeling a slight shiver run through him as he did so. Reaching into his pocket, he plucked a pre-made, hand-rolled cigarette from a filter box, placed the box back from whence it came, and retrieved his petrol lighter, flipping the lid and the flint in one smooth movement. A party trick that no one had ever asked to see, but one that he was always pleased with when he pulled it off first time.

Hal took a drag, resting his elbows on the picnic table, lamenting to himself that he really needed to quit.

"Soon. Just…not this weekend," he thought, making the conscious decision that he would seriously attempt doing just that, when he departed Fir Lodge.

*

Kara walked into her room and dumped her case onto her bed, noting the other cases scattered around her. She'd be sharing with Rachel and Jon tonight, as well as Jasmine. She flew back out of the room, shivering slightly at the cool breeze that had just hit her, and past the pool table that was directly outside it. Walking past the double doors that were on her left, she made her way up the central staircase to the upper level, where everyone was congregating.

As she made her way up the staircase, she was temporarily overcome with an unexpected, split-second, of dizziness, as if she had missed a step on the way up, and her stomach lurched. She flicked her short, auburn hair, and bumped into Jasmine on the stairs, who was on her way back down.

'Hey Jas', thanks so much for driving!' said Kara, her dizziness now a mere memory. 'And for stopping for a Macker's breakfast, that was epic.'

'You're welcome,' said Jasmine. 'I'm just glad Will took the lead. I don't think we'd have made it otherwise,' she said, frowning.

Jasmine was relieved the journey was over. Hal had programmed his satnav with the voice of a popular talking car from the 80's, which was fine and all, but the route it was advising her to take seemed to want her to break away from the convoy every time she approached a roundabout. She was relieved that she was able to follow Will for the entirety of the journey. Jasmine flicked her long, black hair, still having to look up at Kara, despite being a step above her on the stairs.

Jasmine descended the central staircase, and popped into her room, noticing the pool table directly outside it.

"Well that's going to be *awesome* at three in the

morning," she thought to herself.

She chuckled at the thought that her sleep would be regularly interrupted with the sound of clacking resin, and loud drunken banter, secretly wishing that she could drink this weekend. As Jasmine walked through the open door into her room, she noticed that someone had already been out to her car and placed her bag on the bed for her. She remembered that a few people already knew about her not-so-secret secret, and smiled at the thoughtfulness, her hand subconsciously resting on the slight bump she was sporting.

*

With their bags unpacked, everyone met on the top floor, a vast space that was split between a large living area, a modest kitchen, and a larger dining section. Long sweeping balconies bookmarked each end of the building, which overlooked the front and rear gardens respectively. Sofa beds lined the far corners of the open space, which would be claimed soon enough by Peter, Fearne, Will, and Stacey.

With the tour of the lodge out of the way, the lads had all commandeered the hot tub before the girls had a chance to protest.

Alex was last to arrive, welcomed by Rachel and Hal, as he pulled up on the driveway. At just over six-foot tall, Alex towered over them. Thanks to Alex's thick, swooping, black hair, it would have been impossible for anyone to assume he and Hal were brothers.

As he closed the driver-side door, Alex could hear that the drinks were already flowing, and loud laughter was emanating from the rear garden, as music began to blare from an unseen speaker.

"I have a really great feeling about this weekend," thought Alex.

*

Jerry stared at the new visitors from the cover of the surrounding trees.

"Not yet…" he thought, "but soon…"

And he slowly retreated into the shadows that were being cast by the expansive canopy of the trees.

CHAPTER THREE

Jerry

Friday Afternoon, 2:37pm

Later that afternoon, the majority of the group headed inside to freshen up and escape the unrelenting sun. Jasmine ran a hand through her long dark hair, as she made her way up the staircase to the communal area. She was all for a bit of sun-worship, but since she fell pregnant, she'd applied an "everything in moderation" approach to how she went about her day.

She took a seat on one of the sofas, grabbing one of the magazines she had brought along with her from the coffee table, and flicked through the various stories that focused predominately on the current wave of pseudo-celebrities. Various fancy weddings adorned the pages, full of staged photos of people wearing more make-up in one photo than she would wear in a year. As she skipped over the majority of the stories, which focused on Shakespearean relationship betrayals, scandals engineered by the agents for the stars they represented, and various articles on two people that wore the same dress to the same event, her eyes glazed over, as the mystery over who indeed *did* wear it best was about to be revealed.

Daisy fell down onto the sofa to her right, pulling Jasmine back into the real world as she did so. Thankful for the arrival of a more stimulating pursuit, she turned to her friend.

'You know, it's a good job I'm not allowed in that hot tub,' said Jasmine, 'considering how much the boys are hogging it!'

Daisy rolled her eyes in agreement.

'Yeeeeah, Robert's pretty much set it up as a forwarding address,' said Daisy, smiling playfully in reference to her newly-aquatic husband, 'he can't seem to get enough of it.'

'Aren't you worried he's going to shrivel up?' asked Jasmine, with a chuckle.

'Nope, he's his own person,' said Daisy, 'I'm just thankful for the peace and quiet to be honest,' she joked, a layer of sincerity in her tone.

Daisy was always looking out for the members of the group; it was in her nature. Always advising them all whenever they were about to do something ill-advised, whether it be smoking a cigarette, or investing in an interest-only mortgage. To the untrained eye, it might have come across as being interfering, but they all loved her for it. She had a heart of gold, and if she was disappointed in you, it was a general rule of thumb that it was a direct result of your own misdemeanor that got you there in the first place, and you did your best to do better next time.

*

Robert sat in the hot tub, unknowingly satiating his wife's desire for peace and quiet. He was patiently waiting for Jon to rectify whatever it was that was causing the jets to keep cutting out, and was already three beers in; well on his way to becoming inebriated.

'Any luck, mate?' he said, calling out to Jon.

The hot tub immediately sprang to life, as if there was a direct correlation to his quandary and the desired outcome. Jon returned, flicking his sunglasses down from his forehead and discarding his white dressing gown to join Robert in the tub.

'Must be something wrong with the electrics,' he surmised.

'Maybe a fuse?' suggested Robert, bringing the exhilarating conversation to its natural end whilst simultaneously masking his complete lack of understanding when it came to anything electrical.

Peter and Will joined them next, having just returned from sourcing more alcohol, and jumped in next to Jon. Due to his always-active lifestyle, Peter was similar in physique to Jon, his short black hair, meticulously-maintained designer stubble, and ridiculously-perfect jaw-line working in harmonious tandem to make him look like a male model. He was always the smartest-looking man in the room, thanks to wearing the latest styles, nailing that edgy, fashionable look that Hal himself could never seem to get right, and his dark brown eyes smouldered, even when he was thinking about a grilled-cheese sandwich. Peter, having just returned from working in Vietnam for the past year, seemed positively glowing that he was back home, and getting to spend some real time with his friends again.

'Cheers everyone,' said Jon, and they clinked their bottles of beer in celebration of their long-overdue reunion.

*

At 3:37pm, Kara, Hal, Jon, and Fearne headed outside into the rear garden to kill some time by blasting a shuttlecock between them, having discovered some badminton rackets stored in the supply shed of the lodge, completely oblivious to the fact that Jerry was about to introduce himself to them, and that his arrival would turn their lives completely upside down.

'Right, we've formed a badminton! Let's do this!' declared Jon, his badminton racket shredding through the air and colliding with the already-beleaguered shuttlecock.

Hal wasn't sure what "forming a badminton"

meant exactly, though he assumed it must have been a "Northern thing." Nevertheless, he accepted the responsibility of whatever that entailed by volleying the shuttlecock back at full pelt, inches above Jon's head, which Jon expertly deflected over to Kara who then, in turn, redirected it towards Fearne. And so it continued, as Robert acted as an intoxicated referee from the comfort of his new, oceanic-themed home.

Jerry approached silently, utilising the tall hedges to cloak his presence. He was so close, he could smell them now. He breathed deeply, memorising their scent. Jerry sensed they would trust him, and he would use that to his advantage.

He stalked ever-closer, actively analysing the entirety of his surroundings for any other people.

They were alone.

"It's now or never," he thought.

Exhaling sharply, now resigned to his plan, he searched inside himself for the bravery he would need in the moments ahead. Impulsively, Jerry ran through the hedges, moving with incredible speed, remaining unseen, despite being in plain sight. As he charged towards them, he experienced, as he always did, the purest joy that came from following his animalistic impulses. With sheer brute-force, he set his sights on the short-haired one, briefly acknowledging the weapon she was brandishing, but not feeling afraid. After all, he'd done this so many times before, and had always reached his prey before they had time to run.

Kara saw him now, but it was too little, too late. He was on her. Tackling her legs, Jerry pinned her down, and extended his tongue, running it across her cheek. Kara screamed in shock at the violation of personal space, laughing loudly.

'Arg! Dog attack!' shouted Kara. 'Good doggy! Are you a good doggy?! Yes you are! Off now! Get off!'

Jerry, a white and red springer spaniel, obeyed immediately, assumed the sitting position, and barked loudly, seeking the customary validation for a job well done, what with him being the embodiment of "a good boy."

Kara rolled onto her front, picked herself up, and dusted herself down, as Jerry barked a second time, growing impatient for what was surely a well-earned reward. Hal went to fetch the football Stacey had brought with her, a crucial part of the costume she would be adorning the next day, and jogged back to where Jon had formed The Badminton Alliance.

Hal tossed the ball to Kara, and Jerry caught on immediately. Jerry barked intermittently, seemingly exasperated that Kara was taking so long to lose her grip on the spherical trophy that he was so desperate to intercept, fearful that she would return it to the man standing a fair distance away before he could strike.

'Wow, if you weren't a dog person, you'd think he was being aggressive, right?' said Hal, raising an eyebrow as he surveyed the dog.

'Yeah, definitely,' said Kara, using an underarm-throw to launch the ball down the seemingly endless garden.

Jerry overshot his mark, and went head-first into a hedge, then launched himself back out, wrestling the ball on his own for a bit. Jon sighed, as the realisation that he was never going to talk Rachel around into having a dog set in, what with her being regimentally concise about being a "cat person."

Hal went to pick up the ball, and Jerry resumed his tirade of barks, refusing to let him pick it up.

'You wanna play kid? Or are you just going to be a jerk about it?' said Hal, causing Jerry's ears to twitch, as he looked up at him.

Kara seized the opportunity to grab the ball whilst Jerry was distracted, taking advantage of Jerry's momentary lapse in judgement, as he apparently mulled Hal's question over. She threw it once more, and Jerry bolted off after it at full pelt, his legs flailing wildly, as if they were working independently from his adorable mind.

Once Jerry has used a fair portion of his seemingly-endless reserve of energy, Kara, Hal, and Jon all took turns fussing over him. Jerry's collar flashed in the sunlight, revealing his name, which was engraved on the front. Kara flipped it over and noted his address, which was etched on the back.

'Anyone else think it's weird that whoever his owner is has just let him roam free out here?' said Fearne, raising a valid point. 'Do you think he's lost?'

Jon gave it some thought, and then dismissed her concerns.

'Nah, probably lived here for years,' said Jon. 'Probably lives close by too.'

'His name's Jerry. Says he lives at number 51,' said Kara, chiming in and referencing the tag. 'No idea where that is though, our lodge doesn't even have a number, does it?'

Jerry's ears twitched once more, as if catching a sound only he could hear. He moved away from them, and shook from head to tail, his comically flapping jowls revealing his teeth, as if he was shaking off water after an unexpected dip.

Having seemingly decided that their fuss and attention was no longer required, he shot off around the side entrance, stopping briefly to examine an interesting scent. Whatever had caught his attention didn't distract him for long, however, and he continued on his way, disappearing from sight.

'Why do I get the feeling that won't be the last we'll be seeing of him?' said Hal with a chuckle. 'See ya later Jerry!' he added, shouting towards the hedges, despite knowing that Jerry was surely long gone by now.

Wrapping up their badminton quartet, they

headed back inside, leaving the current Master of The Seven Seas to his own devices in the hot tub.

*

At 8pm, everyone met in the communal dining area for a sit-down meal, and the luxurious cabin was filled with the sound of clinking wine glasses, laughter, and music.

After their meal, the drinkers in the group moved on to the stronger liquor, indulging in the delights of shots, mixers and the over-powering cocktail monstrosities that Jon was throwing together with reckless abandon.

Not one of them suspected that they were being watched, or that their actions and conversations were being monitored.

CHAPTER FOUR

Bloody Mary

Saturday Morning, 7:59am

Hal stirred from his sleep with a start, momentarily readjusting to his unfamiliar surroundings. The downside of Jess not coming with him was that he had been assigned a room with only single-sized beds to choose from instead of a double. It was a sleep devoid of stolen covers, and dogs stretching, that usually operated in tandem to force him into the one-eighth of sleep-space he was accustomed to. He smiled, noting that it was the most space he'd enjoyed whilst sleeping in a long time, whilst acknowledging that he missed the two ladies in his life, despite the fact that they frequently conspired to ruin his sleep at every opportunity.

Hal reached for his phone to check the time, noting that it was 7:59am. One minute before his alarm was due to go off.

'Rad,' he muttered, rolling his eyes as the dulcet tone of an acoustic rendition of the track "Numb" began to spill from the phone. He killed it instantly, so as not to wake his brother Alex, who was still fast asleep in the bottom bunk of the adjacent bunk-beds. His attempt at stealth was largely negated, however, by the creaks and groans his spring mattress made as he rose.

Safe in the knowledge he'd tried his best, he slipped out of the bedroom into the communal hallway, and ascended the wooden staircase that led to the voices of his friends, who were already up and milling around.

"Having kids will do that to your body-clock I guess," he thought, adding another tick to the column of boxes for reasons not to have them.

The kitchen was alive with the sound of grilling.

In an audacious display of Britishness, crumpets popped from the nearby toaster, and the sound of cereal reacting to cascading milk did nothing to draw his focus away from the nearby kettle. He was a zombie without coffee.

Daisy breezed past him, grabbing the aforementioned crumpets, a tub of butter, and a cup of tea, multi-tasking with natural aplomb.

'Morning Hal!' said Daisy chirpily.

'Mrng,' mumbled Hal, yawning deeply as he opened and closed what felt like fifteen drawers, until he finally struck gold and located a teaspoon.

Popping the cap off the whole-bean/instant blend of coffee he was rocking lately, and using his Terminator style vision to acquire the location of some sugar, he nabbed the milk from behind Fearne, who was clearly in the zone, working with Jon to knock up some epic bacon sandwiches for everyone. Making a mental note to pick these two up first in the event of a zombie-apocalypse, he retreated to the communal lounge area, which was invitingly illuminated by the rising sunshine.

'How's it going boss?' asked Hal, plonking

himself down next to Will.

'Mate, I feel great, we should cut back on the drinking more often,' said Will, almost whispering.

'Yeah, this must be what winning feels like,' noted Hal. 'Mind you, clearly I'm better at pool when I'm drunk. I take it Robert is still recovering?'

Will chuckled as only someone without a hangover would, when looking down from their ivory tower, at Robert's misfortune, who had taken his drinking a notch too far.

'Dead to the world apparently,' said Will, 'I think he pretty much finished that bottle of whisky he brought? He was in that hot tub for six hours straight too. Worryingly, he didn't even get out to take a leak…'

They sipped their coffees, and scrunched up their noses with simultaneous distaste at that revelation.

Hal swallowed his mouthful of coffee, immediately feeling like a red-caped superhero who had recently returned from a long weekend retreat at the centre of the Earth's sun.

'I heard him professing his love for each of us when I popped out for a smoke,' said Hal, recalling the moment that Robert began shouting about how they were all family, and him all but shaking Kara until she convinced him that she really did understand his point.

'Poor chap,' added Hal.

Will laughed, and wrapped up the tangent succinctly by whispering 'yeah, makes a change for it not to be us for once,' as if speaking any louder would remind their nearby friends of their mile-long list of transgressions that no normal group would have forgiven them for.

'Amen brother,' said Hal.

*

Kara awoke with the grace of a startled pigeon that was reacting to the sound of a shotgun going off in the nearby vicinity. Holding her hands against her face, and running them through her short hair, she tried to shake off her hangover with a determined shudder. She reached for her phone and noted it was 8:09am, cursing herself for hitting the drinking hard the night before. She wasn't entirely sure what day it was.

"Saturday…" she realised.

Kara looked over and noted that Jon, Rachel, and Jasmine were apparently already up and out of the room they'd all been sharing, just as Rachel hopped out of the en suite bathroom.

'Heeey you! How you feeling?' said Rachel, in the manner of someone approaching a ferocious tiger.

Kara thought about the question, then dropped her head back onto her pillow, staring at the ceiling and emitting a soft groan of acknowledgement. Kara held up her phone, unlocking it with the fingerprint scanner. A message from Greg singed itself into her delicate retinas. She clicked on the message.

"Hope you had a great night hun! It was so lonely without you last night! Xxx"

She smiled, and made a mental note to reply when she was a tad more vertical, as opposed to her current state of being an occupant on a merry-go-round, one that was apparently localised entirely within her own internal sense of equilibrium.

Sitting up, she stretched and summoned her secret superpower, permitting it to activate. There wasn't a hangover she couldn't power through; all she had to do was refuse to submit to it. She hopped out of bed, made her way to the en suite, and set the shower to a gentle, refreshing, ice-cold temperature, slightly disappointed by the realisation that there wasn't a heat setting closer to that of liquid-nitrogen.

*

Rachel jogged up the stairs and caught Hal making what she knew was surely his second cup of coffee. Her partner Jon was brewing "proper coffee" in a percolator, a device that Hal had never possessed enough patience to try. He had always needed coffee yesterday, and was too impatient to wait for what he knew would be a far superior caffeinated experience. Hal's ambivalence was forever neutralised by his need for instant, albeit granulated, gratification.

Rachel winked at Jon, and he interpreted her signal. Grabbing another cup for her, he placed it next to his own, both cups speaking happily to each other via the medium of an audible clink.

'So, what's the plan of attack for today guys?' asked Hal.

'Breakfast, hot-tub, get drunk,' said Jon, listing off the items on his non-negotiable agenda.

Hal laughed, waiting for the customary one-second to expire, knowing that Rachel would elaborate.

'Well,' said Rachel, 'we're doing the barbeque this afternoon. Robert is doing his trademark paella, assuming he ever surfaces...and Will is doing his beef brisket. Then we're going to change into our costumes.'

Her comment caused Jon to frown.

'And *then* get smashed,' added Rachel, nudging Jon in the ribs playfully.

Several months ago, each of the guests had received instructions to put together fancy-dress costumes for the Saturday. This year the theme was "Idols." It was something of a tradition, and every year, each and every one of them attempted to up the ante.

*

Feeling refreshed and, more importantly, not smelling of tequila, Kara removed her costume from her carry-all and placed it onto her pillow, searching for a top to wear. She skipped into the communal hallway, up the wooden staircase, and into the kitchen, just as Peter was explaining to Jasmine how his recent construction contract in Vietnam had yielded enough monetarily to finance them moving into their first home together.

Coupled with Jasmine's pleasant reveal yesterday, whilst they were driving to the lodge, that her and her husband were having a baby, Kara noted how quickly time was passing.

It seemed like only yesterday that they were all downing prosecco and beers, spending their nights hitting the town. The same nights that had cemented their friendships into bonds that would never be broken.

And then Kara smiled, as she realised that that was literally what they were doing yesterday evening and, perhaps, they weren't all doomed to become full-blown adults quite just yet.

Maybe that was what growing old was really all about. Not betraying your identity to be what you thought the world was telling you to be, but instead imbuing your adult persona with the quirks and idiosyncrasies of your younger self, empowered by the hindsight gained along the way.

It was a poignant thought, one which she expertly

gave credence to, as she bypassed the tea and coffee entirely, reaching instead for some tomato juice, some Worcestershire sauce, some Tabasco, and the salt and pepper shakers. She scoured the kitchen-counter looking for the last, crucial ingredient, experiencing a pang of relief as she located the vodka, and added all of the components together.

"Much better," she thought, as she gulped down her Bloody Mary.

CHAPTER FIVE
Into the Woods

Saturday Morning, 10:52am

The morning passed quickly, as each of the gang applied their own personally-customised brand of hangover cure around their respective breakfasts. Feeling a lot more like themselves, they moved into the rear garden to soak up some sun. Hal remained in the protective shield of shade, cast by the gazebo Jon had erected the day before, whilst Fearne was busy at work, applying the final touches to some intricate Henna artwork to Daisy and Jasmine. Jon, meanwhile, was on the phone to the owner of the property, reporting that the hot-tub was cutting out at sporadic intervals. Ending the call, he informed Rachel that the owner would be popping in later to take a look.

'All done!' said Fearne, finally.

The results were impressive, and both of her customers seemed chuffed to bits.

For the first time since anyone could remember following a heavy drinking session, Will was looking positively recharged and raring to seize the day. Only Hal knew that this was due to their secret pact to dial-back the drinking.

'Right, anyone fancy a walk through the woods?' said Will. 'I want to check out the lake!'

Will had inexplicably purchased some junior fishing equipment, and had been adamant that he would use his impulsive investment at least once this weekend. Everyone knew that he wouldn't get around to it before the weekend was done.

'Count me in,' said Hal, jumping out from the safety of the make-shift barrier of shade that the gazebo was providing, and running off to pack the only provisions he would need for this impromptu trek into the tamed wilderness that was surrounding them.

Jasmine, Kara, Fearne, and Daisy all decided they were also up for the walk, and followed suit, heading to the driveway.

Hal hopped through the front entrance door of Fir Lodge, and joined them on the gravel.

'Right, I'm ready, let's do this,' said Hal.

Kara narrowed her eyes, scrutinising the backpack he was sporting.

'What could you *possibly* have in there that you'd need for a twenty-minute walk?' said Kara.

'Suntan lotion man!' said Hal, as he pulled his shades from the collar around his neck, flicked them open, and popped them on. 'I didn't want to just carry a bottle of the stuff, that would look stupid!'

'Yeah…no danger of that now,' said Kara, mockingly raising an eyebrow.

Hal feigned a look of sadness, as if she had hurt his feelings, then positioned himself in front of his friends.

'Smile everyone!' he said, as he took some selfies of the group, now that they were ready to embark on their expedition.

*

The group of explorers returned half an hour later than planned, due to hitting a dead-end, resulting in them having to backtrack over their entire route to make it back to the lodge. Will had suggested it would have been easier to have just swum across the lake, cutting their return time down significantly, but his partially-serious idea was vetoed by everyone, on the basis that it was terrible.

Their return from the woods heralded the arrival of Michaela and Gavin, and with the final guests accounted for, Jon and Robert headed out to the rear garden to fire up the barbecue.

Rachel and Hal headed down the stairs to greet them, and gave Michaela and Gavin a tour. This was Michaela and Gavin's first real time away from their recently born little girl, but they seemed to be taking the separation in their stride. They were the calmest parents Rachel and Hal had ever seen, and never seemed intimidated or lost amidst their new-found responsibilities. Hal admired their laid-back approach, certain that his own parenting style would have been a combination of uncontrollable chaos and debilitating sleep-deprivation.

Hal waited for the new arrivals to work their way through the group, hoping to steal some quality time with Michaela. Back in the day, he, Rachel and Michaela were inseparable. And whilst their busy lives had inevitably got in the way of them spending as much time together as they may have liked, they knew without a doubt that there was nothing they wouldn't do for each other. If he ever needed to hide a body, these two girls were the ones he'd have on his speed-dial, with Jess as his getaway driver.

'Hey Hal!' said Michaela, throwing her arms around him, and planting a kiss on his cheek.

'It's so great to see you Mich's, how's the little-un?' asked Hal.

'She's all good!' said Michaela, using her index finger to push a runaway bang of her long, blonde hair back behind her ear. 'Mum's babysitting for us, it was *so* hard to leave her,' she added, looking over Hal's shoulder and around the lodge. 'No Jess?!'

'Nah, she's looking after Shelby.'

'Oh no, was really looking forward to catching up with her. Well, it's so good to see you!'

'You too!' he said.

It really was.

After a short catch up, Gavin returned from fetching their bags from the car and moved in for a handshake. Extending one of his tattooed arms towards Hal, they both bailed on that idea and gave each other a hearty hug instead, as was generally customary with the men in the group. Gavin was taller than Hal, his modestly-toned body and handsome features making him an ideal ally for Peter, in the event that either of them ever decided to branch out into the glitzy world of modelling.

With the formalities done and dusted, and the final guests now present and accounted for, Rachel gave Jon the green light to fire up the barbecue, and for everyone else to suit-up into their chosen costumes.

*

The two spectators watched the events unfolding before them, everything playing out in the same order it always did, hoping they had done enough. The young man looked over to the woman standing beside him, a stranger to him now...and yet, at the same time...somehow not. Her presence was simultaneously a comfort, and a horrifying reminder that everything was wrong. He blinked to release the tears that were building up in his eyes, like a wall of doubt, blurring his vision. His throat burned with regret, for a sin he could barely remember, one that he also had no desire to clutch on to any longer.

CHAPTER SIX

The Man in the Plaid Shirt

Saturday Afternoon, 1:53pm

The barbecue was in full swing, with Robert's now-legendary paella going down a storm, not that Robert could really enjoy it, given that he was still gingerly nursing the mother of all hangovers and didn't want to push his luck by eating anything as ambitious as prawns. Using his stocky, muscular frame to his advantage, he had fully embraced being Santa Claus, presenting copious amounts of his own unique brand of hangover-tinged Christmas cheer, four months earlier than anyone was even remotely ready for. A white wig covered his short brown hair, conspiring with his real beard that he'd began sporting several months ago, causing him to sweat in the afternoon sun.

The garden was filled by the tantalising smells of freshly-cooked barbecue food as everyone dug in, sitting themselves down on the benches, and breaking bread together for the first time in far too long.

As everyone finished up their barbecued food, Gavin span onto the scene to top up the cups that were resting on the homemade beer-pong table that Fearne and Peter had brought with them, whilst Rachel headed inside to chuck some chicken wings in the oven, now that Jon and Robert had cooked all of the barbecue food they had brought. Wearing spats, a perfectly tailored yellow suit and, in a show of ultimate commitment, his face painted completely green, Gavin had begun to boil in the baking sun. But, as yet, there were no signs of smoke

Hal and Alex were equally suffering beneath the scorching heat, currently dressed as two ghost-busting scientists, made famous in the 80's. Their matching, tan-coloured boiler suits were emblazoned with rectangular name tags, their names embroidered with red stitching on a black background. Grey belts were wrapped around their waists, with heavy-duty, black chemical-gloves tucked through the belts on one side. Wrapped around their belts on the opposite side were home-made, portable ghost-containment units, attached with customised TV cables. Olive coloured arm pads complemented the look, together with inflatable versions of proton-powered, nuclear accelerator packs, which they wore on their backs. Their costumes were finalised by the thick, black, wellington boots they were sporting.

Hal was distracted from the heat, somewhat preoccupied with making weak excuses as to why he couldn't partake in the next round of the "epic beer pong tournament" that Jon and Gavin had organised. Both were in the process of thrashing Peter and his ghost-busting brother, as Santa Claus acted as referee.

Dressed as none other than his golfing hero Tiger Woods, Peter was a proficient golfer in real life, and regularly spent long weekends away to hit some of the fancier courses. Hal suspected that Peter had used the excuse of needing a costume to fool Fearne, so that he could purchase another wave of golf merchandise.

Jon, meanwhile, was rocking a parody costume of Craig David, one which was made famous in the early two-thousands. His short black hair was covered by a beanie hat, his face covered by a rubber mask that was kept in place by retro headphones, an inflatable kestrel attached to his arm completing the look.

Hal winced, as he remembered the last time he had played. In fact, he found it almost impossible to forget. How they had run out of beer and switched in mojitos to every cup…and how Hal and Alex thought they could take on Jon, a seasoned RAF professional and Gavin, who had years of university experience under his belt. Hal and his brother had failed so spectacularly that, to this day, even the slightest whiff of fresh-mint caused Hal to cringe at the triggered sensory memory. It was not his finest hour, an emotion that Alex clearly shared, as he slinked off inside, under the pretence of helping Rachel.

Luckily, Fearne and Stacey, dressed as Marilyn Monroe and the centre-forward for Colchester United respectively, excitedly stepped up to take on the lads, meaning that Hal was safe for another ten minutes or so.

Fearne appeared at Peter's side, looking breath-taking in her 1950's white dress, which complemented her curvaceous frame, and an eerily convincing blonde wig that covered her naturally brunette hair. Despite her high heels, she still managed to look somewhat shorter than Peter.

No one expected the next ten minutes to play out quite the way they did, however. In the purest demonstration of beginner's luck, and against all odds, Fearne and Stacey methodically, and systematically, destroyed The Mask and Craig David at their own game. The rupture of applause at the hilarious turn of events was deafening.

As the girls demanded a rematch, drunk on their success, unlike Jon and Gavin, who were soon to be drunk in a more conventional sense, their adversaries were honour-bound to down the remaining cups of beer on the table, and rack them up for the next round.

Accepting their fate, they honoured the forfeit and downed their beers. Jon and Gavin then re-racked the cups and refilled them (with a slightly lower amount of beer than they would have done if they had won.)

Their rematch was unexpectedly interrupted, however, as Jerry bounced into the garden, colliding with the table and knocking over the carefully aligned cups, leaving the freshly-poured beer now freshly-soaking into the grass.

'Je-RRRRRYYY!' shouted a stranger from the side of the lodge. The dog's frustrated owner walked into the rear garden, apologising profusely.

'I really am sorry about this one. He tends to wander the woods and likes to hassle the new arrivals,' said the man, as he clocked the barbecue, and voiced his deduction by adding 'though in this instance, clearly he was just drawn by your dinner.'

'Not at all,' said Jon, pulling of his mask. 'He's welcome to join us, as long as you don't mind?'

'Kevin. The name's Kevin.'

Jon and Kevin shook hands. Kevin was taller than most, approximately in his fifties, and had the heavyset build of a man who had worked hard in a profession that possibly involved moving breeze blocks or incredibly heavy timber. Jon wouldn't have fancied his chances in an arm-wrestle contest with the gentle giant. Wearing a blue and black plaid shirt, denim jeans that had been washed a few-thousand more times that was probably recommended, and large, heavy-duty, brown work-boots, he was precisely how you imagined a man who spent the majority of his time in the woods to look.

'Well,' continued Kevin, 'as long as you're sure. If he gets too much for you, just get his attention and say "JERRY. GO HOME."'

The man clicked his fingers, causing Jerry's ears to perk up, and demonstrated by repeating the phrase. Jerry stared at his owner, tongue hanging out, and panted excitedly. He barked, and then went to acquire a sausage from one of the easily-manipulated humans sitting on the picnic benches.

Kara skipped across the grass in a flurry of bright orange, thanks to the colouring of her matching top, and knee-high socks, her red pleated-skirt and retro magnifying-glass combining exquisitely with her nerdy-glasses. With her naturally-bobbed auburn hair, she was the spitting image of Velma, a member of an iconic ghost-hunting team from the 80's, who was often affiliated with a talking dog and an unshaven, loveable waster.

She broke off a piece of sausage, asking for Jerry's paw, and rewarded him accordingly when he obeyed.

Kevin sighed exhaustively. 'Well, it'll work for you when you try it, I'm sure. I'm only up the road if he doesn't let up.'

'Cheers, no worries,' said Jon.

'Right, well, I'll get back to it then,' said Kevin, looking more than a little out of breath, as if he had recently been for a run. 'Hope the sun holds out for you. Nice costumes by the way,' he added.

And with that, Kevin left through the same side access that he'd arrived from, as Marilyn and her professional-footballer partner racked up the plastic cups into a triangular formation, ready for round two. Jon was feeling just a shade too drunk to accept, however, and was begrudgingly forced into admitting defeat, making his way to the hot tub instead.

'Anyone?!' said Fearne, her white dress swishing crazily amidst her newly acquired enthusiasm for The Great Beer Pong War of 2018.

With a mutual nod between them, The Mask and

Tiger Woods accepted the challenge.

CHAPTER SEVEN

The Pink Flamingo

Saturday Afternoon, 2:07pm

With the rest of group dispersed in the rear garden, Alex made his way inside the lodge under the guise of offering up some assistance to their host.

Rachel was preparing some additional food for her ravenous guests, as Alex wandered into the open-plan kitchen to grab himself a beer, twisting the cap and flicking it towards the bin that was situated several feet away. The cap bounced off of the side, missing its intended target, forcing Alex to perform the walk of shame to pick it up, and having to dispose of it in a more conventional, less-flashy manner.

'This place is awesome Rachel. Thank you so much for arranging it,' said Alex.

Rachel thrust an additional tray of spicy chicken wings into the gas oven that dominated the north wall of the kitchen area, utterly unconvinced that one tray alone would be enough, and that only a second, perhaps a third, would suffice. She spun around to face Alex, and leant on the counter, her eyes shockingly bright amidst the red and blue lightning bolt that ran across her face. Alex couldn't get over how spot-on the birthday girl looked, noting how she perfectly embodied the image of the legend that was David Bowie. Dressed in a well-tailored blue suit, white business shirt and yellow tie, the outfit complemented her self-applied face-paint; a flawless recreation of the red and blue lightning bolt that only Ziggy himself could pull off, until now that was. Her electric-red hair now less a reflection of her mood, as it was a carefully thought out and fundamental component to her costume.

'Not too shabby, right?' said Rachel, 'I'm just

thrilled so many of the gang could make it.'

In many ways, the group was as close as it always was, and each of them knew that any one of them could have called on the other, day or night, and they'd be there for each other in a heartbeat. But as they glided into their thirties and beyond, life inevitably got in the way of the weekend-long parties of old. Many of them were parents now, some soon to be. Others were wrapped up in their careers, chasing promotions and various other opportunities. Things that used to drive them, such as buying tequila slammers, ten rounds of Jagerbombs, and dancing in clubs and bars until the sun began to rise, had been replaced with mortgages, parenthood, and the ruthless reality that they just couldn't brush off a hangover sent direct from Mother-Nature quite like they used to in the old days.

"With the exception of Kara of course," thought Rachel, pensively. And yet, they were the cliché in the best possible way. Whenever they got together, no matter how long it had been, it was always as if no time had passed. It was as if they'd pressed the pause button on their last gathering, continuing exactly where they had left off, whenever they next met.

Alex caught a whiff of a familiar scent, and thought it best to ask Rachel if she had noticed it too.

'Can you smell gas?' he said casually, in-between swigs of beer.

Rachel swished her hand in front of her face, as if she were swatting away an invisible fly.

'Nah, it's just this beast of an oven! It takes forever to heat up,' said Rachel.

Alex nodded, told Rachel he'd catch her in a bit, and walked out onto the eastern-side balcony. His inflatable nuclear accelerator smashed into the door frame, causing him to have to walk through the door sideways.

Applying pressure to the wheel on his lighter, which took several attempts for the flint to catch so that the sparks ignited the gas contained within, he eventually lit his cigarette. Looking out over the balcony to his friends in the garden below, he noticed how much cooler it was under the shade of the roof, which extended beyond the balcony itself, and experienced a chill that made him shudder.

It was at that moment that a bright-pink flamingo

flew up to him, and landed at his feet. Which was unusual at this time of year. In England. Whilst in the middle of a woodland area that the species was not even remotely indigenous to.

CHAPTER EIGHT

Scooby Don't

Saturday Evening, 8:34pm

Being the forward planning adults that they were, the gang cleared up the remnants of the barbecue, and took the dirty plates and utensils up to the kitchen, ditching them in the sink, due to the over-filled dishwasher being packed to bursting-point. Jerry had lost interest several hours prior, continuing his adventures elsewhere.

Kara, adopting a persona akin to the Velma costume she was wearing, was currently reviewing a recently accepted case, using her deductions and sleuthing to figure out how the high-tech dishwasher was supposed to work. After pressing every button, the machine eventually showed pity on her, humming to life, and Kara grabbed her bottle of Southern Comfort, contentedly rewarding herself for a job well done.

She saw Gavin scanning the now-communal mobile phone in the dining area, searching for the next track to play, and called out a request to him.

'You got "Spirit in The Sky" Gavin?'

He shot her a wink and, several seconds later, her wish had been granted.

Fearne and Stacey, like many of the others, had shed the more-encumbering components of their costumes, relishing in their inexplicable hat-trick of wins in the beer pong tournament. Stacey grabbed a nearby bottle of Prosecco from the kitchen counter, her Colchester football shirt clashing ridiculously with Fearne's 1950's ensemble. Fearne had discarded her wig well into the second round of the competition, due to it allegedly being responsible for her missing some easy shots, a fact that was seemingly invalidated by her naturally brunette hair, which was as equally as long and voluminous as the flowing wig.

Fearne span around with the bottle, knocking over one of the champagne flutes, which were all lined up precariously on the counter next to Kara, who was pouring a hefty measure of her American liqueur. The glass fell from the counter, causing the other flutes to ripple threateningly and connected with the wooden floor with a sickly clink, shattering violently.

Daisy immediately took charge from the other side of the room and tasked Kara with grabbing a dustpan and brush.

'I'm so sorry!' said Fearne, offering to help pick up the pieces.

'Don't worry, I've got this!' said Daisy, as Kara passed her the dustpan and Daisy began sweeping up the broken pieces. Slightly drunk, Fearne decided more drink was the answer and that she would pour her friends some more wine.

Gripping a nearby bottle of Prosecco, Fearne shook it a little, readying the cork for popping. With a vibrant pop, the cork, being a slave to predetermined physics, flew across the room, down the stairs and into the back of Hal's head.

'Ow. Thanks upstairs,' moaned Hal, hearing the girls giggling laughter from the landing above him. Hal grumbled, attempting to stifle a chuckle, then continued onwards towards his bedroom.

Will and Jon, meanwhile, were starting another round of pool, manoeuvring their way around Peter, who was in the corner, tapping incessantly on the screen of his phone.

Finally, arriving at his room, Hal acknowledged how his thick rubber boots had been a bad choice.

"These things man…" he thought, noting how they were all but filling up due to the mugginess of the evening heat. Wellington boots were definitely not a lifestyle choice he would be switching to in a hurry. He was about to switch into more conventional footwear when Peter called from outside his door.

'Hal mate, can I borrow your charger?' said Peter.

'Sorry dude, I gave up the fruit a while back,' said Hal. 'Try Robert, maybe?'

Peter mumbled something and continued on his quest.

Hal pulled his filter box from his pocket to take

stock on how many pre-rolled cigarettes he had left, discovering that only three remained. He made a mental note to dig out his tobacco from his suitcase to roll some more. Slipping the inflatable nuclear-accelerator from his back and chucking it onto his single-sized bed, he pulled out his phone, noticing that he had a missed call from Jess, along with a pre-recorded video in his inbox. Unlocking his phone, he pressed play, turning the screen sideways. Shelby filled the screen, doing her favourite thing in the world; chasing bubbles, as Jess's voice filled the speakers.

"Say hello to Daddy!"

Judging by the lack of response, Shelby was clearly far too preoccupied with taking down the bubbles for such a task. As the video came to an end, Hal chuckled to himself, then exited through his bedroom door, took a left turn, and headed back out into the rear garden.

As he made his way outside, he heard a strange clunk from Robert's room, which backed onto the hot-tub area. Mercifully for Hal, he was pleased to see that the sun had finally set. With the hot tub cleaning cycle over and done with, Robert had jumped back in for what must have been the thousandth time, having grabbed a beer from the cool box he'd cunningly positioned within arm's reach, the bottle perching precariously on the edge near the control panel.

"Poor tub, having to ensconce this lot," thought Hal, as he punched the dial button and waited for his phone to connect to Jess.

As he walked past the hot tub, still waiting for the call to connect, he looked over his shoulder and saw Peter through the window of Robert's bedroom. Peter's face was illuminated by the blue hue of his smartphone. Paying more attention to Peter than the potential hazards in his surrounding environment, Hal walked straight into one of the gazebo struts.

'Ouch,' said Hal, immediately checking his angles, relieved to see that only Robert was currently in the garden, and that Robert was too busy snoozing in the hot-tub, his Santa hat pulled down low and covering his eyes, to have paid him any attention.

Jess's voice emanated from the speaker of his phone and the ghost-buster rolled his eyes, as the familiar answerphone kicked in. He loved her to bits, but she was the absolute worst at answering her phone. If he was honest (and less tipsy), he would have rationally acknowledged that he too had been the absolute worst at answering his own, having been the one to miss her initial call in the first place.

'Hal, get in here!' shouted Kara from across the hallway which he had just traversed.

Flicking the lid back on his box of cigarettes, he begrudgingly walked back, past the tub, past Robert's room, along the full-length of the hallway, and stood next to Kara, who was standing in front of the stairs, looking out towards the front driveway.

'You okay Kara?' he asked, with the tone of a man that was being nagged, then noticing why she had called him.

'Look!' she said, gesturing with her head towards her feet, as if he had somehow missed the obvious.

'Oh, hey buddy!' said Hal, setting his eyes on Jerry, who was sniffing Kara's shoes. Responding to his name, Jerry's excitement levels increased somewhat, and he took off, running between everyone's legs, sniffing everything he could get near. He began to run up the wooden staircase when Daisy called down at them.

'Can someone grab the dog please?!' said Daisy, clearly more than a little stressed out. 'Don't let him upstairs, there's broken glass everywhere!'

Stacey began to walk down the staircase to assist them, but Fearne lost her balance, all but falling over into her path. Stacey spun round, catching Fearne just in time, preventing her from falling down the stairs, and escorted Fearne to one of the sofas in the living room so she could lay down.

'Wow, looks like the beer pong finally finished Fearne off,' said Kara. 'What should we do?' she added, turning her attention back to Hal.

Will, who had fully embraced his costume, was still dressed as an iconic anchor-man, his bushy, fake moustache completing the full-on Burgundy look, and was currently revelling in his victory at the pool table over Jon. Fed up of Will's lucky streak, Jon was willing to do anything to free himself from the humiliation of another inevitable defeat, and chimed in.

'Didn't that Kev guy say you just have to tell him to "go home"?' said Jon, preparing to ditch his pool cue entirely. 'Here, let me try…'

'Don't think so mate,' said Will, 'you're not getting out of this that easy.'

Alex arrived through the rear doors, taking up a seat next to the pool table and laughed, eager to see if Will's lucky streak would continue.

Being the only two in Jerry's vicinity who weren't battling for bragging rights, or spectating on a battle between two self-proclaimed pool gods, they didn't feel comfortable just kicking Jerry out. Hal stepped outside, the gravel crunching under his cumbersome boots.

'Jerry, GO HOME!' he said, pointing into the darkness in an authoritative manner.

Jerry, who had followed him outside, stared at him for all of two seconds, made an indignant huffing noise through his nose, and then tried to walk back past him into the lodge.

'Yeah, that's not working, shall we take him home? Can't be that far?' suggested Kara.

'Yeah,' agreed Hal. 'To be honest, I don't like the idea of him being outside in the dark on his own anyway. Come on Jerry!'

'You need a hand Hal?' shouted Alex, across the

room to his brother.

'Nah, we've got this, cheers though,' said Hal, taking the lead.

As Kara and Jerry followed him up the driveway of Fir Lodge, Hal stopped suddenly, as Robert's car made an odd creaking noise.

'You hear that?' he asked, directly his question to Kara.

'Hear what? Come on let's get going,' said Kara, taking charge.

It was at precisely that moment that they realised they had no way of knowing which way to go.

'Sooo…which way?' asked Hal.

Jerry trotted ahead of them, turned left and continued along the road a bit further, stopping to sniff a decaying pile of pine needles.

'Left is good,' decided Kara.

CHAPTER NINE

The Cabin in the Woods

Saturday Evening, 8:56pm

Jerry continued to lead the way, stopping intermittently to take care of his business, to sniff at random intervals, and to indulge in other canine pursuits that made no sense to either of the members of his current entourage. Hal had always been amazed by how attuned a dog's senses were to the world. He had read somewhere that they perceived the world in tunnel-vision, possessing the ability to identify smells that had dissipated weeks before, completely imperceptible to those of a more human disposition.

It suddenly occurred to Hal that they had no idea if they had even walked past Jerry's house already and that, for all they knew, Jerry was working on the assumption that he was simply being taken for a walk.

'Did you say his address was on his collar?' said Hal, after a few minutes had passed.

'Damn it, yeah!' winced Kara, as she leant down and reached out for the silver disc that was dangling around Jerry's neck, causing it to glisten in the moonlight. She recited what she deemed to be the most pertinent of the engraved information.

'Number fifty-one,' said Kara.

'Uh-huh. Which would be super awesome if all the lodges didn't have *names* instead of numbers,' said Hal, reaching for his box of smokes.

'Didn't you say you were quitting?' asked Kara.

'That's funny…that doesn't *sound* like something I'd say…' lamented Hal.

'Ha. Wait, that's forty-five there!' said Kara.

Hal pocketed his cigarettes, craning his neck in an attempt to see the house number, which was helpfully illuminated by the interior light from the stranger's living room.

'Huh. Okay...I take it back,' said Hal.

They continued on, Hal feeling somewhat irritated that he hadn't traded his wellington boots for more conventional footwear. His boiler suit was actually protecting him from the evening breeze. He noted to himself that Kara must have been catching a chill in her Velma costume. Kara, on the other hand, not entirely sure why she had bothered bringing her detective style magnifying glass, tucked it into the waistband of her red pleated skirt. Feeling pleased with herself for developing an impromptu life-hack that negated the need for her to hold it any longer, she smiled, finally surrendering to the shiver that had been building due to the cool night air.

'Gah, it's getting chilly!' said Kara.

'Sucks to be you,' said Hal, pulling up the zip of his khaki boiler suit for added effect, 'I know why they call them boiler suits now, I'm proper toasty. You can have my gloves if you like?'

She turned her nose up at the offer, which was clearly a joke, given that the black rubber gloves of his costume were designed more to prevent chemical burns than for retaining heat.

'Hard pass, but thanks for being *such* a gentleman.'

'It's my one flaw, said Hal. 'Well, that and modesty.'

They continued on, and eventually reached what they believed to be Jerry's home. The front door was open, despite all of the lights being off.

'Well, that's not creepy at *all*,' noted Kara.

'Dude, relax,' said Hal, 'with our powers combined we're the greatest ghost-hunters the 80's had to offer. And, he may not be a talking Great Dane, but we have Jerry too.' He pointed at Jerry, who yawned and emitted a traitorous, yet undeniably cute squeak.

'Great. You take him in then,' said Kara, checkmating him with a single sentence.

'Damn, well played,' said Hal, sighing in defeat. 'Fine. I'll be right back.'

Hal grimaced, realising he'd just broken the cardinal rule of horror movie clichés and had inadvertently become an expendable side-character. Half-jokingly, but secretly completely-serious, he made a request.

'Come with me yeah?' said Hal, feeling glad

Jasmine hadn't been around to hear him commit the frankly unforgiveable faux pas. She was a huge horror movie fan, and would have given him a very stern eye-roll. He needn't have worried though, as Kara channelled the spirit of Jasmine, rolling her eyes as she made her way over to him, deliberately orchestrating every step, in order to emphasise that she was not happy about this one bit.

They walked up the driveway to Jerry's home with only the moonlight for guidance, until they reached the front door, which Hal wrapped with his knuckles.

'Hellooo?' cooed Hal, in a voice that was nowhere near as manly as he had intended.

He looked at Kara, who was looking down her black-rimmed glasses at him, utterly unimpressed by the presence he had just tried to project. Clearing his throat, he took another stab at it.

'Hello? Is anyone home?' "*Better*," he thought.

'I don't think anyone's here. In you go, boy!' said Kara, as she ushered Jerry into the house then took a step back, heavily implying Hal could take over.

He looked upwards to the dark, cloudless sky, summoning a little bravado. Gingerly, he stuck his head inside through the dark portal of the doorway, noticing the empty water bowl.

'Ah maaan, hang on,' said Hal, stepping further into the cabin. 'Make sure Jerry doesn't run out will you?'

Picking up the empty water bowl from the floor, he hit the lever of the cold tap on the sink that was directly above the counter with his arm, filling the bowl to the brim. The water sloshed over his hand and over the counter. Repeating the movement in reverse, he turned off the tap, placing the bowl back on the wooden flooring.

'Right, done and done,' said Hal, wiping the residual water droplets from his hands and onto his boiler suit. As he made his way back out, he hit the light switch so Jerry wasn't in the dark, noting that the radio playing in the background would provide adequate company until Kevin came home. Not bothering to look back, he closed the door behind him and pulled his cigarettes from his pocket.

'Well that's that,' said Hal, 'Back to the lodge?'

'Back to the lodge,' said Kara, and they began their journey back to the party.

CHAPTER TEN

Diminishing Returns

Saturday Evening, 9:04pm

The walk back was predictably uneventful, though the coolness of the night air had all but vanished entirely.

"Probably the adrenaline," thought Hal, glad to be done with the place they had left behind.

'Ow!' blurted Kara.

'What's up?' asked Hal, exhaling smoke into the cloudless sky.

'Nothing…' said Kara, 'just got this splitting headache for a second. It's gone now.'

'Weird. I used to get those. "Ice-pick headaches" I called them,' said Hal. 'Hey, check out this fog!'

Kara looked around at the fine mist that lined the ground, barely perceptible, but definitely there.

'Shpooky,' she said, in her best Velma impression, both of them ignoring that it was difficult to tell if it was a good impersonation or not, given that they hadn't watched the cartoon in well over two decades.

Hal pulled out his phone, through habit more than anything else.

'Ah crap.'

'What is it?' asked Kara, gently massaging her right temple, more out of the residual memory of the pain as opposed to anything existing.

'Phone's dead,' said Hal in an irked tone.

'Hate that,' replied Kara, reaching down to her skirt, then remembering it had no pockets, realising she'd left her phone only God knew where.

"At least I still have my detective magnifying glass," she thought to herself, sarcastically.

'You think Jerry will be ok?' said Kara, more to exercise a self-reassuring rhetoric, rather than searching for an actual response.

'Totally, he'll be fine. I'm sure...what was that guy's name?'

'Kevin,' said Kara, helpfully.

'Yeah, I'm sure Kevin will be back soon. Plus, we left the little guy some water, *and* popped on a light. Way better than him roaming around out in the dark.'

They continued their stroll back to Fir Lodge, taking in their serene surroundings. As Hal looked up at the sky, he noticed the stars were out in force tonight. The clear night-sky looked unreal, displaying a level of detail he couldn't recollect ever seeing before. As the stars themselves shimmered with intense white, amber and deep blue hues, the space between them seemed to possess a depth and texture that was unlike anything he had ever seen.

The walk had warmed Kara up a bit, and she couldn't feel the chill of the night air at all anymore. Her mind wandered, as Hal tried the power button on his phone for the fifth time. Seeing Jerry once again made her think of her own dogs.

"They'd have loved this walk," she thought. The fresh air was doing wonders for her; she didn't even feel remotely tipsy from that last glass she'd downed before she had left the lodge. Usually the fresh air had the opposite effect on her, but she chalked it up to her innate superpower.

*

They followed the road back, eventually stumbling upon Fir Lodge, the ten-or-so minute walk coming to an end. They very nearly walked straight past it, and would have done just that, were it not for Daisy and Jasmine being on the balcony. They were laughing about something, the music from the living area and rear garden cutting through the otherwise tranquil forest.

Hal suddenly felt a stabbing sensation in his chest, the feeling reminiscent of heartburn.

'Hgnn!' he groaned, staggering slightly.

'You ok?' asked Kara, largely preoccupied with trying to deduce where exactly she last saw her phone.

'Yeah, just heartburn I think.'

'You're getting old, man,' she said playfully, shooting Hal a wink.

'Made plans for your thirty-fifth birthday yet?' retorted Hal, knowing how much she hated him reminding her that he was a whole year younger than her.

'Nothing concrete,' said Kara, 'all I know for certain is that you're not invited.'

'Ha!' laughed Hal, instantly regretting doing so, as his heartburn flared at the exertion.

Pressing his fingers into his chest, he and Kara walked up the drive, finally reaching the front doors of the lodge. Hal reached out for one of the handles of the now-closed front doors, but it wouldn't budge.

'They've locked us out?!' said Hal, incredulously. 'We've only been gone like, what? Half an hour tops?'

He tried the handle again. Not even a wiggle. He couldn't help but admire the robustness of the doors. They didn't look like much, but were clearly lined with an indestructible alloy of some kind.

Kara tapped on the window, trying to get either Will, or Peter's attention, who were setting up a new game of pool, as Jon spectated from the side-lines, but quickly realised they were clearly being dicks and ignoring them on purpose.

'Dammit guys, can you let us in please?' huffed Kara.

'I don't think they can hear you,' said Hal. 'Either that or they're choosing not to. Let's go around the side, we can get in that way,' he added, offering a constructive alternative.

*

They followed the path round the side leading to the hot tub, as Hal sub-consciously noted the lack of crunch beneath his feet. Rachel, Jon, Stacey, and Robert were currently occupying Robert's second home, as Fearne and Michaela sat on the side dunking their legs.

'I'm gonna go hunt for my phone,' said Kara, 'see you in a bit,' she added, as she trotted off through the open side-door and into the lodge.

The mist emanating from the hot tub had taken over most of the rear garden, the vapour from the tub reacting with the cool night air, and giving it a life all of its own.

'Hey guys, took Jerry back,' said Hal, directly to his friends in the hot tub. 'Just going to grab a beer and a smoke and I'll be right in!'

His hot-tubbing friends cheered but, unbeknownst to Hal, it was more because of something Robert had just said. Hal smiled, having no tangible reason to suspect anything was amiss, and made his way to the nearby cool-box. The lid was ajar, and he reached into the blackness of the box, unable to gain purchase on a beer can.

"Must be running out," he thought, grumbling under his breath.

He tried removing the lid but discovered it was stuck, like a freezer door kept in place by solid ice. The mist billowing from the tub was thickening around him, making it incredibly difficult to see. He swished his hand in front of him, attempted to swat it away, to no avail.

It was then that he heard the ear-splitting, blood-curdling scream.

CHAPTER ELEVEN
The Untouchables

Saturday Evening, 9:13pm

Hal raced into the hall, as his friends in the tub continued to laugh hysterically, an act that was becoming increasingly more unnerving. Everyone around him appeared to be completely unfazed by the fact that something bad was going down inside the lodge.

He decided not to focus on the horrifying contradiction; his friends laughing amidst the haze of debilitating fog, which had all but compromised his sense of spatial-awareness, and the scream that had shredded his nerves, but had seemingly left the rest of his friends entirely unaffected. He knew only one thing; that scream came from Kara.

Scanning the lower level, he proceeded up the central staircase three steps at a time, stopping halfway when he noticed Kara sitting in the corner of the room below him. She was sitting on the opposite side of the pool table in the large entrance area, hidden behind a small chair, in-amongst some outdoor sports equipment. Her arms were wrapped around her legs, and she was rocking back and forth, whispering to herself. Will and Peter added to the unfolding insanity, by completely ignoring her, continuing their game of pool without a care in the world.

'Kara?!' said Hal, 'what the hell, are you ok?!'

He turned on the stairs, just as Jasmine and Daisy appeared before him at the top. Hal stood to one side to let them pass, as they began to descend the staircase.

'Guys,' said Hal, 'what's wrong with Ka–' but his question was cut short by the shock of what happened next.

Jasmine's face was slightly lower than his, despite her being a step above him. Her height became of secondary relevance, however, as she breached his personal space, ignoring him completely, casually continuing her conversation with Daisy. Before Hal could signal his presence to her, her face collided with his, passing through him entirely, followed immediately by the rest of her body. All he could see was whiteness, until the back of her head and hair had successfully cleared the space his head was occupying.

He fell to his knees on the staircase, noticing that the mist from the hot tub had now filled the entire lodge. It was thickening around him with a malignant ferocity now. All he could see was Kara, and the outline of shapes, as his friends swirled away from his line of sight. He had no idea what was happening, the only singular truth he could verify for absolute certain was that the banister to the stairs was still there, due to the fact that he was clinging onto it for dear life, in an attempt to counteract the overwhelming sense of vertigo that was coursing through his entire body.

Blindly, he jumped back down the stairs, relying entirely on his muscle-memory of the layout of the building to prevent himself from running head-first into a wall. Turning to his right, he swung around to face Kara, who was somehow still perfectly visible, helpfully acting as a beacon of light, piercing through the gloom to light his way.

'Kara! I think there's a fire?!' said Hal. 'I…Jasmine…did you see–' but she was still whispering to herself. Something had clearly caused her to snap, and he assumed it had something to do with the fact they'd just taken up residence in Silent Hill. All that was missing was a claxon.

Suddenly, a thunderous wind began to fill the room. Hal found it odd that he couldn't feel the rush of air, and that he could only hear the sound, as Kara, meanwhile, continued to whisper to herself.

'I can't hear you Kara, you've gotta speak up!' said Hal, falling to the floor beside her and attempting to put his arm around her.

He experienced an intense static-shock, witnessing a significant arc of blue light that pierced through the whiteness, like a blast of condensed lighting, repelling him away from her. It was just them and the thick, motionless fog now.

'We need to get out of here!' shouted Hal, but his voice was drowned out by the unabating sound of air which was cascading over them, as if they were standing just on the outskirts of the heart of a tornado.

In all of the insanity, he took a moment to clock the fact that he could still breathe with ease.

"If this was a fire," he thought, but that thought was cut-off mid-flow, as the temporal nexus surrounding them eradicated his entire essence and existence from the timeline he was occupying.

Kara's eyes widened, as every cell in her body was atomised, not having time to question what she had witnessed, given that a dimension could not be comprehended when it no longer existed.

CHAPTER TWELVE

Total Protonic Reversal

1st Restart – Friday Afternoon, 12:01pm

A rush of air, like being in the epicentre of a wind tunnel. A blinding whiteness in every direction, entirely removing their sense of spatial awareness. The thundering, relentless sound of air vacating an infinite echo-chamber of nothingness.

Finally, after what felt like an eternity, the sound ceased, like someone pressing a mute-button on reality. An airlock re-stabilised, after all the oxygen had been vented out into the cold, dark, heart of space.

And then, there was sunlight. As devoid of heat as it was crystal clear. Their surroundings appearing before them with impossibly perfect clarity, akin to an interactive, high-definition image. Everything was swathed in a colour scheme that looked almost hyper-realistic.

Hal and Kara found themselves standing outside Fir Lodge, covering their eyes against the savage brightness of their environment.

'Kara,' whispered Hal.

'Hal,' said Kara, equally disorientated. They both fell to the ground, landing heavily on the shingle of the driveway. Hal was on all fours, dry-heaving, clearly needing to throw-up, but not being able to produce anything. Kara, meanwhile, rolled onto her back, fighting the involuntary hyperventilation that her lungs were trying to engage in, feeling like she'd been hit by a truck full of smaller, baby trucks.

The ultra-bright sunlight reflected off of an equally crystal-clear, large red object, that was moving towards them at speed.

'Ka…Ka!' exclaimed Hal, trying to get Kara's attention, his mind wrestling for dominance over his ability to actually form words. Kara was gradually managing to slow her breathing, dialling back her panic attack from "full-blown" to "pretty-serious."

'Wh-what?' mustered Kara, suffering from the same problematic inability to reboot and regain her senses.

'Ka-car!' said Hal, finally.

The red, family-sized vehicle pulled into the driveway, the displaced shingle sounding like a fuse that was burning ever-closer to a stick of dynamite. In this instance, the dynamite was represented by Kara's head, which was currently lining up perfectly with the oncoming, potentially skull-crushing, tyres.

She rolled to her right, successfully evading the tyre, which was now occupying the space where her head had just been.

The driver killed the engine, opened the driver-side door, and stepped out. The ground crunched beneath his feet, the sound so excruciatingly loud that it forced Hal and Kara to cover their ears.

'Will!' shouted Kara and Hal in unison, the sight of their friend snapping them out of their mutual discombobulation. They breathed a sigh of relief, comforted by the fact that they were no longer forced to deal with what was happening alone.

Will took a moment to stretch, trying to shake off the two-hour car journey, and looked up at the lodge. The place looked beautiful. His wife Stacey stepped out of the passenger side and asked him to pop open the boot. Will clicked the button on his key fob and the boot of the car opened obligingly, the pistons of compressed air supporting the boot door hissing softly.

Rachel and Jon came out to greet them, stepping unceremoniously over Kara's legs. She let out an involuntary yelp, and pulled her legs inwards before they could apply the pressure of their full weight on her, and scowled at her soon-to-be hosts.

'What the *hell* guys,' said Kara, 'help me up!'

Jon and Rachel continued to greet the first arrivals, ignoring her request. Deciding to take matters into her own hands, she pulled herself up, using the side of Will's car for support, and dusted herself down, as Hal tried to get her attention.

'Erm…Kara…'

Kara moved between Will and Jon, who were

shaking hands.

'*Seriously* Jon?!' she said, approaching him with the intent of playfully punching him in the arm.

'KARA!' shouted Hal, causing her to freeze where she stood. Hal never shouted.

'Your clothes,' he said, more calmly.

She looked down at her body, and then back at Hal.

'Yours too!' she said, moving away from the greetings being exchanged, and circling around Will's car so she was standing next to Hal again.

She reached out for Hal's collar, which was dishevelled and needed straightening, but that wasn't what drew her to do so. It was the fact that he was *wearing* what he was wearing in the first place. Upon contact with the fabric, she felt a sizzle of what she assumed was static electricity, and pulled back her hand, as a barely-perceptible blue light tickled her fingertips.

Will and Stacey made their way inside with Rachel and Jon, leaving Hal and Kara behind. Before she could comment about the static-electricity and, respectively, the rudeness of their friends, their joint attention was pulled towards a streak of white, which was moving through the hedges that made up the boundary of the front of the lodge. They quickly realised it was another car, which pulled onto the driveway, apparently aiming for the spot alongside Will's car. The newly acquired, high-definition upgrade to their eyesight that Hal and Kara had only just inherited went haywire. Their perception of the surrounding environment began to shake from side to side, at first from left to right, with furious speed, and then with the occasional up and down directional change thrown in for good measure, presumably just to really sell to them the shared sensation of unbearable motion-sickness.

'I feel like I'm in one of those paint mixer machines you see at the hardware–' said Hal drunkenly, his sentence cut short as he tumbled to the ground, fumbling around on the sea of stones that covered the driveway. To a casual onlooker, it would have looked as if he were looking for a non-existent contact lens, as he tried, with embarrassing futility, to regain his composure.

Meanwhile, Kara was having a whale of a time

trying to get her own shit together. She would've offered Hal a hand, were it not for the fact that someone had seemingly, and rather thoughtlessly, switched the gravity off in her immediate vicinity, forcing her to focus intently on clinging to the ground in order to prevent herself from plummeting all the way down into the sky. Her theory was immediately debunked, due to the fact that, in reality, she was rolling around on the shingle the whole time, a meter or so from Hal.

She and Hal were so busy trying to regain their equilibrium that they had all but forgotten the existence of the other, until they finally collided with each other. The sizzle they had experienced earlier which, to Kara at least, felt like hours ago was a little more "punchy" this time around. In the same way a flame-thrower tended to be a little bit more "punchy" than a recently-struck match.

Blue lightning sparked between their bodies, forcing them apart. Kara flew over the top of Will's car, rolling several meters across the shingle, through an unfortunately-located patch of mud, and onto a beautifully maintained grass verge. Hal was a little more fortunate, as he was flung into the solid concrete support wall of what, he would later remember, was the sauna and steam rooms.

With his vertigo abated, Hal shook his head, as if he'd just downed a can of energy drink and was finally thinking clearly again. He would have noticed, then and there, that he wasn't experiencing the usual debilitating pain that inevitably ensued after a full-blown electrocution, especially one that was followed-up by a chaser of blunt-force trauma, but he was understandably more preoccupied with what happened next.

In Hal's defence, it wasn't a common occurrence to be afforded a front-row seat to bear witness as the existential nature of reality was turned completely on its metaphoric head.

CHAPTER THIRTEEN

Face-Off

1st Restart – Friday Afternoon, 12:03pm

Kara pulled herself up from the perfectly manicured stretch of grass, and instinctively proceeded to brush the mud from her legs, but noted that, oddly, there was none. She met Hal's gaze, who looked as white as a ghost. She closed her eyes, shaking her head at the loaded terminology.

"Nope. Just *nope*," thought Kara. And then she saw it. Or rather, she saw herself.

'That's impossible…' she whispered, moving closer to the aberration that was currently standing a few feet behind Will's impossibly-bright red car.

Kara stared, slack-jawed, at the carbon-copy of herself, now standing behind her frighteningly-realistic duplicate. The imposter even had her hair just right, short and freshly-straightened, her clothes identical to what she was wearing when she had first arrived at Fir Lodge. Even her mannerisms were eerily precise, as if the clone had practised and rehearsed her movements so that they were imperceptible from the real thing. The *real* her.

She continued to observe, as the imposter released a copy of Hal from the confines of the back seat of Jasmine's car.

Jasmine showed signs of perceivable relief that the journey was over, as the other Hal hopped out, and popped open the boot of the car. Their doubles then proceeded to lug their cases into the lodge, with Jasmine following just behind them, saddled with several light bags of food and drink.

Hal's doppelganger was equally convincing. The way he moved, the way he laughed, right down to the way he used his left hand to use his phone.

"He even has the south-paw thing down,"

thought Hal, as impressed as he was terrified by the attention to detail.

Hal waved at Kara to get her attention, but she was understandably preoccupied. He tried harder, waving his arms like he was trying to guide in a low-flying aircraft. She snapped out of her trance but, unfortunately, she noticed Hal's warning too late, unable to avoid Robert, who was positioning his car onto the drive behind her. His passenger wing mirror collided with her hip, the force of impact clicking the mirror into the closed position. She recoiled away from the vehicle, more out of shock than any physical pain.

In order to remove himself emotionally from the insanity, Hal had started to consciously take notes of their surroundings. Of course, he'd have to confront his evil-twin at some point, but he'd seen enough movies to know that there was a right way and a wrong way to approach the sinister usurper of his life. He surmised that the electricity was probably important, as was the fact that he was still wearing his costume from last night.

"Or is that tomorrow?" he thought.

Kara ran over to him and went to grab him, but he took a step back, and she rolled her eyes, realising why.

'Oh, right,' said Kara, with frenzied eyes. 'What are those things?! And why can't anyone see us?!'

Robert exited his car, and was milking a stretch. Kara shouted out his name, fruitlessly attempting to get his attention.

'I'm like ninety-percent certain he can't hear–' but Hal stood no chance of stopping her. She was proper going off on one, like Rachel often did when engaging in a rant over something Jon had done wrong.

Hal followed her, placing his hands in his boiler suit pockets. He felt his phone beneath his palm as he did so, and pulled it out. He stabbed the home button with his finger.

'Dead. Well, that's typical,' muttered Hal.

Then, like a gunslinger from the wild-west, his right hand flew to the outside of his right-side pocket. He could feel the comforting bump of the filter box nestled beneath the fabric, where he stored his hand-rolled cigarettes.

"Every cloud," he thought to himself, as Kara

stomped her way over to Robert.

'Seriously, Robert? You're ignoring me too?! Snap out of it,' she yelled, raising her hand with the apparent intention of giving him a gentle slap.

Hal couldn't be sure from the angle, but he was certain her hand went straight through Robert as she did so, like he was a construct in a virtual-reality game.

"Maybe there *is* no spoon," thought Hal.

He began to stare suspiciously at everything, looking for shades of green-tinged code. After a few moments, he gave up staring at a nearby flowerpot, which was clearly minding its own business in a convincing-enough manner as to satisfy Hal's paranoia. Remaining somewhat suspicious, he begrudgingly dismissed the idea.

'Sometimes there *is* a spoon I guess,' he mumbled.

Judging by the fact Kara was staring at her hand and sporting a frantically confused expression, he made the leap and concluded that he'd actually seen what he thought he'd seen. He walked over to Robert, raising his own hand, like a speedster preparing to reverberate at high speed, held his breath, then plunged his open hand through Robert's chest, retracting it instantly. Hal sheltered his now closed fist, as if nursing a severe burn.

'Are you ok?!' shrieked Kara.

'Oh, yeah, totally. It didn't hurt or anything, I just wasn't expecting that to happen?' said Hal, wincing at the tone in his own voice, as if the inflection of a question mark at the end of that sentence was an unreasonable assumption to make. Luckily, Kara was too busy losing her mind to notice such semantics.

'WHAT IS GOING ON?!' shouted Kara, dispensing a barrage of quandary-bullets in his direction. 'Why does that *thing* have my face? Why are there…*copies* of us walking around in there with our friends? Why are we wearing these stupid costumes?! Why is Robert a ghost now?! And why...why…actually, just answer those first please,' said Kara, knowing that she would have more questions shortly.

Hal had no idea how to answer her tirade of questions. They were apparently now living in a cuckoo-land town, just south of Logic-Ville.

'Well,' said Hal, rubbing his five-o'clock-shadow

chin stubble, and deciding he might as well just go for it. 'I think…I *think* Robert's a hologram, *we've* been cloned, and are also somehow *invisible* for some reason. Honestly? I'm Jon Snow right now, I know nothin'.'

'I don't know what that reference means!'

'Are you being serious right now? Dude, you *need* to start Game Of–'

'Hal,' said Kara, sharply, 'what do we do?'

Hal felt the room, acknowledging that his friend clearly wasn't in the mood for him dropping pop-culture references right now.

'I guess…we head inside? See how this plays out?' he said.

And with no other plan in their arsenal to speak of, Hal gestured towards the lodge and made his way to the entrance.

Kara, still shaking, proceeded towards the front doors as well, flinching at the sound of laughter being generated by their traitorous, evil clones, which was emanating from within. Kara instinctively walked around Will's Car, but Hal didn't see the point after his experiment with Robert. He walked straight towards the centre of the vehicle, expecting to walk through it, experiencing unexpected resistance as his chest smacked soundlessly against the car. Rolling his eyes to mask his embarrassment, Hal tried to pretend he had conducted yet another impromptu experiment.

'Note to self;' said Hal, 'not everything here is a hologram.'

CHAPTER FOURTEEN
Ghosted

1st Restart – Friday Afternoon, 12:07pm

They slipped in through the front door, completely unseen due to a level of stealth that wasn't so much a perfected skill, as it was more an intrinsic by-product of their current disassociation with the universe, watching as their friends and duplicates dispersed throughout the lodge. It was a unique experience, like watching a playback of a video recording of their memories. Only there were details that couldn't have been memories at all, given that they had not been present for some of the things they were witnessing. Hal noted a perfect example of this, as he witnessed a conversation that was taking place between Rachel and Kara. This was something that he couldn't have remembered, because he had been outside with Jon at the time.

One thing Hal and Kara confirmed pretty quickly was that they were, indeed, entirely invisible, but it was taking their minds time to adjust to the new status quo. They instinctively moved out of the way, as the manifestations of their friends and, more horrifyingly, themselves, moved around them. Neither of them wanted to experience the sensation of passing through another human being again any time soon, or, in fact, ever.

Waiting for an opening, to ensure there were no obstructions ahead of them, the invisible spectators ascended the wooden staircase that led to the communal living area, finding a quiet corner that they could observe from without having to constantly dart out of anyone's way. Hal tried to project an air of light-hearted banality by striking up a conversation.

'What made you scream back there?' said Hal, correcting himself immediately, 'back then? Shit, you know what I mean,' he finished, quickly realising that the biggest problem they would need to overcome during their time here was apparently grammar.

Kara's eyes, which were wide with wonder, fluttered slightly, as she regained her composure, locking on to his words as if they were an inflatable lifeline being thrown out to her drowning sanity. She swallowed, expecting her mouth to be dry and croaky when she spoke, but realised it was apparently unnecessary.

'When we got from back from Jerry's, I went to go find my phone,' began Kara. 'Will and Peter were playing pool. They were laughing about something. I asked Will why he was ignoring us, but he just kept playing. I tried to slip past him to get into my room whilst he took a shot, but he turned around and…and…he *literally* walked *right* through me Hal!' She said it again, almost as if she needed to say it out loud a second time. 'He literally. Walked. *Through* me!' her eyes widened again, filled with a desperate fear that stemmed from the thought that he would think she was crazy. 'You must think I'm insane. You have to believe me Hal, please tell me you believe me!'

Hal responded immediately, in the hope he could ease her anguish.

'Kara, I *believe* you. The same thing happened to me.'

'Will walked through you too?!'

'What? How would that even…no, he was nowhere *near* me, it was Jasmine. On the stairs, just before I got to you. It was weird though, she was there, then all I saw was a white mist as she walked through me, then she was…*out* of me, and–'

Kara winced, 'don't say "*out of me*" ever again, that's gross.'

'Oh, I'm sorry,' said Hal, 'what would you rather I call it? I'll amend my lexicon once we've dealt with the universe collapsing in on itself!'

'Jeeze Hal, dramatic much?' said Kara, shooting him a look to let him know she was kidding.

They continued watching their friends with intent suspicion, looking for anything that could give them more insight into who these people were, and what exactly their agenda was. But the most bizarre thing of all was that nothing seemed out of place. Not one of their friends gave any indication that they knew they were being watched, and continued to behave perfectly in-character. They engaged in the same banter they always shared, referencing the same in-jokes that they always did. Hal and Kara's initial suspicion that their friends were somehow carrying out an elaborate charade was largely debunked, as not a single one of their friends dropped the act.

Eventually, they were forced to accept the possibility of the easiest conclusion they could get their heads around; that their friends were exactly who they appeared to be, just a version of themselves from thirty-three-or-so hours ago.

Kara, giving up on Hal, made the conscious decision to be the one to say it out loud.

'I think…I think we're in the *past.*'

Hal struggled to disagree but, despite (or perhaps because of) his love of time-travel movies, he also knew that was impossible.

'Okay…' said Hal. 'Baby steps. So, we've…travelled back in time,' he said, cringing at how absurd it sounded as he said the words out loud, but pressing on regardless, 'as you do. Except, that isn't something *anyone* can do.'

'You don't think…' began Kara, her voice barely a whisper.

'That we're dead?' said Hal loudly, as if doing so would take the power away from the question. 'Thought had crossed my mind. But I think we can rule that one out too,' said Hal, matter-of-factly.

'Okay, I'll bite. How so?' challenged Kara.

Hal took a deep breath, not entirely sure what he was going to run with first.

'Well, for one thing…' he said, pulling out his box of cigarettes from his pocket, along with his phone, a lighter, some chewing gum, and one of Jess's hair bobby pins, which had a habit of turning up everywhere, apparently even inside the pocket of a brand-new costume. He shook away the disbelief, pressing on with his theory. '…despite my current attire, I'm no ghost expert, but I'm pretty sure you leave materialistic knick-knacks at the door before *moving on.*'

In all of the insanity, she had forgotten that they were still in costume. In one swift movement, she pressed her hands to the pleat of her skirt, then remembered, once again, that she didn't have pockets.

'Oh, come *on*,' groaned Kara, 'you get chewing gum, cigarettes *and* a phone, and all I get to bring with me is–'

'Nerdy specs and a magnifying glass?' said Hal, in a sarcastically optimistic tone.

Kara pulled the black rimmed detective tool from the waistband of her skirt, spinning the stem of the magnifying glass in her hand. Then, dismissively, she discarded it on the floor. They watched, as it landed solidly, bouncing several times as it travelled noiselessly across the wooden floor.

'This is total bullshit,' said Kara finally, as she fell back against the wall situated behind her, then stood upright again instantly as her inadvertent discovery dawned on her. Hal smirked once she noticed it.

'Annnnd that. Remember when I walked into the car on purpose?'

'I see your revisionist history course is going well?' said Kara, not buying that statement for a second.

Hal winced. 'Worth a shot,' he said, and then continued. 'Anyway, in what ghost story in the history of ever, has a ghost not been able to walk through stuff? We couldn't open the front door yesterday either. I mean *tomorrow.* I mean, you know what I mean.'

She gave that some thought. 'But we're ghosts to these guys,' said Kara, 'they can't see us, they walk straight through us? We can't interact with them at all.'

Hal had to concede on that part.

'I think we need to see how this plays out,' said Hal. 'If we watch, listen, and try to learn as much as we can, we might be able to figure this thing out. If we wait for ourselves to come back from dropping Jerry off tomorrow night, we can fill in the blanks from what happened to us in the fog.'

'You want to spend an entire day-and-a-half spying on our friends?!' exclaimed Kara. All she wanted to do was wake up from what was clearly a terrible fever dream.

'Well, when you say it like that, it just sounds weird and creepy. I prefer the term "doing research,"' said Hal, checking his box of cigarettes and noting that only three pre-rolled smokes remained. He pulled one from the box, putting it between his lips, flipped the metal lid on his lighter, then hesitated for a fraction of a second, not wanting to be wrong.

"'I'm not wrong,' he thought to himself, striking the flint and staring in secret amazement, as the petrol lighter generated an actual flame. He was even more shocked by the fact that the flame ignited the cigarette paper, just as physics dictated it should have done.

'See,' said Hal, smugly. 'Definitely not ghosts.'

CHAPTER FIFTEEN
Jerry's Secret

1st Restart – Friday Afternoon, 1:27pm

Friday played out exactly as it had before, though Kara and Hal's new perspective certainly kept them entertained. They remained in the corners of rooms, and a good distance away from anyone when in the garden, ensuring they didn't come into contact with any of their friends, avoiding themselves in particular.

Hal was adamant that coming into contact with their "past-selves", a term they had both agreed on for the sake of making their conversations easier, could result in making things worse. Kara wasn't entirely convinced that his theory that "the same matter couldn't occupy the same space" was anything more than lazy science fiction.

She wanted to lash out at the woman who had stolen her life. The prospect that Kara could very well be a time traveller did little to help her shake the feeling that her life was being commandeered by an imposter, even if their working theory did mean that she was the one and only *real* Kara. Throughout the course of the day, she frequently revisited the notion that she had simply lost her mind. The phenomenon she was experiencing had not been documented anywhere as far as she was aware, and she found it hard to believe that she and Hal were the first people to have ever experienced what they were going through. Perhaps that simply meant that no one had ever returned to tell the tale.

Casting the negative implications of that thought from her mind, she looked over at Hal, who was kneeling on the wooden floor of the living room, running his hands across it like it was the most interesting thing in the world.

'Okay, fine. What *are* you doing?' said Kara, her boredom finally causing her to give in after watching him mess about with the floor for the past twenty minutes.

'Nothing. Actually, maybe something. It's... okay, watch this. Ready?' said Hal.

Kara shrugged, indicating he should just get on with it. Hal stood up, and then slammed his foot down on the floor. The action generated a barely audible, notably muffled, thud. Kara stared at him, unsure of what to say.

'I meeean...it's not the *greatest* display of interpretive dance I've ever seen. Sorry, just being honest,' she said, with exaggerated awkwardness.

Hal cocked his head, and raised an eyebrow in an attempt to counteract her mocking tone.

'World's most underrated time-travelling comedian everyone,' said Hal.

'Actually, given that I'm probably the *only* time-travelling comedian, that would make me the best by default, wouldn't it?' asked Kara, surprising even herself by the technicality.

Reluctantly, Hal nodded in agreement. It was hard

to find fault with her logic.

'Don't you think it's weird that we can't generate noise here?' said Hal. 'Like when you knocked on the door last night. And the shingle outside, it doesn't move under our weight. It's like we're here, but not here…' he added, pulling a face of frustration.

He was missing something, a vital answer that was miles beyond the realm of his comprehension. Kara mimicked his earlier action, stamping her two-inch heel down hard on the wood, the transference of force emitting an equal lack of sound.

'Huh,' said Kara. She had to admit, it was a clever observation. Not out loud, or with actual words or anything, but she knew that Hal would know she was impressed.

'Right? It's totally a thing isn't it?' said Hal, sensing her appreciation of his discovery.

*

With the arrival of the late-afternoon came the inevitable arrival of Jerry. They stood in silence, as they witnessed their first encounter with him, the only difference being one of perspective. They hid behind the right-hand side of the building, peering around the corner to watch the interaction, as the event played out exactly as it had done the first time around. Kara watched intently, as her past-self noticed Jerry too little, too late, resulting in her being tackled to the ground by the enthusiastic dog. Kara winced as she heard her past-self scream in shock, her own laugh sounding incredibly alien to her. She cringed at her rambling doggy talk, all but sick of how many times she could ask a dog if he was a good boy. As the following moments unfolded, watching their past-selves and past-Jon fussing over the admittedly adorable dog, Kara made a mental note to dial it down a bit when meeting other people's dogs in future. Not her own, of course. As far as she was concerned, her dogs were the gold standard when it came to being a good boy.

Hal whistled absent-mindedly, his way of reconciling himself with this bizarre out-of-body experience. Jerry's ears twitched and, leaving their past-selves in his wake, he ran towards the time-travellers.

'Erm, Kar'…' said Hal, 'I think…I think he's coming over to us?'

Jerry sprinted across the garden and around the corner to where they were skulking. He sat, seemingly aware of their presence, scratched an itch that was lurking beneath his collar, and sniffed in their general vicinity.

'Can he...can he *see* us?' asked Kara, more for her own benefit than as a direct question to Hal. Before they could find out for sure, Jerry's head dipped to the right. He was looking well beyond them into the distance, as if he was straining to make sense of a sound. Without warning, he set off suddenly, apparently eager to continue his adventure. He stopped at the top of the driveway, sniffing again, rolled onto his back on the same area of grass that Kara had been thrown onto earlier that morning, kicking his legs into the air. Jerry then jumped to his feet and departed, leaving in his wake even more questions for Hal and Kara to sift through.

*

The remainder of their second run-through of their Friday was serenely ethereal, as they traversed through the hyper-realistic, immaculately reconstructed world that they had been transported to. It was as if they were locked within a shared, lucid dream; able to observe, but not permitted to interact with their surroundings. The re-creation of their combined recollections, however, was clearly so much more than a visually-interactive memory. From the amount of liquid in bottles of alcohol that would reduce in quantity throughout the day, to the playlists of music that shifted in the same identical patterns they had done the first time around, everything was perfect.

Hal and Kara spent their time scrutinising every detail, trying to find a chink in the armour of their current predicament that they could somehow exploit, but their efforts yielded one unchallengeable truth; their original assumption had to be correct. They were truly passengers, travelling in the slipstream of their own history, utilising an entirely independent consciousness than that of their past-selves.

As Friday evening drew to a close for a second time, their friends and past-selves finally called it a night and went to bed, leaving the time travellers with little to do but sit in darkness, discussing how little they understood about what was happening to them.

Laying on the now-vacant sofas in the communal living room, Hal and Kara attempted to sleep. However, after much futility, they soon realised that the ability to sleep had apparently been revoked, and was clearly an impossible endeavour in their current state. They'd decided, together, that they would let everything play out tomorrow, just as it had before. They would then study exactly what happened when their past-selves returned from dropping off Jerry.

As the seemingly endless night unfolded around them, they ran out of things to say, and in the end settled on just pretending that they were both asleep, until the morning came.

CHAPTER SIXTEEN

Bubble or Nothing

1st Restart – Saturday Morning, 7:06am

Hal and Kara were eventually pulled away from their day-dreaming, as Daisy kicked off her Saturday morning by popping on the kettle. One by one, the gang made their way to the communal living room, forcing Hal and Kara to resume their position in the corner of the room. Hal had finished all three of his cigarettes the day before, but they were rationing the chewing gum in case they suddenly developed the pangs of hunger. Most of the seats were taken now, but given that they weren't paying attention the first time around, they didn't want to risk getting comfortable and sitting on a free seat, only to end up being sat on.

Kara's past-self emerged from her pit last of all, dragging herself up the wooden staircase and into the living room.

'Wow…I really look like crap,' said Kara, as she assessed the condition of her identical twin, then added 'remind me to quit drinking after we've figured a way out of this nightmare.'

Hal gave her the thumbs up, allowing her to pretend that her request was something he could feasibly enforce.

In the early hours of the morning, they had been discussing a theory regarding their own proximity to their past-selves. Hal felt they should stay out of their own way, whereas Kara wanted to be as close to them as possible, in the hope that their duplicates would say or do something that might shed more light on what was happening to them.

Kara decided to broach the subject once more.

'What I can't get my head around is that we're not even here Hal, I mean we *are* but…we're not solid.

What does it matter if we shadow our past-selves?'

'There's no need to be so matter-of fact about matter Kar', it doesn't matter,' said Hal.

'Do you even *hear* yourself talking sometimes?' asked Kara in exasperation.

Hal scrunched up his face and nodded in the direction of the past version of himself, currently talking to Rachel and Jon in the kitchen.

'Lately? More than I'd care to, if I'm honest,' said Hal.

Kara scowled, and he held up his hands apologetically.

'I'm sorry, I'm sorry, I know just as much as you do. I'm just saying let's not risk it for the time being.'

He pulled out his phone for the hundredth time, a habit that he couldn't kick, despite the battery being completely dead.

'Who ya gonna call?' asked Kara, with a smirk.

'The late-eighties and early-nineties, presumably, to see if either of them wants that joke back,' retorted Hal.

'I miss the nineties…' said Kara wistfully.

'Yeah well, let's not tempt fate, we're still trying to

figure out what to do after jumping a couple of *days* back in time. Besides, I haven't packed much denim.'

*

As their friends prepared for the day ahead, Kara and Hal once more moved their operation into the garden. Kara was watching Fearne drawing freehand temporary tattoos onto Daisy and Jasmine, taking advantage of the fact that she was now invisible, which allowed her to get closer to see how the process worked. Robert was, of course, in the hot tub with Jon, both trying to eradicate their respective hangovers.

With the art session coming to an end, Hal and Kara continued to observe, as their past-selves once again set off for a late-morning walk in the woods with their friends. Reasoning that there was nothing that happened on that excursion that they didn't already know, the chronologically-displaced duo decided to hang back, giving their past-selves additional space. Hal had argued that they would need to be in places they weren't the first time around, if they had any hope of understanding what was happening to them. The more information they had, the better equipped they would be when it came to working out exactly what had caused, as Hal had described it, the "temporal anomaly."

She looked over at Hal, who was standing in the rear garden and staring at the sun for reasons that were totally lost on her.

'I don't think trying to blind yourself is going to help…' she said, jokingly.

Hal turned to face her with yet another look of perplexity on his face.

'Have you noticed how we don't burn in the sun?'

She hadn't really thought about it, but given that Hal was borderline flammable due to his not-so-borderline vampiric skin-tone, she could understand why he would probably notice something like that. Hal had to take sunscreen everywhere he went in the summer months. She was pale in complexion too, but had only dyed her hair a reddish-auburn. Hal, on the other hand, was just a few shades closer to brown-haired to fully be regarded as, what he called, "Metallic Blonde." His preferred terminology for "ginger."

'Actually,' said Kara, 'it isn't hot at all, is it? I

remember burning up a bit in the heat when we first got here.' As she considered the implications of that, she realised there was another sensation that was conspicuous only by its absence.

'Also, are you hungry?' asked Kara. 'We haven't eaten in like…' she looked over at Jon's phone which was streaming music to the speaker, the shade of the overhead balcony allowing her to read the time. "10:55am," she noted to herself, running the maths in her head. '…What, twenty-two hours since the barbecue?' she said, a split-second later.

Hal felt his stomach, as if there was a direct correlation with carrying out the action and making an informed decision, eventually relaying to her what she already suspected.

'I'm not even remotely hungry…' said Hal, finally.

'Me neither. Which is probably just as well, since we haven't even tried to eat food since we ended up stuck in the past,' said Kara, wondering if she could even pick up food whilst displaced in time, let alone actually being able to consume it.

Hal reached into his pocket for his cigarettes, then kicked himself, as he realised that he'd smoked his last one the day before. He chucked the box carelessly in frustration, watching as it flew through Robert's head, and landed in the hot tub. The box ignored the water, and immediately fell to the bottom of the tub, as if the tub itself were empty. Hal hesitated for a moment, and then leant over the edge of the hot tub. His curiosity getting the better of him, he took a deep breath and submerged his head into the water, peering down at the box and staring at the ridiculous paradox before him; With the jets of water obscuring his vision, he could just about make out the small piece of cardboard, which was unaffected by the water entirely, what with it being out of phase with time, and was inexplicably resting on the hard plastic base of the hot tub, instead of floating on the waters of the past. Not even the jets could disturb it from its final resting place.

Pulling his head from the water, he went to wipe the water from his eyes. Instead, he was startled to discover his head was completely dry. He took another deep breath, this time exhaling slowly, in an attempt to remain calm.

'Nothing about this damn place makes any sense,'

said Hal, feeling aggravated by the lack of coherence to the rules this new world appeared to follow. A world he had been thrust into unwillingly.

'As revelations go, this isn't your best work,' said Kara, who had sprung up behind him during his deep-dive, wondering why he was bobbing for apples in Robert's new home in the first place. Hal, realising she hadn't seen what he'd just witnessed, dutifully elaborated.

'The box I was using for my smokes,' said Hal, 'I chucked it in the hot tub, it should be floating.'

'Makes sense I guess, it's out-of-phase just like we are. Why would it?'

'Yeah, I agree, except if that were true, why is it resting on the bottom of the tub?'

Kara stepped closer and stood next to him, then peered over the edge of the tub. Between the bubbles she could just about make out the distorted outline of his makeshift cigarette container. She still didn't really see what he was getting at.

'I'm sorry Hal, I really don't understand why this is a big deal?'

'Well, why doesn't it fall through the base of the

tub?' said Hal. 'Why does it pass through water but not through solid objects? Come to think of it, why are *we* not falling through floors, plummeting to the earth's core, and out the other side?'

'Oh. Oh damn,' said Kara, her mind blown by the point he'd just made. 'You mean why can't we walk through a closed door, or a car, but when it comes to the gang, we pass right through them?'

They stood there, staring at the bubbling water, as the aberration of time gazed back at them from the depths, the answers to their questions remaining as evasive as ever.

CHAPTER SEVENTEEN

Hard Light

1st Restart – Saturday Afternoon, 1:08pm

Kara and Hal remained in the rear garden whilst their friends changed into their fancy-dress costumes. It felt unethical to be floating around, trying to gain intel from rooms they hadn't been in the first time around, whilst the gang were changing their clothes. Now that the remainder of the guests had arrived, and they had all of the puzzle-pieces at their disposal, all they lacked were the instructions on how to proficiently assemble the puzzle itself.

As their friends made their way into the rear

garden, Hal and Kara noticed that the colours of their chosen family's costumes were popping with a vibrancy that they hadn't noticed the first time around.

Hal shielded his eyes, looking away from Jasmine's knee-high silver boots which, despite complimenting her glamorous take on a member of the iconic quartet Abba, were currently channelling what appeared to be the entirety of the sun's electromagnetic radiation, reflecting it straight into Hal's corneas.

Meanwhile, Kara was doing the same thing to avoid making eye-contact with Santa's trousers, jacket, and hat, which were all emitting their own eye-wateringly vivid red laser beams of refracted sunlight. The brightness gave her another ice-pick migraine, her right temple throbbing savagely. She winced at the pain, but it dissipated quickly.

'I don't remember real life being so…*bright*?' said Hal, turning away from the eclectic light show playing out in front of him, choosing instead to stare at the dullest object he could find. He set his sights on a nice patch of mud, situated a few metres away from where they were standing.

'I know,' said Kara, experiencing the same discomfort. 'It comes and goes, but everything seems…it's like the high-definition settings have been set to the max. You want to go inside?' she suggested, eager to get away from the dazzling sights that were bombarding their senses. Hal nodded vigorously, and they made their way back into the lodge like a couple of mole-people.

As they headed up the central wooden staircase and into the kitchen, they heard a gruff man's voice through the open kitchen window calling out to Jerry. They looked at each other, and ran towards the rear balcony. Staring down, they saw the arrival of Kevin play out for a second time. Hal felt a pain in his chest that felt a lot like heartburn, and tried to put his finger on the odd sense he was experiencing that something felt off.

'Is it just me, or does Kevin seem…*off* to you?' said Hal, suspiciously.

Kara was about to say she didn't feel anything at all about the guy one way or another, but then she felt a twinge in her right temple again, and strangely changed her mind.

'Sort of,' said Kara, 'I get where you're coming from actually.'

Kevin, having finished his conversation with Jon, headed off after Jerry, blissfully unaware that he was reliving his Saturday afternoon for the second time that weekend. Hal and Kara remained upstairs on the balcony, their eyes finding it easier to adjust to the brightness of their surroundings now that they were viewing the unfolding events from a distance.

*

Their privacy was interrupted with the arrival of Rachel, who shot up the stairs to the kitchen area to cook some more food in the oven, now that Jon and Robert had blitzed through their barbecuing. Shortly after, Alex joined her, and Hal and Kara remained where they stood, intent on staying out of their way.

Hal heard his brother Alex making small-talk, as he asked Rachel if she could smell gas. Alex then popped a bottle-cap from his beer, throwing it at the nearby bin, and grimaced as he missed the shot, finally making his way onto the balcony Hal and Kara were still occupying.

As Alex made his way towards them, his cumbersome inflatable ghost-busting pack smashed into the door frame, completely preventing them from ducking past him. Kara had managed to sidestep to the right-hand side of the balcony, but Hal wasn't quite as fortunate. Alex, walking with huge strides of intent, was standing right in front of Hal now. The invasion of personal space caused Hal to consider jumping over the edge of the balcony itself, but he resisted the urge, not entirely keen on the idea of being stuck in this time-loop with a broken leg.

Alex lit a cigarette and then, without warning, took another step forward, occupying the same corner of space that Hal was desperately trying to cram himself into to stay out of his brother's way. As Alex's face passed through his own, Hal saw a momentary sheet of whiteness, and then he found himself staring into the communal dining area.

Alex shuddered, unware that a time traveller had just passed through his face. Hal had only one option, and he balled his fingers into assertive fists, clenched his jaw, closed his eyes, and with an irksome whine of resignation he took a step forward, no longer sharing the same area of space as his brother. He was finally free, but required Kara's reassurance before he opened his eyes again.

'Am I through?! Am I out?! Kara talk to me, where do I go?!'

'Calm down Hal, you're through,' she said, trying to resist the urge to laugh, but failing miserably. 'Take two steps forward and you'll be inside the lodge,' she added, her words broken up between snorts of giggling.

With his eyes still closed, he took her advice, and walked straight into the door frame with a noiseless thud, which instantly brought an end to not only his progress, but also his patience.

'Oh, come on! Dammit! R*eally*?!' said Hal, as Kara gave up entirely on trying to mask her enjoyment over his misfortune.

'My bad, sorry!' she said, not sounding very sorry at all.

Hal opened his eyes, and made his way into the dining area, slumping down onto an unoccupied dining-room chair.

'That was...*uncomfortable*,' noted Hal, with an air

that implied serious understatement.

'Did you see his brains and stuff when he walked through you?!' asked Kara, a little too eagerly.

'What? That's where your mind went? No Kara, I didn't "see his brains and stuff", it was just…nothing but whiteness whilst I was all…up *in* there,' said Hal, shuddering at the memory.

'Oh. That seems lazy. Like if that was a movie you'd expect to see all the synapses and stuff firing off, lots of cool colours,' said Kara, an edge of disappointment in her tone.

'First of all, my eyes aren't equipped with microscopic lenses,' said Hal. 'I don't think you could see that much detail just by passing through someone's brain. Second of all, can we please stop talking about how I just walked through my brother's face now please?!'

'Sorry, sorry it's just, I was expecting more than just–'

Hal finished her sentence 'Our friends being little more than a hard-light construct? Like a Green Lantern made them?'

Kara looked puzzled, 'What do you mean?'

Hal ditched the analogy and rephrased his reply.

'Yeah, I expected there to be more to them that just that whiteness too. I'm sorry for being cranky, it's just…damn. That was weird as shit.'

'So, does this mean our friends…aren't *real*?' said Kara, asking the question that was now on both of their minds. 'Like they aren't really here? That they're just projections?'

Hal thought about that for a moment.

'I don't think we can assume anything at this point, said Hal eventually. 'We just need to get through to tonight, wait for our past-selves to get back, and hope that everything realigns with itself.'

Kara agreed, and so it was decided. Just a few more hours and they would be back in their own bodies, everything would revert to normal, and things would be back to how they should be.

She had to believe that was true.

CHAPTER EIGHTEEN

Hal and Kara's Bogus Journey

1st Restart – Saturday Evening, 8:41pm

The sound of a broken champagne flute, the popping of a cork. Both of these things signifying that it was nearly time. Greenbaum's "Spirit in the Sky" echoed throughout the lodge from an unseen speaker, as Hal and Kara feigned patience, waiting for their nightmare to finally conclude. They were sitting on the bonnet of Robert's Car, taking mischievous pleasure from the fact that they knew how much that would have annoyed him.

'Okay,' said Hal, watching through the front door window of Fir Lodge as his past-self rubbed the back of his head and made his way to his bedroom. 'So, I think I go outside in a minute and try to call Jess. Then you call me back in? You're upstairs with Daisy, right?'

Kara nodded.

'Yeah, cleaning up the glass that Fearne knocked over. Which means Jerry should be right about–' and right on cue, Jerry sauntered up the driveway. He cocked his head up at them, looking as puzzled as a dog could look, and growled playfully at them. They remained perfectly silent so as not to distract him, and with an indignant sniff, he continued on his way through the front doors of the lodge.

'Well I guess we know for certain he can kind of see us now,' noted Kara.

'Uh-huh. That's apparently a thing,' said Hal, begrudgingly accepting what he considered to be just another stupid paradox in a very long list of stupid rules they were currently bound by.

They heard Kara's past-self call for Hal and, beholden to the lasso of inevitability, Hal's past-self entered stage right, as the final string of events set themselves in motion. Their past-incarnations exited the lodge, closing the door behind them, and set off on their errand.

'Oh, *you* closed the door when you left?' said Hal, 'so that's why it was closed when we got back...'

Kara shrugged, as their considerably more-corporeal doubles walked obliviously past their time-travelling counterparts, who remained motionless on the bonnet of Robert's car. As they did so, the bonnet of the car concaved ever-so-slightly under their combined weight.

'Did you feel that?!' said Hal.

'Yeah!' said Kara, her mind racing at the prospect.

This was the first time they had interacted with anything since she had inadvertently moved Robert's wing mirror.

'I mean...it *might* just have been the car cooling down or something,' said Hal, not sounding too convinced by his own statement.

Whatever the cause, his past-self had clearly heard it too, looking at the bonnet for a brief second or two.

'You're thinking of *houses* Hal, the car hasn't been used for over a day.'

'Valid point,' conceded Hal, the shared experience raising yet more questions.

'Should we follow them?' whispered Kara.

Hal considered it. 'I don't think so, we don't know how far away we can travel from the lodge, it might mess things up.'

Not wanting to be the one to make a suggestion that could jeopardise the success of their mission, Kara decided to follow Hal's lead on this one, frustrated by the passivity of their plan. It didn't sit right with her, doing nothing in the hope that it would lead to something.

The concept of relativity, often attributed to the passage of time, was corroborated over the next ten minutes, which felt more like ten hours from their perspective. Kara felt grateful she couldn't feel the cold, nor the coolness of the metal bonnet of the car against her bare legs. Spotting a thin mist, that had appeared out of nowhere, and had begun to creep towards them at ground level, Kara drew Hal's attention to it.

'Hal, the fog's back.'

'Okay, we're getting close now. Any second now, we should be walking back up that drive,' said Hal, with such optimism and certainty that he was even starting to convince himself. And so, they waited.

And waited.

The fog was thickening now, rising up above the bonnet of Robert's car like a rising tide. Kara pulled in her legs, which were dangling over the front of the car, as if allowing the fog to make contact with her would somehow ruin everything.

Kara was beginning to panic, and said aloud what Hal was clearly already thinking. 'Hal…we should be back by now.'

'This doesn't make any sense,' said Hal, 'something's changed. We must have changed events somehow…' the slightly erratic, panic-fuelled break in his voice as clear as their vision was obscured.

As the fog thickened around them, they edged closer together, instantly recoiling as their shoulders made contact with each other and a surge of blue electricity repelled them apart.

'Hal…' said Kara, barely able to make out the

hood of the car anymore, now that their surroundings had all but vanishing into the static sea of white. 'What do we do?'

'What *can* we do Kar'? Maybe this is part of it...maybe we just need to let this play–'

Suddenly, they heard the familiar rush of air, experiencing a blinding whiteness in every direction, hammering their senses into submission. The thundering, relentless sound of air working in unison with the fog to systematically obliterate everything around them.

And then, after what felt like an eternity, the sound ceased without warning. Once again, they were dazzled by an intense, heatless sunlight, as they fell to the ground, overcome with an insurmountable wave of extreme dizziness. As their eyesight was returned to them, they could see that, in terms of detail, everything around them remained just as intensely defined as it had done following their first journey back through time.

Hal and Kara found themselves, once again, standing outside Fir Lodge.

'Please no...' said Hal, clearly on the verge of a

breakdown. They waited in silence, knowing exactly what was coming, but still maintaining hope that they were wrong. And then, as Will's car pulled up towards them, they knew for certain what was happening.

They were right back where they started.

CHAPTER NINETEEN
The Third Kara

2nd Restart – Friday Afternoon, 12:02pm

Once they had fully aligned themselves with what they now realised was their second jump into the past, Kara was the first to break the silence.

'Real solid plan Hal, doing absolutely bloody nothing for thirty-three hours.'

Hal was still shaking off the queasiness of his turbulent journey through space and time, though the former was only technically a few metres away from where he had previously been perched, given that he had been on the bonnet of Robert's car.

'We had to try it, if only to rule it out,' said Hal sheepishly.

They surveyed their surroundings, turning their backs on the cars that were arriving before their past-selves showed up, and made their way to a picnic bench at the rear of Fir Lodge.

As Hal slumped himself down onto the bench, he noticed the right-hand pocket of his boiler suit was slightly raised, the fabric vacuum-formed around a rectangular object. Slowly, he reached into his pocket, and removed the cardboard filter box that he had lost to the depths of the hot tub in the previous timeline. He gingerly used his thumb to flip open the lid to the box and peered inside, his hopes and dreams aligning to create a sense of pure elation.

'Kara, check it out!'

She too peered into the box, and saw the three pre-rolled cigarettes nestled inside. Hal pulled one out and fished around for his flip-top lighter, the sound of scratching metal filling the currently empty garden as he lit up, not that anyone but them could hear it.

'You want one?' he said excitedly.

'No thanks, you hang on to them for later,' she

said, wresting her elbows on her legs, and her chin in her hands, in a manner that evoked defeat. Hal tried to break the ice that Kara's sulk was generating.

'Okay, so time has reset, and we're back where we started,' said Hal. 'You were right, doing nothing did nothing,' he added.

'Shocker,' drawled Kara.

'At least we didn't electrocute each other this time, a successful landing! Which, at the very least, is a change of *some* kind?'

Hal's words did little to lift her mood, but she could see he was trying, and dug down deep to find a way to contribute to the conversation. Taking a deep breath, which she slowly exhaled, Kara responded in a slightly more upbeat tone.

'This…*time-loop* thing seems to have put things right back to the beginning again. Even restocking your supply of death sticks, apparently.'

'Yeah, that's weird right? I mean, for all intents and purposes, we assumed we were operating outside of this timeline,' said Hal, 'and yet, we're clearly still…embedded within these…how many hours was it?'

'Thirty hours and change,' contributed Kara, making a conscious effort to dial down her iciness.

'Right. It looks like when we restart, we start again with everything we had before,' said Hal, the gentle hum of the hot-tub drawing his attention, causing him to look over his shoulder to see how much time they had before their make-shift boardroom was commandeered by his past-self.

"We still have time," he thought, then turned his nose up at the terrible choice of words.

Kara reached down to her waist and pulled the magnifying glass that was tucked into the waistline of her skirt, confirming his assessment. It was seemingly identical to the one she'd thrown onto the wooden floor and left behind on their previous jump. She tossed it onto the grass with the same level of contempt she had done the first time around.

'Okay,' said Kara, 'here's what I think. We focused so much of our efforts on avoiding our past-selves last time, this time I say we stick as close to them as possible.'

Given that Hal's previous plan had been a total bust, he didn't have much of an argument to make.

'Agreed. We need to retrace our steps,' said Hal. 'Literally,' he added unnecessarily.

They jumped up off their seats, just as Past-Hal arrived and took over the bench.

'You stay with you,' said Kara, 'I'm gonna go find myself.'

Kara seemed positively reinvigorated now that she had something to do, and a plan of her own design to follow.

'Sounds spiritual,' said Hal with a chuckle. 'Catch you in a bit.'

Kara shot him a smile and headed inside, her mind whirring through all of the data she had obtained so far, trying to organise their experiences into some kind of order. She spun on her heels, a horrifying thought springing to mind.

'Hal, wait! Just how many of us are here now? I mean, there's our past-selves, then us, but what about the last version of us that jumped back on the first go around?'

'I get where you're coming from,' said Hal, 'but this doesn't feel like that kind of movie.' Kara looked at him blankly, urging him to continue.

'What I mean is, when we re-materialised out the front there,' he said, pointing to the driveway currently in front of them to the left of the lodge, 'we didn't land on copies of ourselves right? That's where we would have been after our first trip on the crazy-coaster.'

Kara nodded, wrapping her head around his nerdy, but seemingly sound-in-principle, understanding of their current situation.

'So, we're *it*? You don't think we've been split a third time?' she asked, needing him to say the words.

'I mean damn Kar', it's impossible to say for sure I guess, but we're not having this conversation with ourselves right now, so I'm going with the theory that we're not horcruxes,' reasoned Hal. 'Of course, that being the case, that means anything we did in the last thirty-three hours?' he gave her a thumbs up, then flipped it upside down, blowing a raspberry, and added 'that's probably been erased too. Not that we did all that much.'

'Like you smoking all your cigarettes, and me ditching my magnifying glass!' said Kara excitedly. This time-travel stuff was unexpectedly easy to grasp once she started thinking outside of the box.

'Exactly, hence your sleuthing tool and my smokes being restocked by the time police,' said Hal.

He noticed that Kara suddenly looked troubled.

'What's wrong?'

'Oh, nothing really,' said Kara, 'just…do you think that's a real thing? Time police?'

'Well if it is, they're clearly suffering from the same budgetary constraints as the *actual* police. Surely they would've shown up by now?' said Hal. 'I think we're on our own with this.'

Kara had to agree. If there really was a group of people charged with moderating disturbances and changes to the timestream, they surely would have presented themselves by now. She thought she'd cheer Hal up by saying something she knew he'd get a kick out of.

'I guess that makes *us* the time cops then,' said Kara.

Seeing his gleeful smile, she knew she'd hit the right note, and made her way inside to track down the version of herself from thirty-three hours ago.

"Or was that sixty-six hours ago?" she thought,

instantly deciding that she was not going to count previous time spent between their first and second leap through time.

CHAPTER TWENTY
Just Passing Through

2nd Restart – Friday Afternoon, 12:08pm

Kara had cornered her past-self in her bedroom, the latter of whom was throwing her bag onto her bed. Kara stood there, trying to take everything in, every little detail that might just reveal some kind of Easter-egg that she could somehow exploit. But as far as she could tell, there was simply nothing to see. Her past-self turned around suddenly, and began to walk towards her. Kara clenched her fists and stood there, her feet firmly planted. Her past-self continued on, a game of chicken she didn't even know she was playing. As they passed through each other, Kara heard a sound reminiscent of one of those memory-altering devices used in that movie; about a secret organisation that protected the universe from alien invasions.

As every one of Kara's currently out-of-phase molecules began to resonate, infused with an interdimensional energy that somehow tasted like the colour blue, Kara's past-self seared all the way through her and out the other side, seemingly unaware of the encounter, bar the faint indication of a shiver that she immediately shrugged off as she left the room.

Kara noticed that her saliva now tasted like copper, and that she suddenly felt very different, though she couldn't quite define the reason why. Spinning around, she rushed from the bedroom, feeling the need to confer with Hal. She immediately stopped in her tracks, as Jasmine took over the doorway.

Taking a few steps backwards, Kara allowed Jasmine to pass, then set off into the rear garden, ensuring not to bang into the pool table outside her bedroom in the hallway.

Frustratingly, Hal was nowhere to be found, then she kicked herself realising he must be upstairs. She ran back into the lodge, and up the wooden staircase, where all of her friends were currently congregating.

'Hal!' she shouted, 'have you walked through yourself yet?'

She had to dodge her past-self once again, who began to unknowingly encroach on the space Kara was currently occupying. Pressing herself against the kitchen island, which was laden with food and drinks, her hand accidentally brushed against a packet of biscuits, causing them to roll off of the counter and onto the floor. She stared at the packet, then turned to face Hal.

'How did you do that?!' he said, with a look of awe and confusion.

Her eyes were wide with the implications of what had just happened.

'Holy shit…' she said, 'We can move things in the past!'

*

They were standing in the entrance hall as Hal's past-self, along with Rachel, were greeting his brother Alex. Hal knew what he had to do, but was clearly putting it off for as long as possible, causing Kara to grow impatient.

'Hal, just do it already and stop being a baby.'

Her words did little to expel his unease, as he swallowed dryly, taking up a stance similar to that of a professional runner, aligning himself behind his past-self. After another several false starts, Kara tried a different approach.

'The sooner you run through yourself, the sooner we can test this thing.'

Seeing no sign of him taking the leap, Kara pushed him, a blue spark erupting from in-between his shoulder blades and her hand. Adopting a persona akin to that of a spooked horse, he was off, his hands outstretched in case things went south.

As he passed through himself, he heard a sound that reminded him of the repulsor-blast generated by that superhero who wore a suit made of iron. He felt an odd sensation of tingling all over, as a current of energy flowed through him, and then he was through. Kara noted that Hal's past-self shuddered slightly.

Hal looked at his hands, expecting to see some kind of visible transformative evidence, but was left disappointed, as he clicked his tongue trying to make sense of why he could taste the colour blue.

'I don't feel all that different...' he said. 'I thought I'd feel different?'

Kara sped past their friends in the hallway and onto the drive where Hal was now standing.

'*Finally*,' she said. 'Now we can take this thing for a test drive.'

*

It didn't take them long to realise that there wasn't anything to move on the driveway, so they instead followed the path at the side that led into the rear garden. Staring excitedly at the various items spread out before them, they decided it was best to start small, settling on the beer bottles that lined their favourite picnic bench, which indicated that Jon had clearly started early on the beers. Kara ran at them like an Amazonian warrior, her arms flailing wildly as she attempted to swipe at them. One of them wobbled, but only barely. Rubbing her hands together at chest level, she dived in for a second attempt. This time, the bottle didn't move at all.

It was Hal's turn next, and he swiped diagonally at a nearby bottle, his carefully composed judo-chop resulting in an embarrassingly non-effectual anti-climax.

'Hey, at least you made one of them wobble,' said Hal, sensing his fellow time-traveller's frustration.

After twenty-or-so minutes, Kara was close to giving up, as she swung a killer right-hook once more for good measure, causing the bottle to fly off the bench and onto the grass. As she turned around to make sure Hal was watching, she noticed her past-self walk past, making her way to sit with the girls, who were laying down towels in the rear garden to do some sun-bathing. She put two and two together and presented an observation to Hal.

'Waaaait a second…we have to be *close* to ourselves! It won't work if we're not close!'

Kara took another swipe, knocking another bottle over. Her past-self looked over her shoulder and looked at the propelled bottle. Realising she must have been imagining things, she shook her head, and continued on her merry way.

With every step past-Kara took further down the garden, the remaining bottles increasingly took on the apparent mass of cast iron, refusing to budge no matter how much Kara tried.

*

They spent the remainder of their Friday this way, trying to move mundane objects around when no one was looking, with varying degrees of success, though this meant splitting up in order to maintain proximity to their past-selves. As their friends went to bed, they eventually held a meeting on the roof of Robert's car to share their findings, and to determine any discerning limitations to their game-changing new abilities, with Hal leading the charge.

'Well, I've learnt that we definitely can't physically interact with the gang, *or* our past-selves. Not in any tangible way anyway. How about you?'

'Nope. Same. It seems like we can only move, like, non-*living* objects or something,' said Kara, pointedly.

Hal dropped some more knowledge about another one of their discoveries.

'You were right about having to be close to our

past-selves to interact with stuff,' he said. 'The further away we are from them, the harder it becomes. Did you notice that even if they were right next to us it eventually took more and more concentration to move things? Almost like it's draining us every time we move something?'

Kara agreed. She'd experienced the same sensation of feeling increasingly more exhausted as the day went on.

'I tried walking through my past-self a few times to see if it would...I don't know...*recharge* me or something, but it seems like it makes no difference how many times we do that,' said Kara. 'I'm not even sure we needed to do it in the first place. I think maybe we could move things all along,' she added, casting her mind back to her first restart, when she had inadvertently bumped into Robert's wing mirror, forcing it inwards.

Inside the lodge, someone turned off the last light, casting them into darkness. Their improved vision still afforded them the ability to see clearly, despite being enveloped by the night, and only having the solar system's nightlight, the moon, for illumination.

They had also intentionally avoided interacting with Jerry that afternoon, noting that he didn't stop at the side of the lodge to sniff at where they were standing during their last time-jump. This seemed to validate Hal's theory that things they set in motion were erased once they restarted their weekend.

'How you feeling, anyway?' Hal asked Kara, wondering how she was dealing with everything that had been thrust upon them.

She laid on her back, her feet gently kicking against Robert's windscreen, as she stared at the stars.

'I mean…I feel fine, physically. Or is that meta-physically?' she asked.

Hal shrugged, not really sure how to answer that, allowing her to continue.

'Either way, I'm okay,' said Kara. 'I just don't know how we're going to get out of this loop, you know?'

Hal knew exactly how she felt, because he felt the exact same way.

'I was thinking,' said Hal, 'maybe we could follow ourselves into the woods tomorrow? Get a change of scenery…might do us good?'

'Yeah, can do if you want,' said Kara. The more she thought about it, the better it sounded.

'I like that idea, actually,' she added.

And with that, they decided to turn in for the night, jumping from the roof of the car and onto the gravel in a soundless leap. They made their way to the front door, and immediately realised they were locked out.

'Oh bollocks,' said Kara.

Forced into making alternative arrangements for the night ahead, they made their way around to the rear garden, taking up a spot on the top of the hot tub, which was now fully covered for the night with a solid plastic protective shell, and spent the rest of the night staring up at the stars and waiting for sleep to take them, despite knowing that it wouldn't.

CHAPTER TWENTY-ONE

Lost

2nd Restart – Saturday Morning, 11:01am

Their trip through the woods wasn't nearly as thrilling as Hal had hoped, though the excursion did present an unexpected opportunity. The walk took them directly past Kevin's lodge, another piece to the puzzle that they had yet to investigate. Deciding that having daylight on their side could be useful, they broke away from their past-selves to check it out.

The front door was locked, of course, so all they could do was peer through the windows into the perfectly ordinary home. By the time they had made their way around the perimeter and discovered a back door, their past-selves were too far down the road for the time-travellers to try turning the handle. Deciding it was a fruitless endeavour, they cast the idea aside, and joined up with their friend's to continue onwards into the picturesque woodland.

Kara was thankful that the copious amounts of stinging nettles that lined the walkways couldn't harm her exposed legs, though Hal noted the practicality of her attire was hardly any different from the shorts her past-self was sporting. They followed several paces behind their friends, as they ventured deeper into the woods, chuckling at the dramatic irony as their past-selves realised that they'd reached a dead-end and had to turn back.

Upon returning to Fir Lodge, the remainder of the morning went unusually quickly. As destiny dictated, everyone adorned their iconic costumes, and Hal and Kara decided to split up, determined to observe the afternoon from different vantage points. An unfortunate by-product of doing so was that it made it slightly more difficult for Hal and Kara to identify which one of themselves was who. More than once, Hal had engaged in conversation with Kara's past-self, only for *his* Kara having to resort to signalling him, so that he was aware that he was talking to the wrong person. Despite being out of phase with time, visibly they looked identical, in both opacity and density, to their more corporeal twenty-eight-hour-old selves.

"Or was that fifty-six hours?" thought Hal.

He hadn't decided if it was advisable to keep count of the exact measure of time they'd been there, but it was already giving him a headache. Kara seemed equally vexed by something time-travel related, as Hal noticed she was rubbing her temples again.

'Headache again?' he asked, already knowing the answer.

'Yeah, comes and goes,' said Kara. 'Where are we at?' she asked, referring to where they were in the current loop. 'Kevin should be arriving in a bit, right?

'Mm-hm. You wanna follow him for a bit? Maybe get a closer look at his place? If he opens the doors for us, we may even be able to sneak inside...' suggested Hal.

Kara wasn't so sure it was a good idea.

'I thought the plan was to follow our tracks,' she replied. 'Also, we need to make sure we follow ourselves to Kevin's tonight,' she added.

'Relax,' said Hal in a reassuring tone. 'We've got hours before we head off to take Jerry back' he said, referring to their past-selves

Reluctantly, Kara responded with an "okay, why not" kind of shrug.

'Okay, if you're sure,' said Kara.

*

Like clockwork, Kevin arrived, and then departed, only this time he had two time-travellers on his tail. Unfortunately, it was slowly becoming a theme that when it came to Hal's ideas, things didn't quite go to plan.

As Kevin navigated the woods in pursuit of Jerry, who had run off ahead of them, he took them further away from Fir Lodge than they'd been thus far. This resulted in them focusing more of their attention on trying to keep up with Kevin's brisk pace than the route they were taking.

Their progress was hindered at numerous points,

as Hal tried to step around the protruding brambles that obstructed their path, despite Kara's protests that they could just walk through them unscathed. It transpired that plant-life fell into the tick-box of "Living matter", meaning they couldn't directly interact with it.

They eventually stopped at the edge of a lake to regroup, as Kevin stopped and pulled a plastic bag from his pocket, and proceeded to pick up some of Jerry's recently deposited business.

'Would you look at that view,' said Hal, staring out across the wide expanse of water in front of them.

Kara was about to question what was so breath-taking about watching Jerry taking a dump, when she realised Hal was referring to the rural skyline stretching out in front of them.

They sat down on a nearby log, taking in the serene beauty of the fir trees that ran across the horizon. The late afternoon, orange-tinged sun reflecting the vista before them into the water of the lake, like a shimmering mirror-image of a duplicated snapshot in time.

A few minutes later, it was Kara who noticed the

one thing missing from this interactive postcard that they were diverting all of their attention to.

'Hal, where's Kevin?'

Hal quickly looked over his shoulder, then his other shoulder, finally standing up with an air of urgency.

'Oh man,' said Hal, running a hand through his hair. 'I guess now we know how the parents felt in Home Alone.'

'He can't have got far,' said Kara. 'Let's go catch him up.'

*

After what felt like a couple of hours searching for Kevin without success, Kara was the first to voice her uneasiness about the way their day was progressing.

'I think we should head back, Hal,' she said, as she looked behind her and realised they had stepped well-beyond anything resembling a beaten track.

Hal, who was about as reliable with directions as he was with contributing informative opinions relating to football, offered up his thoughts on which path they should take.

'Yeah, you're right, we need to suck it up and sack

it off,' said Hal, who had also had more than enough walking for one day, and they proceeded back the way they came.

*

An hour or so later, they found themselves back at what appeared to be the log they had sat on earlier that afternoon.

'Kara, do you know where we're going?' asked Hal eventually.

'Not funny Hal, I've been following you this whole time,' said Kara.

Hal gave some thought to their current location and said 'Well, I *think* our lodge is on the other side of this lake…maybe?'

'Oh, that's just perfect. So now we're lost in time, *and* the woods,' exclaimed Kara, her definition of perfection clearly differing greatly from Hal's. 'So, what're you suggesting, we swim across?'

'Man, these woods are way denser that you'd expect for a holiday retreat. Not to mention, every path looks the same,' noted Hal, sensing he may need to begin formulating a case for his defence.

'They're trees Hal, of course they look the same.'

Not for the first time that day, she'd wondered why she couldn't have been caught in a temporal anomaly with Jon instead of Hal.

'Well, we can't swim,' said Hal, 'even though we wouldn't get wet, we'd just drop to the bottom of the lake-bed. Without knowing how deep it is, we might not be able to climb up the embankment on the other side,' he added, basing the entirety of his opinion on The Great Cardboard Case/Hot tub Incident of their first restart.

'It'll be getting dark soon, we're wasting valuable time,' said Kara nervously. 'Let's just head that way,' she added, pointing towards the path that looked most like the one they had trekked down before they had lost track of Kevin.

'If we keep the lake on our right, we can use it to guide us,' she said, vaguely recalling that she'd seen someone do that on a documentary once.

Unfortunately for Kara, she failed to realise that the "documentary" she was citing was actually a movie about a small town called Burkittsville, infamously known for having a spot of bother, thanks to a rather rambunctious Blair Witch.

*

Despite maintaining a brisk pace, and also discovering that they apparently had endless reserves of energy, the journey was a long one. Not having to stop to catch their out-of-phase breath did little to combat the sheer amount of distance they had to traverse. Hal stopped for a moment, a severe burst of heartburn stopping him in his tracks. Kara slowed her pace and walked back over to him.

'Heartburn again? You haven't even eaten anything in days,' said Kara, more out of concern than resentment.

'I don't' know…It's like your headaches I guess.'

They both knew that they didn't seem to get hungry or thirsty in this place. Nor could they feel the heat or cold. Why they kept experiencing the similar symptoms of pain left Hal as mystified as Kara. Feeling better, he motioned that he was ready to get going again.

Sticking to the edge of the lake had yielded results; they'd reached the other side just as the sun had set. However, from their current view-point on the edge of the forest, they could see the glistening of water a long distance away from the current body of water they were using as a landmark.

Kara took a deep breath, then vented the temporally-displaced non-air from her lungs.

'Kara...how many lakes are there here?' asked Hal, as he recalled their first walk, where they had hit a dead end and Will had noted there was a second lake on the horizon.

'Well, it's called Pentney *Lakes*, so I'm guessing more than one?' said Kara.

Every path they took seemed to lead them further and further away from where they needed to be. Several huge errors had clearly snowballed until, eventually, they were acres away from where they wanted to be. They were now truly and utterly lost, finally understanding the expression of not being able to "see the forest from the trees."

A static fog began to line the floor, undisturbed by their legs, as they kicked their way through it.

'No, no, no, NO!' yelled Kara, shouting into the thickening mist that was surrounding them. It was then that the all-too-familiar sound of rushing air made its attack on their eardrums.

'Oh, for *fu*–' but Hal's profanity was cut short, as the ruthless fog swallowed them up and, once more, they disappeared into the past.

CHAPTER TWENTY-TWO
Restarting from scratch

3rd Restart – Friday Afternoon, 12:05pm

They sat on their picnic bench, Hal smoking the first of his freshly restocked trio of cigarettes. It was Kara's turn to break the ice.

'It was a good plan Hal, it wasn't your fault we got turned around.'

'Thanks Kar', but it was a terrible plan. Though I do appreciate you caring enough to lie.'

They shared a smile, and looked out across the tree line to the rear of their lodge. Oddly, the mist hadn't fully dissipated following the restart. It was barely noticeable, but with their heightened sense of sight that had been bestowed upon them since arriving in their personal bubble of repeated time, they could see it. It was merely a wisp in terms of density, but very much there.

'What do you think the deal is with the fog?' Hal asked Kara. 'I mean, besides it being a literal manifestation of Robert's sardonic wit,' he joked, taking another drag. The damn cigarettes didn't even do all that much for him, it was like breathing in air.

'God knows,' said Kara, 'It's never followed us back before...has it?'

'First time I've noticed,' said Hal, shaking his head. 'It usually only shows up as a useless early-warning system before it whisks us back to the start.'

'It's kind of...*static* right?' added Kara, waving her hand through the scarcely perceptible mist, which refused to move under her admittedly ineffectual touch.

She scrunched her eyes shut, then opened them again, trying to ignore the whiteness, as if it were the lines on a heated windscreen of a car that she had to cast from her mind so that she could, once more, concentrate on the road ahead.

'So, I've been thinking,' declared Hal, as he turned to face her with a look of excitement on his face. 'We need a name.'

With his past-self talking to Jon at the hot tub, Hal and Kara stood up and made their way to the free deckchairs to the right of the tub. They knew through experience that they'd have access to them for another ten or so minutes without being interrupted.

Kara dropped onto a deckchair, eager to continue their conversation.

'How do you mean?' she asked.

'This thing we're doing, jumping through time, it's kind of like a superhero thing,' said Hal, 'and all the best teams have a name.'

The light-hearted distraction was actually a welcome one to Kara, and she decided to entertain the notion.

'What, you mean like "the dynamic duo"?'

Hal scrunched his nose up at that.

'We can do better than that. Something that relates to what we're going through. Time-Travellers is a bit...one-dimensional, no pun intended.'

'How about "Time Ghosts,"' suggested Kara, earnestly.

'I meeeean…something like that. Only *not* that,' said Hal, administering an immediate veto.

'What's wrong with Time Ghosts?!' asked Kara, clearly hurt that Hal didn't see the potential.

'Because, how can I put this delicately…it's terrible,' said Hal with a smile, and offering her a playful wink. 'For one thing, we're not ghosts, and secondly, well, it's depressing as all hell.'

It was Hal's turn to give it a try. 'Time Jumpers?'

'That's boring,' said Kara, getting her own back.

'*You're* boring,' whispered Hal, feigning a sulk.

Kara took another stab at it. 'Time Rid–' but Hal cut her off without hesitation.

'That's *definitely* taken,' said Hal, recalling the urban-myth he had once read about on an obscure forum. 'We don't want to mess with those guys, they'd probably erase us. Besides, I was thinking more along the lines of what we're doing. *Restarting* specifically.'

They continued to sit there for a while, running various names past each other, until they eventually found a winner. It was so obvious that they kicked themselves that it had taken them so long to get there.

'How about Restarters?' suggested Hal.

'Nah,' said Kara dismissively. 'How about...*Restarters*?' she added, a mischievous smile appearing on her face.

'That's literally what I just said,' said Hal.

'Yeah,' admitted Kara, 'but if we ever get to tell our story, now everyone will think *I* came up with it.'

'No one's going to buy that,' chuckled Hal.

'Time will tell, I guess...' said Kara.

Standing up for dramatic effect, and putting on his best movie trailer voice, he took it for a test-drive.

'In a *world*, where *time* itself is broken, caught in a *loop* that no one else can perceive, only *The Restarters* can restart the past...'

'...to save the future,' added Kara, in an equally dramatic voice.

'You know, as tag-lines go, that's surprisingly not terrible,' said Hal. 'Unlike your trailer voice. How embarrassing for you,' he added, pretending to cringe.

'You're ridiculous!' said Kara, laughing. 'Besides, we haven't done much future-saving. All we've done so far is get lost in the woods and push some beer bottles over.'

'Every elite team has to start somewhere,' said Hal with a shrug. 'Besides, we're kind of writing the rule book as we go along. We'll figure this thing out.'

Kara wasn't as convinced. 'Uh huh. Right. Come on then *Restarter*, let's get to work. We need a plan for today.'

They began by running through the list of things they knew, which, as it turned out, was a relatively moderate list. They had learned that they could move things when in close proximity to their past-selves, but only inanimate objects (or as Kara defined it, "Nothing living.") Following their first restart, they had also discovered that their past-selves hadn't returned to Fir Lodge after taking Jerry back. Hal speculated that something must have happened between them dropping Jerry home and their return to the lodge, and that this "event" had put them out-of-phase with time itself. He reasoned that, as a result, they wouldn't be able to see themselves after the event happened, as they would be out of sync with their personal timeline.

Despite Hal's innate ability to make even the most straight-forward of sentences overly complicated, she thought she saw what he was getting at.

'Sooo, you think things went south for us during the walk home?'

'That's exactly what I just said,' said Hal, completely unaware that he'd taken the long way around with his explanation.

'Makes sense I guess,' said Kara. 'In that case, I think we need to wait for our past-selves to arrive with Jerry at Kevin's place, then we can follow ourselves back to see exactly what went down?'

Hal liked that idea. 'Oooh! We could stakeout Kevin's place from across the road? Get an early start tomorrow, follow ourselves on our walk to the forest, only this time, break away and stay by his lodge. Sound good?'

'Motion seconded,' confirmed Kara.

'Motion carried,' said Hal.

CHAPTER TWENTY-THREE
Stakeout

3rd Restart – Saturday Morning, 9:02am

They found their spot at around 9am that Saturday morning, and settled in for the long haul ahead of them. The Restarters had perfect line-of-sight to Kevin's lodge, and were excited by the prospect of rigging the system in order to see just what had happened on their walk home. They began sharing their theories on what they expected to uncover, each more outlandish than the last. In the end, they decided to make a bet.

'So, we're agreed?' said Kara, reiterating the terms.

'If our past-selves are greeted by time-travellers, and jump through a swirling portal into the past–'

'A *green* swirling portal,' corrected Hal.

'Fine. A *green* swirling portal. If it's that, you win, and we'll follow them through it on the next restart. And if it's literally *anything* else, *I* win, and get to keep your pack of chewing-gum.'

They shook hands, the fizzle of blue light preventing them from indulging in doing so for longer than a second or two.

At approximately 11am, their past-selves could finally be seen approaching from the road to their left. Kara took the opportunity to punch Hal in the arm to snap him from his failed attempt at sleeping, the electricity far more potent now, given the proximity to their past-selves, causing him to bolt upright.

'*They're here*,' she whispered.

'Jeeze, thanks creepy child from Poltergeist,' said Hal, rubbing his arm.

'Don't you think we should get closer to Kevin's place?' asked Kara. 'Why are we sitting so far away, it's not like anyone can see us?' she added.

'*Because*,' said Hal, 'it's a *stakeout*.'

The reality was that Hal wanted to feel more connected to the world. Sitting further away created the illusion that they could be seen, and that induced a feeling that the stakes were higher than they would have been had they just waited on Kevin's doorstep.

'Gah, this is so exciting isn't it? Just a couple of time-travellers, staking out a key moment in their own history? We're like proper detectives!'

Kara shrugged.

'I'll be more excited once we find out exactly what happened to us,' she said.

*

Hal's excitement wore off exponentially as the seconds evolved into minutes, and the minutes graduated into hours. They learned pretty quickly that the idea of a stakeout was much cooler in theory than it was in practice. Precisely nothing happened until the late afternoon, when Kevin pulled up on his driveway, in what Hal assumed to be a four-wheel-drive pickup truck of some description. He wasn't all that au fait with vehicles, so couldn't make out the model, but it looked relatively expensive, despite the worn exterior. A midnight blue, two-seater vehicle, what it lacked in passenger practicality it more than made up for with its open-top storage area. The paintwork looked like it could use a touch-up, as if to indicate the vehicle had really been put through its paces. What was surely once a shiny exterior was now more dulled and matte-like.

Kevin looked around shiftily as he opened the door of his truck, allowing Jerry to jump out from the passenger side. Moving to the rear of his vehicle, he unlatched the back panel of the truck, and pulled a long black bag from the back. He slid it all the way out, until it collided noisily with the ground. Hoisting it onto his shoulder, Kevin awkwardly made his way to his front door, unlocking it with his free hand. Once inside, he kicked the front door closed behind him after Jerry was through, but the door failed to catch, and was left ajar by a few inches, failing to shut fully.

'What do you think he's got in there?' asked Kara, intrigued by Kevin's seemingly suspicious demeanour, coupled with his apparent eagerness to move the large black fabric container into the house as quickly as possible.

‘I bet you any money it’s doughnuts,’ said Hal, still salty over the fact that the stakeout just didn’t feel cliché enough without them.

‘Hal,’ said Kara, pinching the bridge of her nose, ‘for the last time, even if we had access to doughnuts, we couldn’t *eat* them even if we’d found a way to drag them here. Let it *go* already.’

He hummed something about the cold not bothering him anyway and stood up, brushing the grass from the back of his boiler suit, despite the fact that foliage debris wouldn’t have adhered to the material anyway.

‘I’m gonna go peer through the window, you coming?’ asked Hal.

Kara stood up, following Hal’s lead, as he made his way across the road, and they both took up position at separate windows, peering through into Kevin’s home. Kevin was unlocking a door to the left of his kitchen and, moving backwards, he pulled the big black sack in after him. Hal and Kara could hear the faint sound of Kevin talking to himself and then, shortly after, Kevin reached from the darkness of what lay beyond the door and slammed the door shut.

Jerry barked at it incessantly.

'Well, that wasn't creepy as shit,' said Kara solemnly.

'Yeah, real glad we did this, it's been fun,' said Hal, walking away from the lodge at a pace that was just slightly too brisk for someone trying not to look freaked out.

'We should get in there, see what he's up to, suggested Kara. 'The front door is partially open, maybe we can squeeze through…'

'Hard pass,' said Hal. 'I don't care what he's up to. Let's stick to the plan and keep an eye out for this swirling time portal, or whatever it's going to be, okay?' but she ignored him, staring into the dimly-lit cabin.

'Kara, snap out of it yeah, let's head back to our spot.'

Begrudgingly, she pulled herself away from the window, and they made their way back to the patch of grass directly opposite the increasingly mysterious lodge.

*

Jerry had forced himself out of the front door an

hour or so ago, staying true to his own timeline, and making his way to Fir Lodge. They couldn't shake the tenseness, as the evening slowly approached, knowing that their past-selves would be directly in front of them soon. Despite not having a watch, or a working phone, to confirm exactly *when* they were in the current restart, they knew they didn't have long to wait now.

As if right on cue, their saint-like perseverance had paid off. There they were; Velma and a ghost-busting scientist, casually walking towards Kevin's lodge, being lured there by Jerry. A few houses away, Kara saw her past-self lean down to check Jerry's tag.

This was it, any second now.

They held their breath in unison, as they watched themselves walk up the short driveway, the past incarnation of Hal calling out to see if anyone was home. The Restarters were so focused on watching events play out, that they failed to notice the thickening fog that was rolling across the grass behind them, dispersing through the fir trees like a viscous, yet entirely intangible liquid. As it moved across their line of sight, they drew their focus away from their target for the first time in hours, sensing that something wasn't right.

'It's too early, why is the fog here already?!' Hal asked Kara, despite knowing she knew as much as he did, and wouldn't have the answer.

'It's so thick, what do we do?!' responded Kara, the panic in her voice putting Hal even more on edge. If the fog was here, a restart wouldn't be far behind it.

'We make a run for it,' said Hal, 'to our past-selves!

Having come too far to allow the omnipresence of time to steal their reward out from underneath them, they stood up, and began to run across the road, realising all too late that they'd lost sight of themselves. In their frantic attempts at trying to locate their past-selves amidst the debilitating fog, their eyes eventually landed back on Kevin's lodge.

Being the only landmark that was currently visible, they moved towards it, but barely made it two steps before the sound of rushing air brought them to their knees.

Kara felt like her head had been split open with an actual ice pick. Meanwhile, Hal was rolling on the floor, unable to catch his breath, due to the excruciating sensation of a trapped nerve being plucked like a harp-string in his chest. Their surroundings were shaking now, from side to side, and for a brief moment Hal thought he was going to fall into the sky, as if it were a bottomless ocean beneath him. And then the pain, along with the temporal distortions, retreated just as quickly as they had taken them down, the fog lessening in its opaqueness, albeit only slightly.

'Where are *we*?' said Kara.

Hal knew she was referring to their past-selves. He pointed into the distance, where they could just about make out the faint outline of themselves walking back to Fir Lodge.

'They're getting away!' shouted Hal.

Hal and Kara immediately pulled themselves up from the ground, and headed off in pursuit, the answer to their biggest question still within reach. The fog began to thicken again, causing the outlines they were chasing to disappear from sight. They picked up the pace, but the road seemed to go on forever. It was then that they realised they had run completely past

Fir Lodge. The sound of rushing air arrived once more, at first a mocking whisper, gradually increasing in pitch and severity, attacking them from all sides.

'Oh, you sonuva–' Hal shouted, both into the night, and at the deafening crescendo that followed.

CHAPTER TWENTY-FOUR
A Trip Through Time

4th Restart – Friday Afternoon, 12:01pm

'Bitch!' finished Hal, landing in the next restart with the grace of a man doing a teddy-bear roll after drinking two bottles of tequila.

He stormed off to their favourite picnic bench, running through various expletives with frustration. Kara caught up with him, and sat down next to him, as he sparked up the first of his three cigarettes for this restart, and waited patiently for him to calm down.

'We were so damn close!' said Hal.

Kara hadn't seen him lose his cool quite like this before. Even when they had first arrived here, in this cursed place, and considering what they were up against, Hal had always seemed relatively calm and collected.

'If it weren't for that damn fog rolling in…' he continued, playing through the events in his mind. 'We were *right* behind our past-selves! You saw them walking back to our lodge too, right?!'

Kara skimmed through her recent memories, then realised she didn't actually know what she saw.

'I mean…I thought I could see us, but the fog was so thick. It was barely an outline…'

'Well, this isn't working, I think you were right all along,' said Hal. 'We need to be more proactive here. We need to go on the offensive. Whatever is causing this clearly doesn't want us to have all the facts,' he added, throwing his cigarette over his shoulder as he realised he wasn't getting anything from the clearly fake tobacco.

'What did you have in mind?' asked Kara in a soothing tone, trying to get him to calm down.

'I think we're going about this all wrong,' said

Hal. 'Instead of trying to find out what *happened*, I think we need to prevent it from *happening* at all. We need to stop our past-selves from leaving Fir Lodge. If we don't go, we can't end up in this mess.'

Kara considered the concept, then shook her head as if she was shooing a wasp out of her hair.

'Can we even change things like that?' said Kara, 'I mean, the most we've been able to achieve is making our friends shiver when we walk through them. We're hardly the masters of our own destiny in this place.'

Hal looked over his shoulder and saw his past-self talking to Jon by the hot tub. It was then that he remembered something. It was so obvious, that he couldn't believe he'd missed it the first three times. Then he remembered that they hadn't made it to the garden early on, during their first restart, which meant it was technically only two restarts that he needed to berate himself for having missed something so crucial.

His past self-was leaning against the hot tub now, the sound of the jets rumbling gently, just as they always were at this time of the morning. Except, they weren't rumbling at *all* the first time he arrived.

He shot up without warning, and sprinted towards the sauna room to the left of Jon and his past-self, his cumbersome rubber boots colliding soundlessly on the tiled flooring. His eyes darted frantically, as he scanned the room for what he needed, and then he saw the closed cupboard door in the corner of the room. He ran to the door and reached for the handle, his past-self being close enough to allow him to interact with it. And there it was; cast in darkness, a tiny black plastic switch, the initials "HT" emblazoned above it in a humble font that failed to do justice to their significance.

Reaching out, he flicked the switch to the "OFF" position, and heard the stream of jets slow down, eventually grinding to a halt. He waited, as he heard past-Hal and Jon discussing what had happened.

Hal counted to ten, then flipped the switch back to the "ON" position, causing the motor to restart, and filling the jets with life. Stepping out from the cupboard, Hal closed the door behind him, a ridiculous grin on his face, then walked back out to Kara.

"This is going to blow her mind," he thought to himself.

*

'What's with the ridiculous grin?' asked Kara, as Hal popped the collar on his boiler suit, walking towards her with a swagger that lacked the desired cool factor he was going for, given that she had no context for its usage.

'Every morning we sit here, I can't believe I missed it!' said Hal, gearing up for a good old ramble.

'Missed wha–' began Kara, but Hal cut her question short.

'We move out of the way to make room for past-me, who sits *right* where we're sitting, something always niggled me about that. I think on a sub-conscious level I felt it, that the timing was off. Then I noticed the jets! I can't believe it took me three damn restarts to spot it! The *jets* Kara!'

'Hal, you're rambling. It's annoying. What jets?'

'On the hot tub! When we first got here, as in the first time around, to Fir Lodge, I came out and chatted with Jon. Whilst we were talking, the hot tub cuts out, right? The power tripped!'

Hal was talking even faster now, his tone indicating that this conversation contained the greatest discovery since the instant-coffee that fuelled the very existence of his former-self.

'That's…a cool story,' said Kara, pulling a face that she usually only used moments before pushing a panic button, to signal the help of a security guard that would descend on the situation, rescuing her from a crazy person that had approached her at work.

'Kara, those jets haven't cut out at this time of day for the past three restarts. But they did just now. Because *I* tripped the power.'

Kara stared at him, her mouth slowly dropping open. She understood now. Hal smiled as he saw the realisation dawning on her face.

'We've been changing the original timeline all along through our own *inaction*,' said Hal excitedly, 'by doing nothing at all. Imagine what we can do when we actually try!'

Kara was having a hard time getting her head around Hal's bombshell. Hal, on the other hand, was clearly in his element. Kara had so many questions, which Hal happily countered with a volley of answers.

'But how is that possible?' asked Kara. 'I mean, if you were the one, in a restart, that turned off the hot tub, how was that the true timeline? That would mean that we, us, *Restarter us*,' she barked snappily, irked by how hard it was to form a sentence when referencing herself whilst she was occupying two periods of time simultaneously, 'that would mean *we* were already here before whatever happened sent us here?'

'Exactly,' said Hal, without missing a beat.

Kara scrunched her eyes closed, unsuccessfully faking the appearance of patience via the medium of a clenched jaw. 'You can't just say "exactly" like it explains everything!'

Hal laughed, 'But that's exactly it! It's a paradox! We were *already* travelling through time *before* we arrived here for the first time. And by me not tripping the hot tub, we've been changing the true course of events purely by accident. Me tripping it just now has put things back on the course they should have been since the beginning.'

Kara surrendered to his relentless certainty that there was logic hidden within his words, rubbing her temple as a preventative measure for the headache she was surely about to get.

'Okay,' said Kara, 'so, our actions here can directly affect our…original timeline. Before the restarts kicked in…'

'That's right!' said Hal.

Kara knew Hal well enough to be able to tell that he was gearing up for a mic-drop moment.

Hal finally took a breath, then said 'and if our inaction can change the past, it stands to reason that our actions here can undoubtedly affect the future!' he mimed the action of dropping a microphone, precisely as Kara had predicted.

'Okay, settle down Obama,' she retorted. 'So, assuming we can change something larger than the destiny of a trip-switch, how the hell are we going to manipulate–' she paused, running the numbers in her head, and continuing once she'd cracked it, '–all *twelve* of our friends? Fourteen if you include us. That's a *lot* of meddling.'

'You're thinking too big Kar', all we need to manipulate is *this* guy,' he said, pointing at his chest with his thumbs, 'and *that* girl,' he added, gesturing towards her by shooting imaginary bullets of knowledge from his fingers.

'Uh-huh,' she said, with a smile. 'Okay cowboy, so what's the plan?'

Hal shook his hands, then holstered his imaginary six-shooters.

'It's simple. We just need to find a way to stop ourselves from leaving the lodge tomorrow evening.'

And with that, they began to sift through their combined memories to find their window of opportunity, trying to pinpoint the exact sequence of events they could set in motion that would change their past, in the hope that they could somehow save their future.

CHAPTER TWENTY-FIVE

The St Nick of Time

9th Restart – Friday Afternoon, 5:32pm

Throughout the anthology of restarts that followed, the glamour of being elite time-travellers with the power to alter the course of reality itself had worn thin pretty quickly for them both. In fact, it mostly amounted to Hal tripping the hot tub whenever his past-self was in close-enough proximity to the sauna room, which housed the breaker switches. Whilst it initially seemed like these acts of time-manipulation would send the course of their self-contained history spiralling into chaos, it seemed that time itself was not having any of their shit, deploying counter-measures to ensure their antics equated to little more than the equivalent of turning your watch back by an hour in accordance with daylight savings time, in that whilst you were technically travelling backwards and forwards in time by an hour, it made little difference to anyone but the wearer of the watch.

Events generally unfolded in the following way; Hal would trip the switch, some of their friends would exit the tub, engaging in conversations that were either identical to what they would speak about later in the day, or completely tangential. These erratic, spin-off discussions tended to end quickly, and ultimately led their friends back onto the predetermined course they were destined to follow for the day. Though their experiments seemed frustratingly fruitless in the grander scheme of things, they did discover one indisputable truth to their newly-found capabilities.

Hal approached Will's car, casually stepping onto the rim of the protruding number plate, onto the bonnet, and fell with a noiseless thud onto the roof of the car. He grabbed his second cigarette of the day, lighting it as Kara clambered up onto Jasmine's car.

'Right,' said Hal, 'it seems altering the course of history sends everyone off on different tangents, but it only lasts a little while before they steer themselves back on track.'

His fellow time-traveller had experienced the same, irritating phenomenon.

'Same as upstairs,' said Kara, recounting how she had knocked over some glasses, delaying Rachel and Fearne for a little while whilst they cleared it up, eventually resulting with them both ending up where they would have been anyway.

They thought on that for a little while, until Kara interrupted their contemplative silence with another of her many observations.

'You know, our rooms are basically at either end of the pool table? Whilst our past-selves are sleeping, that whole area is wide-open to manipulation. We'd be close enough to them over a prolonged amount of time. Maybe we could…I don't know…*use* that time to move things above them, around them.

'Holy crap, that's genius!' said Hal. 'I think that's

the problem though isn't it,' he mused. 'For this to work, we need to change the natural order of things *just* before we leave Saturday night. Anything we do before that will just get smoothed over by time.'

They were in agreement. Nothing they did seemed to matter. All that mattered was what they did just before their past-selves were due to leave. Changing the events that led to that moment was the only sure-fire way of freeing themselves from an eternity of restarts.

*

Having resisted the temptation to mess with their past too much throughout the next few hours, they spent most of their tenth Saturday waiting impatiently for the evening to arrive, and observing the natural order of things as they attempted to isolate what they could exploit and manipulate to achieve the desired result.

In the end, they decided to keep things simple. Kara would cause a scene upstairs to distract her past-self enough so that she wouldn't see Jerry, Hal would run through Robert's bedroom, through the shared shower room adjoining his room, and would hold the bedroom door closed from the inside, preventing his past-self from exiting the room.

Kara started proceedings, by dutifully knocking some plates off the island in the kitchen, sending her friends into a panic upstairs whilst, more importantly, keeping her past-self busy in the process. Meanwhile, Hal watched eagerly, as his past-self entered his bedroom and Peter knocked on his door asking for a phone charger he could borrow.

"Come on, come on," thought Hal, needing Peter to open the door to Robert's bedroom so that he could nip through and prevent past-Hal from leaving his own room. Hal didn't want to spook Peter by opening the door to Robert's room in front of him, as there was no telling how that would change things.

Peter sauntered along at an excruciatingly snail-like pace, as he made his way to Robert's room, with Hal in hot-pursuit, struggling to resist the urge to physically push Peter along.

As Peter opened the door, Hal noticed a wisp of blue light, which sprung from his own hand, causing him to shiver. Whilst residing within a restart, a temperature change within his body shouldn't have been possible, but Hal was far too preoccupied to notice that he'd felt anything at all.

Slipping into the room in Peter's wake, Hal noticed the bedroom door close behind them, reasoning that the incline of the building must have created the illusion that the door was closing of its own volition. Hal slowly opened the bathroom door, which connected to the bedroom his past-self was currently in, but stopped as he saw Peter, who was pressed against the bedroom wall.

A faint blue sizzle of energy was radiating from Peter's eye sockets, contrasting eerily against his black skin thanks to the dimly lit room, resulting in only his eyes and cheeks being illuminated. A memory flashed through Hal's mind, before his life had been consumed by all the madness of repeatedly travelling back through time. He remembered how, just before he had called Jess that Saturday evening, he had looked through Robert's bedroom window, as Robert had lazed about in the hot tub. He recalled seeing Peter's face illuminated by a faint blue glow. At the time, he had assumed it had been emanating from a phone screen, but clearly there were far more sinister forces at work here.

Something was seemingly holding Peter in place, preventing him from moving, and that *something* appeared to be directly connected to the blue energy that kept Hal and Kara apart.

Suddenly, Peter whispered, causing Hal's heart to skip a beat.

'Ha-Hal?!' said Peter and, for a brief second, he thought Peter could see him. 'Um-su..sorry.'

Whatever was going on, Hal didn't have time to help Peter. He had spent too long here already, his past-self now visible outside the bedroom window and walking past the hot-tub.

'Shit. Peter, I'll come back for you,' said Hal, as he ran through the bathroom and out of his now-open bedroom door. Meanwhile, Kara's past-self was making her way down the staircase, as *his* Kara shouted out to him.

'Hal, I'm sorry,' said Kara. 'Smashing the plates didn't work!'

He nodded, making up a plan B on the fly.

Running past the pool table, around the side of the lodge, and rushing past the hot tub with impressive speed, he accidentally knocked Robert's bottle of beer over with his arm.

Robert lifted the rim of his red Santa hat that had been covering his eyes, and grumbled at the tell-tale sound of glass connecting with wooden decking, as his beer clinked against it.

'Ah man, beer fell off,' said Robert, groggily.

Rising out of the water, Robert reached over the side of the tub, wobbling significantly, planning to retrieve another beer from the cool box. It was then that Robert lost his footing, the perpetual current of the water causing him to land hard on his knees, with a sickening crunch. He grabbed clumsily at the edge of the tub, trying to grip the side to pull himself back up, but his wet hands, pruned from the water, refused to latch on and slipped from the edge of the tub to the control panel. Losing his balance entirely, Robert slipped into the water, now fully submerged, pulling the control panel of the tub from its socket and into the tub with him.

Hal raced to the cupboard, which he had opened earlier to save time. Meanwhile, his past-self had finished up his failed attempt to phone Jess and was already walking back through the hall in response to past-Kara, who was summoning him. Robert's predicament remained invisible to him due to the obstruction of the hot-tub cover blocking past-Hal's view.

"This can still work!" Hal said to himself, unaware of what his actions had set in motion, as he flipped the switch, causing the light bulbs to pop in the sauna room, plunging him into complete darkness.

He rushed outside for the next phase of his improvised plan, but was stopped in his tracks at the sight before him. Robert, now face-down in the hot tub, was twitching violently, as the electrical current coursed through his body. All of the exterior lights on the same breaker were out, and with the rest of his friends currently inside Fir Lodge, there was no one there to help. Hal heard his past-self and past-Kara walking away up the driveway, duty-bound by fate to take Jerry home, blissfully unaware that their act of kindness was about to curse them by sending them to a purgatorial prison that would displace them entirely from their current perception of time.

Kara sprinted up to Hal from the side of the lodge, appearing from the driveway entrance.

'What happened? All the lights are out,' said Kara.

Hal cleared his throat. 'I, erm…I think I messed up.'

Robert stepped up behind Hal, completely dry and wearing nothing but swim-shorts and a Santa hat.

'Doesn't sound like you mate,' said Robert, raising his arm to slap Hal on the back. 'What have you done now—*owwww*?'

Robert's hand recoiled, as the intense blue energy repelled them apart.

It was at that precise moment that they had been exposed to an intoxicating possibility; that Robert could *see* them, which in turn meant that Hal and Kara had made it back home.

But their elation was short-lived, once they realised that there were now two Roberts, one of which was bobbing up and down in the hot tub in front of them, very much dead. What truly shook the Restarters to their core, however, was the inescapable revelation that this could mean only one thing…

That *they* were dead too.

CHAPTER TWENTY-SIX

Hot Tub Crime Machine

9th Restart – Saturday Afternoon, 8:47pm

Kara acted quickly, standing in front of Robert so he couldn't see past her and into the tub, where his dead body was, rather awkwardly, bobbing up and down. They only had twenty or so minutes before the restart. Eleven minutes for their past-selves to reach Kevin's lodge, and the same amount of time for the walk back. That wasn't nearly enough time to explain the predicament Robert was about to find himself smack, bang in the middle of.

Hal was currently frozen in time, as if the act of imitating a mannequin would absolve him of the consequences of what had just happened.

'HAL! I need you with me,' said Kara. 'We need to get jolly ol' Saint Nick as far away from here as possible.'

Hal snapped out of his reverie, realising she was right. They didn't have time to answer all the questions he was about to bombard them with. Shaking his head to clear his mind, he attempted to compose himself.

'Rob, mate,' said Hal, as casually as he could muster, 'we need you to come with us okay?'

Robert shrugged, and peered over Hal's shoulder.

'Sure, whatever, let me just grab my beer,' said Robert, attempting to walk past Hal.

As he unknowingly moved closer to his own crime scene, Kara stepped to her right and blocked him from proceeding.

'Robert,' she said softly, 'please come and help us for a minute, would you?'

She maintained eye contact, and slowly moved further to his right, as if she was trying to herd a wild animal by ensuring he wouldn't bolt off in the wrong direction, gesturing towards the expansive rear garden. 'We need to go down here, right now. To get more bulbs for the lights that have just blown,' she added, as an additional convincer.

'There are bulbs at the end of the garden?' questioned Robert, not convinced at all.

'Yup. In the shed, at the bottom,' lied Kara, flawlessly.

'Okay,' said Robert, 'but I don't know why we need to worry about the lights, I can see everything perfectly clearly? It's really bright out here…'

They led him down the garden, spacing themselves out a few paces behind him.

'I was wrong,' Hal whispered to Kara. 'I mean, after seeing what we saw with Robert…we *have* to be dead right?! It's the only logical–' but she cut him off, whispering quickly.

'Sshh. Not *now* Hal. I'm not ready to go there just…not now okay?'

He nodded vigorously, taking the hint.

'You know,' said Hal, continuing to whisper, 'this might be a good opportunity for us.'

'Explain to me how *murdering* Robert is an *opportunity*?!' she hissed, with an unexpected, lightning-quick velocity.

'All I'm saying is, having a fresh perspective on this thing might be just what we need,' explained Hal. 'Follow my lead.'

Once they were far enough away from the others, Kara stopped walking and they stood there in silence. Robert coughed awkwardly.

'Guys…you're acting weird. And you're strange people anyway, so for *me* to notice, something's obviously wron–'

'Robert,' said Hal, interrupting him, trying to break this down for Robert in a way he knew he would understand. 'You remember that episode of Stairgate, where they go through the gate and then relive the same day over and over?'

The question, as well as Hal using his full name, caught Robert off guard, distracting him from Kara's now-obvious lie, given that there was no indication of a shed at the end of the garden. Being a not-so-secret sci-fi geek himself, he was happy to respond.

'Why are you saying it weird, it's *Starga–*' but Hal cut him off a second time.

'I'm not saying it weird, you're *hearing* it weird.

Anyway, Kara and I saw this movie recently. Basically, two friends come back from a long walk, right? Only when they get back, their friends can't see them. They're invisible. And they can't interact with anything.'

'So, they're dead?' said Robert, letting out a fake yawn. 'That's boring. Way too predictable.'

Hal bristled a little. When Robert was in one of these moods, it was virtually impossible to steer him towards a more receptive mind-set.

'No! They're not dead you dick. I mean, they *might* be dead…but that's not…it doesn't matter, what I was *going* to say is–'

'Blatantly dead. Next question,' said Robert.

'*Fine,*' replied Hal icily. 'Fine, they're dead. Then every day, at a certain time, they travel back in time to the beginning, and have to relive the same day over and over again–'

'What's the film called?' interjected Robert, once again.

'Restarters,' said Kara.

'That's a terrible name for a movie,' said Robert, constructively. He stretched, breathing in the night air, noting to himself how odd it was that he didn't feel even the least bit cold, given his current attire.

Hal pinched the bridge of his nose, scrunching up his eyes, which Kara took as a sign to take over, seeing where Hal was going with his approach.

'So,' said Kara, 'they relive the same day over and over. If they're dead, they don't know it. They try to retrace their steps, but nothing seems to indicate they died. They just return home and the restarts…well, *start*. The film ends on that cliff-hanger. We just wondered what you thought? What could they do to find answers to what was causing them to relive the same day over and over?'

Robert thought for a moment, before replying to Kara's question.

'Did they stop off anywhere on their walk?' he asked. 'That's a terrible place to end a movie by the way. What was it called again? I want to avoid having to watch it.'

'It doesn't *matter* what it's *called*,' said Hal, all but completely losing patience.

'It matters to *me*,' said Robert, sniffing to clear his nose. 'I've got a second kid on the way Hal, I can't be wasting Robert-Time on a movie that–'

'They did stop off briefly at a…a cabin, I guess,' interjected Kara, aware that time was a factor.

Robert rolled his eyes. 'Oh, so two kids stop off at a creepy log cabin, get back home and realise they're stuck in a time loop?! Guys, how have you not figured this out.'

'Figured *what* out?!' replied Kara and Hal, in unison.

'Wow. Stupidity in surround-sound. Whatever caused it obviously happened in the creepy-arse cabin,' said Robert, in a tone that implied he was attempting to teach his Grandad how to send emails via a smartphone.

'Settle down Santa, they didn't go into the lodge,' said Hal. 'I mean, just inside the doorway to take a…*cat* back inside,' he added, wincing at the pointlessness of amending such an irrelevant detail when the truth would have done just fine.

'Well, clearly they did, and they just don't remember or something,' said Robert, confident is his problem-solving abilities. 'On their next rewind, they should just head straight to the house and watch things unfold from inside. Front row seats. Job done. I'm going to get my beer.'

Robert began to make his way back to the lodge, when a scream broke through the night, making its way to the three of them.

'That sounded like Daisy?!' said Robert, picking up the pace and then, inexplicably, collapsing onto the ground in a heap, his arms tingling. He realised Hal and Kara were on top of him, ripples of faint blue energy erupting from their hands and into his arms.

'Guys, what the hell?!' said Robert, squirming under their combined weight.

'We're sorry Robert, really we are,' said Kara, tears running down her face. 'You really don't remember what happened?'

'What are you *talking* about?!' shouted Robert, effortlessly pushing them off him, as an arc of electricity temporarily pulsated around his hands.

Robert was a lot stronger than them, an attribute that clearly had transferred over and carried notable weight, despite him now being out-of-phase with time.

'ROB!' shouted Hal, brushing off the imaginary grass from his boiler suit once again, an old habit that, much like the three of them, clearly refused to die. 'Robert,' he said, softer this time, 'I know I never really say it, you make it so hard. But you know we're mates, right?'

'*Acquaintances*,' said Robert, correcting him.

Hal looked at the surly Santa, standing there in swim shorts and a hat and looking utterly ridiculous. Hal thought for a moment, trying to find the words that would not only show Robert he cared about him, but that would also appease Robert's cantankerous nature and inability to open up.

'You're such a bell-end Robert,' said Hal finally, with a smile.

'Ha!' said Robert, 'True. What's with this fog anyway?'

Kara threw her arms around Robert and kissed him on the cheek.

'Ouch! You just gave me major static Kara, get orf me!' said Robert, just about managing to hide his smile, his love for his friends betraying his pointless show of bravado.

'Hey, want to see a magic trick?' asked Hal.

Robert grimaced, partly because he hated Hal's magic tricks, but also because he needed to check on his wife.

'Can you just show Kara,' groaned Robert, 'and I'll pretend to watch after I've checked on Daisy?'

'Nah man, trust me,' said Hal convincingly. 'Daisy's fine, and you'll really like this one.'

Hal raised his hand in an attempt to draw Robert's attention from the fact that the fog had begun to erase everything around them now, with only the three of them remaining fully-rendered in the lifeless space. As the sound of rushing air invaded their ear-drums, Hal clicked his fingers. Not that any of them could hear the click.

'Shazam!' shouted Hal, in a display of perfect choreography, as all three of them were erased from time, sent hurtling thirty-three hours into the past. A brand-new timeline being forged from nothingness, reserved for just the three of them.

CHAPTER TWENTY-SEVEN
The Flutterby Effect

10th Restart – Friday Afternoon, 12:02pm

Hal stared out across the rear garden of Fir Lodge, struggling to find just the right combination of words that could fill the awkward silence, one that he had brought on himself as a direct result of his actions.

'Well, one thing's for sure, we need to be way more careful,' said Hal, as he took a panicked drag on his second of three cigarettes, having never been so glad to be in a fresh restart as he was right now. Despite it not providing him with any nicotine, the routine was no less of a comfort. Kara shot him a look that wasn't a million miles away from smugness.

'Who's *we*? You got a mouse in your pocket?'

'Funny. You know what I mean,' said Hal, who was starting to get the feeling he wouldn't be living this one down in a while.

'All I'm saying is, it wasn't *my* time-travelling finger on the fuse board,' said Kara, helpfully ensuring the blame was assigned correctly.

'Okay, we can both agree this was *my* fault. Can we please go over what we've learnt now?' pleaded Hal, still shaking from the traumatic experience.

Hal and Kara were sitting on their picnic bench, their past selves having just arrived. The ever-so-faint static fog that they'd noticed several restarts back was more noticeable now. It seemed to Hal that every time they restarted, the fog got incrementally thicker. Hal blew smoke into it, to disguise the problem they would no doubt have to confront in the upcoming days ahead, given that they had far more urgent matters to discuss.

The discovery of the hot tub jets had proven that they could change the course of past events, but accidentally killing Robert changed everything. It meant they could truly impact the past in ways they had never imagined. Hal echoed his thoughts to Kara.

'What happened to Robert changes everything,' he said.

Kara leaned back on the bench, looking into the contradiction that was a perfectly clear sky tainted by the thin veil of static fog. They really needed to talk about that soon.

'It didn't change *everything* though did it?' pointed out Kara. 'I mean, we still ended up restarting, just like we always do.'

'Thank *god*,' exclaimed Hal. 'Can you imagine if we had broken that chain of events? If past-us had found Rob's body and not left Fir Lodge? We may not have been here right now, but Rob's death would have been irreversible!' he added with a shudder.

'We don't know that...maybe he would have inherited the restarts?' said Kara.

'Maybe. But he would have been on his own, with no guidance, no support network...he could have been stuck here forever.'

'Like we are,' murmured Kara, vehemently.

Hal activated his selective hearing, as if Jess were asking him to take the rubbish out.

'He could have gone insane Kara. Think about that…'

And she did for a moment. 'Nah, he's way too stubborn to lie down and take a punch in the face from space-time.' But, secretly, she agreed. 'The big question is, why didn't he come back with us?'

Hal had been thinking about that, and offered up his thoughts on the matter.

'My guess? His death didn't stick because we restarted. Our past-selves still went to Kevin's and…whatever happened there…happened again.'

Kara raised an eyebrow.

'So…you think that, because the timeline carried on as normal, everything went back to how it was before?' she said.

Hal nodded.

'So as long as you don't kill him again today, like by dropping an anvil on his head or whatever, he'll be perfectly fine?' asked Kara.

'Funny. But yeah, basically, I think that's how it works,' said Hal. 'But it's highlighted a serious problem; we *really* need to start considering the butterfly effect…'

'The Kutcher movie? That was great!'

'Yes Kara. I want us to form a film club and discuss the filmography of the unsung heroes of perfectly okay movies.'

She filled her cheeks with air and pulled a silly face, indicating she was ready for whatever it was he was getting at, as Hal sat up and began to explain the concept.

'The idea is that small causes can have larger effects–'

'I *know* that Hal, I'm not an idiot,' said Kara, cutting him off. 'A flutterby flaps its wings in, Tibet or wherever, which then causes a tornado in Peru or something.'

'Precise– wait, did you just say *flutterby*?'

'Clearly a better name for an insect that literally flutters around,' said Kara, straightening up in her seat. 'I mean, it was such an easy win, why the hell did they settle on *butterfly*?'

Hal stared at her incredulously.

'I…well, shit. Okay, I'll give you that one. I can't

argue with that.'

Kara was beaming; she loved it when someone came around to her way of thinking over things she didn't really care about.

Hal flicked his cigarette over his shoulder with reckless abandon and continued.

'My point is, that in our desperation to change events, we could inadvertently make things a billion times worse. Our lives are not worth anything if it means risking the safety of our friends.'

'Obviously I agree with you,' said Kara, as a thought occurred to her. 'What I *don't* get, is that you've tripped that hot tub countless times, causing everyone to get out, move around, change the order of small encounters and interactions. Why did *that* one in particular cause such a huge discrepancy in the lead up to a restart?'

Hal cast his mind back to the frantic events of the previous evening.

'I think…I think I knocked his beer off the side as I ran past?' said Hal, trying to piece it together. 'He must have leant over the edge to check it out, slipped maybe? The control panel was in the tub with him, wasn't it? It all happened so fast.'

They sat there in silence, once again, as Hal's past-self entered into their line of sight through the back door, striking up a conversation with Jon, as the repetitive rhythm of the jets continued, entirely undisturbed.

Kara thought she should lighten the mood, feeling a little bad about chastising Hal as much as she had, and decided to highlight how the means of what had just happened may well have actually resulted in justifying the end result.

'Santa made a good point though,' she said. 'If we wait inside Kevin's place, we can sit right by the door, see if there's something we missed.'

Something deep inside of Hal wanted to change the subject, to talk about *anything* but this. But Kara continued, preventing him from formulating a solid argument against it.

'I mean, I know we've followed ourselves back when we dropped Jerry off, but we've always kept our distance. Become distracted. The restart kicks in as it always does. If we're already inside...'

Hal thought about that, an icy chill running down

his spine.

'What could possibly be in there Kara? We took Jerry back, we walked back to our lodge, that's when all this mess started!' He hadn't noticed that he was standing now, his past-self getting ever-closer to claiming their current spot, as Kara jumped out of past-Hal's way just in time.

'Hal, calm down, you're kind of shouting a bit...'

'Because you're not *listening* to me Kara, you're just coming up with distractions when we need to be focusing on more important things, not this STUPID expedition into the DAMN–' Hal saw her slightly frightened face, and he stopped talking immediately, covering his mouth with his hand.

'Kara, I'm so sorry! I have no idea what got into me,' said Hal, noticing that she had taken several steps back from him during his tirade and was looking at him with a face that was filled with both concern and unease, as if she didn't recognise him.

She couldn't remember ever seeing him this angry before.

'Hal…it's cool, everything's cool…I think it's pretty obvious at this point what we're going to see there...'

Suddenly, whatever had been keeping him from concentrating, whatever untold force was clouding his mind, forcing him to deter them from pursuing this line of thought, slowly dispersed, like a fog being sucked away through a jet engine. He swallowed, his mouth dry, not entirely convinced that he could get the words out without something preventing him from doing so.

'Kara...' his voice barely a broken whisper, as true terror enveloped him and caused his eyes to water, as the realisation of the truth set in. He cleared his throat, determined to release the words from their captivity.

'Kara...I think something *terrible* happened there.'

And then Kara felt it too. The fragmented images that kept popping into her head, the ones she'd never told Hal about. Her ice-pick migraines that lasted for only a second. All of the pieces began to swirl in her brain, like a kaleidoscope coming into focus, as the images gained solidity in her mind. Her redacted memories daring her to ask more questions. In that moment, they were so lost in their own personal terror that they hadn't noticed the static fog thickening around them, or that their surroundings had evaporated almost entirely. With Fir Lodge itself nowhere to be seen, their happy place slowly began to abandon them.

*

As the fog began to dissipate, they realised they had been transported to somewhere new. Had their vision not been so exceptional, the darkness may have blinded them. But with their heightened senses, they could see everything with perfect clarity; the wooden panelling of the walls surrounding them, the faint light of the porch outside all but burning their retinas. Hal noticed that the kitchen counter to their left was immaculately clean, and that the usual suspects adorned the countertop; an old-fashioned cream-coloured kettle, with matching containers indicating their contents; an archaic radio was playing a familiar tune. The tinny reverberations of the music did little to lift the suffocating mood and oppressive claustrophobia of their new environment.

It was then that they saw him. Standing behind a wooden support beam to the left of the kitchen, in front of a blue door that led further into what they now realised was a lodge. And then they saw themselves. They saw Hal calling from the doorway, stepping one-too-many steps into the living area next to the kitchen, bringing Jerry inside the house.

It was then that they saw how they died.

CHAPTER TWENTY-EIGHT
The Man Comes Around

Saturday Evening, 9:01pm

Everyone thinks they'll be ready. That in the event that something atrocious is about to befall you, you'll react efficiently and effectively. That perhaps you won't truly know what you're capable of when the time comes until you're tested. But that wasn't the case for Hal.

The blade, and the man wielding it, appeared without warning, without conscience, and with a primary agenda that no rational-thinking human could ever predict, let alone plan for. The cold, tempered steel perforated his upper torso with such speed and force that he didn't even have time to consider if it had cut through a major artery.

Hal looked downwards, as his own blood pulsed from his body, a wet blackness glistening in the dark, as the force of nature responsible twisted the blade counter-clockwise, then clockwise, the jagged teeth of the blade causing irreparable damage to his soon to be vacant body. Though it was the internal bleeding, that coursed up through his oesophagus and out through his mouth, simulating the sensation of drowning, that really hit home that this was truly the end.

He flailed his arms, grabbing at the assailant's hands that were now working together to drive the hilt of the blade forward, even further into his weakening frame. Hal fell to the ground, staring with wide, desperate eyes as the looming shadow strutted with malicious intent towards Kara, who had proceeded further across the threshold of the doorway and, unknowingly, closer to a hell reserved just for the both of them.

"Could she not see what had happened?!" thought Hal, one of many thoughts that were swirling amidst his mind, as he was consumed by the pitch-blackness permeating throughout the cabin.

Hal tried to shout out to her, though the result was a dull and breathless gurgle that was nullified by Cash's "The Man Comes Around", which was spilling out from a radio he couldn't see, coupled with the defiant barks of a nearby dog.

"Shelby? Run Shelby!" thought Hal, as his oxygen-deprived mind became muddled amidst the unfolding insanity, fearful his attacker might focus his attention on the barking dog instead of him, desperate for the innocent pup to escape.

The beast was on her in an instant, his wraith-like strides morphing into an arm-shaped shadow that, from Hal's perspective, looked as big as a tree. In one swift movement he grabbed her head and smashed it against the kitchen cabinets.

Dazed, and understandably confused, due to the monumental concussion her nervous system was trying to make sense of, the ringing in her ears drowned out the unearthly grunt made by her assailant. But as the stars and ever-increasing black spots in her peripheral vision conjoined, acting as the first real early-warning system that something was terribly wrong, her personal harbinger of impending death arrived far too late.

The moonlight glinted off what must have been a second blade, which the demon plunged into her neck with such ferocity that Hal was certain she must have died instantly from the blow. She lay there, silent and still.

The monster, breathing heavily, let out what seemed to be an almighty roar, and stood there, looming over Kara, panting emphatically. Hal closed his eyes, praying that he could summon the strength to stand so that he could avenge his friend. He had always considered himself to be a good man, flawed of course, immensely flawed, but he would fight this evil standing before him. He would destroy him for what he had done. He would stand tall and go toe to toe with this ungodly goliath and he would do…precisely nothing.

As the giant's hands clenched around Hal's throat, draining the last breath of air from his body, the only thing he could do was bleed-out the remaining reserves of his blood, pint by pint, knowing that he had failed his friend.

Images of Jess swirled in his mind. Their first touch, the electricity he had felt. The first time she smiled at him. Her laugh, her eyes…eyes he would often get lost in.

"I'm sor–" but his half-finished thought, much like his time on this earth, was cut short.

And mercifully, finally, it was over.

Kara and Hal were dead.

*

Hal and Kara stood there, staring at their past-selves. Their eyes wide, unable to find the words, given that there was nothing that could be said after witnessing their gruesome deaths, as an all-too-familiar fog began filling their tomb, seemingly erasing their dead bodies from time itself. They closed their eyes, as the maddening ethereal force engulfed them, claiming them once again as it always did, whisking them away to what they now realised was their eternal purgatory.

CHAPTER TWENTY-NINE

The Chain

11th Restart – Friday Afternoon, 12:01pm

The restart happened around Kara as it always did. But, for the first time since this nightmare began, she felt disconnected from it. Like a spectator, rather than an active participant. She didn't wait for the restart to set in. She walked as if she were on auto-pilot, directly into the oncoming red car, yet again playing a one-sided game of chicken, given her current invisibility, with no regard for consequence. She was vaguely aware of Hal calling her name, but the sound barely registered in her mind.

She felt the familiar surge of energy shoot through her arm as someone, presumably Hal, grabbed her by the wrist, which she deep-down acknowledged as being an act of misguided kindness, as he attempted to pull her out of the path of the rapidly approaching vehicle. But even the pulsating energy couldn't eradicate the numbness in her heart.

Her *unbeating* heart.

She was *dead.*

Kara felt an intense pang of anger, and the shimmering blue light connecting her and Hal throbbed wildly, forming a spherical shape that expanded to encompass both of their entire arms, as she continued to drag him along on her new mission.

Will's side mirror collided with her hip, and exploded into pieces. She inattentively took on-board that "The Chain" was bellowing from Will's car radio. Hal must have let go of her arm, because the rapidly-intensifying sensation of being electrocuted ceased immediately.

She continued onwards, towards her goal.

"No more. This ends today," she thought to herself.

Or maybe she screamed it. She honestly didn't know anymore. Forwards. All that mattered was moving forwards.

*

The restart displaced Hal, as it always did, back to the start. He fell to his knees, though it wasn't due to being drained exponentially from the time-jump, He was getting used to that now. It was starting to feel like being a passenger in a car, and suddenly dropping down a steep incline without warning.

'Shit,' he said out loud. 'Son of a damn bitch.'

He remembered it all now. Why had those memories been kept from him? This changed everything. Once again, they'd been going about this all wrong. He lashed out at the ground beneath him, driving a fist into the stones. How many times had he said that? That each new discovery "had changed everything?" That he had been wrong. Again. They weren't joyriding time travellers. Nor were they superheroes, blasting their way through time with mutant powers that had only just manifested. He wasn't Marty. They weren't any damn thing. This wasn't even air he was breathing.

He forced himself to snap out of his self-inflicted cycle of negativity, realising that something wasn't quite right with Kara. She was walking directly into the path of Will's car, which was fast approaching.

'Kara?' he said softly. 'Kara?!' he projected louder this time. 'Kara, move out of the way, it'll hit you.'

Entirely unsure of the ramifications of what would happen if they collided with a few tons of fibreglass and metal that was moving at twenty miles per hour, he jogged to close the distance between them.

'KARA!' he shouted.

Could she not hear him? He reached out instinctively to pull her out of the way of the car, electricity immediately erupting from the connection, but he didn't let go. He gritted his teeth, pushing through the sensation that could only be described as two insanely over-powered magnets trying to repel each other. He yanked at her arm, but she was like solid marble, her arm barely moving, despite his desperate efforts. And then the car hit her. The side-mirror splintered into countless shards, as if hitting a brick wall. He released his grip, accepting that he was making this worse.

Will did an emergency-stop, clicked on the hand-brake, and jumped out of the driver's seat, as Hal noted that Fleetwood was blasting out from the speakers of the car.

Will was clearly alarmed, searching for the object he had apparently collided with, as Rachel and Jon came running out of the lodge, reacting to the sickening sound of a car being struck. On closer inspection, Hal noticed that Kara had somehow carved away the paint on the driver's-side door.

He set off after her, not knowing what he would say when he reached her.

*

Kara was at the beginning of the driveway now. She closed her eyes, not slowing her pace, as Jasmine's car shot past her. She couldn't bear to see her own face, laughing, joking and knocking back a beer. Jealousy took over her soul for a moment, but was quickly replaced by despair. But she kept walking.

She screamed, a bone-chilling scream that was a mixture of defiance and hate, aiming her weaponised anger at the road ahead. She screamed until there was no more air in her lungs. As the tears streamed down her face, she realised that she could scream forever…after all, there was no air in her lungs to begin with. She closed her mouth, savagely swiping at the tears on her cheeks. That wouldn't do. She had work to do, and the tears were little more than a hindrance, blurring her vision.

The lake appeared on her right-hand side. That wasn't possible, was it? She was much further away from Fir Lodge than she should have been, based on her pace. She put it down to her determination, and being distracted, soldiering on regardless. Her boyfriend Greg was waiting for her, and she'd kept him waiting long enough.

*

Just as Hal caught up to Kara at the top of the drive, she flitted out of sight, then reappeared ten metres or so ahead of him, like an old videotape on fast-forward, her bright orange and red outfit shimmering, as if she were out of phase with even him.

"Damn she's fast,' he thought, as a piercing scream shattered the peaceful woodland. It was like nothing he had ever heard. Almost like a banshee from that videogame he'd spent far too many hours on, about a monster-hunter in search of his silver-haired daughter, but *far* more unnerving. If there had been blood in his body, he was certain it would have either frozen from the sound, or erupted from his ears, which he was incidentally covering, despite it making no difference to the decibel level.

He shouted her name, not that any sound could have countered the sheer power emanating from his friend's clearly agonised soul. He tried to keep up with her, but she flitted again, seemingly gliding in seconds along terrain that was taking him twice as long to traverse by running. He was losing her. He could feel it.

*

Infuriated, Kara suddenly realised she didn't know the way to the exit of this damn maze. She stopped at a road sign, but it was unhelpfully showing the way to both the river, and the fishing lake. She growled at the sign that was of precisely *zero* use to her, punching the thick wooden tree that supported the directional signs.

Everything they had learnt dictated that the tree

wouldn't budge, no matter how much force she exerted. Not least because of how far away she was from her past-self, but also because the tree was technically alive, and could not be interacted with in their current out-of-phase state. The tree must have missed the memo, however, as the trunk splintered under the force of her punch. She punched it again, more debris erupting from the spot where her fist had collided with the enormous fir tree.

Hal sprinted around the corner, not out of breath, such things were no longer a concern for him after all, but nonetheless desperate not to lose sight of Kara. And then, with relief, he saw her, standing at the crossroad that led to…somewhere. The timber support of the sign had been broken cleanly in half, along with a significant portion of the tree it was affixed to.

"Did Kara do that?!" he thought, as he began to close the distance between them, but just as he was in arms-reach, she phased again, her outline juddering as if her entire body was undergoing some bizarre form of signal-interference. She was there, and in a flash, she was gone. Hal stood there, alone on the open-road, with no idea as to which path to follow to find his friend, or if, indeed, he should even try.

CHAPTER THIRTY

The End of the Road

11th Restart – Friday Afternoon, 12:52pm

Accepting that what Kara needed more than anything right now was space, Hal reluctantly made his way back to Fir Lodge. Armed with this new information about his untimely demise, he was forced to re-evaluate everything he thought he knew.

He walked through the double entrance doors of the lodge, instantly realising he had no desire to be around his friends right now, deciding instead to head out into the back garden. He continued walking, and, for the very first time, became determined to see just how far the garden went.

After a while, he reached the perimeter, rummaging in his pocket for his trusty, makeshift cigarette-box, extracting the first of the three smokes he had to see him through until the next restart.

“Assuming there’s going to be another restart,’ he thought to himself.

Hal shook his head, once again shaking off the negative notions, forcing them to behave themselves. He couldn’t think like that. Sure, he’d just received a form of closure on what had caused this whole mess, and every movie in the history of ever had taught him that a bright light would probably appear at any moment, beckoning him forth into a potentially peaceful, paradisal, afterlife.

He closed his eyes and contemplated that for a second, draining his cigarette with a grossly-extended, single inhalation, then asked himself if he would be able to accept those terms; if he was ready to leave this place, his friends, Jess and Shelby behind.

Opening his eyes, and exhaling a steady stream of smoke, Hal was relieved to discover that a portal to the beyond had not manifested in front of him.

'Balls to that,' he said, as he flicked his dog-end into a hedge, safe in the knowledge that the biodegradable implications were a moot point.

Another thought occurred to him; contrary to the echo of the music, that was hauntingly making its way to his ears from the lodge situated behind him, he realised that for the first time since this nightmare had begun, he was truly alone now.

He lit his second cigarette.

*

Kara had got turned around. The walk (or rather the supercharged time-dilation she was unwittingly utilising to move so quickly) at the beginning of this restart had helped greatly, allowing her to gather her thoughts. She was moving at normal speed now, though her goal had not changed; she needed to be with her family. She needed to be with Greg. Maybe if she could just be around them one last time, she could find some kind of peace. She had to break the chain. She needed to shatter the endless cycle.

Picking a direction at random, she continued towards what she hoped was the exit to this purgatory.

"Could it really be that simple," she thought, hoping that the secret answer to leaving Fir Lodge behind forever was finally within her reach.

*

Seeing no use in giving in to the prospect of the crippling loneliness that was sure to befall him, Hal decided to go over the sequence of events in his head. Namely, Kara "levelling-up" and achieving things they hadn't even known were possible.

How was she able to destroy the car mirror, despite her alive-self being so far away from her? Hal theorised it must have had something to do with the following factors and, deciding to indulge in one of his all-time favourite pastimes, he began to formulate a mental list;

"Flash Fact Number One: We were both in contact with each other when Kara collided with Will's car," thought Hal.

"Variable Number Two: Kara was clearly experiencing an intense level of emotion at the time of said collision."

Hal hadn't had time to consider this before, what with all the commotion during the incident with

Robert, but the way Robert had pushed them off of him a couple of restarts ago had all but proven his new theory; that emotional intensity appeared to amplify the blue energy that coursed through their temporally-displaced veins. He continued onwards with his thought process.

"Fact Of The Day Number Three: We may be stronger than we first suspected at the start of a restart than we are by the end of one."

Hal felt better already. He really loved making lists. He found that formulating them generated a cathartic sense of productivity within him, freeing up the problem-solving section of his brain and allowing him to...

"In contact...The energy!" he thought, excitedly.

His theory implied that their combined density increased whilst they were super-charged. They'd never remained in contact for so long until now, except perhaps at the beginning, during their first restart. But the fact remained that a direct result of extended contact seemed to destabilise them. The way Kara was moving...phasing in and out of their jointly-perceivable spectrum... he remembered her scream, and shuddered.

*

Kara felt as though her heart had skipped a beat, as she finally reached the wide, open grass-verge that led to the literal exit of this godforsaken place.

She exhaled, her breath shaky and uncertain. But she pulled herself together, and made her way across the grass, walking into the road.

Kara could see the slip-road that would eventually lead to the winding country roads that would, in turn, lead her to the motorway. More importantly, it would lead her to Greg. It would be a long trek, but she was ready.

She continued along the centre of the road, beginning to pick up speed, a gentle jog that quickly became a run. Not needing to stop would be a huge game-changer for the journey ahead, and she found herself smiling. This was the right thing to do.

'Good luck Hal…I'm sorry…' she whispered, hoping that he could somehow hear her.

As she zoomed past the "Welcome" sign for the complex of lodges, she heard the tell-tale beginning of a rush of air.

“*No…*” she thought.

‘NO!’ she screamed.

*

Hal was laying on the picnic bench, taking advantage of the extended privacy afforded to him by the changes Kara has caused to the timeline. The subtle change of obliterating Will’s wing mirror had sent the chronological order of events askew, and his friends were all in the communal living room, retelling the story to each other, trying to figure out what had happened.

It was then that he heard it; the sound of rushing air.

He sat up immediately, legs sprawled out on the top of the picnic table.

‘Kara…what did you do?!’ he said, staring at the sky, then lowering his eyes, looking out across the lawn in front of him, as the static-whiteness bled across it, immersing everything it touched, wiping it from reality.

Hal rolled off the table, his eyes darting from side to side, as the sinister mist stalked him, hunting him down, with the sole intention of reclaiming him.

There was nowhere to run. Whatever was happening, he was powerless to stop it. It was way too soon, he had at least thirty odd hours until the next restart was due to occur.

And then, along with everything else, he too was erased from the timeline.

CHAPTER THIRTY-ONE

The Edge of Time

12th Restart – Friday Afternoon, 1:14pm

Kara stood a fair distance away from the "welcome" sign to the lodge complex, standing in the centre of the road, staring out across the wide expanse which led, as she'd just learned, precisely nowhere.

The walk to the edge of Pentney Lakes was an unpleasant one. After Hal had gotten his opinions off his chest and finally allowed her to speak, Kara had explained to Hal what she'd discovered. They didn't exchange a single word for the entirety of the walk, and the tension hanging in the air was thick enough to cut.

Hal was squatting two metres ahead of her in the centre of the road, wary that standing any closer would trigger another restart, and resting his wrists on his legs. He stared pensively, as if he was trying desperately to locate the glimmer in the shield, like the lead-actress in a movie about tributes having a class-system grievance, risking their lives for the entertainment of wealthier districts.

'What are you looking for exactly?' said Kara quietly, unsure if he was ready to engage in conversation.

'I'm not really sure. Something...anything...' said Hal, as he removed his dead phone from the pocket of his boiler suit, and tossed it towards the deceptively normal-looking open space in front of him. He winced, as the thrown object reached the boundary line, waiting for the inevitable restart that was sure to follow.

Instead, the phone dematerialised into a billion fragments of light-blue sparks as it crossed the threshold, like a celebratory explosion of glitter.

'Woah,' said Hal, marvelling at the beauty of their prison door. Suddenly, he noticed a dead weight in his pocket. He reached inside the pocket of his boiler suit a second time, and retrieved a fully-restored facsimile of his phone, which was, of course, still devoid of power.

Hal presented it to Kara, his free hand performing an impromptu jazz-hand-esque shake, which he rounded off with an obligatory "Ta daaaa!"

'What the fu…how'd you do that?!' she said, her eyes wide with wonder.

'Classic misdirection,' said Hal, 'I had two phones all along.'

'Really?!' said Kara, utterly bewildered that he'd managed to keep that secret for the entirety of twelve restarts.

'What?' said Hal. 'Of course not! You've literally been with me this whole time, it was obviously the portal thingy!'

'Oh,' said Kara, feeling embarrassed. 'I knew that.'

'Uh-huh. Well, you were one-hundred-percent right about one thing, it seems our Restarter…*manifestations* are bound by the location…we ain't getting out of Dodge anytime soon.'

Kara slumped to the floor next to him.

'So, we're stuck here? We can't leave?' she asked, utterly disheartened that her escape-plan had been demolished by her ever-present arch-nemesis; time. 'We really are dead aren't we…this confirms it.'

Hal clucked his tongue and thought for a second.

'Well, clearly yes. But also, maybe it's not as clear-cut as that?' said Hal, scrunching his nose at the unfortunate use of the word "cut", then added 'but regardless of the finer details, I think it's pretty obvious what's happening here.'

Kara stared at him with a patience-level of zero-percent. Hal felt the sharpness of her glare, and spat out his theory.

'Well, think about it from a global perspective. Having two people with our…*condition*…roaming around without limitation. Seeing time unfold, possibly interacting and altering the lives of others. It makes sense…as far as any of this makes sense…that our reach would be finite.'

'Why would time care if we left?' said Kara, 'It's

not like we'd be able to alter anyone's life, or interact with anything at *all* in fact, not if we were so far away from our past-selves.'

'You *say* that, but what if we managed to manipulate our past-selves to stay within our proximity…if they left *with* us I mean…' said Hal.

'But if we managed to do *that*, we wouldn't end up being trapped here in the first place!' scoffed Kara.

'That's kind of my point,' said Hal.

She sat down on the dirt-covered concrete, and allowed herself to fall backwards, now lying on her back in the middle of the road.

'Time travel is *total* bullshit,' she said.

Hal nodded in agreement.

'Um, Kar', do you think it's a good idea to be lying in the middle of the road like that?'

She scowled at him, and he dropped it, as she continued onwards with their previous conversation.

'As much as I hate that we're complete prisoners right now, I can see what you mean. You know, that would actually explain a lot about paranormal activity in general. What if ghosts, or Restarters or whatever…what if the reason they *haunt* specific locations is solely because they're bound by similar laws and stuff?'

Hal was chuckling.

'What'd I say?' said Kara, feeling embarrassed. 'You think that's dumb?'

Hal sighed the sigh of someone realising a joke had outstayed its welcome.

'No, not at all! I actually think that's a genius theory! It just sounds like something I would say, that's all.'

'Clearly you're a bad influence on me,' she said with a soft smile, not quite ready to allow herself to laugh just yet, what with everything they were dealing with. 'So, tell me what happened whilst I was–'

'*Deserting* me?' said Hal, finishing her sentence for her with the only two words she would never have chosen herself.

Kara let that one slide, primarily because he wasn't totally unjustified in that assessment, and sat quietly as he filled her in on everything he had experienced whilst they were apart.

*

Kara listened intently, as she processed the three

notable facts that Hal had come up with whilst she had been "busy" on the previous restart, a busyness that Hal had, rather passive-aggressively, defined as her "going rogue."

As if reading her mind, Hal shot another cannonball her way, as he turned his back on her to face the time-barrier, not wishing to make eye-contact.

'You really left me in the shit back there you know,' he said in a quiet, yet forceful tone.

'I know, I know...look,' said Kara, 'I'd just reached a point where I needed to get home. I needed…I *need* to see my family, to see Greg! It's been so long since I've interacted with another human-being other than, well, you…and, no offence, but it's driving me insane!' she said, trying to explain how seeing their murder had completely broken her, and adding 'I thought that if I could just get away from here–'

'That you'd break the restart loop, or at least spend your restarts with your family. I get it. I do…'

They sat there in silence for a while, allowing the memories of their last two restarts to wash over them.

As the soft wind displaced the leaves of the trees, the afternoon sun cascaded down on them, the shimmer of the heat against the road rising up to create a haze reminiscent of a mirage, not that either of them could feel the heat. Hal noted to himself for the hundredth time that his past self would be burning in this heat, his pale skin forever rebelling in its reluctance to allow for a normal tan, instead resting somewhere between a beetroot-purple and ridiculously-vibrant red. Once again, he took mild solace in the fact that he didn't have to apply suntan lotion these days, though he did wish that he'd picked up his shades before snuffing it. It was peaceful though, and they allowed their minds to drift.

Several minutes later, or perhaps hours, Kara pulled the rip-chord on their counter-productive daydreaming.

'Well, let's do this thing then,' she said, standing up and dusting off the imaginary dirt that hadn't adhered to her out-of-phase legs, and making her way to the presumably-fluctuating breach in reality that would trigger the next restart.

Hal stood up, taking a single step towards the

boundary-line of their permissible existence, then stopped, turning to face Kara.

'You know what, it really is a beautiful day,' said Hal, noticing that even the fog wasn't as noticeable when mixed with the direct sunlight.

Kara agreed with a casual shrug.

'Maybe we just sit this one out today?' said Hal. 'Take a walk to the lake, and you can tell me how you and Greg met? You've never really gone into that much detail before.'

As her eyes welled up, she hugged him with all she had, generating a huge spike of electricity that forced them apart.

'Ouch,' said Hal. 'What was *that* for?'

'I'd *love* that,' said Kara, wiping a lone tear from her cheek.

Not for the first time, Hal wondered how they could generate such a large feedback of electricity when they were so far away from their considerably more-alive past selves. He thought back to the three things he had observed, just before Kara had triggered the last restart.

"Variable Number Two…" he thought to

himself.

The Restarters turned around, leaving the barrier that separated their timeline from that of the outside world behind them.

As they made their way to the nearest lake, Kara began telling Hal everything about the past six months of her life, with added details that she had never told anyone before. Just two friends catching up, with not so much as a whisper about time-dilation, flutterby-effects, or their plans for manipulating their self-contained pocket of space-time.

CHAPTER THIRTY-TWO

Lodge This

13th Restart – Friday Afternoon, 12:17pm

The scales that were balancing both the list of things Hal and Kara did and did not know experienced a notable rebalancing, as Kara uttered three, simple words.

'It wasn't Kevin,' said Kara.

They were sitting on the grass that ran along the edge of the rear garden of Fir Lodge, not wanting to have to move or be disturbed. Hal had seen it too, but was waiting for her to be ready before broaching the subject. They had been on completely the wrong track by assuming their dilemma had been caused by something Kevin had either done, or was doing. They had felt uneasy when in his presence, but now they knew it was more due to their lives being interconnected with him in a way they could never have imagined.

'Yeah. Not Kevin,' said Hal, who was both lost in his own thoughts, and giving Kara the space she needed to steer the conversation in whatever direction helped her come to terms with things the most.

'So now we know. All this…' said Kara, lifting her arms and gesturing out towards the huge garden, to Fir Lodge, and up into the sky. 'It's all fake. It isn't real. Just a snapshot of time we've fabricated as some kind of *coping mechanism*, until we finally decide to…let go.'

Her eyes welled up, and she suppressed the burning in her throat by coughing forcefully. Hal flicked open his cigarette box and offered her one of his newly-printed three smokes. She fumbled with the box and grabbed one, as Hal chucked her his lighter, then took one for himself.

As they stared out across the large garden at the faint mist that was haunting them with increasing vigour from restart to restart, Hal exhaled the artificial smoke and offered a counter-argument.

'I don't think that's true, Kar'. It's real. This place, our friends, all of it,' said Hal, clearly gearing up for another one of his patent-pending mic-drop moments. 'And I'm going to prove it to you,' he added, jumping up and extended his hand, offering to pull her up.

She scoffed, and pulled herself up, not wishing to be electrocuted.

'I've had just about all the shocks I can handle for a while, but thanks. So, where are we going?' asked Kara. But Hal was already off, heading back up the garden, and taking the side-exit to the driveway.

'Urgh. Such a drama queen,' she said, addressing Hal's past-self as he sat on their bench, completely oblivious to her presence. She sighed, and set off after her fellow restarter.

*

After about fifteen minutes of walking, he turned around to face her, and began to make his point.

'This bubble of time we're in, it extends all the way to the boundary line. Acres and acres of land, right?' he said, stopping at a literal crossroads, pointing in the general direction of the time-barrier that was situated over a mile away in the opposite direction to where they were heading.

The dirt road before them split into four directions, large logs acting as dividers between the road and the surrounding forest. 'You ever been down any of these roads?' he asked her, in a playfully challenging tone.

'You know I haven't,' she said, staring at him with a suspicious glare.

'Right? Neither of us have,' said Hal. 'We arrived here two days ago, relatively speaking, and we spent most of our time at the lodge.'

He recounted how they had originally driven in from the other end of the lakes, where Kara had discovered the portal that acted as a restart-point. They were working on the assumption that the barrier surrounded the entirety of Pentney Lakes.

'But we've been here, what…twenty-six days now? If we include every restart,' said Hal, taking much longer than it would have taken Kara to work out the maths. 'And we've never headed off in this direction. There hasn't been a need to come here.'

Kara held up her hands, as if to indicate she was waiting for the big reveal.

'Let's go. Try and keep up,' said Hal, as he set off at a sprint, choosing at random to head off down the road veering left.

'Where are we going?!' shouted Kara, as she set off after him.

*

Eventually, they came to a building they'd never seen before. It was different, in a lot of ways, to Fir Lodge, which was designed in a much more traditional log-cabin style, feeling more rugged and welcoming, due to the natural colouring of the wood. *Homely* even. The sides of *their* lodge had been designed to create the illusion that they were comprised of logs that were piled on top of each other, with the balconies extending out beneath the traditional triangular roofing either side of them, supported by clever structural design rather than any visible supports.

The property currently in front of them, however,

was on the other end of the spectrum. Rectangular in shape, and devoid of flair, it was a minimalist approach to design, coated in a slick, black colouring. With enormous, sleek-looking, sweeping windows that were as wide as the surface area of the entire walls, what it lacked in character, it made up for in its chic demeanour.

'Okay, confession time,' said Hal, who was clearly revelling in the theatrics. 'I think it's time we open up to each other about any structural-engineering or design degrees we've been hiding from each other?'

She had to admit, she was actually enjoying not having to spend the day memorising probability patterns, or the ramifications of cause and effect. Kara replied robotically, speaking loudly to an imaginary audience as if she was an unwilling participant in a poorly implemented cruise-ship stage-show routine.

'I can confirm that I do not have a degree in structural engineering or design, and neither do you.'

'Come with me madam!' said Hal, and they proceeded to the back of the high-tech-looking black lodge.

Two young children were running up and down the garden, their parents chucking lunch together in the incredibly expensive-looking kitchen.

'Recognise these people?' asked Hal, knowing for a fact that she didn't.

She shook her head, and Hal ducked in through the patio doors, making his way into the living room. Hal seriously hoped the current occupants were the owners of the lodge, and not just guests that were renting it for the weekend. And then he saw it; a family photograph on the mantelpiece. Hal gestured with both arms, to add emphasis to the photo-frame, finishing with a completely gratuitous bow, as the point he was trying to make began to make sense to her.

'You get it now, right?' he asked her. 'We walked down a road we've never been down before, to a lodge we've never seen before, occupied by a family we've never met, having a conversation about–' he listened to them intently for a few seconds, '– correction, having a hipster *argument* about who forgot to bring the kale. Jeeze, if only they knew what a real problem was,' added Hal. He sat himself down on an uncomfortable chair by the kitchen counter that, presumably, cost hundreds of pounds, and addressed the strangers directly.

'Seriously guys, things could be worse, you could be trapped in a time vortex!' said Hal, turning his attention back to Kara. 'So, all of this?' he said, gesturing to the living room, the lodge they were in, and to the apparent absence of over-priced kale, 'these events are happening all around us whether we're here to witness them or not. Why would our minds bother? How would our brains even be able to maintain this level of detail over hundreds of acres of woodland? It just can't–'

'Can't just be our imagination,' said Kara. 'We couldn't create detailed buildings, or people we've never seen or met before,' she added, a great big smile gradually appearing on her face. 'You couldn't just tell me that? You had to bring us all the way out here?!'

'No one can be told what The Matrix *isn't* dude…you have to see it for yourself.'

'I got that reference!!' said Kara, pointing at him enthusiastically.

'Besides, I had no way of knowing for certain. I

don't know what this place is Kar'. I don't know if we can get back. All I know is, we *have* to try. And I think we need to start by finding out what the connection is between Kevin and that brick shit-house that murdered us.'

And for the first time since she saw herself die, she felt something deep inside that she could latch onto. She felt a sense of hope.

She moved closer to Hal, a look of unprecedented excitement on her face.

'Can we do another one?' she whispered, causing Hal to laugh.

'Hell *yes* we can do another one!' he said, equally excited by the prospect of getting to indulge in a once in a lifetime opportunity to play a game of people-watching, their currently inherent invisibility providing them with a uniquely unrestricted access to the inner-sanctum's of the unsuspecting residents of Pentney Lakes.

CHAPTER THIRTY-THREE

Repeating Peter's Paradox

14th Restart – Friday Afternoon, 12:01pm

They landed unsteadily into their next restart, as Hal attempted to maintain his composure, and commenced walking immediately, apparently losing his bearings, as he walked straight into the exterior wall of the sauna room.

'Ow,' said Hal, more out of embarrassment than through the pain they both know he couldn't feel.

'Why do you always try to walk off as soon as we land here?' asked Kara, a barely concealed smirk plastered across her face.

'You'll think it's stupid,' said Hal sheepishly.

'As stupid as walking into a wall, or falling over every time we land?' asked Kara.

'Okay, fair point. It's just…I'm trying to pull off a time-traveller landing. As we materialise in the past, it's just so much cooler if we're walking somewhere with purpose don't you think? Like, "Damn! There go some competent time-travellers right there!"'

'Uh-huh. Your argument would hold more water if we weren't completely invisible to every single human person in this timeline, but I'm sure any wildlife nearby would be blown away,' replied Kara.

Hal shrugged dismissively. Nothing could ruin his good mood today. In fact, The Restarters had both been instilled with a feeling of positivity, the tragedy they had witnessed pushed slightly further back from the forefront of their thoughts, as the possibilities before them suddenly seemed infinite. They had a purpose now; to learn more about the relationship between Kevin and their murderer. But Hal had a more pressing matter he needed to discuss with her. With everything they had been through, it hadn't seemed all that important in the grander scheme of things until now.

'Something weird happened a few restarts ago,' said Hal.

'What happened?' asked Kara, 'and which restart?' she added.

'Well, not to sound like the title of a nineties sitcom, but "The One Where Hal Murdered Robert."'

'Ha. Good one,' said Kara. 'Nothing about that night *wasn't* weird, but go on.'

Hal shrugged off what he was certain was a double-negative, and cut right to it.

'Peter…he was…' Hal was struggling to find the words, realising that it would be much easier to show, rather than to tell. 'Listen, how do you feel about holding-fire with following Kevin? We don't know how far that will take us, and I really think you need to see this,' said Hal, acknowledging that he was asking a lot of her, given that it would mean sacrificing another restart.

'Sure,' said Kara. 'If you think it's important, I trust your judgement.'

If she was being honest, she wasn't entirely ready to get back on the Restarter horse just yet anyway, and if she could put off witnessing her own murder for a second time, she was all for it.

*

Early that Saturday afternoon, they positioned themselves to ensure they had a good spot in Robert's room. Kara had tried to get Hal to spill the beans on what to expect, but Hal was adamant this was another one of those "You have to see it for yourself" kind of deals that he had apparently invested shares in, given than this was the second time in as many restarts that he'd taken this approach.

They spent the day planning how best to proceed in terms of stalking Kevin, and had decided they would follow him Saturday afternoon for the duration of their next jump into the past.

The day dragged for the most part. They had to endure some awkward moments, such as Daisy, Robert and various other members of the group hopping into the room Hal and Kara were occupying. They averted their eyes, as everyone changed from their swimwear, into regular clothes, to fancy dress costumes, and back again. The whole experience had firmly cemented Hal's theory that they were truly witnessing the past, rather than an artificial dreamscape of their own concoction. A conclusion that became a solidified truth by the fact that Hal was adamant he had no point of reference to so accurately manifest the sight of Robert's manhood, swinging in front of them like a pendulum of perpetual punishment.

After what felt like an eternity, Peter finally entered the room. Hal sat up, berating himself for not having the foresight to have died whilst clutching popcorn.

'Okay, here it is! Watch closely!' said Hal.

'Oh, now? Really? I was actually planning to look away after seven straight hours of waiting,' said Kara breezily.

Hal rolled his eyes at her for the millionth time, as Peter made his way to Robert's bedside table, searching for a phone charger. Kara noted the door closing on its own.

'That's weird, don't you think? The door closing like that?'

But Hal was flapping his arms in Peter's direction, panicking that she would miss what came next.

Suddenly, Peter seemed to lose his balance, and fell against the bedroom wall. A faint blue sizzle of energy appearing around his eyes, as an unseen force kept him in place.

'Woah,' said Kara, as Peter began to whisper something.

'Ha-Hal? Karrr? M-my f-ft. Mist…' said Peter, trailing off.

Kara moved closer, trying to make out what he was trying to say, her face barely an inch away from his, as the blue light continued to spark savagely within his eye-sockets. She reached up to his eyes, her fingertips mere millimetres away from the energy coursing through him.

'Kara no! Don't touch him!' said Hal, his voice full of alarm.

But she needed to. Being this close to the blue energy, she could see detail she'd never seen before, like a blue universe, swirling within, yearning to be released.

The energy ceased suddenly, and without warning, causing Peter's eyelids to flutter as his consciousness reverted to a state that didn't appear to be channelling the entirety of the cosmos, no longer a conduit to whatever it was that had taken him over. Startled, Kara recoiled, but it was too late. Peter walked straight through her, shuddering as he made his way to the door, leaving his phone behind to siphon off a more conventional form of electricity from the power sockets of the mortal realm.

'Gah, I hate it when that happens!' cringed Kara, shaking her body, as if doing so held the secret to expunging the residual essence of Peter's past-self passing through her. 'Well that was creepy as shit!'

'I know, right,' said Hal. 'I mean, the only thing that was missing was a 360-degree head-turn and some luminous green projectile vomit.'

'So, was that us? In the past, or future, are we…interacting with him?' hypothesised Kara.

'I can't see how,' said Hal. 'What happened to Pete happened *before* we started restarting.'

'Same with the hot tub jets though,' said Kara. 'They were tripped by you before we started restarting. How is this any different?'

'True,' said Hal, 'but unlike the hot-tub jets, it carries on regardless without our intervention,' he added, recalling how Peter was being held in place in every timeline, whereas the hot tub jets would only cut out on Friday afternoon if Hal actively chose to intervene and deactivated them manually.

'The blue energy though, that's *so* our thing,' said Kara.

Hal had no idea, but one thing did occur to him.

'I guess now we know that this blue stuff can reach across and affect living things in this timeline,' said Hal. 'Now we just have to figure out how.'

CHAPTER THIRTY-FOUR

It's a Trap

15th Restart – Friday Afternoon, 12:01pm

The first thing that struck them, as they landed in a fresh restart, was that the colours were less vibrant than before. The sun that regularly blinded them upon arrival was far less intense, *duller* even. It wasn't just the sky that seemed off either, everything around them seemed slightly more saturated. What was once a day showered in beautiful sunshine, now appeared to be a day that was slightly overcast. Additionally, the now ever-present mist was even more prevalent than their previous forays into the past. It was as if their connection to this place and to their friends was waning. They both noticed it, but neither saw the benefit in mentioning it.

They set off immediately for Kevin's lodge and, upon their arrival, they were glad to see Kevin's door was open. They needed to see just what his connection was to their killer, reasoning that if they were working together, Hal and Kara might be able to use that to their advantage.

The place was empty, and being unable to interact with anything, Hal dropped into an armchair, sparking up the first of his three restarted-cigarettes, with Kara choosing the sofa opposite. All they could do now was wait for Kevin to show.

*

Kevin returned late that Friday evening, the lights from his pickup truck filling the living room where Hal and Kara were waiting for him. The light bounced around the room like a searchlight. Hal held up his hand, noting that it didn't cast a shadow on the wall opposite him, as Kevin walked through his open front door, Jerry following his master close behind.

'Good boy Jer-Bear, Dinner time,' said Kevin

happily, pulling open a cupboard door in his modest kitchen, which ran along the back wall and almost all the way to his front door. Pulling Jerry's dog food container from the cupboard, he gave it a little shake.

'Uh-oh, no dinner for you, we're all out!' said Kevin, grabbing the keys from his pocket. The jingling noise caused Jerry's tail to wag, clearly a result of him associating the noise with what came next, as Kevin walked to the door to the left of the kitchen.

Hal and Kara were on their feet immediately, ready to act. Kevin unlocked the door, reached around the door frame to switch on the light, leaving the door wide open as Kevin and Jerry descended the staircase.

'Well, that's convenient,' said Kara, unable to believe their luck that they were finally getting to explore more of the lodge. With another piece of the puzzle within their reach, they descended the staircase, pursuing who they were certain to be the accomplice of their killer, with fiery resolve.

They realised that they were now in a basement, under the living room they had spent the past countless number of hours in, whilst waiting for

Kevin to return.

The area was deceptively large, with wooden work benches against each wall, lined with various projects either half-finished or half-forgotten. As Hal and Kara spread out to give Kevin and Jerry space, Hal nearly tripped over a long, wide black object. Trying to prevent himself from falling, he made matters worse for himself by standing on a small box on the floor, which remained perfectly in place beneath his black, rubber boot. As Hal stood there, his arms spread out like a surfer catching some waves, trying to regain his balance, Kara couldn't help but laugh at him.

'Real smooth Hal,' she said, still chuckling.

She ran her right hand over the counters, brushing past and over the various tools and knick-knacks littering the surface, the items refusing to move under her touch. Despite looking a little untidy, everything looked perfectly normal, and boringly ordinary.

'Pssst,' said Hal, getting her attention and wincing at himself for choosing this precise moment to utter "pssst" for the first time in his life, as he pointed at

Kevin, who had walked through another side-door, and out of sight.

Jerry was far too busy waiting on the, as yet, incomplete promise of food to give them much thought or attention, as they followed Kevin through the doorway and inside the new room. They realised, all too late, that Kevin was coming back out, his arms filled with a large bag of dog food. Acting on instinct, they pressed themselves against the back wall of the room, so as not to pass through him.

'No, no, NO!' said Hal.

But it was too late. Kevin had closed the door behind him as he left. Kara ran to the door and grabbed at the handle, but being so far away from her past-self, was unable to interact with it. She looked back at Hal, her eyes wide with the realisation of their mistake. They were trapped.

*

'Well this is surely a contender for *Worst Restart Ever*,' said Kara, pacing the three strides she could make before walking into a set of shelving, turning on her heel and repeating the process relentlessly.

'I guess that's what we get for attempting this on

our thirteenth go,' said Hal, lighting up his second cigarette for the day.

'Fifteenth,' corrected Kara.

'No shit, really? I had us at thirteen?'

'Trust me, it's fifteen.'

'Damn, I guess it's true what they say. "Time really does fly when you operate outside of conventional physics,"' said Hal, extremely happy with the fluidity of his joke.

The worst part of their accidental incarceration was that they had no means of escaping from the confinement of the small storage room, until either Kevin returned to open the door, or their past-selves were in close enough proximity to allow them to interact with the handle. The silver lining was that they knew their past-selves would be just about close enough at 11am the following morning. A solution largely negated by the fact that they were in a pitch-black room that made following the passage of time all but impossible. Hal lit his lighter again, the flame illuminating his face, but not spreading to the rest of the room as it should have done, were his lighter in-phase with the room around him.

'Oh wow,' said Hal, 'another bullshit time-travel rule! Light doesn't travel universally, only within the confines of the timeline it exists in!' he added, his voice thick with sarcasm. 'Awesome. Hey Kar', can you stop pacing? You're making me anxious.'

'I didn't know I was freaked by confined spaces until now,' she said, slamming her fist against the brickwork. She rolled her eyes at the barely-audible, muffled thud that the action generated. Turning around so that her back was resting against the wall, she took a deep breath, then slid down to a sitting position, accepting temporary defeat.

And so, they waited, discussing their theories on their killer, what they had witnessed with Peter, the portal at the edge of Pentney Lakes that had prevented them from leaving, and everything in-between.

*

The remainder of their Friday revolved around listening to Kevin pottering around upstairs. Their hopes ignited early the following morning, as they heard the door at the top of the stairs open, their accidental-captor walking towards them, teasing them with the possibility of early parole for their good behaviour. Hal and Kara were waiting by the door, ready to bound their way through as soon as the opportunity presented itself. Instead, they were treated to the odd sound of a large sack being lifted, then dragged across the floor, up the stairs, culminated by the sound of the basement door closing once again, acting as a sour cherry on top of the already-dire turd that was their current situation.

'Awkward,' said Hal. 'Okay, my turn…I spy, with my little eye, something beginning with–'

But Kara didn't listen for the letter, she was too busy trying to resist punching him in the throat.

*

They took the next few hours in shifts, waiting for their past-selves to walk by thanks to their scheduled trip into the woods, attempting to turn the handle every couple of seconds to make sure they didn't miss their small window of opportunity. Despite neither of them knowing with any certainty if they would be close enough to make it work, the door unlocked with ease at what must have been around 11am. When the door finally opened, it seemed almost farcical. But here they were, free from their imprisonment. They laughed together, more out of a combination of relief, and what was arguably a mild case of cabin fever, more than anything else. Suddenly, Kara's smile dropped, as she thought of something that Hal clearly hadn't. She ran up the stairs and reached for the basement door handle, frantically trying to turn it. Either the door was locked, or their past-selves were once again too far away. She swore at the door, pounding it with her fists.

'Dammit! Trapped again!'

'It's okay Kar', at least we're right where we need to be for tonight. This is good. I mean, it's not *great*, I'd rather be upstairs too, but we can work with this.'

'*Worst. Restart. Ever*,' reiterated Kara. 'What do you think was in that black sack he keeps carting around anyway?' asked Kara.

'At this point,' said Hal, 'I wouldn't be surprised if it's my own dead body. You know, because time-travel, or whatever.'

'How would that make sense?' asked Kara, who couldn't quite tell if he was joking or not.

'We're a couple of ghosts and/or time-remnants,

currently locked in the basement belonging to the person who murdered us and his accomplice, unable to interact with a *door*, because the past versions of our considerably more-corporeal selves aren't close enough to allow us to do so, dressed as a ghost-buster, and a ghost-*hunter* respectively. You're telling me there's not a chance it's *me* in that body-bag?' said Hal, breathlessly.

'Fair point,' admitted Kara.

*

Several hours passed before the basement door flung open. A heavy-set man appeared, closed the door behind him, switched on the light, then plodded down the stairs towards them, eyes firmly set on Hal and Kara.

Instinctively, they took a step backwards, as their self-preservation overrode the knowledge that they knew he couldn't see them. As he strode towards them, they moved out of his way, as he threw a large carry-all onto the counter. The sound of the slowly-opening zip echoed throughout the basement.

He removed various items, and placed them next to the bag; A small black rectangular box, a folded-up sheet that appeared to be made of rubber, and two thick A3-sized plastic folders.

Hal and Kara nervously moved closer to get a better look, as the muscular man reached out for the rubber sheet. As he held it from the top-corner edges, it unravelled in front of him. Placing the hoop around his neck, he methodically tied the dangling straps around his waist, looking over his shoulder at the perfectly symmetrical bow he had just created, then instantly undid it. He repeated the act a second time. Then a third. And then so many more times, that the invisible spectators gave up on keeping count.

Finally satisfied with the last attempt, the man took a deep breath, and exhaled with a tone that indicated he was content. Opening the folders, he began pulling out what appeared to be newspapers. He reached into the plastic folder and removed a new packet of tack, which he used to attach multiple sheets of paper to the walls of the room. A room that, with each passing moment, was starting to feel a *lot* more like a dungeon.

After thirty-or-so minutes of them watching, as the bulk of a man initiated a seemingly endless cycle of placing, taking down, then placing again the various papers, the man took a moment to take stock, and surveyed the display he had created. He made some final adjustments to ensure each page was precisely positioned an equal distance from the neighbouring page, then reached back into his black bag, removing two alarmingly-sized sheathed blades.

'Great,' whispered Kara, 'we were murdered by *Rambo*.'

Hal gestured for them to move closer to the papers lining the walls, eager to see what was printed on them. The tall, dark haired man picked up the small rectangular box, opened it, then placed it back down next to his bag. Kara noticed the glint of a reflection, as the light bounced off of the contents. She moved past the man, and saw three syringes, each filled with a sickly-translucent green liquid. Plastic caps covered the end of the needles, all of which rested disconcertingly in a box that was clearly custom-made to hold the syringes securely.

'*Kara, get over here,*' whispered Hal.

'Why are you *whispering*? He has no idea we're here!'

But as she saw what was written on the papers adorning the walls, she knew exactly why he was being so overly cautious.

'*Oh*,' said Kara, as she too sub-consciously lowered the volume of her voice. 'Oh, this is *much* worse than we thought.'

CHAPTER THIRTY-FIVE

The Murderer's Apprentice

15th Restart – Saturday Afternoon, 3:25pm

Judging by the newspaper articles, this man had been operating in secret for quite some time. Hal and Kara made their way backwards through the display, until their eyes fell upon the first article. Perfectly-executed calligraphy adorned the sheet of newspaper, as it did with all of the others, though the comments on this one in particular were unique in that the words "You did this" were written in every free margin and dead space on the page. The newspaper was dated with the year 1995, though the rest of the date had been redacted with a black marker pen.

One thing was clear; the article referenced a tragic road collision, the faces of the victims oddly covered in so many scratches that they were no longer recognisable. Hal thought he could just about make out a name, but the lack of a substantial light source made it difficult to be certain.

"Ophelia maybe?" thought Hal.

As they made their way across the additional articles, they realised that they spanned multiple towns, counties and even an incident abroad. The Restarters quickly realised that each and every one of them highlighted the man's perverse record of achievement. The display was as terrifying as it was devoid of any obvious pattern. Age, sex and race didn't seem to factor into it, leading Hal and Kara to believe he was little more than an opportunistic bastard.

'He's a serial killer,' whispered Kara, the words feeling false in her mouth. It felt like something out of a movie, rather than a statement based on real life.

Hal struggled to read the smaller text on the

pages, given the dimness of the lighting.

'This one is dated March 2000. It says the victim was…' he stretched over the counter to read the tiny font. 'Melanie Jenkins. "A graphic designer, found dead in her home" yadda yadda,' he skimmed the article, jumping ahead. 'Died of *natural causes* apparently.'

Kara read another. 'Jacob Murray, "a traffic warden, found dead in his flat in Kent in 2009." *Suspected* suicide.'

Hal's eyes were drawn to a third article.

'Hey, check this one out; "Abigail Shaw. A twenty-eight year old theoretical physicist from Cambridge." Now *she* sounds like someone we could use right about now…' he said, noting the date of the newspaper article. 'Says here she was found dead in her car near…Cavendish Laboratory in 2012.'

'Jesus Hal, do you really think he killed all these people?'

Before he could answer, they were interrupted by the sound of a car pulling up on the driveway above them. Their killer's head dropped to an angle, as he listened intently.

He moved like a panther, in remarkable silence given his size, gliding up the stairs of the basement, three at a time, and waited out of sight by the side of the door frame.

Kevin opened the basement door, and began hoisting his giant black sack, the same one that may or may not have contained a dead version of Hal, down the stairs.

The killer was on him instantly, grabbing Kevin in a choke-hold. The steps of the stairs seemed as if they would buckle under the duress of the combined weight of the two men, but the steps refused to yield.

Their would-be murderer reached out with his free right-hand, and dragged Kevin back up several steps, reaching out for the handle of the basement door, and slamming it shut. Kevin seemed to be losing his connection with consciousness as his frantic kicks and gurgles grew less and less intense, until he finally went limp. The large entity then dragged his prey down the remaining steps, sidestepping the large black sack that was obstructing the stairs.

Setting Kevin down on the floor, he paused,

seemingly to review his options. He stared at Kevin's wide array of tools, and the do-it-yourself accessories that were adorning the walls. Finally, he settled on the tried and tested heavy-duty black tape, which he grabbed, moving back towards his rectangular box of–

'Oh no, not the death juice!' said Hal, covering his eyes, but still looking through his open fingers. 'Kara, we have to stop this!'

'How?! What can we do?'

'Maybe if we join hands or something, use the energy somehow, we have to try!' said Hal, grabbing her by the hand and swinging wildly with his fists at the sadistic cause of all of their problems. His arms flew through the killer's body and head, but the monster didn't so much as shiver. He did, however, stop in his tracks, looking around the dark room suspiciously, as Hal continued to throw harmless punches at Kevin's attacker, completely ineffectual in his efforts.

Ultimately, it was all in vain, as the man refocused on the task at hand and pulled the plastic cap off of the syringe with his teeth. Wrapping things up, he punctured Kevin's neck with the needle, pressing the plunger without a semblance of remorse, as the sickly-green liquid flowed into Kevin's bloodstream.

The man then proceeded to bind his victim's hands and legs, and dragged him into the small room that Kara and Hal had spent almost the same amount of time in than it would have taken to experience a small city-break. Finally, he locked the storage-room door with the key that was helpfully in the lock, and pocketed the key.

'Oh c'mon!' said Kara, as the reality of the situation dawned on her. She could tell by Hal's face that he was thinking it too. 'It's been hard enough trying to figure out how to save ourselves from Kevin and this murder-bot from hell, but now we have to save Kevin too?!'

'Kevin was innocent all along,' said Hal, 'this definitely complicates things.'

'Switching car insurers complicates things Hal, we're literally running out of time, or time's running out on us. This isn't a *complication*, this is the definition of impossible.'

And on that sombre note, they waited for the

personification of their cause of death to leave the basement, both of them flitting away from the glorified coffin that was Kevin's home at the soonest opportunity.

CHAPTER THIRTY-SIX

Kevin

Saturday Evening, 10:59pm

Kevin awoke, his mind swimming amidst a nauseating grogginess. His thankfulness that it was pitch-black quickly dissipated, devolving into panic, as his need for a dark room to sleep off this hangover-from-hell transformed into a complete lack of spatial awareness.

A sliver of blue-hued light cut across the floor, two metres away from him on his right-hand side. His brain quickly processed a list of likely options, and he slowly realised it was shining from the other side of a doorway. As his eyes adjusted to the dark, familiar shapes began to crawl into focus. The fogginess of the pounding headache that was debilitating his eyesight began to retreat, allowing him to assess his surroundings more deductively.

He felt a sharp pain in the back of his neck, like a blunt blade of a guillotine. He pulled his head away from the cold, jagged metal, and attempted to use his hands to push himself up. It was then that he noticed his hands would not separate, bound by a force he could not see.

Bringing his hands up to his face, he tried to ascertain what he was up against. The light from the crack under the doorway glistened against his wrists, and for a terrifying moment he thought it was blood. Kevin inhaled deeply, which sent him off-balance and caused his neck to collide once more with the thin metal surface. Expecting the feeling of inertia to afflict him forever, he was relieved to discover that his mind was able to focus once again.

He brought his hands back up, then realised it wasn't blood.

"Tape," he thought, allowing his panic to subside.

Instinctively, he then tried to move his feet apart, rolling his eyes at the fact that, predictably, they too were bound. Kevin tried to yell, the noise a feeble whimper that was dampened by the fact that that he was also gagged. Kevin tried to push his fingers underneath the tape wrapped around his head, but eventually gave up.

Dragging himself forward, he rolled onto his side, edging towards the slice of eerily-glowing light that was creeping beneath the bottom of the doorway to his right. There was barely enough of a gap for him to see a hint of the other side, but it provided Kevin with just enough information for him to know precisely where he was.

'Um herrrrm!' he muffled, then instantly froze, realising how stupid he was for disturbing the silence. What if *he* had heard? What if he was coming for him right now?

Now he knew he was in his own home and, more specifically, in the storage room of his own basement. He realised the sharp metal was actually the shelving unit for his old paint tins, discarded creosote, and reserves of dog food that he kept a safe distance away from the potentially hazardous chemicals. He also knew that he wasn't going to escape by doing a MacGyver, and creating a ballistic weapon with crusty old paint and wood preservative.

He shimmied along to the far corner of his prison cell, searching for anything that he could use to aid his escape. Eventually, his hands fell upon an old coffee table, concealed under what he remembered to be a dust sheet.

Using his head and hands to form a pincer, he pulled at the sheet to reveal it. The table was ready to fall apart, and the wooden legs would have made a poor weapon, as he recollected why he had demoted the thing to the basement in the first place. The table was held together with wooden dowels, cheap glue, and a hefty dose of willpower. He grimaced, as he realised there wasn't much in the way of resources.

Kevin continued his quest, remaining prone as he did so, back to the metal cabinet. As he attempted to use the edge of the shelving-unit to cut through the tape, he discovered that he had clearly done far too good a job at sanding them down when he'd built them a couple of years ago.

After what felt like an eternity, he realised there was nothing he could use to escape. It was then that he began to come to terms with the fact of how screwed he was. Kevin heard a muffled sound of what seemed like crying, realising Jerry was upstairs, alone with the monster that had dragged him here.

A tear rolled down his cheek. Pulling himself together, now more determined than ever, he began searching the floor of the room all over again, inch by inch.

His boy needed him.

CHAPTER THIRTY-SEVEN

The Punxsutawney Purgatory Paradox

18th Restart – Friday Afternoon, 12:07pm

They watched in silence, as the afternoon sunlight edged ever-closer to their favourite picnic bench at the rear of the lodge. It was a fresh restart, and their friends, as well as a past incarnation of themselves, were arriving in their respective cars.

Jon had just finished welcoming Will and Stacey for the nineteenth time, and was now, true to form, tinkering with the hot tub behind them, which meant that they had about five more minutes before they'd have to free up the bench.

It was an odd sensation, the once-beautiful but now-saturated haze of the afternoon sun flickering between the leaves of the trees, acting in unison with the ever-thickening, static white fog to create a notably dismal ambience.

Hal, once again, stared deep into the whiteness. Seemingly reading his mind, Kara broke the silence, pulling Hal back down to earth from his racing thoughts.

'The fog's getting thicker with every restart. It's getting harder to see stuff,' said Kara.

'That can't be good,' said Hal. 'It definitely feels like we're not as tethered to this place as much as we were at the start.'

Kara nodded and contributed another observation.

'And those guys,' she said, gesturing over her shoulder with her thumb towards the lodge, where her friends were congregating, 'their voices are definitely getting more muffled, it's getting harder to hear the gang talking…'

'Except the music, it's as clear as if we were in-phase with them…' said Hal, referring to the never-ending playlist that echoed throughout the lodge on a constant cycle whenever their friends were awake.

'Yeah…that *is* weird,' agreed Kara. 'Why do you think that is?'

Hal rattled off an overly-complicated theory involving decibel levels and reverberations, which immediately caused Kara's eyes to glaze over, making her feel sorry that she'd asked. She sat up straight, and Hal stopped his trademark tirade of techno-babble, knowing her well enough to know that she was gearing up to share an idea.

'We need to try something different, instead of trying to change the events that lead to us leaving to take Jerry back to the murder house. Each and every time the flutterby effect–'

'You can't change the butterfly effect to flutterby effect Kara, it's never going to stick,' said Hal.

'But you agreed that butterflies should *so* be called flutterby's. It's literally all they do.'

'Yeah, but you can't jump out of your blue, police call-box–'

'Time-travelling car, surely?' interjected Kara.

'*Fine*, whatever your time-machine of choice may be, shouting that the "flutterby effect" is…I can't remember what I was getting at, but my point is it doesn't sound as cool.'

'Can I finish what I was saying now?' she asked, wishing to finish her thought before she too forgot what her point was. It was getting harder to concentrate in this place, she couldn't decide if it was a side-effect of prolonged time-travel, or if there was a more sinister reason behind it.

Hal casually mimed the shooting of duel pistols in her direction, with his elbows resting behind him on the picnic table.

'Each and every time the flutterby effect,' said Kara, ignoring Hal, who was rolling his eyes, 'stops us from achieving any notable change. It's like time wants us to fail, maybe because we also need to save Kevin?'

It was true that, with the exception of accidentally murdering Robert, every change they tried to make was ultimately corrected by an unpredictable counter-measure, presumably deployed by time to counteract their meddling. Every time they thought they were successfully causing a ripple, they realised all they were really achieving was adding the tiniest water-droplet to an ocean of pre-determined, and perfectly orchestrated, destiny.

Kara continued. 'What if, instead of trying to change things *here,* we need to be changing things *there*?'

'You mean where it happened?' asked Hal.

'Yeah!' confirmed Kara.

'Go on,' said Hal, pulling his elbows away from the table and sitting up.

'What if we can change things *where* we are due to die *before* our past-selves get there?'

'You know that's impossible,' said Hal, shooting down her plan. 'Our past-selves are too far away for us to interact with the environment. We'd have the combined physicality of a kitten's burp.'

'We would initially, but what if we practice, focus on increasing our range?'

'I don't think there's much we could achieve in the sixty-odd seconds our alive-selves are going to take to walk up Kevin's driveway…'

'What if one of us was distracting Jerry?'

suggested Kara. 'To buy us more time? Still in range, but delaying the arrival of our past-selves at Kevin's lodge, just enough for you and I to make changes in the basement?'

Hal had to admit, it was a good idea, in principle at least. By maximising the duration of their proximity to their past-selves, they could theoretically increase the amount of time they were able to interact with their environment. Hal wasn't entirely convinced, however, by what they could actually change in the basement.

'But what can we really change whilst our killer is getting his kill-room oh-so just right? All we're really achieving is giving him more time to sharpen his psycho-knife. Maybe even allow him to get a few more reps in with his dumbbells so he can drain the air out of me just that bit faster?'

'Oh, I'll tell you what we're going to do,' said Kara, rising from the bench and adjusting her superfluous spectacles, positioning her legs shoulder-length apart, and placing her hands on her waist in a full-on Darth Vader pose.

'We're going to follow his every move for the

next two days, memorise everything that happens before zero hour–'

'Zero hour. Nice. Did you know that was the title of this cool comic abou–' but Kara cut his interruption short.

She needed to say the words out loud. To give life to her thoughts.

'Hal, we're going to *kill* the bastard.'

*

'Damn dude, that was so dramatic!' said Hal excitedly. 'Like, even the sun was behind you, casting this totally boss shadow. Don't get me wrong, the whole "hand on the waist Vader thing" looked damn impressive and all, but…there's a huge difference between pushing things over, flipping switches and, well, killing a man dead with, what? Light-petting?'

'Gross. I hate the word "petting", Hal.'

'I know, that's why I said it I think…'

'Douche.'

'Ha! Plus,' added Hal, 'there're the ethical implications of committing a murder…'

'I think our conscience can be pretty clear on this one,' said Kara, a look of ferocity in her eyes. 'Not least, because of the fact that we wouldn't be committing the crime in the physical world, given that we're time-travelling astral-projected photocopies of ourselves.' Kara smiled, extremely pleased with herself for how that sentence came out. It was the sort of techno-babble that Hal was so fond of using.

'You've been spending too much time around me, now you're *really* starting to sound like me,' noted Hal, also sporting a smile, 'I'd have gone with "facsimiles" rather than "photocopies" though, but that's just me.'

Kara was on too much of a roll to entertain Hal's vernacular hijacking to stop now, eager to win Hal around to her way of thinking with another fact.

'Not to mention, by the way,' said Kara, 'that the only reason we're even *having* this conversation is because of the guy, you know, *killing* us in the first place!'

Hal had to agree, this wasn't exactly a black and white moral dilemma, it was matter of survival.

'Okay…settle down, Agent 47. Assuming we can remain close-enough to our super-fine past-selves long enough to instigate a chain reaction that could lead to taking out our murderer, what would happen next?' There was no way he was even going to consider this unless they could be certain of where the outcome would leave them.

'The past versions of *us* will drop off Jerry,' said Kara, 'then…I guess they'd walk back to Fir Lodge–'

'Leaving Jerry at home alone with a slowly decaying murderer?' interrupted Hal, 'Whilst his owner is trapped forever in his own basement?'

She winced. 'That…*is* a concern, I agree…'

Hal shifted in his seat uneasily, glanced over his shoulder, and offered up his seat to his past-self. He gestured towards the expansive garden, and they started walking, deciding to plan their first ever murder-plot on the go.

'So, to summarise,' said Hal, 'our plan is to practice extending our range so we can operate unhindered by the laws governing this…*paradoxical Punxsutawney purgatory*?'

'You're proud of that one, aren't you,' said Kara, more as a statement than a question.

'More than a little,' said Hal. 'You know, like in Groundhog Day, the town they were in was called–'

'Nobody cares Hal,' said Kara, cutting him off

with a smile.

Hal continued. 'Right, anyway, then we have to devise a way to kill a man, the *one* thing we can't interact with in this place I might add, using *only* an empty basement. Then, finally, we have to free *another* man from a locked room, *before* the timeline readjusts and erases *us* from existence entirely? Just so I'm clear on what you're proposing?'

Kara stared at him defiantly. 'Well, when you say it like that, it sounds stupid, but…yes. That's our plan.'

Hal smiled devilishly. 'I *love* this plan. And I'm excited to be a part of it. When do we start?'

'Unless you have somewhere you need to be, I was thinking right now?' proposed Kara.

Hal took out his ghost-like phone, which was still as dead battery-wise as *he* was pulse-wise, and proceeded to scroll through his imaginary calendar app.

'Nope, I'm free.'

'Wow,' said Kara, with another one of her trademark eye-rolls. 'You really committed to the bit there.'

'Let's just hope I can commit murder with the same vivacity,' said Hal.

'To be fair, your vivaciousness has never held you back before.'

Hal let out a thick chuckle, stood up, then stretched. It did nothing for his muscles, but mimicking the process was oddly comforting, if nothing more than for the small hit of nostalgia it gave him.

'Damn Kara, do you ever just take a moment sometimes, trying to take in how insane all of this is?'

'Not nearly enough. Which part in particular?'

'That's what I mean,' said Hal. 'There are *so* many parts. I mean, this is *Norfolk*. It's hardly somewhere you'd expect to find an other-worldly hub full of batshit time-anomalies. And yet here we are, dressed like *this*, doing these things…'

They had come here to get drunk, and relax with their friends. Instead, they had somehow become time-travellers dressed as ghost-hunters, on a mission to stop a real-life serial killer. Kara had to admit, the whole situation sounded utterly ridiculous. Hal's mood was surprisingly infectious, however, and she found herself giggling too.

'Busting ghosts with scooby-snacks,' said Kara whimsically, realising, for the first time, that Hal must have been really in his element. 'Admit it, you're secretly loving every minute of this aren't you.'

Hal balked at the accusation, though his smile betrayed the authenticity of his reply.

'I mean…I was considerably *more* comfortable before we settled on committing *time-murder…*'

Kara screwed up her nose in an inquisitive manner, pulled out her magnifying glass, and brought it up to her left eye.

'Don't say it,' said Hal, but there was no telling her. 'I mean it Kara, don't.'

And in her best attempt yet at a Velma impression, she uttered but a single word.

'Jinkies!'

CHAPTER THIRTY-EIGHT

Haunted

Saturday Morning, 3:01am

Jasmine was having difficulty sleeping. Rolling onto her side, she glanced at her phone to check the time, grimacing at the display which told her it was 3:01am.

'Urgh,' she said to herself quietly, not wishing to wake her roommates. Kara was asleep in the bed opposite her, tossing and turning in her sleep, presumably trying to combat the impending hangover that had no doubt already begun to dig its claws in. Jon and Rachel were out for the count in the double bed in front of her, with Jon's snoring bouncing off the walls and into her eardrums.

Up until now, she'd been fortunate that her pregnancy had gone easy on her, but it seemed that was about to change, now that it had finally begun messing with her sleep patterns. She saw her near-empty glass of water on the bedside table, illuminated by the intermittent flashing blue light of her phone, the moonlight casting a shadow of the glass onto the wall.

Jasmine reached for the glass, drained what was barely a mouthful and frowned, knowing she would need more. Using her legs, she pushed the duvet cover off of herself and begrudgingly pulled herself out of bed, being careful not to disturb the multiple sleeping-beauties, and made her way to the bedroom door, prising it open quietly. As she turned around to gently pull it closed, she noticed an object moving in the dark. It was Jon's wireless speaker, which had seemingly fallen over. Jasmine shrugged, knowing that the shadows were clearly playing tricks on her, and made her way up the wooden staircase, being careful not to walk into the adjacent pool table.

As she made it to the communal kitchen, the cold-water tap on the sink burst to life, obliterating the silence. A dark figure dominated the kitchen, the moonlight affording her eyesight nothing more than a silhouette.

'Oh, hey Jas'! Just grabbing some water,' whispered the entity. 'You're up late?'

It was only Hal. She berated herself for being so jumpy.

'Hey, yeah I know,' said Jasmine. 'Same here,' she added, raising her empty water glass.

Hal extended his hand, and she gave him her empty glass. The noise of running water erupted once again, stopping abruptly, as he passed her back the refilled glass.

'Well, g'night!' said Hal.

'Goodnight,' she whispered back, noting that Fearne and Peter were dead to the world in the far corner of the communal dining area, engaged in a deep sleep on one of the sofa beds. Will and Stacey mirrored their inactivity, on the sofa bed situated on the opposite side of the room.

As she heard Hal descending the stairs, the steps

emitting noticeable squeaks under his weight, she stood in the darkness for a moment. Jasmine stared out through the kitchen window, into the black, night sky, resting with her back against the stair-rail, waiting until she finally heard Hal's bedroom door closing with a gentle click.

It was then that the fridge shook violently, as the door opened, bathing the kitchen in an amber light. She stood their frozen, staring at the inexplicably-open appliance. It shook once again, less violently, though this did little to ease her frayed nerves. She stepped towards the fridge, the light meeting her face, casting a sickly glow upon her.

She stepped backwards, then towards it, her instinct to retreat overridden by her practical, adult mind, knowing that if she didn't close it, the small amounts of food wedged between the ridiculous amount of beers would potentially turn bad in the night.

Closer now, she reached out to the fridge door, her fingertips mere millimetres away. But before they could make contact, the door itself was pulled away from her, slamming inwards into its frame. The bottles of various spirits resting on the counter above it rattled violently.

Her scream was suppressed beneath her hands, which she had impulsively covered her mouth with. Her eyes wide with confusion and terror, she backed away from the fridge, not entirely convinced that it didn't now contain a terrifying creature, like a movie she had seen many years ago. As yet, there were no eggs frying on the counter at least.

Taking the long way around the stairs, she doubled back on herself, and power-walked down the wooden stair-case, covering her ears as she was forced to walk directly past the malevolent appliance, almost expecting it to chase her.

As she reached the lower level, she turned left, desperate to get back to the sanctum of safety that was her bed. Looking back up the stairs, expecting to see something no-one living ever should, she was relieved that there was nothing to see or, more importantly, no *one.*

Taking a moment to catch her breath, she rested her left arm on the stair-rail at the bottom of the stairs for support, whilst she shook off what was clearly a waking-dream of some kind.

It was then that she saw it; a black rectangular object above a table it had previously been resting on. Jon's speaker again, in itself not intimidating in any notable way, except that it was currently levitating three feet above the table, with no apparent support.

'That's…not possible…' she whispered to herself, in both amazement and terror.

Jasmine suddenly felt a solid object behind her back. She had automatically walked backwards, and into the wall that backed onto Hal's bedroom. The small cube of chalk, that men always seemed to dramatically apply to pool cues when they wanted to look professional, rose up from the wooden edge of the pool table, until it was perfectly level with her terrified face. Slowly, it bobbed towards the blackboard that was intended for score-keeping but, in reality, was used for new guests to write messages on.

The cube of blue chalk connected with the board with a soft, shrill squeak, moving downwards. Disconnecting from the blackboard, the chalk bobbed two inches upwards, then erratically changed course, moving horizontally. The process repeated, mirroring the first step. A poorly drawn letter 'H' now adorned the board. But the cube of condensed powder was not done with her. It began the next stage of its journey, creating a forward slash, then a horizontal line, culminating with a crudely drawn back-slash. The seemingly erratic movements now seemed less random, forming a word:

HA

That was enough for Jasmine. She ran past the speaker, knocking it out of the air, making a mad dash for her room. Something sinister was clearly laughing at her. She woke her friends, begging them to come with her, to witness concrete evidence of a world beyond their own. Jon and Rachel came running out with her, though Kara was still dead to said world.

Jasmine pointed to the speaker, which was now on the floor, following her collision with the entity that had previously been taunting her with it. Then to the board, which was indeed adorned with the letters 'H' and 'A' respectively.

It took over an hour before they managed to calm Jasmine down. In the end, they had all concluded that her mind had been playing tricks on her, despite her being adamant that she had truly seen what she had seen. But as they spoke their calming words of reassurance, she relinquished her hold on the accuracy of her memories, questioning their authenticity.

After all, the mind is a funny thing. When presented with the impossible, it's quite reasonable and natural for a false memory to overwrite a true experience. Especially when the alternative could pull everything you thought you knew about reality into question.

CHAPTER THIRTY-NINE

Exorcising Caution

20th Restart – Saturday Morning, 6:23am

'Yeah...might have overdone it with the chalk…' said Hal, saving his smokes for later and chomping on a piece of gum instead. Whilst they had learned early on that their teeth didn't get dirty here, it still felt awful not getting to brush them twice a day.

They were both lying on the covered hot tub, waiting for dawn to get its act together and arrive so that their friends would wake up and embrace yet another Saturday.

'You think?!' asked Kara, clearly in a rhetoric mood.

'Oh, I'm sorry, it's cool for you to go all Magneto with a speaker, but I try and make contact in written-form and suddenly I'm Swayze's traitorous best friend?!'

'I actually get that reference, it was very well put together.'

'Thanks. I was quite proud of–'

'But why write "HA"?' She must've thought some demon thing was laughing at her.'

'Oh, c'mon Kar', isn't it obvious?! I was writing "HAL", and I would have got to finish it–'

'If it weren't for those pesky kids?' said Kara, unable to resist interjecting with a perfectly-timed Scoob quote.

'I was *going* to say, if she hadn't bailed on us,' said Hal, torn between given her a high-five for her excellent one-liner, and his frustration at having to explain himself. In the end, he conceded by switching out a high-five for some straight-forward praise. 'But yes, that was very good. Well played.'

'I know,' said Kara, unknowingly landing a killer

blow with a flawlessly executed Captain Solo quote. Hal decided she didn't need the points.

Their biggest window for experimenting was at night. The central communal-area was directly in-between where their past-selves were sleeping, and it created a "sweet spot" of sorts. But they hadn't accounted for the consequences of their friends witnessing their antics, and potentially losing their minds. The last thing they needed was for the gang to get distracted by thinking the lodge was genuinely haunted, despite the fact that, technically, it kind of was.

They sat in silence, Kara wanting to throttle him for chewing his gum so loudly. She sighed, then asked 'so why didn't you finish writing? Maybe opening a dialogue with them isn't, well, the worst idea we've ever had.'

Hal spat out his tasteless gum, much to Kara's relief.

'Something weird happened when they all piled into the room. Even though I was near to my past-self, I couldn't grip the chalk. It's like…'

'Time was fighting back?' said Kara, finishing his

sentence for him. 'Shocker,' she added.

Hal shook the notion from his head, and offered a counter-argument.

'Not really, it just took all the willpower I had to pull off two letters.'

'I'm telling you, it's time fighting back. That was the boldest thing we've attempted since you killed Robert,' said Kara, chirpily.

'That wasn't my…' but he refused to bite, telling by her smile that she was just winding him up. 'It's probably more a case of the universe in general, maintaining boundaries.'

'How so?' asked Kara.

'Well, I mean, if we move something inconsequential and no one sees us, who cares right? But communicating between timelines…we're not just messing with time, we're reaching across an entire dimension.'

Kara jumped off the hot tub.

'Yeah, well, I'm going to go check you didn't break Jasmine. Seriously, she's probably a jabbering wreck right about now. See you in a bit?'

'Yeah, you know when to find me,' said Hal.

*

Despite being a little subdued, Jasmine didn't show any notable signs of stress, and Hal and Kara had decided to let events play out, to see if their cross-dimensional shenanigans had any adverse, or positive knock-on effects. As it turned out, with the exception of Jon taking the piss out of Jasmine for the majority of the day, everything settled back in to the predetermined order by around midday.

They spent the remainder of their restart testing the limitations of their abilities, focusing intently on extending their range. Following their past-selves around, they attempted to move tiny items, taking a few steps back each time, to test precisely how far away they could be from their duplicates before the carefully chosen objects could no longer be manipulated.

After much trial and error, they had determined that, at approximately thirty-two metres, they could nudge small objects only a minor amount. Being closer, and dependent on how much they concentrated, they could actually move larger objects, and even *lift* smaller ones, as evidenced by their recent antics with the fridge and the speaker.

Eventually, their experiments led to a final conclusion, and they were in agreement that they couldn't extend the distance any further. Deciding it was time to move on, they set off to wait for their would-be murderer, consolidating their efforts to focus on a new mission; to follow the steps their killer had taken prior to him even stepping foot into Kevin's home.

*

It was now their twenty-third restart, and the Restarters were slowly beginning to realise that trying to follow someone in reverse was not as easy as they had expected. They had assumed, wrongly, that simply knowing when and where someone was destined to be would make tracking the route that they took to get there a simple matter of looking up a road, waiting for them to appear, triggering another restart, then starting the process all over again, road by road.

Their first challenge, however, was ascertaining which entrance Kevin's captor had used to enter the lodge in the first place. Despite there only being two entrances, they didn't have a definitive arrival time for, who they had tentatively named, "The Big Bad". They had to take the loss of a whole restart just to determine he had entered through the back door, though they did learn an additional titbit; The Big Bad had accessed the property by utilising a key safe attached to the rear door-frame, which he had forced open with a screwdriver.

'This isn't working is it,' said Hal.

Every time they followed The Big Bad to a new point in his chronological journey to Kevin's, there were multiple possibilities of where he could spring from next. It would have been simpler if they had line-of-sight, but everything seemed to conspire against them. The trees obscuring their view, the multiple cut-throughs to other lodges, not to mention the fog that was mocking them with its ever-increasing density.

'We can do this!' said Kara enthusiastically. 'We just have to split up and keep trying.'

*

'We can't do this,' declared Kara with an air of finality, at last accepting this wasn't going to work. It was now their twenty-seventh restart, and they'd managed to track The Big Bad in reverse, gaining a 30-minute head-start on him, until eventually losing him by choosing an incorrect vantage point.

'How can it be so difficult to track someone's steps in reverse?!' she added.

'I don't think it's the *difficulty* exactly,' said Hal. 'More the trial and error of it all,' he added, as they took stock on how much of a painfully-slow process the entire experience had been thus far.

After seven restarts, they were forced to accept that their idea, though clever in theory, simply wasn't working. Realising that they needed to employ fresh tactics, they adapted their plan, choosing to follow Kevin instead, hoping that The Big Bad would be present somewhere along the way, lurking in the shadows and stalking his soon-to-be victim.

CHAPTER FORTY

28 Daisy's Later

28th Restart – Friday Afternoon, 12:01am

As soon as the sound of rushing air has ceased, and Hal had regained his balance from yet another failed time-traveller-landing, they turned their focus towards the next crucial element of their plan, which was simple, in theory. Armed with the vital information that the killer wasn't actually Kevin, contrary to their initial assumption, all they had to do was find the real murderer, in order to devise a way to change the past. Whilst they didn't know where their killer was in relation to Kevin's lodge on Friday, they knew that he had captured Jerry's owner late that Saturday afternoon.

Hal and Kara headed over to Kevin's late that Friday afternoon knowing, through trial and error, that tracking his whereabouts any sooner was a waste of time. During their multiple attempts at following The Big Bad, they had discovered that Kevin was not at home at the very beginning of their restarts, and they had no desire to scour the hundreds of acres of woodland on the off-chance that they would be able to locate him.

Upon their arrival, they followed Kevin around his house like shadows. Kevin eventually grabbed the keys to his truck and called out for Jerry, until his dog dutifully returned from the woods. They knew better than to get locked in, slipping out of the front door, as Kevin closed it behind him and got into his truck.

Hal impulsively jumped into the back of the open-topped vehicle and gestured for Kara to follow. She followed his lead and, for the first time since they could remember, they didn't have to walk for a while. She positioned herself with her back to the rear axle of the vehicle, as Hal positioned himself at the opposite end of the storage section of the truck, leaning against the rear of the cabin that Kevin was occupying.

As Kevin drove through the winding roads, Hal was trying to get his head around how they could be in a moving vehicle, despite being out-of-phase was time.

'All I'm saying is, it's like when you're on a train. If you jump when it's moving, you don't go flying down the carriage right?'

'Uh-huh,' said Kara, not really paying attention to a conversation that would clearly have been more up Alex's alley than hers.

'I guess it's something to do with everything inside, moving at the same speed as the train itself?' continued Hal.

'Sure.'

'But we can't be moving as fast as this truck if we're not even technically *in*–'

'Hal...'

'–the truck, I mean we're displaced from the physical–'

'HAL!' shouted Kara, pointing to something directly behind him.

Hal stopped talking, and turned around to look out at the road ahead.

Kevin was heading in the direction of the boundary line, hurtling them straight towards where the time-barrier was lurking.

'Shit. Shit! We have to jump!' said Kara, as she perched herself on the edge of the truck, spun her legs over the side, and assumed the foetal position, as she jumped out. Hal looked out at her as she got up and dusted herself down, rapidly decreasing in size as the vehicle sped away from her.

'Okay, okay…we don't feel pain here, just jump,' said Hal, in what was clearly a futile attempt at convincing himself. But after five attempts of counting to three and not jumping, he realised he was caught in an endless loop of over-thinking it.

As the portal to another restart approached at a giddying speed, Hal finally jumped off the side, landing like a crash-test dummy, arms and legs everywhere. He watched, as Kevin drove off into the distance, unrestricted by the same laws that were keeping them here.

As he picked himself up off the dust covered concrete, he realised he had lost one of his boots. Hal turned around, and saw that half of his boot was over the barrier, like it had been cut at an angle with a laser-sword, a blue rim of glowing energy burning around where it had been cut.

Gingerly, Hal reached out for it, pulling the boot towards him. The remainder of his boot had been either sent hurtling back in time, or erased entirely. He held it up to show Kara, who had decided to sit on the grass rather than walk towards him.

Throwing the remaining half of his wellie into the abyss over his shoulder, it vanished with a faint sizzle, comically reappearing on his foot in an instant. Hal marvelled at what must have been the most flagrant misuse of time-travel since a famous witch was given unrestricted access to a time-displacement device to facilitate her request to attend extra school classes.

*

With the arrival of yet another Saturday, the Restarters waited impatiently for Kevin to make his appearance at what was technically now their annual barbecue. The most-frustrating part of being a Restarter was waiting for the moment you wanted, but knowing there was nothing you could do to get to it besides waiting for it to arrive. They had places to be, things to do, but none of it could be accomplished until the correct chain of events began. They had returned to Kevin's lodge the night before, avoiding getting trapped in his storage cupboard, only to discover that Kevin's Friday evening was entirely unremarkable.

Kevin had awoken early, and set off in his pickup truck Saturday morning. Not wanting to repeat their previous mistake, they watched from his porch as he left, then returned to Fir Lodge to await his inevitable return.

'Gah,' groaned Hal. 'This place should come with a remote, so we can fast forward and rewind to where we need to be.'

'Now *that*,' said Kara, 'would be amazing. Hey, I've been thinking. Wasn't it weird how we just jumped to when The Big Bad killed us? It wasn't a natural restart, we were just kind of…*taken* there?'

As Kara continued, Hal chastised himself for

failing to follow up on that. He wondered how he could have missed something so huge.

'What if–' but she was cut off mid-flow by Hal, who had turned all of his attention to the arrival of Kevin.

'Hold that thought Kar', time to bounce.'

'Who says "bounce" anymore?' said Kara, in a playfully mocking tone.

'I don't know, Zumba instructors, presumably?

'I meant in the context of–'

'Tennis-ball manufacturers?'

'I hate you.'

They watched Kevin like a couple of hawks, fearing that letting him out of their sight for even a second would result in him teleporting out of their reach, like some kind of elusive wizard.

With Kevin's introduction to their friends out of the way, they followed him deep into the woods. After what felt like forever, they eventually ended up at a location at the edge of a huge lake. They were surprised to see that Kevin's truck was parked up, a familiar big, black canvas-sack resting in the back, unzipped for the first time since they'd seen the suspicious container many restarts ago.

Hal rubbed his face, like an archaeologist from the movies who was about to swap out a bag of sand for a golden idol, and jumped onto the back of the vehicle. Peering inside, he fell backwards, and rested his arms on his knees, eyes closed and shaking his head.

'What…what is it? What's in there?' asked Kara.

'Come take a look,' said Hal. 'Spoilers, it's nothing like what we were expecting.'

She climbed up next to him into the back of the vehicle, cautiously moving closer, as the shade of the trees and the mist obscured her view, and peered deeper into the dark container. Suddenly, she felt something grab her shoulders, the faint sizzle of blue sparks firing off and repelling her assailant. Hal was laughing.

'You're such a dick,' said Kara, rubbing her shoulder, having just discovered that the bag contained nothing more than fishing equipment. 'Okay, so I think we can say for certain we have to save Kevin. He's just a regular guy.'

'Yup,' said Hal, 'This place is clearly making us

paranoid.'

With the mystery of the black sack resolved, they had at least acquired some valuable information. Piecing together what they had seen, they had a pretty good idea as to what led to Kevin arriving at Fir Lodge that Saturday afternoon. Presumably, Jerry had run off for reasons unknown, and Kevin, not wanting to pack up all of his gear, had proceeded on foot to try and locate him. Ultimately, this had led him much further than expected, eventually bringing him all the way to Fir Lodge. They also now knew precisely where Kevin had been all this time after departing Fir Lodge, which meant that their knowledge of the chronological order of events for Saturday was almost complete.

But there was a still a crucial question left unanswered; where the hell was their killer hiding?

CHAPTER FORTY-ONE

Who Ya Gonna Call?

39th Restart – Saturday Morning, 9:44am

They sat there, staring out across the lake, basking in the early-morning sun as Kevin fished, and Jerry slept on a blanket. It was a fantastic view, with not a serial killer stalking the woods in sight. They'd spent a bunch of restarts scouting the surrounding area, looking for any signs that The Big Bad was hunting Kevin, but after searching from every conceivable angle, for both the mornings and early afternoons, they'd not seen any evidence at all that the killer even existed. It was like he was a phantom, one that only existed during the four hours leading up to their deaths.

'I've been thinking,' said Hal.

'Uh oh, should I stand back and wait for it to blow over?'

'Funny. Seriously, there's too much ground to cover, so much margin for error…we're in over our heads,' said Hal. 'I mean, how can we possibly come up with a plan that has so many moving pieces? We're drowning in variables.'

Kara had to agree with him. They'd spent countless restarts just trying to *locate* their soon-to-be murderer, and had garnered virtually no worthwhile information from their attempts. All they'd really managed to do was confirm the things they already knew.

'What do you suggest?' asked Kara, staring out across the shimmering lake, totally at odds with the static mist that should have been rolling, but was instead just occupying the dead space between the lake and sky.

'We need help. I think it's time to bring in the big guns,' said Hal.

Kara turned to face him with a look of reluctance on her face.

'No… we can't do that, Hal. It's too dangerous. We got lucky last time, *reeeeally* lucky. What if we can't undo it?!'

'I'm not saying we rush into anything, we have to make sure it's perfect, I know that. I'm saying we work it all out, and when we can guarantee, one-hundred-percent, that it won't be permanent–'

'I don't like it,' said Kara. 'We have no idea what lasting effects this will have on Robert as it is. I know the thought of spending an eternity here is terrifying, but to bring our friends into it...it's not right.'

'This has nothing to do with fear Kar'! I mean, you have to admit, having some extra minds on this to work through the problem with us would be a game-changer?'

As much as she hated to admit it, Kara couldn't deny that he had a point. There was only so far that they could get by relying on sheer dumb luck.

'We need help Kar'. The two of us alone aren't equipped to navigate our way through this…this…*whatever* this is.'

'We can't just rely on luck anymore,' said Kara, echoing her thoughts.

'Exactly,' said Hal. 'It's time to adapt.'

Kara turned her eyes back to the river. The static fog was getting thicker with every restart. Their time here was clearly running out. And then there was Kevin. There was also the small matter of there being a serial killer on the loose, who wouldn't just stop with the three of them, would he? Outside of their time bubble, he was probably already planning, or doing, horrible things to other innocents. People who had simply been unfortunate enough to have crossed his path. She turned her gaze back to her fellow Restarter.

'Okay. Hypothetically, who did you have in mind for this... *time-heist* of yours?'

Hal's eyes lit up. He could tell by the look in her eyes that now was not a good time to point out how awesome he thought "time heist" sounded, but he knew she knew how much he loved it.

'I've been giving it some thought, and I think my brother will be useful. And Rachel.'

Kara needed more if she was ever going to agree

to this.

'Why them, specifically?'

'Well, for one thing, we may not have much time once we bring them here,' said Hal. 'And I know I can talk Alex round, he'll trust us at face-value without needing to binge-watch five seasons to get up to speed. Plus, I'm pretty confident he'll be able to get his head around the time-travel element.

'And Rachel?' pressed Kara.

'She's smart. She'll think of all the things we haven't yet. We can't risk Robert again, I don't want to end up giving him *time-cancer* or something. And the rest have kids. It's as simple as that.

'What about Peter and Fearne?' asked Kara. 'They don't have kids?'

'Tiger and Marilyn? Well, given that Peter spends the final stint of each restart doing his *God of Thunder* impersonation, I'm not entirely convinced we should be involving him at all. At least not until we know more about what's causing him to glitch out like that. With Fearne, I honestly just don't know how she'll react.'

'Hmm, agreed,' said Kara. Peter and Fearne were

an unknown quantity right now. 'So, we've nailed down the *who*, we just need the *when* and the *how*,' added Kara, causing a mischievous smile to appear on Hal's face.

'Oh, I think I know exactly *when*,' said Hal, 'the *how* is going to be the tricky part.'

CHAPTER FORTY-TWO

Ashes to Ashes

52nd Restart – Saturday Afternoon, 2:06pm

It was a beautiful Saturday mid-afternoon. The birds chirped in the gently swaying trees that were being kissed by the summer breeze, as if auditioning for an Attenborough production. The tranquillity was almost tangible; everything was as it always was, and as it always should be. Soft laugher drifted out across the woodland backdrop from the rear of Fir Lodge, accentuated by the muffled hum of a hot tub. Everything perfectly encapsulated Norfolk at its finest; a calm, relaxing, picturesque location to stay in, entirely removed from the hustle and bustle of city-life. A place where those who were weary of the day-to-day grind could take a break, put their feet up, and revel in meditative contemplation as the world passed them by.

Which made the following explosion of Fir Lodge all the more alarming, as the billowing flames engulfed the building, and soared into the afternoon sky, the roaring fire spitting and hissing with such ferocity that the orange glow could be seen from miles away, even in broad daylight. The dense smoke swirled furiously, so thick that it was impossible to tell the difference between a temporal fog-anomaly and a…well, Hal couldn't even settle on a corroborative noun that would do it justice.

'Fucking Hell, Hal,' said Kara, staring directly into the fiery abyss that her friend had just opened.

'Yeah, that...escalated quickly,' said Hal. 'Might've overdone it a bit. Sorry,' he added sheepishly.

'How did you even generate that much of an explosion?!' she said, finding herself shouting to be heard, as one of the load-bearing support beams of the building collapsed in on itself with an ear-splitting crunch.

It had taken Hal no less than twenty-five restarts, five of which were spent locating a suitable accelerant, but he'd finally cracked it.

'I won't bore you with the details on my apparent affinity with the dark arts,' said Hal. 'Besides, we have guests.'

Rachel and Alex ran from the building, covering their mouths through fear of smoke-inhalation, with looks of sheer terror on their faces. Rachel's face-paint remained oddly un-smudged and immaculate, considering she'd just burst forth from a burning cabin. Alex was screaming to Kara and Hal, something along the lines of "Get the duck back fire boom", and looking decidedly less pristine due to the inflatable backpack he was wearing, now a molten-mess of congealed plastic.

Kara took a deep breath.

"Here we go," she thought.

The newly-inducted Restarters were understandably losing their shit, desperately wanting to run back into the inferno to ensure their friends were okay, but Hal and Kara grabbed them, causing an almighty feedback of channelled energy that sent all four of them hurtling onto their backs.

Hal dragged himself up from the ground, shaking away the power-surge caused by the displaced electricity that was coursing through his veins, and made his way back to the group. Kara was already up, ready to act as a blocker, in case Rachel and Alex made another mad dash towards the lodge. She was worrying needlessly; they were still reeling from the after-effects brought on by the physical connection the four of them had just made, rolling around on their backs, trying to catch their breath.

'Alex. Rachel,' said Hal, speaking quickly and concisely. 'Look at *us*. Not at the fire, at *us*.'

But they were already staring into the smouldering abyss, without context to guide them through the insanity surrounding them. Hal grabbed Alex by the shoulders, fighting against the electrical current that was now working overtime in an attempt to repel them apart.

'Alex! *It's happening*,' said Hal.

Alex stopped resisting, taking in the words his brother had uttered. Seeing in Alex's eyes that he understood, Hal released his electrified grip. Alex covered his own face with his hands, and then ran them through his thick black hair in a crazily-sudden motion, as if he was shaking off a cold chill, leaving it in a dishevelled state, and finally appeared to be completely focused on Hal.

Alex closed his eyes for a second; seemingly trying to wrestle with the immediacy of the situation, and the trust he had for his brother. His eyes fluttered open, the look on his face indicating he'd made his decision.

'Tell me everything,' said Alex.

Kara, meanwhile, was standing above Rachel, who had graduated from lying on the ground to kneeling, breathing heavily and apparently on the verge of having a panic attack, as she stared at the utterly obliterated lodge. Kara could faintly see their remaining friends through the thick smoke, running away through the seemingly endless rear garden, as the sauna area exploded.

"Jeeze" thought Kara, as she attempted to rally the troops. 'Rachel, Alex, we have to go. Now!'

Hal leaned down, fixing his gaze directly into

Rachel's eyes, moving as close to her as he could without triggering electrical feedback, and asked her a simple question.

'Do you trust me?'

Rachel's heavy-breathing slowed, as something clicked in her mind.

'Ye-yes. Of course,' she stuttered.

Hal stood up, not averting his gaze from hers, and smiled in an attempt to reassure her.

'Then come with us. If you want to, you know…live,' said Hal, wincing slightly at his choice of words.

And with that, Ziggy, Velma, and the ghost-busters headed away from the heatless flames, onwards towards the promise of safety, and much-needed answers.

CHAPTER FORTY-THREE

Charging Ahead

52nd Restart – Saturday Afternoon, 2:52pm

Alex and Rachel followed their friends, stealing awkward glances between each other, as Hal and Kara bickered incessantly. Alex caught the odd word on the wind, words such as "death", "murder", and something about "restarting". Whatever they were discussing, it sounded serious.

Kara and Hal had ultimately brought them to an expansive area, which led to the exit of the complex of lodges and woodland. Kara put up her hands, and everyone stopped walking.

Alex pulled off his now-ruined back-pack, which was now nothing more than a clump of plastic with straps, throwing it on the ground, and deciding it was time for answers.

'What the hell just happened?!'

Hal cleared his throat. 'Look, we're going to tell you everything, but you have to understand, it's not quite as sim–'

'Bro'. I've known you literally all my life. I can tell you're rattled. We *all* are. But you said "it's happening", and we always agreed that we'd only utter those words if it was the end of the world. So, talk.'

Hal took a moment to contemplate the current group dynamic; a couple of ghost-busters, a scoob, and one of the most iconic and legendary song-writers of a generation, about to tackle the greatest challenge they'd ever faced. Together, they were basically a real-life league of justice. His brother was right; it was time to drop some knowledge. But he'd honestly not thought about the logistics of how he was going to handle this. His entire plan hinged on his brother Alex understanding the severity of the situation when he uttered the key words they'd agreed on in the event of a zombie apocalypse. Past that point...well that's all he had.

'How about you start,' said Alex, sensing his brother's apprehension, 'by telling us why we're not back there helping our friends?' said Alex, gesturing behind them, and hoping Hal would give them the green light to go back.

'I need to make sure Jon is okay!' said Rachel. 'We need to get back there *right* now,' she added, unable to process why she allowed herself to be dragged away from Fir Lodge in the first place.

'Ok, dammit guys, I wasn't...you've really stepped up to the plate here,' said Hal. 'Better than I could have hoped. We don't have long, half an hour tops. After that, the timeline might divert to the point where what has to happen *doesn't* happen. We could end up leaving, and restarting after our death–'

'HAL,' shouted Kara, interjecting his rambling. 'Baby. Fricking. Steps.'

She was right. Almost always. He shook his head to clear his mind and, setting oxymorons aside, he began with the end. He began with the day they died.

*

Alex reached for his cigarettes, then cursed, as he realised that said cigarettes were currently residing under lord-knows how many tons of smouldering timber. He must have dropped them amidst the unfolding chaos.

'Here, have one of mine,' offered Hal, chucking him the last smoke in his packet. Alex wasn't a fan of hand-rolled cigarettes, but desperate disparities in space-time required desperate measures. Alex found his lighter, still nestled in his pocket, and sparked up.

Taking a deep drag, he looked incredulously at Hal, back to his smoke, then back to Hal again. 'You rolling with air now?'

'Welcome to time-travel purgatory mate,' said Hal, shrugging his shoulders apologetically. 'Turns out that whilst you really *can* take it all with you when you die, it's mostly just tangible memory,' he added, beginning to suspect that his cigarettes didn't actually contain any nicotine at all.

Alex closed his eyes, considering the statement for a moment.

'So, why only half an hour until you…'

'Restart,' said Kara, helping him along.

'Yeah, about that...' said Alex, wincing playfully. 'Restarters? You couldn't think of anything a little cooler?'

'I didn't want to upset any time riders,' said Hal, returning the volley.

'Fair point,' said Alex, recalling the myth his brother had told him about a long time ago.

'Besides,' said Kara, 'I actually came up with it.'

'*Really*?' said Hal.

Kara winked, and offered up a shrug as if to say "why not?"

Pushing his barely-concealed incredulity to one side to focus on the matter at hand, Hal took the time to explain their strict schedule. How their current timeline was already wildly out of control. With the lodge destroyed, it was reasonable to assume that their past-selves could, potentially, all decide to leave at a moment's notice.

'And if they...*we* leave,' Hal said finally, 'Kara and I won't be murdered, meaning we'll potentially disappear. You might even inherit the restarts. That's why we're near the boundary line. If the cars start approaching, Kara and I can jump through, restart the chain of events and–'

'Not obliterate the lodge with you inside it,' added Kara helpfully.

'Risky. But solid. Okay…' said Alex, as he took another drag of his quantumly-disentangled smoke. 'So, you've tried following this Kevin guy, but it turned out he wasn't the killer…'

Rachel stirred from her stupor. 'That was actually a really great idea on Robert's part, getting you to stake out the House of Doom.'

Alex nodded in agreement, as he attempted to absorb what he was being told.

'So, what it all boils down to,' said Alex, 'is that you need to stop the guy, but you can't do it any earlier than this evening, because you can't interact with his surrounding environment in any way?'

'Yeah,' said Hal. 'We can only interact on a very basic level, unless we're virtually right next to our past-selves.'

'Pushing a cup here, steering a few events there,' said Kara, in an attempt to elaborate.

'I mean, I *did* move a fridge once,' said Hal, rather

proudly.

'A fridge?! Maybe you're underselling your capabilities here?' exclaimed Alex.

'I lifted a speaker!' Kara added. 'Frightened the life out of poor Jasmine.'

'Like, off the ground?' said Alex. 'And Jasmine actually *saw* you do it?!'

Alex thought about that for a moment.

'What about another fire?' he suggested. 'Is that an option? I mean, you annihilated an entire building…'

'We can't go that route,' said Hal, shooting his brother's idea down. 'Besides, the lodge was…we were desperate. It took us so many restarts to get the details *just* right. And we can't risk Jerry getting caught in the blast. Add to that, Jerry's actual owner is in the basement.'

It was one thing killing an actual murderer, but killing an innocent was out of the question.

'And that's assuming there's something in the basement we could use to recreate a disruption of that magnitude,' added Hal.

'Which there isn't,' noted Kara.

'What about with the four of us?' said Alex, trying a new angle. 'We could work together to bring The Big Bad down?'

Rachel was the one to point out the obvious flaw with this idea.

'Ooh! Wait, no, that wouldn't fly either,' said Rachel. 'If we work together, Hal and Kara would potentially survive, but that would be *after* we died, meaning that we'd be dead. Like, *dead* dead.'

'Rach' is right' said Kara, 'and now that Fir Lodge is gone, our past-selves may not even cross paths with the killer at all. Whatever we do from this point on *has* to be restarted. The douchebag has beat us again.'

'*Major* Douchebag,' added Rachel.

Hal and Rachel saluted each other, something they always did when a noun was prefaced with a word that was synonymous with a ranking officer, or title.

'Wow,' said Alex, 'you guys have got yourself into a real pickle here. I can see why you felt the need to break space-time to call a meeting.' A thought flashed into Alex's mind. 'Wait, can you possess people?! I mean, we're basically ghosts, right?'

Hal smiled. This was why he needed his brother. He needed a mind with ideas that didn't have a filter, someone who wouldn't be too embarrassed to ask the good questions.

'Ha, no, it doesn't work like that,' said Hal. 'That's not what this is. As far as we've been able to tell, we're more like…residual echoes, displaced in time. We're not really dead, *or* ghosts.'

Kara didn't necessarily share that belief, but thought she would add some vital information.

'There appears to be a rule here that prevents us from interacting physically with anything living,' said Kara. 'Anything biological, even. And on the flip side, we can't walk through walls or stuff either. Doors are our arch-nemesis…'

'Yeah,' said Hal, 'unless we're close enough to our past-selves to interact with them, that is. We have to time it perfectly when pulling and turning door handles, or risk waiting god knows how long before we get another chance.'

Hal and Kara plonked themselves down on the grass verge, and Rachel and Alex followed suit. After a short silence, Rachel raised her hand, and Hal gave her a look that seemed to ask if she was serious, gesturing for her to proceed.

'What's the deal with the not-so-mild electrocution when you grabbed us?' asked Rachel.

'Honestly? We don't know,' said Kara, intercepting the question. 'It only seems to happen when we physically connect with each other in this place.'

Alex sat up, crossing his legs, his mind clearly whirring again.

'It was pretty powerful,' said Alex. 'Is it always like that? When you touch?'

'We don't make a habit of it,' said Hal. 'We were kinda worried it would either trigger a restart, mess with the whole deal and send us back further, or that crossing the streams would just erase us entirely. And it's never generated as much feedback as that before. Apart from once with Kara, she–'

'No, it's never been that powerful,' interjected Kara, not wanting her friends to know how close she came to losing her mind when she had first discovered the truth about how she had ended up in this netherworld.

Hal took the hint.

Slightly unconvinced, Alex geared up to question Kara further, but saw Hal shaking his head in a barely-perceptible manner, and sensed he should let it slide.

'Do you think it's because there were so many of us connecting at the same time?' asked Rachel.

'Undoubtedly,' said Hal. 'I've got to say, grabbing Alex's shoulders earlier was the longest we've been able to sustain a connection so close to our…other selves.'

Alex nodded, more questions clearly brewing.

'Does the potency of the feedback increase when you're closer to your past selves, then?' he asked.

Hal and Kara shrugged in unison, then Kara decided to field the question.

'We'll have to test it out more to be certain, but it seems that way. It's only a fizzle when we're far away from them.'

They could hear the sound of a fire engine in the distance.

'We don't have long,' said Hal, as the siren set off a burst of anxiety within him.

Kara stood up. She didn't want to run through the barrier just yet, but she wanted to be ready if she needed to, in case things went sideways.

'Guys, there's something that's been bothering me,' said Hal, noticing that Alex was looking for a bin for his cigarette. 'Bro, seriously. It'll disappear instantly after the restart. Just drop it.'

Realising Hal was right, he flicked it into a patch of tall grass to the left of him.

'Sorry… it's a lot to take in,' mumbled Alex.

Hal continued detailing his concern. 'Say, by some miracle, we change the past, future, or whatever, and we actually manage to prevent our deaths, but we don't kill the guy, Jerry's owner Kevin is going to be next on a very long list of future murders.'

Hal shuddered, as he thought about the covered walls that seemed to function as some sort of creepy shrine to all of the people the killer had ended. 'But say we actually succeed, and manage to kill this weirdo, Kevin will still be locked away in that basement.'

'You know,' said Rachel, clearly wanting to address something that was on her mind as well, 'I'm not pretending to be an expert on all this time-travel shiz, but regarding your problem with Kevin…I have an idea that might help.'

'Rach', none of us are time-travel experts' said Hal. 'We're all just making this up as we go along. What are you thinking?'

'Well...say you stop this guy, saving Kevin *after* that point is going to be hard,' said Rachel. 'I mean, time itself will presumably be all over the place, what with how much you've screwed around with the natural order of things, no offense.'

'None taken,' said Hal with a chuckle, as Rachel pressed onwards, validating his decision to bring her here in the first place.

'Your past-selves will presumably leave Kevin's lodge safe and sound,' continued Rachel. 'And each step further they take away from *you* will reduce your ability to interact with this place, right?'

Hal and Kara confirmed this with a simultaneous nod.

Rachel closed her eyes, her idea not quite fully-formed, and opened them again, as it solidified.

'I think…you need to find a way to save Kevin

before he needs saving…put something in place well in advance. Does that make sense?'

Hal and Kara mulled that over, letting her words wash over them.

'Yeah…' said Hal, 'I get where you're coming from. That's…that's actually genius Rach'!'

Rachel blushed, and shrugged it off as if it was nothing, but secretly felt pretty bad-ass over finally getting her head around the rules of time travel.

'Can't you call the Poli…' began Alex, then stopped mid-sentence and slapped his forehead for emphasis. 'Nope, even if you could dial out, there's no way you could give the police the heads-up, unless they were running your call through a dedicated EVP filter. Which may or may not be a real actual thing.'

Hal laughed, then said 'yeah, I'm pretty sure that's not a real thing mate. Although, if we make it out of this, we should definitely try and patent it!'

Rachel pretended she knew what an EVP was, and let it slide, trying not to get distracted by the combined nerdiness of the two brothers.

'Will we all retain our memories?' asked Rachel. 'Once you, erm, *restart* us? Or if you beat the guy, will you both remember?' she added, pointing to Hal and Kara.

Hal sifted through his foggy memories. There had been so many restarts since Robert's untimely demise. Eventually, he begrudgingly reached his conclusion.

'Unlikely. If Robert remembers anything, he hasn't let on since he restarted.'

'He did seem to debate whether he wanted to get into the hot tub after the restart though,' said Kara, 'it was only for a second, and you'd have to have watched three or so restarts in a row to really have noticed it, but now he does it every time,' she added.

'You do realise what that means don't you?!' said Alex excitedly.

Rachel was right there with him. 'You *changed* time!'

Kara and Hal looked at her disbelievingly, but she wasn't to be dissuaded.

'Your actions in this world directly led to a…help me out Alex,' said Rachel.

'Temporal constant,' Alex chipped in effortlessly.

'Oh Lordy, where do you come up with this stuff?' said Rachel. 'But yeah, that! You changed one of those! It's a tiny change, sure, but–'

'Now you know that the future is pliable,' said Alex, finishing Rachel's sentence for her, 'this could actually work!'

Alex and Rachel were now hopping around on the spot, just a little bit too enthusiastically, and went in for a high five, then remembered they were self-contained lightning dispensers, and seemed to think better of it.

Whilst the elation they were projecting regarding this revelation was admittedly infectious, Hal and Kara knew better than to read too much into small victories. And yet, Hal couldn't help himself.

'Eesh, maybe, I guess,' said Hal, warming to the idea. 'Yeah. Yeah, okay. I mean he *does* hesitate every single time now...but that's a huge leap to assume we'd remember enough to call the police if we manage to beat this thing and realign with present-time.'

Alex pulled out his phone, out of habit more than anything else.

"Dead like me," he thought.

But as he looked at his phone, he suddenly got

the feeling he was onto something.

'Hal, give me your hand for a second.'

Reluctantly, Hal obliged, noting that the current was mild, undoubtedly due to their alive-selves being well-over a mile or so away, as Alex continued to stare at his phone.

'Come on come on…' Alex said impatiently, eventually conceding. 'Worth a shot I guess,' he said, as he pulled away from Hal and shook his own arm, which was more than a little numb. 'Maybe with more power…if we were closer…'

'What?' said Hal, 'I mean, sure, maybe we could listen to our music, but I'm fairly certain we couldn't make a call even if these things had some juice. I doubt the circuitry is even in there.'

Alex walked over to the boundary line and squatted.

'Alex, be careful, don't get too close!' warned Kara nervously.

'Jeeze, *obviously*,' said Alex. 'Relax Kara, I'm just thinking. What happens if I throw my phone through here?' he said inquisitively.

'Try it,' said Hal, with a smile. Alex obliged,

watching as his out-of-phase phone disintegrated into a thousand tiny blue shards.

'Coooool,' said Alex.

'Where'd it go?' asked Rachel, the sight of seeing an object dematerialising before her very eyes creating a very real sense of wonder.

Hal had forgotten what that must have been like. He and Kara had been here for so long now that remarkable occurrences were relatively commonplace to them. He suddenly felt like a very jaded time-traveller.

'Now check your pocket,' said Hal.

Following Hal's instruction, Alex pulled his restored phone from his boiler suit pocket, his mind suitably blown, and turned back towards the mysterious vortex.

'This blue electricity stuff *has* to be important,' said Alex. 'There's no way something that holds *this* much power over the reality of this…*time-bubble* you're both trapped in is just for show.' Alex couldn't see the point in that. 'Surely, if it's generated by the contact between Restarters, it must serve a purpose, and I'd bet real money that it's the key to interacting with people in the past.'

Hal grinned at his brother for finally embracing the term "Restarters." Hal had almost been on the fence up until now about sticking with it. Their discussion was cut short by the ear-splitting sound of a fire engine, as it sped past them.

'Crap. Guys you've been amazing. But we've got to go,' said Kara.

Alex acknowledged Kara's instruction with a look of determination, and extended his hand, to Hal.

Realising it was time to say goodbye, Hal felt his spirit break a little. He always felt like he had to be strong around his little brother, even though Alex had never expected that of him. Hal cleared his throat, frustrated by all of the things he didn't have time to say. What if he couldn't make it back? Who would look after their sister? Their dad? Could Alex get a message to Jess?

'Boys…' whispered Kara, not with impatience, but merely a mild undertone of urgency. 'We have to go now…before it's too late.'

The brothers ditched the handshake for a hug.

'If you need to talk again, feel free to…erm, *kill*

me again?' said Alex.

Hal laughed. 'We took a huge risk bringing you here, we won't risk your futures by pushing our luck. But thanks.'

Rachel pushed between them, and flung her arms around Hal. Hal hugged her harder, preventing her from recoiling from the now-shimmering blue energy that radiated between them.

'Make sure you come back to us okay?' said Rachel. 'I don't want to lose my best friend.'

Hal smirked. 'Erm, you *do* have Jon, Rachel…you know…your *boyfriend*?'

'You know what I mean, you douche!'

Hal laughed, knowing perfectly well what she meant.

Alex offered Kara a casual salute, but she scoffed and jumped towards him, hugging him tightly, muttering something into his ear.

'Tell Greg I love him,' said Kara, 'I don't think I ever actually said the words…'

Alex frowned at the foreboding tone in her voice.

'You can tell him yourself, when you make it back,' replied Alex.

Kara's eyes welled up, and she clenched her jaw, nodding firmly.

Rachel and Kara ran at each other and hugged, ignoring the mild impact of displaced energy as they did so, and said the word "babe" a few thousand times.

Now it was Hal's turn to act as timekeeper. He coughed softly, and they broke it up.

Hal and Kara made their way to the invisible nexus ahead of them, as Hal looked back over his shoulder and shouted to Alex.

'Bro, I'm *so* Sam Beckett right now!'

'I guess that makes *me* Al'?' said Alex. 'Let's hope this next leap gets you guys home,' he added with a smirk.

'*Oh boy*. Here's hoping,' said Hal.

Rachel and Kara shot each other a look, rolling their eyes, as Hal turned back to face Kara.

'You want to hold hands or anything when we go through?' he asked.

Kara pulled a face that seemed to be assessing if he was drunk.

'Man-up and pull yourself together, Hal.'

'Anyone ever tell you that you're so grumpy just before a restart? On three then?' suggested Hal.

'Who would *possibly* be able to tell me that?! Yeah, on three,' confirmed Kara.

They counted down in unison. 'Three…two…'

Alex's phone pinged to life in his hand. The glowing, white, fruit-shaped logo emblazoning the screen like a perverse product-placement that had just decided this purgatorial afterlife was its new core demographic. Alex raised the handset, his brain trying to formulate words to shout at Hal, who was facing away from him, facing towards the invisible time barrier, but all Alex could produce was an unintelligible, barely-formed sound.

'Fffffffff!'

'…One.'

Hal and Kara jumped into the nothingness, as everyone and everything in the timeline they were currently residing in was indiscriminately vaporised.

CHAPTER FORTY-FOUR

Return of The Pink Flamingo

53rd Restart – Saturday Afternoon, 2:07pm

The entirety of the group were dispersed in the rear garden, with the exception of Alex and Rachel, who had remained inside. Rachel was preparing some additional food for her ravenous guests, as Alex wandered into the open-plan kitchen.

Grabbing himself a beer, Alex twisted off the cap and, in one swift motion, flicked it into the bin that was situated several feet away. He smiled at the satisfaction of nailing the shot.

'This place is awesome Rachel,' said Alex. 'Thank you so much for arranging it!'

Rachel thrust an additional tray of spicy chicken wings into the gas oven that dominated the north wall of the kitchen area, utterly unconvinced that one tray alone would be enough. She span around to face Alex, and leant on the counter. Alex noted that her eyes were shockingly bright, amidst the red and blue lightning bolt that was painted on her face.

'Not too shabby, right?' said Rachel, 'I'm just thrilled so many of the gang could make it. Wait,' asked Rachel suddenly, 'can you smell–?'

As she said it, she immediately experienced a faint queasiness, as a severe case of déjà vu took hold.

'Gas?' said Alex, finishing her sentence. He swallowed his mouthful of beer, and did an over-the-top sniff. 'Kind of, actually. Should we be worried?'

The sensation released its grip on Rachel, and she pushed it to the back of her mind.

'Nah, it's probably just this beast of an oven,' said Rachel, 'it takes forever–'

'To heat up,' said Rachel and Alex, at exactly the same time.

'Ha! Woah, that was weird,' said Alex. 'Well, back in a sec, just gonna–'

'Pop out onto the balcony,' finished Rachel, not knowing why.

'Okay, stop it now, you're being creepy,' said Alex, taking another swig of his beer and walking out onto the eastern-side balcony, moving sideways to ensure his inflatable proton-stream dispenser didn't get caught on the doorway. He stared at his lighter, then hesitated, seemingly in a trance for several seconds, experiencing a sharp, momentary sense of quantum-despondency.

Placing the lighter back into his pocket, he decided against having an unnecessary cigarette, and made his way onto the balcony, overlooking his friends in the garden below. It was a scorching hot afternoon, and he was slightly regretting his choice of costume, as an illuminous, pink, inflatable-flamingo flew up to him, landing at his feet.

'What's up mate?' Alex shouted down to Jon.

'Bring some more booze down will you?' asked Jon. 'We're all out.'

'No worries,' said Alex. 'Be down in a minute.'

*

'Ha!' blurted Hal.

'What is it?' Kara was following Rachel around the kitchen, pretending that she was helping to prepare food.

'Oh, nothing,' said Hal. 'The bottle-cap, the flamingo, little tweaks…'

'Uh huh, sounds hilarious,' said Kara, continuing her fake conversation with Rachel.

'We changed something else, you know,' said Hal. 'Alex. He hesitated before lighting his cigarette. Out of all the restarts I spent following him on the lead up to bringing him to us, I've never seen him do that before. And did you see the way they finished each other's–'

'Sandwiches?' said Kara, turning to face him. 'Yeah, that was weird, right?

'Oh, we're referencing Frozen now?' questioned Hal disparagingly.

But, much like Elsa, he decided to let it go, not least because his recognition of her joke's origin had all but levelled the high-ground he was striving for. After all, who was he to judge.

'Very weird,' said Hal. 'I think this proves their theory that we can create a temporal constant, and influence events permanently…'

'I guess so, sort of,' said Kara, not really seeing how a few conversational changes really made that much of a difference in the grand scheme of things. 'It really was the best thing ever getting to talk to them, wasn't it?' she added.

'Yeah,' agreed Hal. 'I have to admit, it was getting a little boring hanging out with just you if I'm honest,' said Hal, shooting her a wink as he sparked up a cigarette.

'Busting one out a little early today, aren't you?' said Kara, ignoring his comment. She hadn't seen him use his second of three cigarettes this early-on in a restart for a long, long time.

'I'm celebrating. We blew up a lodge, had an *actual* conversation with our friends, *and* came up with some interesting ideas on what to do next. You want one?'

'No thanks, those things will kill you,' said Kara earnestly, the intentional irony of her statement having no less of an impact on Hal, who took it on-board, throwing his cigarette over the edge of the balcony.

He really wanted to quit.

CHAPTER FORTY-FIVE

Breakthrough

56th Restart – Friday Afternoon, 12:01pm

'All I'm saying is, I don't care how good a shot you are, there's no way you'd be able to find enough lemons in the first place,' said Hal, materialising into the next restart and walking to the left of the driveway to avoid the oncoming arrivals, only partially losing his balance, tripping over his own feet, as his body adjusted.

They'd spent the last few weekends at Kevin's place, looking for anything they could use in order to orchestrate the defeat of The Big Bad. Kevin's lodge hadn't shown any evidence of gas leaks, poor electrical work, or even so much as a leaky faucet, resulting in them having to review other options.

'Yeah true,' replied Kara, having allowed a few seconds to adjust to the restart before attempting to walk, and making her way over to stand next to him, as their friends arrived in the order they always did.

'Morning Will!' she said chirpily, waving to Will and Stacey as they arrived.

She found that speaking to her friends every now and then kept her grounded.

'So, putting our murder-plan aside for the day, you still want to focus on helping Kevin pull a Houdini?' asked Kara.

'Actually,' said Hal, 'I've been thinking about what Alex said about this blue energy.' He stared at his palm and flexed his fingers, as if doing so would cause the energy to arc around his hand. 'What if he's onto something? About it having more potential than we realise?'

Kara wasn't entirely convinced.

'I think we would have stumbled across any evidence of that by now.'

'Maybe we have? Take Pete, for example. Maybe he's all whacked out on Scooby snacks because we're using him as a conduit,' countered Hal.

'I thought we were going to avoid entertaining that possibility by not following up on that?' said Kara, reminding Hal of the plan they had agreed on all those restarts ago.

They had decided that they could potentially change the timeline if they left Peter alone, whilst also ruling out the possibility of *them* being the cause of whatever was going on with him in the process.

Hal rubbed his temple with the palm of his hand, trying to keep the inevitable headache at bay, that was sure to follow by discussing the paradox surrounding their friend.

'Yeah, I know that was the plan,' said Hal, 'but I'd like to explore this, unless you're dead against it?'

'Nope. Just dead in general,' she said, causing Hal to wince. She softened her tone, realising he clearly wasn't in the right frame of mind for hard-hitting jokes this afternoon. 'If you want to do this, let's do it,' said Kara, 'just know, the moment we get involved with Peter…well, it means we're confirming that we're probably responsible for what's happening to him.'

*

They had a solid thirty odd hours to kill, before they could investigate what Hal was referring to as "The Peter Paradox", and Hal had another experiment he wanted to try. They had been holding hands for the past forty-five minutes, remaining as close to their past-selves as possible. The blue energy varied in intensity, its volatility being entirely dependent on which of their past-selves they remained close to. At the moment, they were directly next to past-Hal, who was daydreaming whilst waiting for the kettle to boil.

'I th-think we sh-should try linking arms inst-stead!' jittered Hal, who was struggling to maintain contact with Kara, as their hands were being forced apart like industrial-grade magnets.

The energy cut-out whilst they repositioned themselves, then surged back to life as they linked arms. It was all Kara could do not to fall over, as her leg twitched incessantly due to the feedback. Hal was holding up his mobile phone upwards towards the ceiling. Kara couldn't help but smirk at how ridiculous he looked, as if he were trying to find a signal in the middle of a reception dead-spot, like a yuppie on a train with delusions of self-importance.

'An-any ba-bars?' she said, struggling to get the words out, what with the more-than-mild electrocution she was experiencing. She imagined it was akin to being shot with a taser.

Hal scowled at her, or at least that was his intention. Due to the current running through his body, it looked more like he was trying to wink at superhuman speed. And then, without fanfare, the sweet-spot he was waiting for finally presented itself, as past-Kara skipped up the wooden staircase and into the kitchen.

'I've got a ba-baaad feeling ab-bout this…' stuttered Kara.

They gripped their arms tighter, bracing themselves for the inevitable shockwave that was sure to hit them like a freight train to the face, but were nonetheless caught off-guard, as Hal's past-self turned around and walked into them, just as past-Kara walked into her time-travelling other-self at the same time.

The explosion that followed didn't disappoint. The Restarters would probably have perceived it as a thing of beauty, had they not been flung in opposite directions across the top floor of the lodge. Hal got off lightly, as he flew into the kitchen counter. Defying physics, he rolled over the top of the work-surface, and into the window above the sink, causing the glass to shatter. Fragments of glass rained down onto his past-self and past-Kara, who were now cowering below him, as the sink taps bent inwards at awkward angles under the pressure of his recently gifted weight and substance.

Kara, meanwhile, was considerably less fortunate, as she was flung away from her past-self at an incredible velocity, colliding with the wooden banister rail, which splintered violently. This did little to end her journey, however, as she went head-first over the wooden railing, and tumbled down the stairs, banging ferociously as she descended the staircase, and finally colliding with the left outer-wall of past-Hal's bedroom with an audible crack.

It was at precisely this moment that every rule they'd ever learnt, in their self-contained vacuum of space and time, crumbled. As they surveyed their friend's facial expressions, and the unprecedented destruction they had caused, the gravity of the situation began to dawn on them.

No longer out-of-phase with time, they had broken not only through a kitchen window and banister, but also through the barrier that had kept them separated from their friends and their past-selves, their arrival generating unprecedented pandemonium.

CHAPTER FORTY-SIX

The Choice

56th Restart – Friday Afternoon, 2:46pm

Hal had never had reason to wonder what breaking time actually meant. Nor had he given much thought to if it was even possible. But as he sat there, with his arse wedged through a window frame, staring down at his past-self, as all of his friends were thrown into chaos, he realised three things; The first of which was that, despite his gentleman's agreement with Will that he wouldn't overdo it in terms of drinking too much, he had still managed to find a way to be the one to ruin Rachel's thirtieth birthday. The second realisation he had was that he was pretty sure that he'd just killed Kara, making this the second time she had died on his watch. Lastly, it occurred to him that he needed to get to the restart-point immediately, before any of this escalated any further out of control. Not that any of what was happening fell within the realm of things he deemed could reasonably be described as being "under control".

Jasmine and Daisy were standing in the communal living-room, and were staring at past-Hal and past-Kara with looks of horror on their faces, making this the second time that the Restarters had broken Jasmine's perception of reality in as many weeks. Jasmine ran to the top of the staircase, and stared at something that Hal dreaded to imagine. There was something about the way she reacted, to having just witnessed a wooden banister explode of its own volition, that seemed to have broken her mentally. Hal didn't have time to feel bad about that. Past-Hal and past-Kara were cowering amidst the debris that had been generated by the antics of their future-selves, as Hal pulled himself from the impromptu vertical seat he had created with his rear-end. It took him longer than he would have liked to free himself, due to being wedged-in pretty hard.

As he jumped from the kitchen counter, he realised he had accidently showered his past-self with another layer of glass.

'Sorry buddy,' he said to himself, literally.

He ran around what was left of the banister, and sprinted down the stairs to check on Kara, noting that Jon and Peter were staring at the dent she'd made in the wall. She was in the process of pulling herself up, and dusting herself off, as fragments of wood fell to the ground from her clothes, causing Peter and Jon to take a step backwards.

'You see that?!' said Jon.

Peter nodded, his face pale with dread.

'Kara!' shouted Hal. 'Bloody hell mate, are you okay?'

She scowled at him, flicking the hair out of her face. Jon and Peter were staring at the splintered wood in her hair, and the dust covering her glasses. Jon ducked his head behind her, seemingly looking to check if she'd split her head open.

‘Well, I’m not dead, so that’s something,’ said Kara. She waved her hand in front of Jon’s face, and then tapped him on the shoulder when he didn’t respond. He recoiled from her touch.

‘Holy shit,’ said Kara, ‘We’re back!’

*

Jasmine and Daisy were midway through listing off the things they most resented having to give up due to their respective pregnancies, when they noticed Hal was making coffee. They turned around to ask him if he’d mind making them a cup of tea, just as the window behind him exploded, and shards of glass cascaded down onto the counter. This was shortly followed by the sight of the wooden banister rail erupting into splinters, the force of its invisible assailant causing the whole floor to shudder.

Jasmine heard the sound of someone falling down the stairs, and rushed over to help. She looked to her left at Hal, who was cowering by the kitchen cupboards, and then to the window above him, as the sound of more falling glass filled her ears. Her eyes followed the invisible presence that had seemingly crawled through the window, as it landed with a thud on the kitchen floor. She took a step back, hearing footsteps connecting with the wooden flooring. Whatever it was, it was stalking its way towards her.

Meanwhile, Jon and Peter had dropped their pool cues, as they heard the impact upstairs, and an unseen presence tumbled down the staircase, colliding hard into the wall next to them, the impact shaking the entirety of the ground-floor. They made their way to the point of the collision, staring at each other, and then back down at the small fragments of wood. Fragments that were floating several inches above the ground.

'You see that?' said Jon, Peter's pale face responding with a mere nod.

The fragments then hovered higher, up to waist height, and then sprinkled to the ground. It was then that both Jon and Peter took a step back. At head height, Jon could see additional tiny pieces of wood floating in mid-air, and he ducked his head around behind the gravity defying objects to check that the sunlight wasn't playing tricks on him. Doing so merely allowed him to see something else, as clear as day; two odd shapes of floating dust, like frameless sunglasses, were staring up the stairs, also hovering in mid-air. He felt a sharp stab in his shoulder, and recoiled.

'Peter,' said Jon, 'get Rachel, and tell everyone. We're leaving immediately.'

*

Hal felt a vibration in his hand and realised his phone was working again. He held his thumb on the home button, unlocking it, and the familiar home-screen singed his retinas. He checked the signal, but was dismayed to see that he still had zero bars. He needed to call Jess. The battery indicator showed he had a full battery, but it immediately shot down to eighty-percent. Pocketing his phone, he jogged down the stairs to assist Kara, as everyone around him continued to run frantically around the lodge.

'Guys!' shouted Hal, 'It's okay it's–' but he was cut short as Robert shoulder-barged him. Robert turned on the spot but kept going, a look of horror on his face. 'Kara, what's…'

'Hal,' said Kara, her voice filled with urgency, 'listen to me, they can't see us, they're leaving! Now!'

Hal watched, as their past-selves ran past them,

on a mission to grab their things.

'Wait, but…my phone? They saw you! I saw it!' said Hal, as his confusion merged with denial and evolved into defiance.

'We've broken something Hal!' said Kara, frustrated by Hal for not seeing what she was seeing. 'Something went wrong. If we, *past-we*, leave, we've broken the chain, we'll be free, but…'

'This is what we wanted!' said Hal. 'This whole time Kara, we've been trying to find a way to escape these restarts. If we leave–' he pressed himself against the wall to avoid Fearne from walking into him. '–If we leave Fir Lodge now, we can't be murdered tomorrow night!' And then he realised what she meant. The elephant in the room that his conscious mind was trying to hide from him. 'Shit.'

Kara nodded several times in quick succession, relieved that he finally understood what she was saying.

'If we leave,' said Kara, 'Kevin will die.'

Hal was shaking, there wasn't much time.

'We need to get to the restart-point, *now*,' said Hal. 'We can discuss it on the way,' he added, as the ground shook violently beneath them.

'Um, Kara? What was that?' said Hal, as the ground vibrated again, this time shaking the entire lodge with such ferocity that objects fell from the counters. The sound of glass smashing onto the hard, wooden-flooring filled the lodge, along with the tingling and clinking of metal, as cutlery shook in the drawers on the floor above them. The sound of smashing ceramics complemented the cacophony of noises, as cups fell to the ground, shattering with equal fervour.

The consequences of instigating such a rambunctious paradox became immediately apparent, as Hal and Kara began to see multiple versions of themselves springing in and out of existence all around them. The trail of the path that each Hal and Kara took leaving a slipstream of residual echoes. Fir Lodge filled with every and any potential outcome of Hal and Kara's afternoon, the noise of every possible conversation they would ever have, all taking place at once in a deafening crescendo of banality.

'RESTART POINT?' a voice shouted, belonging to who Kara presumed was *her* Hal.

She nodded, making a break for the entrance doors of the lodge, but coming in hot and colliding with the door-frame. Her speed was unprecedented, as was the dent she had made in the frame of the doors. She looked back at Hal, whose mouth was agape with amazement.

Having no time to discuss Kara's display of raw, unparalleled super-speed, they ran, taking advantage of their mutually-increased traversal velocity, hoping that their newfound ability would allow them to travel faster than their friend's cars.

*

Jon couldn't put his finger on *what* was happening exactly, whether they were all hallucinating, or if they were actually witnessing some form of attack. In the back of his mind, he hadn't ruled out the possibility that they were in the middle of a potential earthquake, as the structure shook violently around him. All he knew for certain was that he needed to keep his friends safe, and right now they were anything but.

Something was happening. He could *feel* it. If he was over-reacting, he knew his friends would forgive him, knowing there would be plenty of opportunity for him to laugh it away with banter, and by plying them with drinks later. But his gut told him that staying here was not the smart choice. Taking charge, he decided to deal with the consequences later. He knew better than to ignore his instincts, and there would be all the time in the world to apologise if he was wrong.

'I'm not wrong,' he whispered to himself firmly.

Everything else was immaterial.

*

Reasoning that their current speed was being amplified by their retained charge, caused by them making contact with both of their past selves at exactly the same time, Hal and Kara felt like they were trudging through deep snow, and that something was holding them back. The fog had disappeared, suddenly replaced with the familiar vibrancy of colours, which had dutifully returned to their surroundings.

They took comfort in the fact that they knew the quickest route to take, their muscle-memory guiding them through the winding roads. Their muscles burned at the exertion, a sensation they had all but forgotten until now, and it was infuriating.

They frantically dodged out of their own way, as additional incarnations of themselves sprung up without warning, obstructing their passage to the boundary line. Kara cursed at the quantumly-untangled road-blocks, seriously regretting how many times they must have walked down these roads to justify the existence of so many duplicates.

'This is bad, Kar', *really* bad,' said Hal, submitting his entry for the understatement of the year award.

'Ya think?' said Kara, stopping dead in her tracks, like a rugby player avoiding an oncoming tackle, as another one of her time-echoes popped up in front of her. She turned on the spot, dodging out of its way, then continued running. It was then, as the time-barrier came into view, still many hundreds of yards away, that they saw something truly out of the ordinary, even by *their* now-lofty standards.

Hal stopped, as a humanoid shape flickered into existence in front of him, shimmering at such a high speed that the details were hard to make out; a man, leaning over another, much-shorter man. The out-of-phase man was brandishing an object, aimed directly at the other, who Hal now realised was kneeling.

'Is that…a *gun*?!' said Kara.

'Oh man,' said Hal, 'this guy looks badass.'

'When you're done flirting with that time…*echo*,' drawled Kara, 'we need to get the hell out of here!'

'Time-echo?' said Hal, his eyes lighting up. 'Nice!'

'Hal!'

'Yup. Sorry. Right. Unimportant details,' said Hal.

They continued onwards towards the edge of Pentney Lakes, wanting to collapse through exhaustion when they finally reached it, but they fought against their bodies, knowing that their friends could be here in seconds.

Looking back out towards the way they came, they saw countless versions of themselves, phasing in and out of existence. Hal and Kara realized that they were closer than they had ever been to finding out *just* what would happen if their past-selves crossed through the invisible vortex.

'Here it is then,' said Hal. 'We let ourselves leave, and we're done. We'll go home, see Jess and Greg, and probably won't remember any of this,' he added, talking fast, and more to himself than he was to Kara.

'But if we leave, Kevin *dies*, and a *serial killer* continues his rampage,' said Kara, her speech equally frantic. They could hear the sounds of cars revving in the distance.

'Maybe we'll remember everything that's happened?' said Hal unconvincingly. 'We can call the police and...and...' but he knew there was no way of knowing that for sure. They were gambling Kevin's life on a hunch, one that they didn't truly believe.

'Hal, whatever we decide to do, we decide together,' said Kara. 'This is too big for just one person to have weighing on their conscience.'

They could see the glistening sun reflecting on the windshield of a vehicle, as the sound of what they assumed was one of their friend's cars grew louder. Hal stared at the invisible portal that they knew occupied the space in front of them.

'This is our chance to finally be free Kara,' Hal said softly. 'We can go home. It'll *finally* be over. No one will know what we've done, maybe not even *us*,' he added.

Their friends were so close now, ten more seconds and the decision would be made for them.

Kara and Hal had no more words to share, the choice they had to make was clear. As the cars approached, they knew this was the hardest decision they would ever have to make. All they had to do was do nothing, and they'd be free.

Kara and Hal looked at each other, noticing they both had tears in their eyes. Hal smiled sadly at her, making his intentions clear, and Kara nodded in agreement, smiling back at him.

'*No one will know…*' she said, her voice barely a whisper as she repeated his words.

They watched, as Jon drove through the barrier, causing it to shimmer, as the ripples of their prison reverberated against his car. Jasmine's white car was the next in line to pass through, their past-selves clearly visible in the back seat.

And then, as Jasmine's car moved further and further away from sight, all they could see was the familiar whiteness, as they were erased forever. Nothing more than forgotten whispers in time, themselves becoming barely-formed echoes amidst the vastness of the universe.

CHAPTER FORTY-SEVEN

Heroes and Villains

RI Timestamp Error: Recalculating

Hal was lying on his back in the late-afternoon sun, that was beating down over his garden. He was utterly content, despite not knowing exactly why. He could feel the sun on his arms, the cool breeze ruffling his t-shirt, causing him to sigh deeply.

"This is the life," he thought.

Shaking his box of cigarettes, he could tell that only one remained inside it.

"No matter," he thought, "plenty more where that came from."

Raising his lighter, he lit his cigarette and reached for his phone. Unlocking it, Hal began to scroll through his music, settling on Muse's cover of "Feeling Good." He smirked, as a sense of irony washed over him, and pressed play.

The music filled the garden, as he placed his phone back on the grass next to him. The sky was a clear blue, unmarred by clouds.

"Or fog," he noted to himself.

'A bit on the *nose*, don't you think?'

He opened his eyes, and saw Kara leaning over him, casting a shadow, as she blocked the sunlight. He knew she was referring to his choice in music.

'We did a good thing Kar'. I mean, sure we've totally fucked ourselves over,' said Hal, 'but it was the right choice coming back for Kevin. The only choice really.'

She plonked herself down on the grass next to him, and picked up his phone, studying the vibrant home-screen.

'How much longer do we have?' she asked, trying to learn the new rules.

Before he could answer, the music lowered in

volume, then stopped abruptly, the screen turning black in an instant. The feeling of the afternoon sun against her forehead lessened until, eventually, she could no longer feel it at all. The all-too-familiar static fog appeared from nowhere, engulfing them once again.

'Damn, my bad,' said Hal apologetically, and sitting up. 'I was looking through my photos, must've drained the battery. Fog's back,' he added as an afterthought.

'Yes Hal, I'm aware of things that happen directly around me,' said Kara, with a smirk.

He smiled back, knowing she wasn't really angry, and was just having him on.

They had spent the last two restarts experimenting with their newly-discovered ability to super-charge themselves, ensuring they remained a safe distance away from their past-selves so as not to cause another temporal apocalypse, and doing so had some interesting side-effects. Whilst super-charged, they could interact with living things, albeit minimally. They could also interact with inanimate objects to a much higher degree, even breaking them if they wanted. It was as if their density was increased by the energy, and they were more whole, allowing them to interact with the past over a greater distance. Lastly, it seemed to bring them more in-phase with time itself. The fog retreated for up to several minutes at a time whilst they held a charge, and they could utilise their senses again. They could smell the air, feel the sun on their skin, and for the first time in a long time, they felt hunger, and even fatigue when exerting themselves. Once their retained charge dissipated, however, it was business as usual once again.

'Right,' said Hal, standing up, and pulling his boiler suit back up from around his waist, pushing his arms through the sleeves, and zipping it back up over his black t-shirt. 'I think that's enough practise, I think we're ready. Shall we go top-up and head over to Kevin's? We need to check out the basement.'

It was the reason Kara had approached him in the first place, and so they set off, to look for inspiration on how to prevent Kevin's future imprisonment.

*

For once, they didn't mind waiting for the day to play out, as they killed time waiting for Kevin to return on

Friday evening. They had a lot to unpack after their recent foray into accidentally becoming weapons of mass destruction.

'What did we do?' asked Kara. 'I thought after each restart, the time-loop started all over again?'

Hal looked troubled by this new revelation, he knew she was referring to what they were now calling the "Time Echoes."

Up until now, they had logically assumed that every restart wiped what had come before; namely everything they had done within the thirty-three hours leading to their untimely demise. Having ruptured the continuity of the timeline by overloading it with the blue energy they had been attempting to harness, it appeared the truth was a touch more sinister than they had first suspected.

Every jump they had made into the past had seemingly been catalogued, as evidenced by the appearance of every incarnation of their past-selves to date, who were going about their day, completely oblivious to the existence of their temporally-distorted time-echoes. There even appeared to be instances of things that hadn't happened yet, though it was hard to tell, due to the overwhelming noises surrounding them at the time. Hal was certain he had heard snippets of conversations that he and Kara hadn't even engaged in, as if every single one of their choices was recorded, even the ones they hadn't followed through on.

'Do you think the echoes could see us? Or each other for that matter?' asked Kara.

'I doubt it,' said Hal. 'I mean for one thing, I don't seem to have any new memories of seeing a hundred *us's* roaming around during our earlier restarts, do you?' he asked, genuinely curious.

Kara scrunched up her face, as if doing so would help her scrub through her memories faster, like sliding the progress bar of a video, skipping over the adverts. Eventually, she came to the conclusion Hal was secretly hoping for.

'No, I don't remember seeing a ridiculous amount of Velma's running around.'

'Well that's a relief,' said Hal, 'means we haven't *completely* broken our own timeline.'

'I really thought we were home, that we'd made it back, you know?' said Kara, the sadness in her eyes nearly breaking Hal's heart, as her eyes glistened under the water being generated by her acceptance that it wasn't meant to be.

'I know,' croaked Hal, 'me *too*, Kar'.'

*

Kevin finally arrived, and Hal and Kara followed him into his lodge, watching as he carried out his predetermined routine. He finally made his way to the basement door, and with the basement now unlocked, they headed down the staircase. Hal made his way into the small room that would soon be the lodge owner's prison cell. Meanwhile, Kara remained outside the storage area in the basement, ready to open the door for when their past-selves were in close enough proximity, knowing that they would be *just* close enough the following afternoon, when they went for their walk in the woods.

Kevin closed the storage-cupboard door behind him, locking Hal inside, and retreated upstairs to feed Jerry, encumbered with a large bag of dog food. The Restarters had spent their afternoon siphoning off the energy from their significantly-more-corporeal past-selves, ensuring that they remained in contact with each other, to make sure no displaced energy went to waste. Hal, surrounded in darkness, pulled his phone from his boiler suit, and hesitated before hitting the power button. He was confident the charge would have held, but if he was wrong, it was going to be a long and boring evening for him. Shrugging off the self-doubt, Hal held down the power button, bracing himself for the pang of disappointment. The last time he had tried this was with his lighter, which failed to illuminate his surroundings. Hal surmised that a retained charge *may* just change the way in which light refracted between phased and non-phased objects, but he honestly had no idea of knowing if that would be the case.

The familiar logo appeared on the screen, and he waited impatiently as the phone booted up, then activated the built-in torch function. As the light bathed his surrounding environment in an eerie blue hue, he sighed in relief that his theory held water. Seeing the light from under the threshold of the door, Kara was first to speak.

'So, what do you see?'

'Well, we've got walls…a shelving unit with old

paint tins on it, and a sheet covering–' he placed his hand on the sheet and felt resistance, '–a table I think.'

Kara gave it some thought, running the problem through her mind, trying to envision how anything in that room could help someone who was bound and gagged. She decided to start small.

'Anything around the door frame? A key on the inside on the ledge, or whatever?' said Kara, waiting patiently for a response as he checked.

'Oh yeah, there's a key!' said Hal.

'Really?!'

'Of course not,' said Hal, 'that would be a ridiculous plot-contrivance don't you think?'

Hal checked the power on his phone. It had dropped from one-hundred, to thirty-three percent already. He made a conscious effort to stop wasting time with irreverent sarcasm.

'Okay, we've got three brackets holding the door to the frame…' he ran his fingers over them, checking for anything useful. 'Huh…' he said out-loud to himself.

'What do you see?' asked Kara, hearing his mind

churning.

'We may have a winner,' he said, as the light from his phone died, plunging him back into darkness. 'Go check the table behind you, will you?' he added.

CHAPTER FORTY-EIGHT

The Dog-Walking Dead

59th Restart – Saturday Evening, 8:51pm

The focus for the next two restarts was all on Jerry. They had toyed with the idea of trying to keep him away from the lodge entirely, but could only keep his attention for short periods at a time. The allure of humans who were in-phase enough with his reality were, understandably, far more enticing than them, given that they couldn't offer him food, or a good scratch behind his ear. It was only when they tried to interact with him on Saturday evening, minutes before their death, that they started to yield results.

Walking alongside their past-selves, Jerry was far more attentive. They felt sorry for confusing the poor dog, who must have felt like he was seeing double. Torn between following the instructions of their fully-alive counterparts, and the odd facsimiles that were fighting for his attention.

'Here boy! Sit!' said Hal, accidentally brushing through past-Kara's arm, causing her to shiver.

Jerry stopped, squatted, and then followed past-Hal's instruction to hurry up.

'I think we need to get ahead of ourselves and call him to us,' said Kara, 'this is just confusing the poor little guy, being so close to past-us,' she added, as she pulled her arm inwards, realising she had connected with past-Hal's arm, causing him to pull up the zip on his boiler suit to keep out the cold.

'Yeah, agreed,' said Hal, as he gave up and stopped walking, huffing in frustration. 'Okay, let's go.'

The Restarters ran to Kevin's lodge, edging their way through the open front door, as their killer was exiting the basement, seemingly looking for something in the kitchen. Hal and Kara linked arms, and Hal threw a punch in his direction, passing straight through him, his punch connecting with the wooden wall instead. It caused a slight noise, and The Big Bad looked over his shoulder, drawn by the connection Hal had made with the wall. Ever-so-slightly shaking his head, as if he were imagining things, he continued fishing around in the kitchen drawer.

It was then that the man's ears twitched, reacting to the sounds of talking coming from outside. In a single stride, he made his way to the light switch, killed the lights to the living room, and hid by the wooden beam next to the basement door.

As Hal's past-self entered the cabin, and the knife entered his chest, Hal unlinked his arm from Kara's and broke away from her, striding towards his murderer with an unexpected desperation, and began lashing out wildly.

Maybe it was his proximity to his past self, but Hal suddenly felt a burning in his throat, his eyes filling involuntarily with partially formed tears, unwilling to accept the futility of his actions.

'Don't you touch her!' screamed Hal, as the head of Kara's past-self once more collided with the kitchen unit, his words doing less than nothing to drown out the chaos unfolding around them.

Realising that nothing they did would allow them to interact with their assailant, they closed their eyes and covered their ears, as the final moments of their murder played out yet again.

*

It was now their sixtieth restart and, once again, they took up their positions on their bench.

'You okay?' asked Kara. 'No morning cigarette?'

Hal scoffed. 'They're basically air anyway. I'm quitting.'

'Finally! At least something good might come out of this.'

'Maybe once we get back,' Hal added, immediately caving, and lighting a cigarette.

'Uh huh,' said Kara, now knowing how Hal must have felt, every time she said she was never drinking again. 'So, erm…you were pretty wild back there, trying to take out The Big Bad with a haymaker.'

'Sorry, it just hit me harder than usual, seeing us

like that,' said Hal with a grimace. 'But that does bring us to one hell of an issue. How are we meant to take that guy down? Everything hinges on that. All of our planning will count for shit if we can't find a way around it.'

'I know,' said Kara, nodding gravely. 'But we're closer than we've ever been,' she lied.

'I don't get it,' said Hal. 'We were *so* close to our past-selves, why couldn't we do anything? Maybe we just needed more of a charge?'

'I don't think that would've made a difference,' said Kara sadly. 'I think it was more a case of our past-selves…well, not being in any condition for us to draw energy *from…*' Kara decided not to add "because they were dead" to her sentence, but she could tell Hal understood where she was coming from. 'Happy 60th by the way!' she said brightly, in a further attempt at lifting the mood. 'I got you something.'

'Oh god, has it really been sixty restarts already?' said Hal, realising he had given up on counting a long time ago. 'Wait, you *got* me something? How? What? *When*?!'

'Yup, I've been dabbling in our down-time.'

'You've been *dabbing* in your down time?' said Hal, a forced look of horrified distaste on his face.

'*Dabbling*,' said Kara, knowing he was having her on.

'What is it?' asked Hal, curious as to how she was able to access her Amazon account in this place, let alone arrange for something to be delivered.

'You'll have to just wait and see.'

*

That evening, Kara led Hal to the communal dining area as their friends were digging into some dinner. A rock song was playing from the wireless speaker, as Kara gestured for him to come and stand next to her.

Linking arms with him, he was stunned by the surge of energy, what with their past-selves being less than a metre away. She shot him a wink, raising an extended finger above the phone on the counter, which was feeding the music to the nearby speaker. Slowly, she lowered her finger onto the "skip" button, and a small fizzle of blue energy connected her finger to the device. Glenn Miller's "In the mood" erupted from the speaker, overriding the previous song.

'Ta-daaa!' she said, shaking her hands jazz-hand style, and extending her arms in celebration.

Hal's jaw hit the floor. 'That's…incredible!'

'That's not all. Remember the conversation from Friday night?' said Kara excitedly, jolting her head to indicate he should focus on their friends around the dining table. Conversations began to shift, the mood of the song sending ripples through time, and causing the group to go off on random tangents. Jon and Hal's past-selves began singing the song in an obnoxious manner. Everything was the same, and yet somehow…different.

'The Flutterby Effect,' Hal chuckled, as he saw what she meant. 'You're a genius Kar'!'

Kara shrugged as if it was nothing, trying to hide the fact that his words had made her blush.

'I don't know what effect this will have in the bigger scheme of things,' said Kara, 'but at least we can listen to some different music for a change, right? I know it's not much, but–'

'Kara. Shut up. It's *perfect*, thank you!' said Hal, hugging her for a split second, then releasing her, as both of them were repelled from each other.

'You know,' he continued, 'I usually find this sort of music a bit twee for my taste, but I'm kind of glad Jon brought some of this RAF stuff along with him, it's pretty upbeat.'

'Me too, actually,' said Kara.

And so they spent the rest of their evening, playing around with Kara's discovery, watching the miniscule impact and differences their meddling had on their friends.

*

Before Jerry could interact with the group that Saturday afternoon, Hal and Kara blocked his path. By splitting up, they had managed to trick him to run between them, allowing Kevin to catch up with him sooner, resulting in Kevin not interacting with the group at the barbecue, as he had done countless times before.

With no point of reference, it was their hope that their past-selves wouldn't think to take Jerry home when he came back that evening. However, they soon realised that even a seemingly-huge alteration to their personal timelines was no match for the omnipresent malevolence and tenacity of the surging rivers of time.

Jerry showed up as he always did that evening, but Hal and Kara were waiting at the top of the drive. They managed to secure his attention once again, and began walking him around the outskirts of Fir Lodge.

'This is actually working!' said Kara.

'Yeah! Although we should probably wrap it up,' said Hal. 'If we carry on, we might actually save ourselves. but Kevin still needs us. Not to mention, we need to figure out what to do about the big guy.'

Reluctantly, they guided Jerry back to the entrance of their lodge. Hal sent Kara off to the boundary line to trigger the restart, whilst he remained at Fir Lodge to determine the outcome of their impromptu dog-walking. Hal watched, as past-Kara checked Jerry's name tag, having not done so before in this version of the timeline, and sought the assistance of someone to help her take him back. Due to the knock-on effect of the timing, Hal's past-self was not on hand to assist, and Daisy had offered to assist her instead.

'Crap!' said Hal.

They'd messed up in a huge way, inadvertently putting Daisy in the firing line. He had no idea how close Kara was to the restart point, and all he could do was follow them to Kevin's lodge.

Several minutes later, they were getting dangerously close.

'Come on Kara, come *on*...what's taking you so long?' Hal said to himself.

They were far too close now. Less than a minute away, and Hal began to panic. With his past-self so far away, he could barely keep Jerry's attention, trying to slow them down in an attempt to give his friends the precious seconds they needed.

As Kara's past-self and Daisy approached the driveway of Kevin's home, Hal was forced to run the numbers on what impact it would have if Daisy died instead of him. Would he be free of the restarts? Would Kara keep her memory of everything they had been through? Or would she too be back to square one, with no prior knowledge? Would Daisy restart with her? Or be stranded in a separate hell, occupying a timeline all of her own?

It was then that he heard it; The approaching sound of rushing air, the whiteness thickening around him. But Daisy was already crossing the threshold...

CHAPTER FORTY-NINE

Daisy Chain

61st Restart – Friday Afternoon, 1:24pm

Kara sat there, staring across the garden, until eventually she turned her attention to Daisy, who was laying on the grass in front of her. She had no idea what approach she would use to explain everything to her. There was no easy way to tell someone they had been severed from time, and discarded into an alternate dimension, like a copy of an e-mail, deleted from the recycling bin of the universe, forever unable to be retrieved.

She looked back behind her at Hal, alive and well,

and blissfully unaware of what the future had planned for him, as a voice broke the silence, pulling her back from the nightmare scenario she kept replaying over in her mind, as she searched for the answers that remained eternally out of reach.

'There's no way you could have known that would happen Kara, stop beating yourself up. You don't have to deal with this alone.'

She remained silent, not willing to forgive herself for what she had done.

'There's no way *either* of us could have known,' added Hal.

'We nearly killed her, Hal. We nearly sentenced her to a lifetime here. All because we were playing with forces we should have left *well* alone,' said Kara, once again tormenting herself over how close they had left it to the designated restart time. It was idiotic, and they should have known better.

'I know,' he whispered, as he took another drag on his cigarette. 'We'll do better next time. We'll be more care–'

'No,' said Kara, cutting him off. 'We became complacent. Maybe we just need to accept that this is what is *meant* to happen. We haven't even *entertained* the possibility that we were *meant* to die!'

Maybe the reason they couldn't change anything was because that, if they did, if they *truly* succeeded, there would have to be a price…a life for a life.

'I'm not prepared to make a deal with the devil to get our lives back, are you?' said Kara, with an intensity that caused her whole body to shake.

'Of course not!' said Hal, deeply hurt by the accusation.

Their mutual silence allowed the severity of their mistake to wash over them, until Kara finally broke the deafening quietness.

'Do you think they're trapped here?' she asked, pointing towards their friends. 'Locked in time, destined to repeat themselves, over and over again?'

Hal had given this some thought, and whilst the logical probability did little to ease his mind, he needed to bring Kara back from this precipice of self-doubt.

'No…' he said finally. 'I think Sunday rolls around, they realise we're missing…they look for us. They call the police. But ultimately, I think they go home. Live long lives, and learn to live without us.'

'That's…as heart-breaking as it is reassuring,' said Kara. 'I don't want them to be trapped here like we are.'

'I know, right. I just can't imagine this…bubble, or restart, or whatever you want to call it, holding everyone inside it indefinitely,' said Hal.

'Maybe that's what the fog is all about,' proposed Kara. 'When it finally consumes everything, taking us with it, maybe it ends. It'll all be over.'

'If that's true,' said Hal, 'what do you think will happen to *us* when that time finally comes? When our time literally runs out?'

And they thought about that for the rest of the restart, too scared to meddle with the past, afraid to roll the dice at the expense of their friend's safety.

One thing was certain. They were adamant that never again would they play with the lives of others so flippantly. If they were going to make any changes at all, they would do it carefully, deliberately and calculate the end results, ensuring they would take into account even the smallest, seemingly insignificant, of details.

CHAPTER FIFTY

For Pete's Sake

98th Restart – Saturday Evening, 8:45pm

They hit the ground running on their ninety-eighth restart. Their nearly-fatal mistake with Daisy had changed the way they approached almost everything. They became experts of their own past, paying attention to even the most seemingly-meaningless of conversations, learning where everyone was at all times, as if studying an artificially-intelligent simulation, looking for weak spots in the code.

One thing they couldn't help but notice was the

static fog, which was somehow even more menacing than ever. They thought it had been bad before, but there were even more insidious side-effects to their exposure to it.

At around their seventy-fifth restart, they noticed that it had become difficult for them to concentrate. At first, they had put it down to trial and error, and had assumed that, given the amount of information they were attempting to memorise, it was to be expected that they would become forgetful over certain facts and timings. It soon became clear, however, that they were finding it harder to focus during certain restarts. Their minds would wander, replaying memories prior to when the time-jumps had started, daydreaming about a life post-restart, and getting lost in the illusion.

They had discovered that one constant could keep them grounded though, and that was music. Whilst the voices of their friends became increasingly muffled and muted, music tore through the fog like a blade. They found that they could keep themselves anchored to the task at hand, so long as they concentrated on a track that was playing. They had also learned that sticking together helped negate the effects, and they relied on each other to correct false-memories when they presented themselves.

It started off small; they would struggle to find the words they needed to finish their sentences. But as the side-effects took a stronger hold on them, the severity of their plight became increasingly more distressing. During one restart in particular, Hal had forgotten some of the surnames of their friends, followed by their ages. But as long as there was music, their plan always came flooding back to them. Charging themselves also helped, it forced the mist to retreat, and gave them a clarity of thought they desperately needed when making important decisions.

It was during one of their more charged moments that they remembered a crucial encounter, that seemed more like a bad dream than an actual memory; the incident with Peter, in Robert's room. They had planned, and then unwillingly forgotten, to follow up on this issue multiple times now. It was time to rectify that once and for all.

They followed Peter for the entirety of the restart, but spotted nothing that would indicate anything was leading up to a temporal anomaly of any kind. Eventually, the restart had led them to Robert's bedroom, as Peter arrived to borrow a phone charger. Peter slumped against the wall, and his eyes began to ripple with a familiar blue energy.

'So erm…what's the play here?' asked Hal, feeling embarrassingly ill-equipped to deal with the situation they were presented with.

Kara shrugged. 'He's clearly channelling the same energy that we're bound to. He's connected to this place somehow.'

'I mean, shall we just link arms and dive right *in* there, or...?' suggested Hal, unable to provide a suitable alternative. Kara didn't have any better ideas either, so they linked their arms, continuing to deliberate, as a familiar energy surged through them, their proximity to past-Hal giving them a notable spike in potency.

'Allons-y,' said Hal, as he placed his right hand on Peter's temple, as if he was performing some kind of Vulcan mind-meld. Kara mimicked the action, placing her left hand on Peter's right temple.

Their stomachs lurched in unison, as the colour

from their surroundings was sucked away. Everything was present and correct, only painted in an immaculate white. They were met by the terrifying sight of two, pitch-black silhouettes, which were connected to Peter and standing directly next to them. One of the outlines was pressed against Peter's body, seemingly holding him in place, the other had their hands plunged directly into Peter's brain.

The entities were made up entirely of a swirling darkness, and were in complete contrast to the surrounding whiteness, as ripples of blue energy exploded from their hands, just as it did from Hal and Kara's. Suddenly, the taller of the two dark figures turned its head and looked directly at the Restarters.

Straightening up, the figure towering over them both, the featureless face began leaning in towards Hal, clearly disturbed by their presence and eager to get a better look at the intruders.

That was quite enough for Hal, who promptly pulled away from Peter, gasping for breath, and utterly spooked by the horror of what he had witnessed.

'What the actual *fuck* was that?' said Hal. 'Did you

see that?! Those *things*? Was that *us*?'

Kara staggered backwards, her arms in a protective pose around her body, the shock of what she had witnessed clearly hitting her just as hard.

'I don't…they didn't have a face. It was just…pure nothingness!' she said, shaking a little.

Facing Kara, Hal was still standing relatively close to Peter, who casually spoke faintly into Hal's ear. 'Still…s-sorry.'

'Argh!' shouted Hal, jumping backwards. 'If that's time travel humour, I am NOT loving it! Can we get the hell out of here please? That's about as much weird-ass shit as I can handle right now.'

On cue, Peter came back to life, seemingly unaffected by any form of temporal dysplasia, and grabbed a charger, plugged in his phone, then happily left the room. Hal and Kara slipped out behind him, their past-selves now well on their way to taking Jerry home.

'You know, in hindsight,' said Kara, 'our plan to *not* follow this up, so as to prevent the possibility we were involved, seems like the right call.'

'Well, too late now Kar',' said Hal, 'we're through

the bloody looking-glass on this one. I think we should steer clear of him from now on. That was messed up.'

'Yuh-huh,' agreed Kara, not wishing to visit that otherworldly version of Fir Lodge ever again. 'And I thought *restarts* were weird, that place was a full-on hell-scape!' she added.

Eventually, they had to accept that there was no explanation for what they had seen. They waited for the restart to claim them, in the hope that it would wash away the heebie-jeebies they were currently saturated with, both in agreement that Robert's room was officially out of bounds from here on out.

CHAPTER FIFTY-ONE

A Fistful of Restarts

100th Restart – Friday Afternoon, 12:17pm

Kara and Hal had spent their ninety-ninth restart preparing for the tasks ahead. It was finally time to transition from talking about what needed to be done, to actually implementing their decision. They had been putting it off for a reason, not least because they had no idea on how they were going to stop their murderer; a living entity, that was out-of-phase with the time and space they were occupying. The second reason was more a question of existential morality. Even if they could kill him, should they? They reasoned that, in the end, it came down to one simple fact; it was self-defence. Though they both felt the justification was still a little tenuous. The defining factor was that it wasn't just themselves they were trying to save anymore, it was Kevin as well. That fact alone made it a mathematical question, rather than an ethical one. How many more would fall to the whim of their killer, if they allowed him to continue on his current course?

Once they made the conscious, mutual decision of what needed to be done, next came the how. It was time to see just how much power they truly wielded. It was time to stop holding back.

*

Hal found it difficult to physically accost his friends, despite Kara's argument that the act would restart anyway, and that it would literally be erased from time. In her eyes, this meant it didn't count. Hal, however, wasn't so convinced.

'Bloody hell Hal, you literally killed Robert, Rachel *and* Alex! Why are you being such a baby about this?' said Kara, laughing at his plight, whilst curled up in a ball beside the hot-tub directly behind

Jon, who turned suddenly, and tripped over her in spectacular fashion.

'It just feels wrong man, I can't explain why,' said Hal. 'I think I'll focus on my past-self instead.'

'Are you sure that's such a great idea, I mean the last time we did that, we nearly erased ourselves entirely,' said Kara, a look of concern on her face, as she remembered her friends fleeing to the edge of town, where the barrier resided. She shuddered, as she remembered the time-echoes.

'It'll be different this time, you and I won't be connected,' said Hal unconvincingly.

With the retained charge that they had spent the early hours of the morning building upon, he ran at his past-self, who was minding his own business, sitting on their favourite picnic bench, finishing his second cup of coffee. Hal threw a punch, aiming for his own face. As it connected, a blue shockwave rippled across the garden, and all the way through the lodge. Hal's past-self recoiled in agony from the broken jaw he had just sustained, as his Restarter self was thrown fifty-yards into the air, and into a nearby hedge.

'Jeeze Hal, way to start small,' said Kara.

'Oh god, they're going to take me to a hospital, aren't they?' said Hal, referring to his friends, as Jon rushed over to see what was wrong with Hal's past-self. Kara winced at the sight of past-Hal's jaw, which was drooping lazily.

'Restart point?' suggested Kara.

'Restart point,' agreed Hal.

*

Will lined up his shot, resolute in his prediction that he would be able to sink the yellow, despite his distance from the pocket. He pulled back the cue and aimed true, but as he moved to strike the ball he felt a sharp push in the small of his back, causing him to collapse onto the pool table. His cue falling to the floor, Will turned and looked behind him, as Jon stared, and then erupted with laughter at him.

'Damn Jon, that hurt mate!' said Will.

'I didn't touch you,' said Jon, 'that was all you.'

As Will clambered up off the table, he slipped on his pool cue, smashing his head into the table, and falling to the ground with a sickly thud.

'Eesh, that doesn't look good. Restart point?'

suggested Hal.

*

As Robert ran frantically around the garden, the flames billowing across his apparently highly-flammable Santa costume, it occurred to Kara that landing an uppercut infused with interdimensional energy, whilst Robert was standing in front of a barbecue, was clearly one of her more reckless moves. Eventually, Robert collapsed in a burning heap, as their friends tried to extinguish the flames.

Hal and Kara stood there covering their mouths, feeling terrible that they'd now killed Robert *twice* since they got here. A curmudgeonly Santa Clause startled them from behind, catching them completely off-guard. This time, Robert was wearing his full Santa outfit, not just swim-shorts and a hat.

'Worst. Magic trick. *Ever*,' said Robert.

'Robert?! You're here? Wait, what magic trick?' said Hal, unnerved by the trauma of seeing Kara having just killed him.

'The fog routine?' said Robert. 'You both disappeared. Clearly a smoke machine. Hey what's that over there? Why is everyone screaming? And why is it daytime now?'

Hal pursed his lips as he tried to find the words. 'Erm…Okay don't get mad…but Kara just killed you.'

'That was totally not my fault,' interjected Kara. 'If anything, you need to sue the costume company for…wait, you remember the last time we spoke?'

'You *killed* me?! That's like…a euphemism, right? And yeah, of course I remember, it was literally a few seconds ago.'

'If anything, you mean "metaphor",' said Hal, 'and no, you are, quite literally, dead. Again. First one was on me, sorry bud. But on the bright side, at least Kara and I are even now,' he added.

'What are you talking about?!' said Robert, unable to wrap his head around what was happening, and becoming even more irritable than usual. 'And why is there a fire in the middle of the garden?'

'Tell you what mate, better if I show you. Fancy a walk to the edge of town?' said Hal, as they dragged him away from getting too close to his own burning corpse.

*

'Interesting don't you think?' said Hal, giving no indication as to what he was referencing.

'That we haven't killed anyone today? I'd agree, but the day *is* young…' noted Kara forebodingly.

'Yeah, I mean, that too obviously, but I was thinking more about how Robert seemed to remember his first restart with us?'

Kara shrugged. 'Nothing surprises me about this place anymore. If anything, it just highlights how little we really know about how time works here.'

'Plus, his clothes? He was in costume,' said Hal. 'Not just wearing those fetching shorts of his. Someone really needs to run a course on the…' Hal paused, as he concentrated hard to put the sentence together, then continued. 'Chronological implications of interdimensional phase-shifting,' he said proudly.

Kara found it worrying that sentences like that were effortlessly deciphered when they reached her ears nowadays. Their adventuring through time had seen to that.

'Oh yeah, bet that would sell like hot cakes,' said Kara, implying a course of that nature would not indeed garner as much interest as freshly-baked treats.

'Well, I think we're ready, don't you?' said Hal, standing up from his seat at the picnic table, and stretching. 'Enough practise. We need to put everything we've learnt into the correct order and see what we have.'

Kara gave him two thumbs up, knowing that his optimism was misplaced. Now they knew exactly what they were going to do, setting things in motion to get there in the right order was going to take far more restarts than even Kara could have predicted.

CHAPTER FIFTY-TWO

Tequila Killer

165th Restart – Friday Afternoon, 12:01pm

With a rush of air, and a brief trip through the white oblivion that lay between the edges of time, separating presumably countless timelines from each other, ensuring the stability of reality as humans perceived it remained immaculately-intact, they landed without the faintest sense of queasiness. Hal set off on his customary brisk walk to nowhere in particular, stopping after a few metres, and turned to face Kara.

'Wow, tensing your stomach really helps with re-entry!' noted Hal, remembering the early days, when it made him want to throw up the non-existent contents of his temporally-displaced stomach.

'Yeah,' agreed Kara, thinking that it would almost be a shame if they managed to pull off their plans on this restart, never getting to take advantage of that little gem a second time.

'You've finally nailed the Time-Traveller-Landing by the way,' she added.

'Really?!' said Hal, his smile positively beaming. 'You wouldn't just say that would you?'

It was then that the unexpected eeriness of their most-visited holiday destination, albeit by default, hit him like a truck. 'Holy shit, the fog…it's–'

'Erasing everything!' said Kara, finishing his sentence for him, as she stared out into the bleached-white yonder.

They took in their surroundings with expressions that were equal part wonder, and barely concealed fear, as Will's car pulled up onto the driveway of Fir Lodge. Only this time, the car appeared to be a dark grey, instead of the vibrant-red they knew it should have been.

As Will exited his car, his words were a barely-audible muffle, though Fleetwood could still be heard, booming through the gloom from the car speakers, as clear as their vision was obscured. Upon closer inspection, it wasn't just the fog that was hindering their vision, everything in their vicinity seemed to lack detail. It was as if someone had smudged the edges of the lodge, the cars, trees, and even the shingle beneath their feet. The voices of their friends had also been affected, as if they were covering their mouths and making strange noises, rather than using fully formed words. For a horrifying moment, Kara wondered if their friends were actually talking in a dialect she didn't understand, or if that dialect was actually English, she'd just forgotten how to speak it…

As their past-selves arrived, Hal and Kara were shocked to see they could hear them just fine. Still blurry visually, and their clothing devoid of any notable colour, they took comfort in the fact they were clearly in-sync just enough to their past so as not to be completely disconnected from it. For all their planning, they now had to contend with the obstacle of the removed audio-cues they had been utilising to keep track of precisely when, and where, they needed to be, for their carefully mapped-out plan to work, as *well* as decreased visibility. Not for the first time, they wondered what exactly they had done to piss off the universe so much.

*

As they prepared, for what they feared would be their last chance at attempting a flawless run of their mission, they took the opportunity to voice any last-minute concerns or curveballs they thought they might encounter. If their plan worked, there was no telling what would happen to this version of themselves, or if they would retain their memories.

'Do you think we'll just disappear?' asked Hal, as he lit his first cigarette of what he hoped would be his final three. 'I mean, if we prevent the events that brought us here in the first place, we should just cease to exist right? Our past-selves should continue on, none the wiser.'

Kara shrugged.

'Or worse, maybe we'll stay here forever,' said Kara. 'I can't imagine time just allowing us to return to the present, not with the all the knowledge we've gained. There's probably a reason no one has ever spoken of an experience like we've had before. Maybe the reason we've never heard of it is because–'

'No one's ever made it back,' said Hal.

Not wishing to allow that sentence to hang in the air any longer, he promptly put an end to it.

'I don't think that'll happen Kar', It's more likely that once our past-selves step over the boundary line, the loop should end. On top of that, we wouldn't be harbouring *time-secrets* if we were never here to experience them in the first place.'

They sat there quietly for a while, mulling over the countless possibilities. The truth was, it didn't matter what the future held for them, it didn't change the fact that their plan was the only thing they had left to keep them going. Without a goal to work towards, they were little more than time-echoes themselves, and they refused to accept that they were nothing but forgotten residual memories, floating through a timeline that not only didn't want them, but had put a full-stop on their respective destinies altogether.

*

It was their one hundred and sixth fifth restart, which meant that they had been jumping through time for almost a year, give or take. With their intention being never to return after the events they were planning to instigate the following evening, they spent their Friday charging themselves, and listening to music, which helped them greatly with maintaining their focus. Whilst charged, the fog retreated for short bursts, which allowed them to concentrate more succinctly on the precise order of events they would need to set in motion.

As their friends turned in for the evening, in the early hours of Saturday morning, they had waited for Jasmine to get her evening glass of water and return to bed, not wanting to frighten her again. With Hal's past-self and Jasmine finally out of the picture, they were free to occupy the kitchen in peace. The kitchen of the lodge being directly above the sweet-spot between the rooms that Kara and Hal were occupying in the past made it an equally ideal location to continue charging the powerful blue-energy for the day ahead of them.

It was then, that an unusual idea occurred to

Kara, as she spotted the various bottles of spirits lining the kitchen counter. She smirked mischievously, and made her way to the alcohol.

Sticking her tongue out slightly to concentrate, she reached for the bottle of Tequila she'd bought over three hundred days ago, and pulled it towards herself on the counter. Hal was curious to see where her thought process was leading her, and leaned against the island in the centre of the kitchen, a raised eyebrow of perplexity on his face.

Kara marched onwards, using her finger to rest on the edge of a shot-glass, moving it closer to the bottle. She repeated the process with a second shot-glass, then tilted her head to the side, as if to indicate she needed some more charge. Checking over his shoulder to ensure Peter, Fearne, Will, and Stacey were still sleeping soundly on their sofa beds at the other end of the lodge, Hal kicked off from the island he was leaning on, and placed his hand on her shoulder.

A respectable surge of energy coursed through them, and Kara seized the opportunity it afforded her, by quickly unscrewing the cap of the liquor bottle, causing it to fall towards the counter, which Hal caught in his free hand to prevent it falling onto the stainless-steel sink.

They couldn't risk anything waking their friends, it could lead to them having to restart, and they honestly didn't know how many more restarts they had left at their disposal.

'Nice catch,' she said.

'Thanks,' he replied softly.

Holding the neck of the bottle, she attempted to lift it off of the counter. With his free Hand, Hal supported the bottle from underneath, and in one swift motion they tilted the bottle, filling one glass, then the other. In unison, they returned the bottle to its upright position, and then pushed the bottle back into the corner, not bothering to mess around with putting the cap back on.

'I'm not even sure if we'll be able to retain the liquid,' said Kara, 'but I think it's pretty clear that, one way or another, this could end up being one of, if not *the* last restarts,' said Kara, 'and I'm sure as hell not leaving before I have at least one more shot of tequila.'

'Uh huh,' said Hal, 'figures.'

Kara punched him in the arm playfully, and they positioned their hands closer to the shot-glasses.

'We should toast to something,' said Kara.

Hal nodded, as a troubled look crept across his face.

'What's up?' asked Kara, sensing something was wrong. If Hal had any doubts or concerns, she'd rather know about them now, rather than out in the field.

'We joked before, when we brought Alex and Rachel to us, you called it a "Time Heist", remember?'

'Umm, *yeah*,' said Kara, 'I remember, because it was an awesome name that I came up with. What about it?'

'Very awesome,' said Hal, smiling weakly. 'But a few hours from now? That's going to be the real deal. We're essentially trying to *trick* time, before it has a chance to catch up with us. We're stealing our lives back Kara. Do you…do you think it will really work?'

Kara inhaled deeply, turning her gaze to the night sky, visible through the kitchen window. What he was really asking her was if the two of them had what it would take to pull the rug out from underneath a force that had stalked them relentlessly. A power that had hindered them at almost every turn, and reclaimed them more times than she could count. They had even been shown a display of their failed attempts in a visible form, when they had witnessed their time-echoes, playing out the decisions they had made, and perhaps even decisions they were yet to make. Kara exhaled, then turned back to face her friend, ready to address his concerns.

'It's going to work Hal. Because we're not the *echoes*, we're *The Restarters*,' said Kara, in a tone that was so resolute with certainty, that it almost made Hal wonder why he had experienced any form of doubt in the first place.

'Well shit,' said Hal, 'I'll drink to that. On three?'

Kara nodded, and they began the downward count from three. As they reached the designated numerical checkpoint, they both then reached out for their glasses, and downed their shots, gently placing the glasses back on the counter.

'Wow,' said Hal, 'someone really needs to patent

Temporally-distorted Tequila!'

'Smooth, right?!' said Kara.

And with that, they made their way to their chosen sofas in the communal living area, safe in the knowledge that someone would clear up the two splashes of Tequila that were currently lining the kitchen floor, feeling only mildly guilty knowing that it would probably be Rachel or Jasmine who would draw the short, metaphoric straw.

CHAPTER FIFTY-THREE

Best Laid Plans

165th Restart – Saturday Evening, 8:47pm

Hal and Kara had no trouble shaking off the innate desire to over-analyse the existential paradox of seeing themselves several minutes before their untimely death, and decided instead to refocus their attention onto the next phase of their plan.

"Okay," thought Hal, taking stock. With Kara's past-self clearing up the spillage from the bottle he had knocked off the table upstairs, and Stacey blocking past-Kara from using the stairs, combined with Hal's past-self conversing with Robert in the rear garden, they had earned a thirty-nine-second head-start. This meant they were on the right track to ensuring their killer would have headed back down to the basement by the time their past-selves arrived at Kevin's. But all *that* would count for nothing, if they were unable to nail the next part of the plan.

Kara mouthed the word "Go" at Hal, but he knew precisely when and where he needed to be, shooting off into the night.

Her eyes glazed over, as the conversation between her and Hal's past-selves played out before her as it always did. Leading to the *conclusion* it always did. Leading to them agreeing, as they *always bloody did*, that it was too dark to just lock Jerry outside and that, as always, they would be worried for the poor little guy's safety *blah blah blah*, she thought to herself.

She wasn't sure if this restart was moving slower than the rest, or if she was just utterly fed up with the boringly-repetitive nature of the conversation.

And then, after a single minute in real time, but what had felt like one hundred restarts all rolled into one for Kara, their past-selves had eventually decided on the outcome that, unbeknownst to them, was irrevocably inevitable. Kara wearily gave a second, half-hearted salute, this time to herself, at their unparalleled decisiveness.

'Go team,' she said to the fog.

'Go team!' said past-Kara, a split-second later, causing the Restarter to raise an eyebrow.

"Well, that's new…" she thought, then refocused her mind, concentrating on the music.

Her next task was dead simple; distract Jerry at specific intervals to give Hal the time he needed to ensure everything happened precisely *when* it needed to. All she had to do was concentrate. Focus on the music. And then she experienced a sensation of true terror.

"What's my last name?!" she thought, her heart suddenly beating in her chest ten times faster than it ought to have been.

She hopped onto the edge of the pool table, accidentally potting the black ball with her arse, causing Will to win the game by default. Jon began barking something about how Will must have knocked the table. Had Kara been paying attention, she would have noticed that the fog was thickening in density. But she was lost in her own memories now, desperately trying to kick-start the specific cerebral-synapse that would grant her access to her full name.

Her past-self had departed with Hal and Jerry, just about the time she'd first noticed her missing memory, and were now well on their way. As her ability to form new thoughts was gradually taken from her, she fleetingly wondered if she was merely a time-echo after all. Doomed to repeat the thirty-three hours leading to her death on a continuous loop, no different from the countless shimmering outlines of herself that she had seen when she and her friend...

What was his name?

Had...done...*something*...

But her thoughts were refusing to form fully, her mind becoming too foggy for her to remember.

*

Hal raced up the winding roads, flitting between the shadows of the trees like a flash of lightning, seemingly tapping into the force of speed itself. Despite still being partially charged, his stamina felt boundless, perhaps due to how much was at stake. Though he much preferred running without a charge at all. One of the rad things about being stuck in a Punxsutawney purgatorial paradox was that you could run as long as you wanted, without getting a stitch, regardless of how out of shape you were. The other cool thing was that you could get away with using words like "rad" without being judged by others.

Hal flew through the woods like a bullet, winged a dozen or so turns and finally arrived at Kevin's lodge. Racing up the driveway, he tried to ignore the eerie lack of audible feedback that should have been emanating from the displaced shingle beneath his feet, realising that he would clearly never get used to that.

The front door was open, as it always was, helpfully pushed open by Jerry before he had departed. Apart from that one time during their one-hundred-and-twenty-third restart. Hal cast his mind back to that day. They'd managed to position themselves just close enough to their past-selves to free Kevin from his restraints, but it was too little too late. They still ended up falling victim to–

"Shit. Focus!" thought Hal, slapping himself around the face. The here and now was all that

mattered. "*Or should that be here and then…*"

He slapped himself again, and ran through the front door. Their killer had just finished clearing the remnants of the plate that had fallen from the kitchen counter and was transferring the pieces from a dustpan into the kitchen bin. They never did manage to find out what had caused that plate to fall and it still bothered Hal.

Kara reasoned that sometimes a falling plate was just a falling plate. It was more than likely that Hal was starting to see patterns where there weren't any.

The killer let out an irksome sigh and stared out of the window into the mild illumination afforded by the kitchen light. Hal's defiant face reflected back at him, as Hal stood behind the killer's left shoulder. Not that his adversary could see him of course.

Now it was all up to his fellow Restarter.

'Run, Kara…*run*,' he whispered.

CHAPTER FIFTY-FOUR

The Jaws of Time

165th Restart – Saturday Evening, R.I

Timestamp Error: Recalculating

The music brought her back, though she had no idea how long she'd been gone.

'Crap! Run, Kara...*run*!' she said to herself, claiming ownership of the here and now once more.

Hal was depending on her to distract Jerry to give him the time he needed to bring The Big Bad back down into the basement. She flew to the front entrance, which was mercifully still open, and across the driveway of Fir Lodge. With a sigh of relief, she could see her past-self only just stepping off the yellow, shingled road and taking the left turn that led to her imminent death.

She clenched her fists, pulling herself together. Everything they'd been through together had led to tonight. They'd thought of everything, and nothing had been left to chance.

'*Not an echo*,' she said, spitting the words as if they were poison.

She ran ahead of her past-self, and stopped at the first checkpoint, calling for Jerry, moderating her tone into a soothing purr.

'Hey Jerry! Oh, good *boy*!' she said, as he trotted over to her. She stroked him gently, her tangibility greatly increased thanks to her super-charged molecular composition.

Jerry didn't seem to mind the coolness that ran through him under her touch, rolling onto his back and kicking his little legs at her hand in a playful manner. Not for the first time, she wondered if all dogs were interacting with other Restarters when they rolled around on their backs like this, seemingly playing on their own. She and Hal had remained in contact for every spare second they had, when they weren't busy manipulating the day's events.

She refocused her mind, suddenly aware that she was drifting again, replaying things she knew, over and over in her brain. Hal was of the opinion that it was an indication of how they could tell they were getting close to winning, that *time* was fighting back, that it knew what they were up to. Kara was more cynical. She knew deep down it was just a matter of restarts before they were erased forever, and that there would be no more do-overs. The reason for which–

"Dammit," she thought, slapping her face.

Kara continued to delay Jerry, and by extension, past-Hal and past-Kara, at four more designated points. This gave the Restarters the precious seconds they needed for the final stage of their plan.

The *Big* One.

Not for the first time, she wondered if they would be able to live with themselves once the dust settled. Of course, that was assuming *any* of what came next would actually work at all.

With the last stalling tactic complete, she ran to

Kevin's lodge for what she hoped would be the last time. She wasn't religious by any extent of the imagination, but her agnostic sensibilities were leaves in the wind to her now, and she prayed for the strength she was going to need for the upcoming battle.

*

Hal watched in silence, as the serial killer grabbed the scissors he was searching for from the kitchen drawer. Hal continued to stare, as the man turned, then made his way back down to the basement. It was at this point, in Hal's original timeline, that his soon-to-be killer had heard them approaching, utilising the darkness as a cloak to remain invisible.

Hal winced, then breathed out through his nose, jaw-clenched, as he realised Kara had successfully delayed their past-selves *just* enough. They'd spent countless restarts getting this part right, but this was the first time they were able to test the perfect sweet-spot out in the wild. They would only get one attempt at orchestrating the perfect storm.

Staring at Kevin's four-minutes-fast wall-mounted clock, Hal noted that the actual time was 9:01pm.

Only they weren't dead. Hal had secretly hoped that just surviving beyond their original time of death would have been enough to end it all. However, the fact he was still present, and engaging in these thoughts at all, proved that he was wrong. There was only one way to finish this.

The downside of reliving the same period of time, over and over, was that as soon as the timeline altered, the Restarters were effectively powerless. They had no way of knowing for sure what would happen next, having no point of reference. So, it was in this precise moment, as the beast faced the basement door and hesitated, like a shark catching the scent of blood across a vast expanse of water, that Hal was just as blind to the future as any normal person.

The man cocked his head to one side, then the other, as if lifting his opposite ear to try harder. Hal continued to hold his out-of-phase breath and realised, for the first time, that he didn't feel a burning sensation in his lungs. This late in the game, he shot a dark smile towards their killer at the utterly pointless discovery; Hal didn't need to breath at all.

“Who knew,” he thought wryly.

It had taken them five restarts alone just to get this moment right. They had underestimated the man’s abilities before. Adding to his shark-like traits, he seemed to be able to read the environment, attuning his senses to his surroundings like nothing they had ever seen. Only this time there was nothing but silence for the predator to work with, causing Hal’s smile to widen.

‘Nice work Kara, right on time,’ he whispered, elated that their persistence had paid off, but still not brave enough to talk loudly in such close proximity to the animal before him.

‘Now open the door you piece of shi–’ but his sentence was cut short, as Kara slipped through the open front door. Hal had a momentary disconnect, and for a split-second thought it was the wrong Kara entering the cabin.

‘Jeeze Kar’ I thought that was–’

‘The other me. You say that *every* time,’ she said in a bored tone. ‘Have a little faith.’

‘Says the atheist,’ said Hal dryly. ‘And to be fair, sixty percent of the time, it’s the *wrong* you *every* time.’

'Agnostic actually. Settle down Burgundy. Head's up, he's going for the basement door!'

'Oh!' said Hal excitedly, 'say it!'

'I'm *not* saying it, it's stupid,' said Kara, with stubborn resolution.

Hal gave her a brief attempt at puppy-dog eyes, and she caved like a bad soufflé, adopting a lifeless tone of indifference.

'Oh for *fu*…fine. *Open the pod-bay doors please, Hal.*'

Smiling like an idiot, he waved his hand with his fingers and thumb in an "L" shape, like a knight of an old republic, using an unseen force. Hal's action coincided perfectly with their killer, as he finally seemed to accept that there was no prey in the vicinity and opened the door to the basement.

Hal and Kara swooped in behind him, passing through his arm as they did so, though the man didn't shiver. Not for the first time, Hal wondered if this man was even human at all, as they descended into the dimly-lit cavern of death below.

Kara saw no point in stating out loud what she was thinking; that only time would tell if they were destined to succeed. After all, time already knew.

CHAPTER FIFTY-FIVE

Blue Lanterns

165th Restart – Saturday Evening, 9:03pm

There was an unnerving stillness to their surroundings, as the basement door closed behind them. For a few seconds, it was as if they were peeking behind the curtain, whole once again, and fully in-phase with time.

It had taken them one-hundred and sixty-five restarts to get this far, the odds had seemed eternally stacked against them. They felt like they were breaking countless rules just by being here; at a point in time that they hoped was as pliable as they needed it to be, and not carved in stone like they secretly suspected.

To the best of their knowledge, no one had ever attempted something like this before; manipulating the flow of time, to change the destiny of not only themselves, but for Kevin too. Potentially, they could be saving countless others in the process. The ripples their actions would surely cause, from the present and into the future, were mind-boggling to Hal. The Restarters were the personification of the flutterby wings that were about to cause a tornado, one that was monumental in scale.

Their intervention, in terms of cause and effect, would not be isolated to just one location either, they could be changing the world in ways far beyond their ability to predict or comprehend. As their retained charge diminished, the thick static fog that had hounded them since the early days returned, slowly but surely, permeating through the walls, obscuring their vision, and clouding their minds once again. It had taken them many restarts to learn *exactly* how long they could operate before the blue energy depleted fully from their out-of-phase bodies, and they were relieved that they had timed it perfectly. They needed to be powerless for what came next.

'It's gone,' said Hal.

'For a second there, I thought the charge was *never* going to leave us,' said Kara.

'And we're still here…' said Hal.

'Which means,' said Kara, 'we have no choice. We have to take the next step.'

Their faces turned a little green at the prospect, as they looked down the stairs into the darkness below.

'Kara, I…' Hal was struggling to the find the words.

After all the time they had shared together, hurtling through time from restart to restart, he felt a sharp pang over all of the things that had been left unsaid. How he couldn't have made it this far without her working the problem with him, how the oppressive *feel* of their self-contained time-bubble would have surely driven him insane without her constant support. But, perhaps most importantly of all, how everything they had achieved together had finally brought him a mere hop, skip, and a time-jump away from seeing Jess again, something that literally would have been impossible had he been stuck here alone.

He must have conveyed all of these feelings through the look he gave her, because she was looking back at him in exactly the same way. She didn't have to say anything at all, no words were necessary.

It was then that they heard the voices of the only two people in this timeline they could still hear clearly through the dense fog. Their past-selves were close, the delay tactics they had implemented officially expunged. Their killer had clearly heard them too, deep in the dim light, being cast by a bulb that surely could have done with being a higher wattage, they could see his tell-tale, shark-like, jerking head-movement, as he listened intently.

Grabbing a menacingly large knife, the killer made his way back towards the staircase they were still standing on.

Hal pulled up the collar on his boiler suit, and tried to click his neck by turning his head in a circular motion, the dramatic effect he was going for not lost on Kara.

"Ever the showman," she thought to herself with a smile.

Then, pulling a thousand-yard-stare in their target's direction, she looked over the rim of her detective glasses, dramatically pushing them up the bridge of her nose, much to the delight of Hal.

'Let's go to work,' said Hal, impersonating his favourite iconic vampire with a soul from the early two-thousands.

'Time to make it rain,' said Kara, like a gritty, time-travelling superhero.

'Oh, that was *great*!' said Hal. 'Did you practice that, like was it prepared before-hand or did you just freestyle–'

'Hal, the killer?' said Kara, motioning towards the monstrous hulk of a man that was making his way towards them.

'I ruined the moment, didn't I?'

'Little bit,' said Kara.

'Dammit.'

And with that, it was time.

*

As their past-selves drew ever closer to Kevin's lodge,

Hal and Kara took up position around the serial killer, who was staring up at the ceiling, seemingly judging whether to ascend the staircase, or remain down in the basement. Hal stood in front of him, with Kara getting into position behind. As the beast took a step towards the staircase, the Restarters realised it was now or never.

Plunging his hand through the monster's chest, he signalled for Kara to grab onto it from the other side of their target. As their fingers interlocked, the blue energy shimmered erratically. Kara realised she needed to move closer, slowly moving her hand back to the area of space where their murderer's heart resided, pulling Hal along with her. As their past-selves drew closer, the energy intensified, electricity coiling and spiralling like the surface of a miniature, blue sun.

The demon growled, apparently settling on the decision to ascend the stairs, but remained in place, moving incredibly slowly. Either he was caught in an internal deliberation, or…it was *working*. He was held in place, just like Peter had been.

'It's…w-working!' said Hal, shaking from the

reverberations caused by the connection.

Hal experienced an intense panic, as the killer relaxed his fixated stare from the basement door above him, and gradually lowered his gaze to meet Hal's, looking directly through him.

"*At* me, more like…" thought Hal.

Their past-selves were at the front door now, shouting into the lodge for Jerry's owner to see if anyone was home.

'Two st-steps right!' said Kara, through gritted teeth.

They needed to align themselves to ensure they were directly underneath their past-selves in order to maximise their charge and, together, they were on the move. They made their way slowly to Hal's right, ensuring they maintained their connection. If they gave in to the force between them that was repelling them apart, this would all be over before it had even begun.

The man between them followed Hal with his eyes as they moved, and for the first time in their lives, they finally heard him speak.

'Aaaaaaaaiiii' said the killer, in a thick deep voice

that dripped with malice and venom.

'Ca-can he s-see me?!' asked Hal, his voice breaking slightly, causing the power of the energy between them to dip in intensity. Something only Kara seemed to notice.

'HAL! F-focus! Don't t-talk to him–' but the billowing voice of evil cut her off, not wishing to be silenced.

'*Ssseeeee youuuuu*!' his voice, though only a whisper, nothing but unparalleled rage.

The energy dipped again, and the murderer began raising his knife towards Hal, who pulled away instinctively, but Kara held on tight, pulling her partner's hand back into the man's chest.

She could tell she was losing Hal, neither of them had expected this level of interaction, but Kara was fortunate in that she was unable to see the man's face.

She closed her eyes, and focused on the music that was still playing on the upstairs radio. Back in the days before his voice became synonymous with a countdown clock to her death, she used to love Johnny Cash

And then she remembered. Or perhaps she was

reliving, it was hard for her to be certain. That day when they had first witnessed what had truly happened to them. Then the restart after, where she had to escape. She was moving faster than she ever had before…her rage had been boundless that day.

She remembered how Hal said he couldn't keep up with her. Then, without warning, something clicked in her mind. It wasn't just rage. It was fear, it was love, it was hate, it was *all* of those things. But most importantly of all, it was her *will*. Her *will* not to accept the world as it was, not to be bound by the confines of the world around her based on the rules they had thought they were beholden to. Rules they had unknowingly shackled themselves to, based on their prior *physical* existence and experiences.

For the first time in her life, she realised that this must have been what experiencing an epiphany felt like. They were not bound to this place by *time*, it was their desire to get home to their loved ones, their friends, everything they had left behind, that gave them power.

"Power…" she thought to herself. "We need more *power*…"

With her eyes still closed, she focused her mind on the things that mattered most to her in the world.

Her friends appeared to her first, as she replayed her most recent memories of them. Their time together at Fir Lodge flickered past in her mind's eye, like a camera roll of highlights, running at an accelerated speed. She scrunched her eyes up harder, as she attempted to reach more-powerful memories.

The images sped up even faster, travelling further and further into the past. Memories of birthday meals and Christmas get-togethers with her friends flashed before her, then images of her sister, then her parents. She thought of her wonderful two dogs, which were her world. Everything she was fighting to get back to was cycling through her heart and soul, as she desperately sought the emotional resonance she needed to infuse the blue energy with everything she had.

Everything she *was*.

Hal sensed a significant boost to the arcing lightshow being generated from his hand, which was still interlocked with Kara's, and could see over the serial-killer's shoulder that she was concentrating hard on something. Hal made the conscious decision to block out every other distraction around him and, mimicking his fellow Restarter, he closed his eyes as well.

His mind was instantly flooded with visions of his friends, of Kara with her sister, of Kara's dogs, of a really epic handbag he was once given as a gift from the girls.

Hal shook his head, realising these weren't his memories, instantly understanding what she was doing; that she was bolstering the energy with the most powerful memories she could muster. He focused on Jess, and his dog Shelby, which immediately caused an energy spike that nearly flung him across the room, but he resisted, and held on tight.

With his apparent telepathic connection to Kara, he learned quickly what worked, and what didn't. The day he first became friends with Rachel; the time Robert broke character and bought him a thoughtful gift after a bad break-up; the day he collected Shelby from the dog rescue centre; passing his driving test after an embarrassing number of failed attempts;

getting his first promotion at work and seeing how proud his father was of him…

Suddenly, the thunderous noise being generated between the three of them ceased, and a voice cut through the unsettling silence.

'Hal, it's over.'

He opened his eyes, and was alarmed to see Kara, who had undergone something of a transformation. The details on her clothing remained intact, but she looked like the manifestation of pure, blue energy, as if her entire body was now made of it.

He looked down at his outstretched hand, and realised it too had been equally transformed. He could see dust motes suspended in the air, the entire room bathed in a blue sheen, so bright that it almost hurt to look at anything directly.

Their murderer stood between them, suspended in both place and time. Hal had no idea how he knew, but he knew that time had literally stopped. They were no longer in a restart, they were in a pause *between* moments, outside of time itself.

They both relaxed their interlocked grip on each other, and dropped their arms back to their sides. The large man between them fell to the ground in an undignified heap, sprawled out before them. And, with a bitter realisation, they knew that they had just become the *one* thing they had spent so much time trying to defeat.

They were now *murderer*s themselves.

CHAPTER FIFTY-SIX

Malcolm in the Middle

Saturday Evening, 9:05pm

His eyes blinked open instantly. Noticing that he must have dropped the knife he was clenching, he stretched out his fingers, then closed his hand again, clicking his knuckles, one by one.

Malcolm ran up the staircase of the basement, feeling uncharacteristically off-balance, reached for the door, and moved silently through it, leaving it ajar. His surroundings were illuminated, his senses seemingly heightened; as if everything he looked at was an incredibly clear photograph, sitting under an extremely-florescent light.

Blinking again, he thought he could see the outline of two young people behind him, standing at the base of the stairs he had just ascended. Oddly, this was the only part of his surroundings that appeared slightly out of focus. He strained his eyes, moving closer to the source of the odd anomaly. Yes. They were two of the young ones, from one of the many lodges he had been surveying. The creature had kept running around the woods ever since he'd stored his owner in the storage container below. Always running off trying to make new friends…and now here were those very *friends*, standing directly in the middle of his current workspace.

Malcolm barked a laugh. He couldn't help himself. They had no idea how short their remaining time on this earth would be. Moving closer, he decided that he would not need the knives, and that he would do this with his bare hands. They were intruders. It was dark. He would be protecting himself. It would be self-defence. Yes. He would recite and memorise that in greater detail, as he mopped the congealing blood from the cracks of the rickety cabin, in the event that questions were asked. Not that it ever came to that, he was always long gone before his victims were discovered, but he always revelled in planning ahead. He would incapacitate the young man first. Then the young woman.

And then he heard it; a girl's voice coming from outside the doorway. He noted that the front door was open.

"The creature must have pushed his way out again," thought Malcolm.

'Hellooo?'

His eyes shot to the left, and then back to the dark space of the stairway that led to the basement of the cabin. The same people? Only far more vibrant. A mechanic of some kind? Or perhaps someone had called a pest-extermination service? He hadn't recalled seeing any rats. He always double-wrapped his projects in order to prevent odours, and by extension the unwanted arrival of vermin. The other wearing orange. Glasses. Was she his secretary? His manager, perhaps?

Then the same voice again, only manlier. Louder.

'Hello? Is anyone home?'

He then heard an actual girl's voice.

"Correction," he thought, "a young woman's voice," as the orange secretary spoke.

'I don't think anyone's here,' said the woman. 'In you go boy!'

Following her instruction, the rat-catching mechanic ushered the creature through the door, then closed it.

This all felt very familiar to Malcolm. He felt…disoriented. He couldn't advance on the young couple at the door, not with the witnesses in the basement below staring back at him.

He looked back to the two people at the base of the staircase, barely being able to contain his fury at what was slowly becoming a missed opportunity. Malcolm thought he could detect one of them smiling. The young woman at the bottom of the stairs slowly raised her left arm, like a ghost harbouring a tragic secret.

She was pointing to something behind her, on the floor, and the young man next to her was holding something. It was at that moment that Malcolm realised the young man was not holding anything, and that he was actually extending his middle finger.

The audacity of the obnoxious child was maddening. Looking back at his unwanted guests by the doorway on the upper level, the young rat-catcher stuck his head across the threshold of the entrance.

This young man, stepping into *his* domain? Could he not see him standing right before him? Perhaps he just did not care?

"The *arrogance*!" thought Malcolm.

The rat-catcher spoke. Something about the creature escaping. The young intruder reached for the creature's water container, then proceeded to use the kitchen tap to fill it. Malcolm noticed his name tag; three red letters, embroidered onto a black patch, which read "HAL". He made a mental-note of the name, knowing through experience that it would be useful for finding them again at a later date.

Placing the bowl on the floor, water spilled from the edges. The mess being generated was too much for Malcolm to bear, and he clenched his fists, having to avert his eyes. He looked back at the young man, who switched on the living room light as he left, momentarily blinding Malcolm, as his superior vision had already completely-adjusted to the dark.

The light was excruciating, his uninvited trespasser's reasoning for turning on a light completely lost on Malcolm. He heard them outside now, stating they were returning to a lodge. He looked back to the identically-dressed phantoms at the base of the stairs, only to discover that they were gone.

Malcolm noticed something glistening on the floor below, and deduced that it must have been what the young woman had been pointing to. Taking several, large strides towards the staircase, he closed the door behind him, and once again descended the wooden steps to the lower level.

All of his art still adorned the walls and work spaces. Each and every one of his masterpieces and paper cuttings. The fact that the intruders had seen these items was a problem he would have to address. They had more than likely seen the plans, deceptions, and lures he'd used to bring the many subjects to his canvas.

"Elegant," he thought, taking the time to marvel at his life's work. "Masterful, beautiful, and…what on *earth* is that on the floor?"

For a brief moment, he thought his genius perfection had sent him teetering over the edge. That all of his masterpieces had grown too much for his perfect soul to comprehend, as he found himself looking at *himself* for the first time in a very long time; A strong man for sure. His vigorous training regime had seen to that.

But, more than anything, it was the face that startled him the most; Dead black eyes, dishevelled hair, and a face that looked gaunt, like not enough papier-mâché spread over too much wire.

"It's *you*, idiot," Malcolm thought to himself, the impossible realisation at odds with his analytical mind.

The room began to fill with a static fog, his previously-impeccable clarity of vision distorting slightly, like an image going out of focus. He moved quickly, stepping over his own body, to reach for the door on his left, the same door which was concealing his current project away from prying eyes.

He had left the newest edition to his collection bound, gagged and, most importantly, heavily sedated. Malcolm turned the handle of the door, instantly remembering that it was locked. He fumbled in his pocket to retrieve the key, relieved it was still there, and plunged the key into the lock, noting that something was wrong; it wouldn't grip the internal mechanism. Had he reached for the wrong key? He never made such mundane mistakes as that. Everything in its proper place, that's how it was for him, and how it always would be. Disorder led to *unpredictability*, unpredictability led to *mistakes*, and mistakes led to *failure*. A concept that was no longer in his vocabulary.

And yet...

He tried again, but it was as if the key was made from air. Meanwhile, the fog was thickening; seemingly growing in density the more he panicked, a black and menacing mist that both swirled as it filled the corners of the room, and absorbed any light that it came into contact with.

"I'm not finished here!" he thought, a sudden desperation causing a crack to appear in his carefully-balanced mental state. And for the first time in what felt like a lifetime, he was afraid.

He sectioned that part of his mind away so that

he could concentrate, not wanting to give such a flaw the satisfaction of his attention.

Malcolm ran to his legacy, reaching out for the papers on the wall, and the journals on the desk. They fluttered as he plucked at them, but wouldn't remain in his frantically-moving fists. Instead, they floated to the floor, seemingly lost forever in the ever-expanding static fog.

Falling to his knees next to his ill-looking corpse, which was now only barely visible, he gasped for air, then immediately regained control of himself.

"Weak. Don't be weak," he thought to himself.

And then there was only darkness. He couldn't see his own hands in front of his face.

"I'm not *finish*–"

And then he was gone.

*

It was then that he heard a deafening rush of air, like falling from an airplane, thousands of feet above ground-level. His senses were bombarded by a terrifying blackness, attacking him from every direction, entirely removing his sense of spatial-awareness. His eardrums filled with the thundering, relentless sound of wind, being expunged into eternal nothingness. And then, after what felt like an eternity of timelessness, the sound ceased without warning, like someone pulling the plug on a ridiculously-loud electric saw.

And there he remained, with nothing but the darkness for company.

CHAPTER FIFTY-SEVEN

A Tornado in Peru

Saturday Evening, 8:38pm

Kara approached the dishwasher, determined to avoid having to wash up the plates from the barbecue by hand. Having no prior knowledge on how the appliance worked, she expected it would take her a while to figure it out, but she sussed out the buttons with little effort. The machine hummed to life, and Kara grabbed her bottle of Southern Comfort, safe in the knowledge that she'd done a good job.

She saw Gavin scanning through what was now

the communal mobile phone from across the room, searching for the next track to play. She was about to call out a preference to him, then hesitated. Gavin saw her brain ticking over, and sensed a request was imminent.

'Any requests?' he asked her.

'Spirit in the–' said Kara, then hesitated again. 'Actually, not right now, you decide Gav, I'm good…'

Gavin shrugged, and pressed a button, activating a random playlist. As music erupted through the speakers, filling the room, the track skipped without warning to a familiar ditty, presumably from Jon's Royal Air Force playlist.

An inexplicable blend of foreboding and uneasiness swept over her, causing a slight chill to run down her spine. She shuddered, and the feeling retreated.

Stacey span around, armed with a bottle of prosecco, knocking over one of the champagne flutes that were all stacked precariously on the counter next to Kara, who continued pouring a hefty measure of her American liqueur. The glass fell from the counter, causing the other flutes to ripple threateningly.

Without looking, Kara instinctively grabbed the falling glass before it could continue on its collision course with the floor, and casually placed it back on the worktop.

Grabbing her drink from the counter, she took a sip, then flinched, as a large bottle of wine collided with the floor next to her, the glass shattering viciously.

'Dammit,' she said, looking over each shoulder in search for a tea towel to wipe up the mess. She looked over at Daisy, who was standing on the opposite side of the staircase, dutifully changing her trajectory and making her way over to help clean up the mess.

'Oh,' said Stacey, waving at Daisy, 'can you pass me that glass on the side babe?'

'Sure thing,' said Daisy.

As she walked around the opening of the staircase, a huge balloon in the shape of a number "three" dipped in altitude, obstructing Daisy's path. Daisy successfully dodged out of the way of the balloon, only to find herself accosted with a second helium-filled nuisance. The "zero" shaped balloon bounced off of her face, causing her to lose her footing, resulting in her accidentally tipping the glass of prosecco she had in her hand all over Stacey.

'Oh my god, I'm so sorry!' apologised Daisy, feeling incredibly embarrassed.

Fearne, more than a little tipsy, tightened her grip on the currently-sealed bottle of prosecco she was holding, and shook it with far too much enthusiasm, readying the cork for popping. With a vibrant pop, the cork dutifully flew across the room, down the stairs, and set off on its preordained trajectory, which in this instance meant into the back of Hal's head.

*

As the music kicked in from the speaker above, Hal felt a strange sense of uneasiness that, unbeknownst to him, was equal to what Kara had just experienced. He couldn't quite rationalise what had triggered it, as he reached behind his head and plucked a cork out of the air, turning on the spot and throwing it back up to the girls, who were on the floor above him.

Reacting to his incredible display of ninja-like reflexes, Jon stood there frozen, his pool cue suspended mid-shot. Jon stared at Hal, slack-jawed, until eventually he was able to shake off his disbelief and laughed, as the pool-balls on the table moved of their own accord.

'Mate, that was awesome,' said Jon.

'That's the coolest thing I've ever done in my life,' said Hal, 'I'm glad someone saw it.'

Heading to his room to discard the more cumbersome components of his costume, the sense of déjà vu was diluted somewhat, and he continued on his way, unaware that Peter was following him.

Peter arrived, then left, after Hal had advised him on where he could potentially source a phone charger, and Hal headed out into the rear garden. He could see Peter through Robert's window, illuminated by the blue-hue of his smartphone, and he once again experienced another surge of familiarity coursing through him, as he casually dodged one of the gazebo struts that were obstructing his path without so much as a second thought. Hal chuckled at the sight of Robert, who was snoozing in the hot-tub.

*

Remembering that she had seen a broom propped up amongst the sports equipment in the storage area downstairs, Kara stepped over the broken glass, and made her way to the staircase. Her progress was halted, due to the pile up of people now blocking the stairway, so she waited patiently for the chance of clear passage to present itself.

Eventually, she saw her window of opportunity and skipped down the stairs, as Jerry trotted past her, making his way to the pool table. Jon was standing there, having just opened the front door, a look of happiness on his face that their guest had returned.

*

Checking his phone, Hal decided Jess would probably be busy, but reached for a cigarette regardless. He noted that he only had three left in the box, and ultimately decided that he didn't really need another one. In fact, he strongly considered that maybe now was the time to finally quit. As if to insinuate that some divine force agreed with him, it was then that he heard his name being called.

'Hal, get in here!'

Pocketing his box of cigarettes, Hal walked back, past the tub, past Robert's room, and approached Kara via the hallway. Suddenly, apparently stirring from his dehydrated slumber, he heard Robert calling for his brother Alex to restart the tub. Had Robert not called out for Alex, Hal wouldn't have known that he needed assistance.

'Don't worry bro, I'll sort it,' shouted Hal.

Walking back out into the rear garden, he made his way into the sauna room, and flipped the switch back, causing the hot tub to spring to life once more.

'Cheers Hal!' said Robert.

Hal gave him a mock salute, and headed back to Kara.

'You okay Kara?' he asked, with the tone of a man that was being nagged.

'Look,' she said, pointing to Jerry.

'Oh, hey buddy!' said Hal, as his line of sight locked onto the mischievous pooch, who was busy darting between everyone's legs, sniffing everything he could get near. Jerry began to run up the wooden stairs, when Daisy called down at them.

'No Jerry! Don't let him upstairs, we're still cleaning up this mess,' said Daisy, uncharacteristically stressed out.

From his poor vantage point, Hal was unable to

see the smashed bottle of wine that had fallen off of the counter. He heard Daisy utter an apology to Stacey, who was currently sporting a damp top for some reason.

'What should we do?' asked Kara, directing her question to Hal.

She didn't feel comfortable just kicking him out.

Hal stepped outside, the gravel crunching under his large boots.

'Jerry, GO HOME!' he said, pointing into the darkness.

Jerry stared at him for all of two seconds, and then tried to walk back the way he came, clearly eager to return to the warmth of their lodge.

'Yeah, that's not working, shall we take him home? Can't be that…far?' suggested Kara, the familiar, strange chill taking hold of her once again.

'Yeah I don't like the idea of him…' Hal trailed off.

Something didn't feel right.

'Being outside in the dark on his own like this?' said Kara, finishing his sentence. 'Same. Come on Jerry! '

Hal took the lead, as Kara closed the door behind her, and they proceeded up the driveway of Fir Lodge. Neither of them asked the other which way they should go, they didn't even need to check Jerry's collar. They knew exactly where they were heading. They just didn't think to ask each other *how* they knew.

*

As Hal and Kara reached the end of the driveway, the handle of the entrance door to Fir Lodge, which Kara had just closed, moved downwards. Submitting to an unseen force, a barely audible click could be heard, and the door then opened outwards slightly, as if caught by the wind, despite there being no breeze to speak of.

CHAPTER FIFTY-EIGHT

Turning the Screw

Saturday Evening, 10:59pm

Kevin awoke, his mind swimming amidst a nauseating grogginess. His thankfulness that it was pitch-black quickly dissipated, devolving into panic, as his need for a dark room to sleep off this hangover-from-hell transformed into a complete lack of locational awareness.

A sliver of blue-hued light cut across the floor, two metres away from him on his right-hand side. His brain quickly processed a list of likely options, and he slowly realised it was shining from the other side of a doorway. As his eyes adjusted to the dark, familiar shapes began to crawl into focus. The fogginess of the pounding headache that was debilitating his eyesight began to retreat, allowing him to assess his surroundings more deductively.

He felt a sharp pain in the back of his neck, like a blunt blade of a guillotine. He pulled his head away from the cold, jagged metal, and attempted to use his hands to push himself up. It was then that he noticed his hands would not separate, bound by a force he could not see.

Bringing his hands up to his face, he tried to ascertain what he was up against. The light from the crack under the doorway glistened against his wrists, and for a terrifying moment he thought it was blood. Kevin inhaled deeply, which sent him off-balance and caused his neck to collide once more with the thin metal surface. Expecting the feeling of inertia to afflict him forever, he was relieved to discover that his mind was able to focus once again.

He brought his hands back up, then realised it wasn't blood.

"Tape," he thought, allowing his panic to subside.

Instinctively, he then tried to move his feet apart, rolling his eyes at the fact that, predictably, they too were bound. Kevin tried to yell, the noise a feeble whimper that was dampened exponentially by the fact that that he was also gagged. Kevin tried to push his fingers underneath the tape wrapped around his head, but eventually gave up.

Dragging himself forward, he rolled onto his side, edging towards the slice of eerily-glowing light that was creeping beneath the bottom of the doorway to his right. There was barely enough of a gap for him to see a hint of the other side, but it provided Kevin with just enough information for him to know precisely where he was.

'Um herrrrm!' he muffled, then instantly froze, realising how stupid he was for disturbing the silence. What if *he* had heard? What if he was coming for him right now?

Now he knew he was in his own home and, more specifically, in the storage room of his own basement, he realised the sharp metal was actually the shelving unit for his old paint tins, discarded creosote, and reserves of dog food that he kept a safe distance away from the potentially hazardous chemicals. He also knew that he wasn't going to escape by doing an Ethan Hunt, and creating a ballistic weapon with crusty old paint and dog biscuits.

He shimmied along to the far corner of his prison cell, searching for anything that he could use to aid his escape. Eventually, his hands fell upon an old coffee table, concealed under what he remembered to be a dust sheet.

Using his head and hands to form a pincer, he pulled at the sheet to reveal it. The table was ready to fall apart, and the wooden legs would have made a poor weapon, as he recollected why he had demoted the thing to the basement in the first place. The table was held together with wooden dowels, cheap glue, and a hefty dose of willpower. He grimaced, as he realised there wasn't much in the way of resources.

The blue light reflected back at him. He cocked an eyebrow, and shuffled his way under the table. He felt around in the darkness and felt something square.

"Cardboard," he thought.

Oddly, it was weighed down by something heavy, making it difficult for him to move it easily. Using his free pinkie-fingers, he felt his way up to the top of the container, then used them to drag the box closer to his face. He dunked his hands inside the box, and recoiled in pain, as whatever it was inside punctured the tips of his fingers. The sudden motion as he recoiled caused his wrists to snag on the box, spilling the contents all over the floor. Wincing at the noise, which to him sounded like a million ball bearings tumbling onto a corrugated tin roof, he lay there in silence, listening intently to see if his clumsiness had attracted the unwanted attention of his captor.

Realising he hadn't exhaled for as long as his lungs could tolerate, he quietly allowed his breath to flow between his pursed lips. Rolling onto his stomach, he felt the ground around him and discovered the sharp objects that had previously filled the box.

Good, ol' fashioned, four-inch-long wood screws he realised, as the inanimate objects quickly climbed the ranks to become his best friend in the whole wide world, second to Jerry of course.

It took more attempts that he would care to admit but, after he set aside his frustration, he had finally managed to find the perfect method to pierce holes in the tape between his bound wrists. Each hole he made brought him closer to the end result. Eventually, the holes amassed to form a jagged line in the crude, yet irritatingly effective, handcuffs. Deciding that he had caused sufficient damage to the structural integrity of the tape, he felt bold enough to make an attempt at pulling his hands apart. The tape buckled under the pressure, the holes joining to form a satisfying tear, until eventually, the elongated tacky glue surrendered to his persistence.

Kevin stretched out his arms, revelling in the newfound freedom his upper body was now able to indulge in, and he applied himself to phase two; freeing his legs. To his joy, it was a much quicker process with two free hands.

He could hear Jerry crying for him upstairs, as he made short work of the tape around his ankles.

'I'm coming boy,' he muttered, his focus shifting from merely saving himself and onto reaching his faithful, admittedly ill-behaved, best friend.

Attempting to stand, a spell of dizziness brought him back down heavily onto his backside.

Compromising with himself, he decided to kneel instead, as he made his way towards the doorframe.

Trying the door handle, he was predictably whelmed by the fact it was locked. Using the door for support, Kevin pulled himself up and felt around the frame, looking for anything that would indicate a weak spot on the door. A weak spot he knew wouldn't exist, because he set this door himself.

He stretched his arms out against the door, looking down at the floor, trying to get his next plan together. His foot knocked something that wasn't a screw…something bigger. Leaning down, and exercising caution, he reached out into the darkness, as his left hand make contact with a cold, plastic baton that had no place being there. Bringing his right hand up to inspect the object, he realised it was a screwdriver.

"Probably a cross-head" he figured, certain the universe wasn't done with toying with him just yet, if at all.

But it wasn't a cross-head, it was a flat-head, one that would soon graduate to become his most favourite inanimate object of his entire life, his fickle friendship with the wood-screws now little more than a distant memory.

Kevin licked his lips pensively.

Bringing the screwdriver up to the metal bracket at the top right-hand side of the door, and using his fingers to guide the edge of the tool, he positioned the screwdriver into the indentation of one of the screws that kept the bracket in place. The first of many that prohibited his escape. As the head of the object connected cleanly with the head of the screw, he carefully turned it to the left, being careful not to shear it off by being too enthusiastic.

Slowly, in the smallest of increments imaginable, the screw began to turn.

CHAPTER FIFTY-NINE

Time Heist

165th Restart – Saturday Morning, 4:59am

They stood outside his front door, their bodies poised to act, as the faint fizzle of blue energy sparked angrily between their interlocked fingers. Hal held his phone in his free hand, still staring at the door. They had the slimmest window of opportunity to get this right, and it had taken them five restarts just to get this part down.

On the first restart, their task was learning what door Kevin would leave through. They had both covered a door each, only to learn that it was, of course, the front door, but they had to be sure. On the first go around, they let events play out until the next time-jump. But on the second try, when only Hal had managed to make his way through the front door, leaving Kara outside, he sent her to the restart-point to trigger their next attempt, instead of waiting all day just to watch themselves die horribly once again.

Hal and Kara waited, neither of them wanting to talk, in case it caused the other to lose focus. At 6:57am, they could hear Kevin navigating his way around the humble kitchen, fixing up what they knew to be his one-hundredth-and sixty-sixth cup of coffee.

At 7:04am, they heard him let Jerry out through the back door. It wasn't an option to run around the back and gain access from the rear, Jerry had seen them when they had tried this, and it resulted in Kevin coming to look for him, sending everything out of whack. Kevin had locked the back door, as well as the basement door, taking the keys for both with him, costing them another restart.

At 7:14am, Hal and Kara stepped sideways, breaking contact for the first time in over three hours, taking up position either side of the doorframe, each of them ensuring the doorway was free from the obstruction their bodies would cause. They were almost corporeal now, what with the charge they were storing up, and Jerry wouldn't run through them in their current state. If they hid at the side of Kevin's lodge, like they had on a previous attempt, they would be too far away to get to the door before he closed it.

Another restart.

At 7:15am, Kevin opened the door, calling Jerry in from outside, and pulling the back-door closed, forgetting to lock it and, more importantly, leaving the key in the lock of the basement door. He held the front door open for Jerry, ushering him outside. Jerry dutifully obeyed, running to Kevin's pickup truck, sensing that they were going for a walk.

As Jerry rushed past them, the Restarters walked briskly through the now-open front door, Hal steering clear of Kevin entirely, but Kara being forced to brush past him. Kevin shivered, looking down at his arm, and then back through the doorway into his home. Shaking it off, he closed his front door, walked to his truck, and clambered inside, slamming the car door shut behind him.

Jerry ceased sniffing a nearby patch of grass and, under his faithful owner's encouragement, jumped into the passenger seat via the now open passenger door that had been opened by his best friend.

Thanks to five whole days of trial and error, Hal and Kara were now inside Kevin's lodge. Five restarts, just to get into the house. Countless more for what came next. But this was important, if they didn't set these events in motion, stopping their killer would be irrelevant, and they'd have to restart again anyway.

Kara positioned herself by the currently closed, but unlocked, back door, one arm outstretched towards the handle, the fingers of her right hand still interlocked with Hal's.

Hal, meanwhile, waited like a statue by the door to the basement, which despite being ajar, couldn't be moved with his past-self being so far away. And so, they waited, for three hours and forty-five minutes, resuming physical contact by holding the other's hand.

*

At 11.00am, going by the clock on Kevin's mantelpiece, which was infuriatingly four minutes slow and not to be trusted, having already cost them a restart, the blue energy they had been so afraid of for so long was now their ultimate weapon.

'Punch it,' said Kara.

Hal dutifully hit the power button on the now fully-charged, residual-energy-construct that was his phone, causing it to spring to life. Waiting the customary 10 seconds for it to fire up, he then cycled through the menus searching for something in particular, and pressed play. The room filled with the sound of The White Stripes' "Seven Nation Army", their minds clearer already, thanks to the extra focus afforded to them by the audible anchor.

'See?' said Hal with a grin, '*so* much cooler with a soundtrack.'

Kara rolled her eyes playfully, her tapping foot betraying her allegedly unimpressed demeanour. Hal ensured he remained in contact with her, as she turned the handle and pulled the back door open. This would facilitate their escape later.

"Two restarts," thought Kara with a grimace, kicking herself as she remembered how they had become stuck in Kevin's lodge with no way out.

Remaining in contact, the energy continued to build, becoming more vibrant as their past-selves drew closer to their current location. They moved towards the basement door, Kara now maintaining contact with Hal via the medium of a ridiculous-looking two-person conga-line.

Hal pulled open the basement door, and they made their way down the stairs, continuing the conga-line so the energy would continue to build, pocketing his phone, which was belting out a rousing chorus, the noise failing to be dampened by the out-of-phase material of his boiler suit.

Kara moved swiftly, and stood by the door to the small room at the bottom of the stairs which Kevin would soon be occupying. The door to Kevin's future prison wasn't currently open in this timeline, as their act of freeing themselves many restarts ago had been wiped. Due to them not being locked inside this time around, it had remained closed ever since Kevin had retrieved the dog food.

Their charge had been significantly reduced by the bold exertion of opening the doors, and interacting with their environment was largely ineffectual now, at least until their past-selves were closer. Only then could they get their edge back. Clicking his fingers a few times, and rubbing his hands together, feeling the beat of the music, Hal leaned down to the box of screws that was sitting on the floor of the basement, the same box he had stumbled over during their first visit to the underbelly of Kevin's home. Hal took comfort in the fact that the killer's weird-ass shrine of death was not yet lining the walls, what with his arrival not taking place for a few more hours.

There was no need for Kara to keep watch this time. She knew their past-selves would be passing their current location shortly, and it was almost as if they were now able to tell when they were getting close. Hal believed they had a developed a sixth sense for it, but Kara knew it was just sub-conscious time-keeping.

Hal tapped the box of screws impatiently, in time with the music, until the cardboard flap finally moved under his touch.

It was time.

Hal nodded, and Kara opened the storage-cupboard door in front of her, moving quickly back to his location. She placed her hands inside the lip of the cardboard box, preparing to pull the box across the room. Seven restarts to get this part right. Another four for what came next.

They moved as one, as Hal pushed, and Kara pulled, moving the box across the full length of the basement floor, both letting go of the container as it aligned perfectly with the doorway of Kevin's storage room, on the opposite side of the basement.

Then, at the precise moment that their past-selves were directly outside their current location, they let go of the box altogether, focusing instead on the screwdrivers lining the worktop. It had to be the flat-head. Hal had discovered many restarts ago during one of their intel-gathering missions that the screws on the brackets were of a certain size and type.

Selecting their tool of choice, they once again continued to move as one, dragging the screwdriver to the edge of the counter, angling it perfectly so that it fell straight into the box of screws.

The Restarters turned their focus back to the box on the floor, the screwdriver now sticking out like a mast on a very-poorly designed pirate ship. And, as the final chorus kicked in, they began pushing the box, which was now increasing in heaviness, as their past-selves moved further and further away as they set off towards the woods. They dragged it all the way to the door of the storage room, over the threshold and under the table in the corner of the small room, pushing it through the sheet that was covering the table. With a quick flourish, Hal pulled the dust sheet back over the box, so it was completely concealed from view.

They began to feel the energy dissipating, no longer acting as conduits for the mystical force. As if to highlight the point, Hal's phone cut off, as it used up the last of the energy that had been fuelling its paradoxical anti-matter battery. Their past-selves had moved too far out of range for them to generate anything more than a fizzle now, but for the first time in countless restarts, the first part of their plan was a success.

'You're welcome Kevin,' said Kara, with a look of almost palpable defiance on her face.

'Nice one Rach',' said Hal, catapulting his heartfelt gratitude both forwards and backwards through time to his friend for coming up with the idea, hoping she would somehow sense it.

They were finally winning.

CHAPTER SIXTY

Double-Tap

Saturday Evening, 11:46pm

As Kevin methodically loosened the screws of the bracket, he berated himself for picking a bracket with five screw-holes in the first place, all those months ago.

He then chastised himself for having affixed the door with three brackets.

And for painting *over* said brackets, resulting in him having to scrape away the excess paint from the grooves.

In the dark.

Because he hadn't bothered to install a light.

With the top bracket finally disconnecting from the interior wall, he set to work on the middle bracket, and then the last one at the bottom of the door.

It was incredibly slow-going, but with the brackets removed, after what felt like an entire evening's work, Kevin pushed the screwdriver into the gap between the door and the frame, bending it back on itself to pull the frame away, using the tool as a makeshift chisel where needed.

With the frame now heavily damaged, he then set the screwdriver into the widening gap, and used his weight as leverage to pull the door open, utterly terrified that he would snap the only thing that could get him out of this mess if he applied too much pressure. The lock on the left-hand side of the door drew out the process, but eventually he had freed enough of the right-hand side to fit his hand through. He began to wedge his right leg through the gap, and then, gradually, his upper-torso. His large stomach was putting up a fight, holding him back from truly escaping, but Jerry's cries spurred him on.

Eventually, the door gave up the fight and caved inwards, the metal lock erupting from the left door frame, and Kevin stepped across the threshold, in the manner of a man who had been served two life-sentences, but had finally been awarded parole for good behaviour.

From the faint slits in the adhesive tape that his captor has placed across the windows, he could see streaks of moonlight, which beamed across the room and illuminated the cause to the entirety of his relentless woe; In the centre of his basement lay the muscular monster that had abducted him, looking considerably deader than he had done the last time they had crossed paths. Kevin clenched his fist around the screwdriver, turning it in his hand as if it were a knife, ready to use it if he had to.

He kicked the serrated knife, which was resting on the man's motionless hand, away from the threat lying before him, so that it was truly out of reach of the psychopath. He leaned in closer to the body before him, all the while ensuring that the screwdriver could be brought down into his adversary's flesh at any moment.

Unbeknownst to Kevin, there was surely a version of Jasmine, on some plain of existence, rolling her eyes at what was clearly a rookie mistake. Had she been there, she would have reminded him to "always double-tap before getting too close." But, in fairness, he didn't know Jasmine, and wasn't an avid movie buff.

With his free hand, he pressed his fingers against his captor's neck, and counted to twenty, then to thirty, and finally to forty. Finally accepting that there was no pulse, Kevin took a step backwards, and rested his gaze upon what he now truly believed was a dead body.

Slowly, silently, he backed away, and made his way up the staircase. Having not taken his eyes off of his captor, he made himself jump with shock when his hip finally connected with the door handle of the basement door. He fumbled behind his back for the circular handle, and backed out into his own living room, closing the door gently in front of him, pressing his hand against the door, and applying his full weight against it. Jerry jumped up at him, licking his hands, and growling playfully for attention. Kevin grabbed him by the waist, and fled to the front door of his home.

As he stepped into the cool night air, breathing in the calming scent of the surrounding fir trees, he thought frantically over what to do next. And then he ran into the darkness, as far, and as fast as he could, wishing to put as much distance as possible between himself and death, as quickly as his legs, and ageing heart, would allow him, holding Jerry in his arms like a feisty toddler, as tears of relief filled his eyes.

CHAPTER SIXTY-ONE

The Road Less Travelled

Sunday Morning, 10:07am

Jon was leading the convoy this time, discussing where they had gone wrong at beer-pong that weekend. Both Peter and Fearne had decided to drive back with Jon and Rachel for their return journey, and Fearne was fast asleep in the back with Peter, still not feeling too clever after her recent migraine had incapacitated her the night before. Jon continued to outline what they could have done better, whilst Rachel programmed in their route home from the front passenger seat.

'All I'm saying is, we need to run more interference to throw them off in future,' said Jon, turning around briefly to face Peter, 'know what I mean?'

'Yeah,' said Peter with a nod of confirmation. 'Absolutely shocking that Stacey and Fearne beat us, I'm gutted,' he added.

Rachel yelled at Jon, screaming at him to watch the road, as a man walked straight out in front of them with his arms in the air. Jon slammed on the brakes and swerved, nearly colliding with the wooden logs that lined the road and acted as woodland-themed curbs.

The man stared at them, his eyes wide, and his appearance implying he hadn't seen a shower in a while, his unkempt clothes indicating that he probably hadn't slept in a long time either.

The sound of the windscreen wiper brushing against a dry windscreen filled the cabin of the car, along with a soft clicking noise that surrounded them, indicating that someone, amidst the excitement, had pressed the hazard button on the dashboard. The ironically-calming, mundane repetitions of the combined noises were completely at odds with the currently-frayed nerves of those inside the vehicle, as Jon tried to distract everyone from the fact that they had nearly all been involved in a fatal accident, due to the stranger's clear disregard for his own safety.

'Is that…the dog guy?' said Jon, clicking off the windscreen wipers that he must have accidentally activated, during his expertly executed emergency stop. 'Kevin right?'

Rachel nodded, still trying to calm herself down, as the adrenaline coursed through her body. Jon clicked a switch, and lowered the electric-powered window, the noise making a muted buzzing noise as it retracted into the door frame, and stuck his head out of the window. 'You okay mate? You need some help or anything?'

The man stared at Jon with wild eyes, as if he was harbouring a dark secret he was finding it impossible to articulate. Kevin shook his head erratically, turned to face the road ahead, and continued waving his arms, as the blue flashing lights of what appeared to be police cars and an ambulance came into view, previously obscured from Jon due to the bend in the road. The cars surged past them, around the corner, and out of sight, just as Rachel regained her ability to speak.

'Do you think we should…I don't know…go and help or something?' said Rachel.

Fearne's eyes sprang open, suddenly fully-awake and alert.

'NO!' she shouted at Rachel, her bellowing voice filling the car and making them all jump out of their skins. Each of the passengers shouted an expletive at the unexpected attack to their eardrums.

'Jesus Fearne, night terrors much?!' said Rachel, her heart pumping so fast in her chest she could literally hear it reverberating in her ears.

'Ignore Fearne, bad dreams and all that. She does that,' said Peter, and then added 'I think we should probably leave all that to the professionals. We'd probably just get in the way.'

In mutual agreement, Jon turned off the hazards, and hit his indicator to signal his convoy of friends behind him, who had pulled over in response to witnessing Jon's near-collision with Kevin, and followed him as he pulled out to continue onwards on their journey.

As Jasmine drove past the turning where the police were congregated, Kara experienced a brief sensation of pain in her temple, an ice-pick-like headache that was gone as quick as it had arrived.

Hal stared through the car window, wondering what could have warranted such a high turn-out of police and medics. He thought he caught sight of a glimmer of light, reflecting on what appeared to be a weapon of some kind, being held by one of the officers. It was incredibly unusual for a police officer in the United Kingdom to be wielding a gun, and he automatically assumed he must have imagined it. Just as he lost line-of-sight to the incident unfolding at Kevin's house, he saw a stretcher being wheeled out to the ambulance.

Whoever it was that had sustained an injury, he hoped they would be okay.

CHAPTER SIXTY-TWO

Changing the Future

Sunday Afternoon, 12:14pm

As Jasmine pulled up outside Kara's home, she allowed herself to take a sigh of relief that the worst of the journey was behind her. She would soon be home with David, and her entirely self-sufficient cats, whom she loved more than anything.

Kara jumped out of the car, freeing Hal from his three-doored prison, and he stumbled out as gracefully as a man who had been cooped up for two hours could ever hope to be. He stretched, milking the martyrdom he clearly believed he was owed, for a little longer than was socially acceptable.

'Thanks for sitting in the back!' said Kara, in a breezy tone that clearly indicated there was never really going to be another option in the first place, merely the illusion of democracy.

'My pleasure!' lied Hal.

He held up his arms, and went in for a goodbye hug, the connection generating a large static-shock that erupted between them, causing both parties to recoil.

'Ouch,' said Hal, 'did you see that! Actually saw a blue spark there! Jas', you need to add some mud-flaps to this thing, to ground your car or something.'

Jasmine stepped out of the driver's seat to give Kara a hug.

'You *do* realise how you sound,' said Jasmine, 'when you try to talk about cars as if you know the first thing about them, right?'

Hal laughed.

'Sheesh, alright scrappy, settle down!' said Hal.

'Thank you so much for driving by the way!' said Kara.

'You're most welcome,' said Jasmine, giving Kara

a heartfelt hug, as Hal pulled Kara's case from the boot of the car for her and placed it beside her.

'Cheers Hal,' said Kara.

'No worries,' he said, as he shot her a wink and clambered into the passenger seat, buckling himself up.

'Are you going to pick up the dogs today?' asked Jasmine.

'Nah, no need,' said Kara. 'My sister's bringing them over later for me.'

The only plans she had for the afternoon were taking a long, ice-cold shower, and meeting up with Greg.

As she made her way up her modest driveway, she spun around to offer a wave to Jasmine and Hal, as Jasmine beeped her horn and they waved back. Kara stood there at her door for a moment, an icy-chill running down her spine, causing the hairs on her arms to stand up. She looked over her shoulder, out across the road behind her. A perfectly ordinary, lazy Sunday afternoon. But something felt wrong. Her stomach grumbled, and she dismissed the thought, reasoning it was merely a direct result of hunger.

As she placed the key in the lock to her front door, the handle lowered of its own accord, the door rapidly pulling inwards and away from her. Besieged by two assailants, she instinctively took a step back, but it was too late, they were on her in an instant.

Her two Jack Russell's charged at her without a second thought, sniffing her shoes, trying to determine precisely where she had been for the last few days, piecing together the entirety of her journey, which she had unforgivably made without them.

'Down Zack, get down Billy,' said Kara, both surprised and delighted that her dogs were there to welcome her.

Greg was standing beyond the threshold, a big smile on his face, clearly elated that he'd successfully managed to surprise her.

'What the hell are you doing here?!' said Kara, her words at odds with the obvious affection and happiness in her voice.

'Your sis and I thought it'd be a nice surprise,' said Greg. 'She dropped off Zack and Billy and let me in,' he added, suddenly fearful he may have overstepped the mark.

Kara dumped her bag and hugged him, a single tear rolling down her cheek, for reasons she couldn't quite fathom or explain.

'Did I do the wrong thing?' asked Greg, noticing her glistening cheek.

'No, you idiot,' said Kara, attempting to compose herself. 'I've just really missed you is all.'

Greg mumbled something unintelligible, then made an excuse to hide his relief, breaking away to pop the kettle on.

Kara made her way into the kitchen, grabbed a treat for her dogs, and leaned against the kitchen counter. Taking a breath, she exhaled slowly, watching as Greg made her a cup of tea.

"It's so good to be home," thought Kara.

*

One hundred-or-so yards away, a dark-haired woman stared intently, having taken up a bench situated on the grass verge opposite Kara's home. The woman checked her wrist, then reached into the pocket of her dark blue coat, retrieving a notepad. Pulling a pen out from the spiral binding, she flipped open the pad, recording the exact time.

A much-older man, wearing a coat of matching colour, took up a spot next to her on the bench she was occupying.

'You didn't need to come yourself, you know,' she said to the man. 'This is basic admin.'

The man remained silent, his stern face staring out across the expansive grass verge. He reached up to his neck, undoing the top button of his shirt, and loosened his dark-red tie. Relaxing his arms, he leant forward, resting his forearms on his legs.

Noting his stony glare, she nodded, the reason for his presence dawning on her. She closed her notepad, then nestled it safely away back into her jacket pocket. They sat there in silence, neither one of them feeling the need to fill the communicative void with small talk. They had known each other too long to feel awkward, listening instead to the rustling noise being generated by the breeze, as it swam across the leaves of the trees and danced across the open stretch of grass before them, like a river of perpetual motion.

*

As Jasmine pulled up onto the driveway of Hal's house and killed the engine, Hal jumped out and made his way to the boot of the car.

Jasmine stepped out from the car, just as Hal moved in for a goodbye hug.

'Thank you so much Jasmine,' said Hal. 'I really appreciate all the driving you've done this weekend!'

'You're welcome,' said Jasmine. 'No point in us taking more cars than we needed.'

The front door of Hal's home opened, and he was bombarded with kisses from his small, black, Staffordshire Bull Terrier, who was jumping up and vying for his undivided attention.

'Ha-ha, I've missed you too girl, get orf me!' but Shelby refused to listen, she'd clearly missed her daddy.

Jess came out shortly after, and gave him a hug, then chatted to Jasmine, whilst Shelby continued to jump up excitedly. As the girls departed, Hal sighed contentedly, taking in the fact that he was finally home.

'Feels like I've been gone a year,' said Hal, rubbing Shelby's belly.

'You've only been gone since Friday, weirdo,' said Jess, shooting him a loving wink.

Hal made his way into the house and, ensuring he resolved his number one priority, popped the kettle on. Jess closed the door behind him, and chirped her request as she always did.

'Coffee pleeeeease,'she shouted, as she shot off out of sight, and into the living room. Hal rolled his eyes, grunting under his breath, but secretly smiling.

Encumbered with a cup of coffee in each hand, he made his way to the living room, experiencing a cold shiver, which caused some of his hot beverage to slosh over the side and onto the carpet.

'Oops,' he said sheepishly, passing a cup to his fiancée.

'Finally found us a window cleaner,' said Jess. 'Reasonably priced too.'

Hal feigned interest, slurping his coffee, and wondering if anyone had ever uttered a sentence more painfully-British that what Jess has just said to him.

'Sweet, you've been on about that for ages,' said Hal.

Jess shot him a playful scowl, and Hal switched out his slurp for a sip out of politeness, remembering how much that drove her crazy.

'So, tell me all about it,' said Jess, curling up on the sofa. 'What did I miss?'

'It was great,' said Hal. 'The lodge was amazing. Oh, Peter and Fearne are getting their first place together. And Jasmine is having a baby bo–'

The end of his sentence was cut-off by Shelby, who rudely interrupted him via the medium of an uncharacteristic growl, which she was directing towards a large plant situated in the corner of the room.

'What's up with Shelby?' asked Hal, taking another swig of his coffee-flavoured sugar-milk, and making a mental note to finally bite the bullet and look into getting some proper coffee into the house.

'Eesh,' scoffed Jess, 'ignore her, she's been growling at that plant all day.'

'We've had that thing for over a week now,' noted Hal, 'you'd think she'd be used to it.'

'Tell me about it. Don't stop, carry on, what did I miss,' said Jess, eager for him to continue so that she could experience the weekend vicariously through him.

As Hal continued to fill her in on everything that had happened during his stay at Fir Lodge, Malcolm stared at Shelby, who was blocking him from progressing any further towards her dad. From the corner of the room, he looked up from her, and stared at Hal. His eyes dropped down to his left hand, and for the one-hundredth time, he inspected the pink plastic rectangle of information, reading it out loud once again.

'Harold Callaghan, 165 Kent Street, thirty-three years of age,' he said out loud, despite having already committed it to memory.

He looked up from Hal's driving licence, placing it back into his out-of-phase pocket, and reaffixed his gaze back to his murderer. It had taken him an incomprehensible amount of time to get here. Countless years spent planning his revenge, obsessing over every detail; what weapon to use, whether he would kill the orange detective first, or last.

"Better to make him watch," he had thought.

He suddenly realised that his left-hand had drifted unconsciously to his waist, and was now gripping the hilt of the large blade that was tucked into his belt.

Malcolm blinked to clear his mind, and then grinned, baring all of his teeth like a hungry shark.

Raising his right hand, he aimed his gun at Shelby, miming the act of pulling the trigger, and blowing the sound of a fake gunshot through his pursed lips. Unable to help herself, Shelby responded by rolling onto her back, and playing dead, hoping to be rewarded with a treat, a customary reward for a trick well done in her household.

Raising the weapon towards Jess, he mimicked the action of firing off another pretend bullet into her forehead, then one at Hal, just for good measure. He despised guns, they were so…impersonal.

"Much better to be up-close," he thought, as he remembered the blood that flowed from–

'Focus Malcolm,' he said to himself sternly.

The black, liquid-like fog often sent his thoughts spiralling into tangents that were not currently relevant.

Lowering the gun back down to his side, he *felt* the darkness before it arrived. It swirled around his body, eager to claim him once more, but he wasn't in the least bit concerned. He had what he needed.

The all-too-familiar sound of rushing air filled his eardrums, as his surroundings were systematically obliterated from his vision, with Hal himself being the last to vanish.

'See you *soon*, Harold,' he whispered into the dark, black fog, his words thick with iciness, and tinged with resentment.

And with that, he was vaporised from the timeline, sent hurtling back into the past, with a single, simple agenda; to restart the past, and change the future.

The Restarters will return.

Acknowledgments

Great Scott, so many people to mention, without whom I would never have got any of this off the ground, and adequately hovering on quantum-entangled propulsion drives, but here goes.

First and foremost, thank *you*, dear reader. Thank you for taking the time to read the first part of this story. I hope you enjoyed it, and will join me for what comes next. I also hope that maybe you will spread the word by passing this book to friends, family, or perhaps even just in the form of small-talk to your local barista. I have some big ideas for where the Restarters are heading next, and if you can find the time to leave a review, it will really help in terms of keeping the lights on.

It would be remiss of me not to start by thanking my editors; Beverley Hatchman, Amanda Gliddon and Christopher McMahon. I can't thank you enough for all of your hard work. The journey to reaching this version of the story wouldn't have been possible without you.

A special thank you to Rebecca Greenwood, my first ARC reader. Your feedback and enthusiasm has been truly invaluable to me.

My sincere thanks to Danny Wyatt, the builder and owner of the real Fir Lodge, who was so enthusiastic and supportive when I pitched him the idea, despite not knowing me at all. For more information on how to book a weekend vacation at the real-life Fir Lodge, please visit my website, which will link you to their bookings page. I have it on good authority that he has since installed a time-dilation dampener around the lodge, so there's no danger of potential visitors being sent hurtling back to the beginning of their weekend. Though by the end of your time there, you'll wish you could do just that.

Special credit must go to my graphic designer, Sam Moore, who patiently took my concept for a book cover and made it a reality (and then had to put up with me calling on him every forty-five minutes for the past several months.) See you soon for Book Two, Sam!

Thank you to my fiancée Gemma. Your patience and support has been instrumental in this book ever seeing the light of day. For every evening where I said "Just one more page", for every cup of coffee you brought me, despite me clearly having had far too much already, and for the hours we spent dog-walking where you reassured me, for the billionth time, that the term "Restarters" worked just fine, I thank you.

A special shout out to Janine and Victoria, who spurred me on to take an idea made in jest, and to run with it to write an actual novel. It is a fact that you wouldn't be reading this now if it weren't for them.

Lastly, but by no means least, thank you to Russell Whitcombe, a very talented photographer and friend who was instrumental in securing the additional photos I needed weeks before launch.

Well, time for me to find a Restart Point. I hope to see you for Book Two, which will be called—
Wait, can anyone else hear the sound of rushing air?...

Your friend in time,

Sean McMahon

Become A Restarter!

For news, giveaways, exclusive content, or even just to reach out to me, why not visit the Restarter's Lodge at www.restarterlodge.com

Thanks to the internet, you can also follow the Restarters in a number of other ways, by punching the following into your communicative weapon of choice. What a time to be alive.

On Twitter @Restarterlodge
On Instagram @Restarterlodge
Or, if none of that is your bag, why not try the official Facebook page which you can find, you guessed it, @Restarterlodge

About the author

Sean McMahon has saved the world countless times.

From the comfort of his sofa.

Utilising a controller, as a conduit for his actions.

He also believes he invented the concept of the digital photo-frame, but has no way to prove it.

Sean lives in Essex with his family. In his spare time, he loves watching movies, reading, is an avid gamer, and enjoys walking his ridiculously-energetic Staffordshire Bull Terrier, Mindy. He also spends his quieter moments making contingency plans for surviving in the event of a potential zombie-apocalypse.

Sean also once took a leak standing next to Simon Pegg at a press event. To this day, nobody cares.

Dear Sam,

Thank you for all your support!

It's an honour to have you as a potential reader.

I hope you enjoy the story!

Your friend in Time,

Sean

S

10805942R00323

Printed in Great Britain
by Amazon